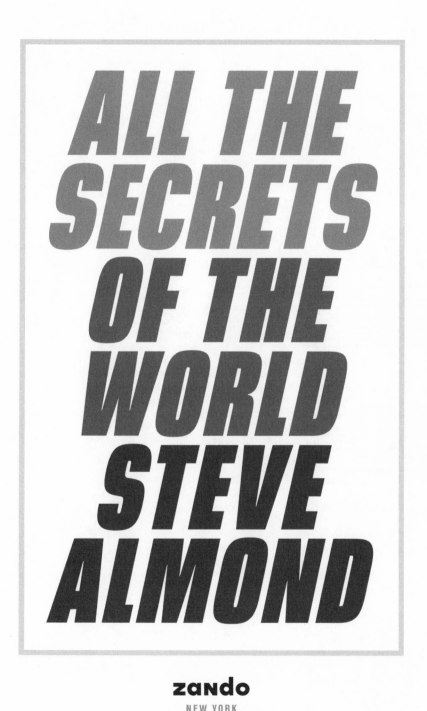

ALL THE SECRETS OF THE WORLD

STEVE ALMOND

zando

NEW YORK

Zando Projects
zandoprojects.com

First Edition: April 2022

Cover design by Evan Gaffney
Interior design by Aubrey Khan, Neuwirth & Associates, Inc.

The publisher does not have control over and is not responsible for author or other third-party websites (or their content).

Library of Congress Control Number: 2021953082

ISBN 978-1-638-93002-0
eISBN 978-1-638-93003-7

10 9 8 7 6 5 4 3 2 1

Manufactured in the United States of America

To Paul Salopek

"*Three may keep a secret,*

if two of them are dead."

—BENJAMIN FRANKLIN

BOOK ONE
WELCOME TO SCORPIONVILLE

BY THE TIME SHE WAS thirteen years old, Lorena Saenz had learned how to make herself invisible. At school, she sat in back and kept her head down, even in second-period science, her favorite class. The teacher, Miss Catalis, was loud and eager and faintly absurd. She wore hippie dresses that bunched at the hips and told long, loopy stories about unsung female scientists.

"Did I ever tell you guys about Maria Mitchell?" she would say. "She was this totally brilliant schoolmarm who lived on Nantucket and loved stargazing. One night, she snuck onto the roof of the tallest building in town with her telescope. And guess what she spotted up there? A comet. A flipping comet! She went on to become the most famous female astronomer in America."

The pleasure Miss Catalis took in such tales was excruciating. She strode up and down the rows, waving her arms, her bracelets clacking. Then she would freeze, dramatically, and demand to know what her students thought. "I'm looking for a deduction. What do you *deduce*?"

Eventually, someone would observe that Mitchell was kind of a rebel.

"What if she simply saw something nobody else could? Is that really rebellion? Sometimes you have to break the rules, if you want to prove the world wrong." At this point, Miss Catalis would pause and let her eyes drift across the desks until they settled on Lorena, who would look down and squirm with a pleasure that confused her. It was an unnerving sensation: becoming visible.

A few months into the fall term, Miss Catalis announced partners for the annual science fair. Lorena would work with Jenny Stallworth. The pairing was so unexpected that a few students snorted. Jenny was blond and willowy and rich; braces lent her mouth a swollen insolence. Lorena was short and pudgy. She lived in a small apartment at the edge of the district with her mother, who was from Honduras. In the world of television, her complexion might have been described as a kind of fancy wood, walnut or mahogany, though in the world she occupied it was merely a shade darker than that of her Mexican friends.

Miss Catalis hoped that Jenny would be inspired by Lorena's passion for science. But the class saw it differently. They were certain that Miss Catalis had seized upon the fair as a chance to unite two girls of vastly different backgrounds, temperaments, and social standing. It was the kind of thing certain eighth grade teachers did, part of their idiotic fairy-tale agenda. Lorena felt the eyes of her classmates upon her; the pity lit her cheeks.

Jenny greeted the union with a poise that would have pleased her mother. "This'll be fun!" she assured Lorena. "We'll come up with something cool."

A week later, Jenny peeled away from the cluster of beauties with whom she commandeered the breezeway, and approached Lorena. "Wanna come over? Like, to my house. My mom thinks we should talk to my dad. About the science fair. He's a research professor."

"What does he study?" Lorena asked.

Jenny smiled without showing her braces. "Scorpions," she murmured. "Totally gross, right?"

Lorena recognized the invitation as a compulsory kindness, yet it was also an opportunity to see Jenny's house, and perhaps to better understand the ease with which she carried herself through the world.

It was the winter of 1981. Ronald Reagan had just been sworn in as president. On the outskirts of downtown Sacramento, where the girls lived, a portrait of the former governor still hung in the classrooms at Sutter Junior High. He gazed down upon them with his eternal smile, like an indulgent father, confident that no manner of evil would ever intrude upon the prosperous kingdom they shared.

THE STALLWORTH MANOR was a mint-green Victorian. It sat on a majestic lot in a tree-lined neighborhood known as the Fabulous Forties. Lorena had biked past the place on her way to school. Mrs. Stallworth met them at the door. She was even more elegant than Lo had imagined, her hair elaborately feathered, honeyed highlights, the sort of woman who might appear in a commercial for perfume. She inspected Lo with a frank and indulgent gaze. "How nice," she said.

"You have a beautiful home," Lorena replied softly, though she had seen only the foyer. Inside, light poured through a bay window, onto a pair of polished end tables. Fresh flowers had been arranged in a cut crystal vase.

Mrs. Stallworth's name was Rosemary but everyone called her Ro, so the two of them were going to get along, Ro and Lo.

Jenny snickered.

"Must everything embarrass you?" Mrs. Stallworth said.

Jenny's room was huge. Rock stars glowered from the posters on her lavender walls. Stuffed animals had been ranked beneath the lace canopy of her bed. The girls thumbed through magazines and listened to Blondie, the band all the white girls listened to. Jenny asked Lo her birthdate, then nodded like it all made sense. "You're a total Virgo. Earth sign. That means you're grounded."

Jenny was an Aries, a fire sign. Passionate and courageous, but maybe also a little impulsive. She was the baby of the family and could have exploited this, but she had been well-bred. She wasn't cruel; she hadn't any cause for cruelty.

Lo listened to Jenny and gazed at her astrology charts, dizzy with arrows and stars. She told Jenny that she had a grandma who was a *curandera* and could curse people with the evil eye. It involved killing a baby goat. Jenny lamented the notion of a murdered baby goat, then made a list of the people she might want to curse, which included her older brother and a boy who had teased her about her braces.

Jenny's father was supposed to be home by four but he forgot. Jenny's mother was mortified. That was the word she used. She called her husband and left a message with the department secretary and invited Lo to stay for dinner. They were having steak. Did she like steak?

Lo preferred not to impose but Mrs. Stallworth smiled and clapped her hands and instructed Lo to phone her mother. Lo's mom wasn't home, so she faked the conversation, and Mrs. Stallworth promised to drive Lo home; they could put her bike in the back of the station wagon. It was the least they could do.

Mrs. Stallworth had this way about her. She put people at ease by seizing control of situations. She had served as president of the PTA; there were plaques of appreciation discreetly placed amid photos of her children.

It was after five when Mr. Stallworth pulled into the driveway. He drove a Jeep, which didn't strike Lorena as the sort of car a professor would drive. His manner of dress was likewise odd: shorts, hiking boots, a field hat that cast his face in shadow. He strode across the foyer, nodding sheepishly at his wife's scolding, and uttered a distracted apology to the girls, who watched him from the top of the stairs. Then he took off his hat and Lorena sucked in her breath. He had a sturdy jaw, dark whiskers, pale brown eyes. *Swarthy*. Was that the word?

"My God, Marcus, go take a shower." Mrs. Stallworth gestured at the stains under his armpits. "You smell like an animal."

Lorena stared at his calves as he retreated.

Later, the girls were summoned to his basement office. He was wearing a polo shirt and thick black glasses. Jenny announced, rather defiantly, that they wanted to pursue a project on astrology.

"It's smart to pursue a topic that interests you, but astrology isn't exactly science." Mr. Stallworth smiled shyly. He was turning a paperweight in his fingers; the tendons on the back of his hand made the muscles of his forearm dance. "You need a hypothesis. And you need proof. Evidence. What do you think? It's Loretta, right?"

"*Lorena*," Jenny said.

"We could have people fill out a survey to see if their personality traits fit with their sign," Lo said. "If there's a correlation."

"A correlation. Good. But we're not always the best judge of our own character, are we?"

"What if other people fill out the survey?" Lorena said quietly. "To correct for bias."

Mr. Stallworth looked at her curiously.

Jenny released a sigh of theatrical impatience. "It's the science fair, you guys, not the national academy of whatever." She took up the idea of a survey at some length, while Mr. Stallworth closed his eyes and listened.

The walls of his office were covered with topographical maps, each of them riddled with colored pushpins. They looked like the connect-the-dot drawings Lorena had done as a kid as she waited for her mother to return from work.

"Why not aim for something a little more empirical?" Mr. Stallworth suggested finally.

He glanced at Lo, seeking an ally. She felt caught gazing at the cleft in his chin. Mr. Stallworth stood abruptly and announced that he needed to start the fire for the grill.

"I knew he was going say that," Jenny said, after he'd left. "*Empirical* is like his pet word."

Lo waited for Jenny to turn away, then picked up the paperweight. It was a coffin-shaped lump of amber with a tiny scorpion suspended inside. By some trick of light, the scorpion looked as if it were shrieking. She felt a sudden urge to slip the paperweight into her pocket and press it against her thigh.

JUST BEFORE DINNER, Jenny's brother, Glen, arrived home. Muddy cleats hung from his shoulders. He was a senior in high school, impossibly glamorous. Mrs. Stallworth scolded him for tracking grime into the house. She wasn't really mad. It was a fond performance, something moms did on TV, the kind who poured fresh-squeezed orange juice into tall glasses.

"Who are *you*?" Glen grunted at Lo.

"That's Lo," Jenny said. "Try not to be a dick."

"Language!" Mrs. Stallworth called out from the kitchen.

Glen sauntered up to Lo and let his eyes roll down her body. "Do you think I'm a dick?" He was gone before she could answer.

The meal itself was elaborate: glazed carrots, fresh rolls with chilled tabs of butter, a salad that had nuts and crumbled cheese on it and steaks from the grill, one for each of them. The

Stallworths sat around a huge oak table, with place settings for everyone. The children were expected to summarize their days in a crisp paragraph as the feast steamed. Jenny ate nothing. Glen annihilated his food.

"Jennifer has a special friend over tonight," Mrs. Stallworth commented.

"Everyone can see her," Jenny scoffed. "She's not invisible."

"Nonsense," Mrs. Stallworth said pleasantly. "Tell us a little about yourself, Lorena."

Lo felt her mouth go dry. Her shirt didn't fit right. Mrs. Stallworth, all the Stallworths in fact, were looking at her. It was ridiculous, like an audience with royalty. "I'm in Jenny's science class," Lo said cautiously. "Obviously. I live with my mom. She works at Mercy. The hospital. On the labor and delivery ward."

Mrs. Stallworth clapped. "Isn't that lovely! She helps babies get born!"

Lo did not correct this impression.

"And your father?" Mrs. Stallworth said.

"He lives in Florida. He got remarried a while ago."

Mrs. Stallworth smiled, as if Florida and remarriage were just splendid.

"Do you have any brothers or sisters, Lorena?"

"Quit grilling her," Jenny said. "God."

"Asking questions isn't grilling," Mrs. Stallworth said patiently. "It's taking an interest in someone."

"I have an older brother. He joined the navy. He's training to work on a submarine."

"It's just you and your mom, then?" Mrs. Stallworth said.

"We get along pretty well. She works double shifts sometimes, so I make dinner for myself."

"Who stays with you?" Mrs. Stallworth said.

"We have a neighbor I can call if something comes up."

"You're *alone* there at night?"

"No. No. My mom always gets home before bedtime. It's not that big a deal." She glanced at Jenny. "I'm a Virgo, so I'm pretty independent."

Nobody said anything for a few seconds.

"What do you make for dinner?" Glen said suspiciously.

Lo meant to tell the truth. Toast pizzas. Beans and rice, doled from the pot that lived on their stove. "Spaghetti," she said. "Hamburgers. Nothing like this. Thanks again for having me."

Through all this chatter, Mr. Stallworth said nothing. He hacked at the meat on his plate and shoveled carrots into his mouth. There was something awkward in how he held his cutlery, as if, left to his own desires, he would have gone at the steak with his hands, then lapped at the red puddle beneath. Lo didn't realize she was staring until she noticed Mrs. Stallworth staring at her. She held her blade aloft, almost like a baton. Lo cast her eyes down at her plate. She felt a shiver of fear, and this fear, for some unfathomable reason, pleased her.

"SHE'S SUCH A phony," Jenny said, after dinner. They were back in her room.

"About what?" Lo said.

"Everything. It's all just this big display. Lucia does all the real work."

Lo wanted to ask who Lucia was, then she understood.

"My mom used to work," Jenny added. "She sold real estate. But her family is loaded. That's the secret formula around here."

Lo nodded. "I lied about my brother," she said suddenly. "It wasn't a lie exactly. He is in the navy. But he signed up cuz he got kicked out of school."

"Why was he kicked out?" Jenny whispered, with a gleeful solemnity.

"He kept cutting classes. Then he kind of joined a gang."

"For real?" Jenny put her hand over her mouth.

Lorena knew it was wrong to talk about her brother's troubles. But it was a kind of preemptive offering, one that allowed her to protect the most important secret of all: that Tony and her mother were undocumented, that he'd enlisted in the hopes of earning a path to citizenship.

"Don't tell anyone, okay? Promise?"

Jenny promised.

MR. STALLWORTH DROVE Lo home in his Jeep, turning south onto Alhambra. She watched the trees of East Sacramento give way to the shrubs of Oak Park, then farther south into Fruitridge Pocket, with its Eichlers and pavement. Lorena had never been in a Jeep before. The wind tore at her hair. Potholes rattled her bum. Mr. Stallworth stared at the road ahead, his hands clamped to the steering wheel.

They pulled up to her apartment building. A Styrofoam takeout box, whipped up from the gutter, hugged the chainlink fence.

"How do you know about bias?" Mr. Stallworth said suddenly.

"Our science teacher. Miss Catalis. She has these sayings. *The enemy of truth isn't falsehood. It's bias.* That's one of them."

Mr. Stallworth was smiling. "Listen, Lorena. I'm going to let you in on a little secret: astrology is nonsense. You know that already, don't you?"

"I guess."

"You don't have to play dumb," he said gently, almost reluctantly. "It's okay to be smart."

They sat in silence for a moment. Then Lo thanked Mr. Stallworth for the ride.

"Of course. Do you need help with your bike?"

"Not really."

"Of course you do."

Mr. Stallworth reached across Lo and jerked at the door handle. "It gets stuck," he murmured, nudging the door open with his knuckles. Lo's seat belt had tugged at her shirt, exposing a band of belly skin, against which the hairs of his forearm brushed, ever so lightly. A dark possibility rose between them like a coil of smoke then dissolved. It was that quick; Mr. Stallworth withdrew his arm. "In any case," he said formally. "It's nice to see Jenny spending a little time with a serious young lady."

"MY MOM LIKES you," Jenny said, in her mocking tone. They were in a corner of the library, supposedly researching. "My brother says you're getting tits."

This was true. They were tender all the time; they bumped into things.

"What a pig." Jenny picked at her braces and oinked. "Boys are all pigs. Let's go to the bathroom."

"Why?"

"I want to see them. I could see them in gym if we had the same period. I'll show you mine. They're so lame."

Lo thought of the Jenny Stallworth who lived in her mind, the tall, stylish girl who glided through the cafeteria in Esprit jeans, a different color for each day of the week, who enthroned herself upon the bench that overlooked their little junior high quad and nibbled at a Twix bar and stared with glamorous apathy past the rich jocks wrestling each other for her attention. Jenny with the magazine home, the gracious mother, the dark handsome father. That was Jenny from the outside. But inside were all the secret boxes that made up a human being, boxes made of envy and curiosity and shame.

In the bathroom, they crowded into a stall and Lo lifted her shirt and unhooked her bra. Her heart was thumping.

Jenny regarded them with undisguised awe, then her slender hand reached out and took hold of the left one, testing its heft for a second. *"Otsa lotsa mozzarella,"* she sang out, the tagline from a TV ad.

Lorena wondered if this was what it meant to be rich, that you were allowed to take possession first and ask permission later. It was like the scientific method in reverse, the conclusion before the hypothesis.

"Your nips are kind of big," Jenny went on. "Has anyone felt them? Like, a boy? Who?"

"A friend of my cousin," Lo said softly. "He lives in San Jose."

Lo made it sound like a date, though it had been a game in her cousin's basement. She didn't know the boy. His tongue tasted of pizza and Binaca. His fingers were bony and fumbling.

Jenny was still squinting. "Does your mom have big ones? That's how you know what yours are going to look like. My mom's a fucking A-cup. She said you don't want them too big or they get all saggy." Jenny began to tug nervously at her shirt.

"You don't have to show me," Lo said.

"Whatever." Jenny lifted her shirt and peeled back the padded cup of her bra and out plopped one of them. It looked small and terrified, like a baby mouse with one pink eye. "Peter Stinson wanted to touch them. He thinks he's such hot shit because his dad is a surgeon. Big deal. He's gay." Jenny carried on like this until they heard the bathroom door swing open. They listened to another girl enter the stall next to them and pee and let out a small glissando of farts, which sent them into convulsions.

"That should be our project," Jenny said, on the way back to the library. "A study of why farts come out in those little blips. How sick would that be?"

"Maybe we should do something on scorpions," Lo said carefully.

"Have you ever *seen* a scorpion? Like, in real life?"

Lo had not. Her mother had talked about them. In the village where she grew up, you had to check your shoes for them. They were supposed to have mystical powers.

"I like the fart idea." Jenny sniggered. "My mom says you should come over for dinner again. She's got a whole idea in her head."

Lo wanted to ask what that meant, but she didn't.

MISS CATALIS DID a weekly check-in on Friday. The science fair was her big crusade, students discovering things, claiming the universe. "Believe me, girls, I'm a huge fan of the horoscope," she said. "But astrology is a belief system. Something more like religion. We choose to believe rather than being compelled by facts. You understand the difference?"

Jenny nodded sullenly.

"Any other ideas?"

The girls exchanged an embarrassed look.

"We were thinking something about gas," Lorena said. "Like, human gas."

Jenny looked down, to keep herself from cracking up.

"To figure out why the byproduct of digestion would be flatulence," Lo continued. "We could examine the specific food groups that lead to a gaseous outcome."

A shadow passed over Miss Catalis's face. "I was hoping for something a bit more ambitious from you two."

Jenny made one of her little smirks, the ones pretty girls mistook for indiscernible. Lo could see how stunning she would be when her braces came off. She thought about the scorpion in Mr. Stallworth's paperweight, its tiny trapped shriek.

"C'mon guys. This is your chance to push into the unknown."

JENNY WAS STARING at her tender, unhappy face in the mirror when she mentioned, in the blithe way she had, that her family was going on a camping trip the next weekend and that Lo was invited. "It's, like, Death Valley or whatever. Not the actual place but around there."

This was in the minutes after Science, the brief portion of the day during which Jenny and Lo consorted. They were in the bathroom behind the portable classrooms, where they wouldn't be seen together. Eighth grade was what it was: a tender, blemished version of the world to come.

Lo smoothed a clump of hair.

"You checked with your mom?"

"Duh. It was her idea. Have your mom call if she's got questions."

But her mom wouldn't have questions. Graciela Saenz lived by rituals of caution, avoiding those outside a small circle of neighbors, parishioners, and co-workers. It was enough to know that Lorena was spending time with a good family. The one she worried about was Tony, who had inherited his father's reckless temper.

Lorena had slept outside plenty of times, setting a thin blanket on the porch, or a patch of lawn, when summer rendered their apartment broiling. But she had never camped in the desert. Jenny said she didn't need anything besides tennis shoes and a change of clothes. Her dad had all the equipment.

On the appointed morning, Lo arrived at the Stallworth home bearing corn dumplings in honey. She claimed her mother had made them, though she'd bought them from a bodega. Mrs. Stallworth made a big production.

Mr. Stallworth had left to pick up Glen from a soccer tournament, so Rosemary drove the girls in her Cadillac. They sat in the back seat, as if they were being chauffeured, and zoomed south into the hot belly of the state, the highways that stunk of cow shit and garlic, the wide green fields where Lorena's father had picked crops when he first arrived. Mrs. Stallworth listened to KFRC, the Top 40 station. She sang along to "Bette Davis Eyes" and "Queen of Hearts" and the other hits Jenny pretended to hate.

"You don't even know who Bette Davis is, do you girls?" Mrs. Stallworth said.

"Here we go," Jenny murmured.

Mrs. Stallworth kept right on talking about Bette Davis and her horrible smoking and what it had done to the skin around her eyes. She had that talent of certain mothers, to ignore the static of her children, to pretend everyone was a bit happier than they were. It was more than that, though. Mrs. Stallworth wanted to talk about herself, those years when pop songs and movie stars still defined her. Jenny experienced her mother's nostalgia as an affront, a galling reminder that her own youth would someday dissolve into such tiresome monologues.

But Lo was happy to hear her stories. She asked questions while Jenny stared out the window. Mrs. Stallworth had grown up with money, back East, on something called the Main Line. She had studied ballet and been a fashion model. An Italian designer spotted her at a club and led her onto the dance floor and by the end of the night he had asked her to come to Europe.

"He wanted to get into your pants," Jenny said.

"Of course he did," Rosemary replied. "What do I always tell you, Jennifer? Women don't enjoy the privilege of stupidity."

"What happened?" Lo said.

"He wanted to design some clothing. He needed a model. He selected me because of my height. And my shoulder blades."

"Don't tell me you stripped naked for this greaseball."

"Alright. I won't tell you."

Holy shit, Jenny mouthed.

"Did you go to Europe?" Lo asked.

"Of course not." Mrs. Stallworth glanced into the rearview mirror, as if Lo had misunderstood the point of the story. "I got married."

After a time, Jenny began whispering about Peter Stinson, whom she liked, or thought she maybe liked, though she sort of hated him, too, while Lo studied Mrs. Stallworth's mauve sweater and tried to figure out what might distinguish her shoulder blades to an older man.

"Your father has a surprise for you two," Mrs. Stallworth said.

Lo pondered where everyone would sleep that night. She was struck by an absurd question: Was she now a member of the Stallworth family?

IN THE PARKING lot of the trailhead, Glen and Mr. Stallworth heaved equipment from the back of the Jeep. Lorena stared past the tiny kiosk with its faded map, into a pale expanse rippling with heat; her gaze fixed on the distant spot where the sky met the white of the trail, the vanishing point. Mrs. Stallworth, Rosemary, hugged Jenny, then got back in her car.

"Isn't your mom coming?" Lo whispered.

Jenny laughed. "Hey, Mom! Lo wants to know whether you're coming with us."

Rosemary smoothed her face into a smile. "I'm afraid the out-of-doors isn't my milieu, dear."

"Her milieu is, like, the nearest Hilton," Glen muttered.

They walked for a long time through desert the color of bone. Everything—the plants and rocks, even the sand—had been bleached by the sun. Glen stripped off his shirt and tied it around his head. He wanted the world to see his muscles glisten. He was that sort of animal.

Mr. Stallworth trudged beneath a massive pack. His thick, hairy legs pumped away. The girls staggered behind. Lo expected Jenny to complain. But a different set of rules applied to her father. Suffering was the price of his company. Late in the afternoon, they turned off the main trail. She could feel the earth's heat through the rubber soles of her tennis shoes.

At dusk, they struck camp and made freeze-dried stew and rice, which they consumed with a keen hunger, along with the corn dumplings. After dinner, the girls crawled into their tent to put on sweaters.

The darkness brought a bite to the air. Mr. Stallworth stood by the fire. "Come on over here, you two." He reached into his giant pack and drew out what appeared to be long plastic shin guards. Then he bent down and began strapping them onto his daughter's legs, like armor.

"What are these things?"

"Snake chaps!" Glen hooted. "Rattlers hunt at night."

Jenny turned to her father.

"It's a precaution," Mr. Stallworth said calmly. "You're perfectly safe." He turned to Glen. "Don't test me, young man. I'm not your mother."

Jenny tore off the snake chaps. "No way no way no way." She retreated into the tent and Mr. Stallworth followed. They could hear him speaking to her in soft exasperation.

"What about you? You afraid of snakes, Lo?" Glen flicked his tongue.

She let her eyes linger on his face. He was like her own brother in some ways, engorged with an arrogance that was central to whatever secret he was keeping from the world.

Mr. Stallworth emerged from the tent.

"I should stay with her," Lo said.

"Nonsense." Mr. Stallworth dropped to his knees before her and suddenly his hands were on her calves. He yanked at the straps. She felt roughly handled in a way she knew she shouldn't like.

"Just go," Jenny moaned through the flap. "Leave me the hell alone."

MR. STALLWORTH LED them into the darkness. He lugged an oversized lantern, which he set down on a small rise. "Close your eyes and keep them shut until I say."

"Do it," Glen murmured.

"Okay. Open."

An iridescent purple light gleamed out in all directions. Lo's eyes scrolled an ocean of sand, upon which now lay scattered scores of tiny glow-in-the-dark toys, the sort kids on TV pulled from cereal boxes. Then the toys began to move. These were living creatures, many-legged and scrabbling, like tiny lobsters.

"Welcome to Scorpionville," Glen said.

Lo glanced at the sand around her feet. A scorpion the length of a hairpin labored under the weight of its stinger, which hung like a fanged jewel over the armored segments of its body.

"Don't be frightened." Mr. Stallworth said. He was suddenly right beside her.

"I'm not," Lo replied.

"What do you think?"

"They're—" She cast about for the right word, stunned to find the truth in such a simple one: "Beautiful."

She could feel Mr. Stallworth inspecting her face, trying to figure out if she really meant it. He took off his glasses and began furiously polishing the lenses with the hem of his shirt. For a queer moment, Lo imagined grabbing his glasses and tossing them away.

"We gonna take any home?" Glen asked.

Mr. Stallworth pulled a small flashlight from his pocket and swept the purple beam across the sand. "We might as well see who's hunting tonight." To Lo's astonishment, he knelt down and guided a scorpion onto his palm. The animal was the size of a matchbox. Its pincers pawed the air.

"Shouldn't you have gloves?" Lo said.

"You just come at them from behind," Glen said. "They can't sting backwards."

"They're not aggressive animals," Mr. Stallworth explained. "They just want to be left alone."

"Tell her about the dance," Glen said.

Mr. Stallworth let the scorpion scuttle from one hand to the next. "Yes. You might like this. During courtship, the scorpions grasp each other's pedipalps—their pincers. They perform a kind of dance. It's called the promenade à deux. It looks like they're fighting. But it's just the opposite. It's how they select a mate."

"Fuck or fight," Glen whispered in Lo's direction.

His father glared at him. "What did you just say?"

"Nothing," Glen said.

Mr. Stallworth aimed the purple light into his son's eyes. "There's a young woman here, Glen. This isn't some locker room."

"It was a joke—"

"It was demeaning. Apologize to Lorena. Now."

Glen blinked like a scolded dog. "Sorry," he mumbled.

Mr. Stallworth returned his focus to the animal. "You see these little hairs along their legs?" he said. "This is how they hunt. By touch. By vibration. They can register the movement of a single grain of sand from ten yards away."

"Why do they shine?" Lo said.

"Nobody knows. Fluorescence must convey some kind of evolutionary advantage, but it's still their little secret."

Glen asked his father to find a scorpion he could pick up. Mr. Stallworth scanned the ground with his magic light. "These are your best bet," he said. "*Paruroctonus utahensis*. Sand scorpions."

"Aren't they poisonous?" Lo said.

"This species isn't too bad. Unless you're an insect."

She watched Mr. Stallworth gently prod the scorpion onto Glen's hand. The creature scampered along his knuckles. It looked glum, menacing, painfully shy.

"Are *you* gonna pick one up?" Glen asked Lo. "How about that little guy?" He pointed to a scorpion barely larger than a beetle.

Mr. Stallworth crouched for a closer look. His arm shot out and swept Glen backwards.

"What the hell?"

Mr. Stallworth drew a pair of long tweezers out of his fanny pack and plucked up the animal, which twisted fiercely. "*Hadrurus hirsutus*. The desert hairy scorpion. Highly toxic." Mr. Stallworth dropped the specimen inside a clear plastic film canister, then strode to the giant lantern and shut it off. The sand went dark around them and in this darkness Lorena heard the crisp thrashing of *Hadrurus hirsutus*.

"What about Lo?" Glen said.

"I'm sure she's had enough excitement for one night."

"I'm not scared," Lo said. The words came out louder than she intended. More softly, she added, "I'd like to hold one."

Mr. Stallworth switched on the lantern. He stared at her face again, half in wonder, and picked up another one, bluish under the light, a gentle species, he said, its sting no worse than a wasp. She reached out and Mr. Stallworth uncurled her fingers. The earth was trembling beneath her. Then she realized that it was her, and not the earth.

"You don't have to do this," Mr. Stallworth said.

"I know."

"Do you trust me?"

She met his gaze and nodded and Mr. Stallworth lowered the animal onto her.

"No way," Glen said.

The creature clung to the knob of her wrist, like a charm. Slowly, tentatively, it began to move toward her hand, the legs rising and falling like tiny jointed oars. Lorena's pulse lurched. She closed her eyes to keep from flinching. Tiny feet tickled her palm. She felt a dampness beneath her clothes, the dizziness of what was going to happen next. When she could stand it no longer she opened her eyes. The scorpion was perched on her thumb, perfectly still, its stinger hoisted like a tiny scythe.

"He appears to like you," Mr. Stallworth said.

JENNY REFUSED TO join them around the fire; Lorena brought her a toasted marshmallow. She described what had happened, careful to express the proper disgust. "I shouldn't have gone. Are you mad at me?"

Jenny shook her head. "I get it. All my friends cream their jeans over Glen. This was my mom's idea, anyway." She ripped the browned skin off her marshmallow and sucked it into her mouth. "The whole thing is so Holly Hobbie."

"What thing?"

"She wants us to do our project on scorpions, so me and him can *bond*. Duh."

Lorena felt a sudden ache in her throat. To be the object of such a plan, to live within the orbit of such concern. "It would be a cool way to freak people out," she said.

"What would?"

"We could have them, like, stick their hands into an aquarium filled with sand, then we turn on the UV light. The boys would shit themselves."

Jenny laughed tentatively. "That's like a haunted house thing."

"The science could be about why they glow. Your dad says nobody knows. It's like this big mystery." She wanted to say:

Just think about it. She wanted to say: *We could win with your dad's help.*

Jenny thrashed at her sleeping bag. "Don't you get it? Those things freak me out, okay? They give me nightmares. Whose fucking side are you on, anyway?"

LORENA COULDN'T SLEEP; her blood was still roaring. She lay in the tent listening to Glen cast words into the fire, about soccer, the refs, some jerk whose ass he might kick. His tone reminded her of the way Tony spoke around his older friends, as if he wanted something from them, praise, permission, a kind of regard that his neediness pushed away. From time to time, Mr. Stallworth replied with a stern murmur. At last, Glen retreated to the other tent. Lorena counted to two hundred. Outside, Mr. Stallworth stood staring at the flames. He had gathered stones— from where, Lo couldn't imagine—and arranged them around the fire in a perfect circle.

He glanced up at Lorena. "Trouble sleeping?"

She nodded.

"They're remarkable, aren't they? Not everyone can see it." He dumped the dregs of his coffee onto the fire and they listened to it hiss. The fire cast the line of his jaw in bronze. Mr. Stallworth seemed to be trying to decide something.

"If you really can't sleep," he said at last, "I'd like to show you something."

He led her away from the camp, onto an incline. She followed the soft crunch of his footfalls, panting to keep up. Then he stopped, so abruptly that she nearly walked into him. His flashlight showed the earth falling away. They had reached a precipice of some sort. With a click, he cast them into darkness. "Look up," he said.

The stars were gigantic and glinting. Their ancient light pressed down, the space between the brightest bodies speckled with celestial ash. Lo stood, breathless.

Mr. Stallworth pointed to a band of stars directly above them. "Orion's Belt. Do you know the story of Orion?"

"No," Lo said.

"He was a famous hunter. In mythology. He promised his lover he was going to kill every creature on earth."

"Did he?"

"No. The goddess of the Earth sent a scorpion to devour him. He's up there, too. On the other side of the sky." Mr. Stallworth aimed the beam. "You have to draw the lines in your mind. The ancients used these constellations to map the night sky. They had no inkling they were seeing an entire galaxy. The enormity would have crushed them."

"We learned about constellations in our navigation unit," Lorena said. "But it was just pictures in a book."

Stallworth laughed softly, and she worried she had said something foolish. After a moment, he spoke again. "We didn't have navigation units when I was in school. It was more of a religious curriculum. *The Lord looks down from heaven on the children of man, to see if there are any who understand.*"

Lorena recognized the passage. It was one of the Psalms.

"They didn't want us curious. They wanted us obedient."

She wondered who *they* were and what sort of child Mr. Stallworth had been and whether he spoke to his own children in this way. She wondered if she should respond somehow, then realized she didn't have to. They had drifted into an easy silence; she was witnessing another part of him emerge. They stood together, gazing.

"You have to get away from all the light pollution to see them clearly," he said.

"That's why you took us so far out?"

He hummed. After a minute, he added, "Certain kinds of beauty make us disappear."

Lorena had no idea what this meant, but she nodded. She was desperate to remain near him. It made no sense.

She heard the rasp of Mr. Stallworth rubbing his face, his profile faint against the starlight. "Everything back there, it's all made up—the light and the pavement and the products. We just pretend it's real." He was standing closer now, inhaling and exhaling. "You know what I'm talking about. You wouldn't be out here if you didn't."

She listened to him shift his weight. From beneath his shirt came a scribbling against the darkness. The poisonous scorpion in its tiny plastic cell. "You were brave tonight. Not many young women your age would be that brave."

"They're so amazing."

"Dangerous, too. If you pick the wrong one."

Her mouth had gone dry; her tongue groped for words.

"You picked me."

"I'm sorry?"

"You picked for me," she said. "So I knew it was safe."

Her gaze shifted from the stars to his smile, which she could just make out. She smelled smoke, the tang of his sweat, and her breath, when she could breathe again, came hard. It was some power he had: to bring her deeper into herself, to make her feel certain things, to get her confused about what she wanted. He was a grown man. His limbs were thick and covered in hair. The moon was a shard of bone. She cast her eyes on the stars again, struggled to find one that wasn't pulsating.

"We need to get back," he said. "Before it's too late."

LO WAS NOT invited back to the Stallworth residence for several weeks. She sensed Jenny was angry about the camping trip, and accepted this without complaint. Perhaps it was better that she return to the safe boundaries of her life. Still, at night, she thought of Mr. Stallworth, in the desert, under the stars. She felt his hands gripping her calves. She saw the scorpions—they seemed somehow *his*—sprinkled across the floor of the desert like a constellation. What made them glow under UV light? It was a mystery that felt bound up in the mystery of him.

The library at Sutter offered nothing beyond a few picture books. At the library downtown, amid the shelves devoted to snakes and spiders, she found just two works on scorpions. The first was a primer published in 1956. The second was a slender volume, a pamphlet really, titled *Prince of the Desert Night*. An editor's note read, "Compiled by the Poisonous Animals Research Laboratory of Arizona State College," though it was clearly the work of one person. "Who among all the creatures of the world must suffer as the scorpion does?" the author demanded. "This shy sovereign, wishing only to abide the ancient stirrings of instinct, must live as an exile in his own habitat, maligned as repulsive, his venom extracted and analyzed in the cold white of wretched labs." It was like some kind of epic poem, or perhaps a confession of love.

The writer made only passing reference to fluorescence, identifying it as a potential mating signal. That didn't make any sense, though: male scorpions used chemical cues to locate females. So maybe it was an adaptation left over from an era when ultraviolet rays bombarded the Earth. But why then had the glow endured? Why did it exist across every habitat and climate?

Lorena remembered something Miss Catalis had said at the beginning of their zoology unit. "All animals exhibit an essential nature." She thought about the scorpion that had scampered across her palm, the ghostly shiver of the hairs it used to detect movement. Scorpions were exquisitely sensitive creatures. Perhaps their fluorescence expressed this. Photosensitivity. That was the technical term.

The author of the pamphlet seemed to be making the same argument. "Miscast as a fearsome hunter," he observed, "the scorpion is in fact exceedingly wary. Most hours are spent in burrow, safe from the owls and bats who spiral above, eager to feast on the soft flesh beneath his armor."

Lorena began to imagine the scorpion not as the hunter but the hunted. The insight came to her gradually, then all at once: Fluorescence was a protective mechanism, a kind of alarm system. The glow researchers used to find them was, in fact, intended to help them hide. This was why the black light had set them into motion.

She hunched over her notebook, sketching out experiments that might certify this theory. At a certain point, the lights flickered overhead and a drowsy voice on the loudspeaker announced that the library would close in ten minutes. Lorena had been *geeking out*. That was what her brother called it. More than four hours had passed.

LORENA BEGAN TO sneak looks at Jenny Stallworth in class, to track her movements through the hallways, into the bathrooms where she touched up her eye shadow. A dozen times she brought herself to the brink of an approach. She was used to this cycle, the thinking and rethinking of what she might say, anticipating how the other person might react, and, in turn, how she might react to this reaction. These were the loops within which shy people lived, and which made it so exhausting for them to initiate contact.

Then one day, Jenny turned from her locker and marched over to Lorena, who was standing nearby trying to look inconspicuous. "Hey," she said.

"Hey," Lorena said.

"So I know you're stressed about this whole science fair thing. But you don't have to spy on me."

Lorena glanced at the girls around Jenny's locker. "I'm not—"

"Yeah, you are." Jenny reached into her mouth to yank at a rubber band on her braces, then smiled brightly. "You don't have to go all stalker. Come over on Thursday. I've got the books at my house anyway. Cool?"

Lorena rode her bike over. Mr. Stallworth's Jeep was in the driveway; there was no sign of the Cadillac. Rosemary was out "doing her Junior League bullshit." Jenny led them up to her room, where they worked for an hour, Lorena recording the questions for their survey in her notebook. Jenny got restless and turned on some music. Then she got a call from a friend *in crisis*, which she *had* to take in the den. The moment she heard the trill of Jenny's phone voice, Lorena glided downstairs, past the kitchen, where Lucia was chopping something. She had no business sneaking down to the basement. It wasn't how she behaved. She kept telling herself to stop and careening forward, outpacing her caution.

MR. STALLWORTH LOOKED pleased to see her, if a little perplexed. "I heard you might be coming over. How goes the world of the zodiac?"

Her heart beat stupidly. "Okay, I guess. Jenny's on the phone."

"Imagine that." His grin was a little conspiratorial. "Sit, please."

She did a quick sweep of his desk: a notebook, a survey map, a small dish of pink and white candies, Good & Plenty they were called. "I'm sorry we didn't do our project on scorpions," Lorena said, in a nervous burst. "I've been reading about them. A little."

"Have you?"

Mr. Stallworth looked squarely at Lorena. She was glad she had worn her prettiest blouse, which she slipped on in a bathroom before first period because it was cut lower than her mother allowed.

"I couldn't find too many books about them, though."

"Scorpions are not a very popular subject of study, I'm afraid, within my family or beyond. Humans find them repellent. It's an evolutionary response derived from our time as cave dwellers. We don't like creatures that hunt while we sleep, especially if they sting." Mr. Stallworth reached out for the Good & Plenty and stirred them with his thumb.

"I've been thinking about why they light up," Lorena said.

"And what did you decide?"

The words spilled out of her, as if she had been gently tipped. She told him about the theories she'd dismissed, then about her revelation: that the scorpion's glow was maybe photosensitivity, an adaptation to help them find shelter from predators.

Mr. Stallworth leaned back and stared at the ceiling for a minute. "So the cuticle acts as a light receptor," he said. "That's what you're suggesting. A giant proto-eye of sorts. Of course, there are already eyes at the center of the carapace, the anterior median, and several lateral eyes evolved for the express purpose of light sensitivity, which argues against . . ." He cocked his head. "Still. It is possible."

"I was thinking about some experiments," Lorena said. "To test the utility of fluorescence."

Mr. Stallworth smiled. "Of course you were."

Lorena wished she'd brought her science notebook, then she was relieved she hadn't; she knew how silly her sketches would look. She began to describe her most sophisticated experiment, which involved placing scorpions in a terrarium, shifting the light levels, tracking movement.

"That's good," Mr. Stallworth said. "But you would need to simulate all sorts of light. Not just the visible spectrum. Starlight. Moonlight, too. And you would have to establish controls, wouldn't you? That would require occluding ocular capacity in some subjects." He poured a handful of Good & Plenty into his mouth and chewed them absently. "Blocking their eyes, I mean. This would help establish that the cuticle acts as a photon receptor. We would have to measure locomotory activity at different light intervals, as well."

"Could you do all that," Lorena asked. "In your lab?"

Mr. Stallworth laughed. "I don't have a lab, Lorena. I barely have an office. I do fieldwork. To conduct such experiments in a sound way, a verifiable way, would require thousands of dollars in grant money." He laughed again, more gently. "You're disappointed. Don't be. This is how science works. It takes time. Your ideas light the way, but you have to grope around to get at the truth. That takes money."

"Right."

He looked at her and beamed. "Don't you see, Lorena? What's really important here? You have the mind of a scientist."

"I do?"

"You do. If you want to give this subject more consideration, my library is at your disposal."

"Really?"

"Us scorpiologists have to stick together." He stood and beckoned for her to join him in front of the bookshelf. "Most of these are technical journals. But there are a few things you might enjoy."

Lorena's eyes fixed on the pamphlet wedged between two bulky textbooks.

"Hey," she said, "I read this one. It was in the library."

"What did you think?" he asked quietly.

"It was sort of weird and beautiful. Do you know who wrote it?"

"A number of us worked on it, actually."

"Wait, *you* wrote it?"

"As I said, it was a collaboration." Mr. Stallworth cleared his throat, and reached for another book, which he held out to her. "This one would be more instructive."

Lorena took the book and looked up to thank him and for just a second he was gazing down the blouse she had worn for his benefit, at the tops of her breasts, which his own daughter had seen and touched. She knew she should be offended or at least troubled, but she remained still, even leaning forward a bit more, suddenly, thrillingly aware of her body, as if her own skin were one giant eye, glowing under his inspection.

Footsteps sounded overhead. Lorena thanked Mr. Stallworth for the book and turned away. At the top of the stairs, a small figure stepped out of the shadows and startled her. "*¿Te has perdido?*" Lucia asked.

"Lost?" Lorena replied in English.

"I'm asking because this is a big house. A girl like you, who isn't used to such extravagance, might wind up in the wrong place." Lucia was still speaking Spanish. The word she used for girl was *morenita*, which they both knew was meant to draw attention to the darkness of her skin.

"We were just talking," Lorena explained. "Jenny's on the phone."

She tried to get by, but Lucia stepped into her path. She stared at the neckline of Lorena's top and shook her head. In her fist was a feather duster that looked like a dead bird. "You're best not to bother the señor," she said, this time more slowly. "He's a very busy man. I'm sure Jenny would prefer if you waited in her room."

ON A MONDAY in late March, Mrs. Stallworth picked up both girls from school. They were to finish their project, but the moment they arrived at the Stallworth home the phone was ringing and Rosemary picked it up and cried out and dashed to the TV room.

The president had been shot, *assassinated*. That was the word Mrs. Stallworth kept using. She sat in stillness before the TV, which showed Reagan striding to his limousine, grinning exuberantly. Then came a rippling of shots. The man behind Reagan, a secret service agent, set a hand on his shoulder. The camera lurched toward the source of the shots and when it swung back the president had disappeared. The networks aired this sequence over and over, as if it were a magic trick they couldn't figure out. The camera settled on two men who lay facedown on the sidewalk, blood, the dark startling red of it, seeping from the pudgy one onto the pavement.

The president was rushed to a nearby hospital. A bullet had entered his chest and collapsed a lung. Surgeons were operating.

"His chest. Dear God. Think about Nancy, what she must be going through." Mrs. Stallworth turned from the screen and took note of Lorena. "We were friendly when they lived here," she confided. Then, more loudly: "I'm letting you girls watch this because I don't believe in censorship. You need to see what the world has come to. I thought it would stop with Kennedy. Well, he was a Catholic. He had enemies, he and his brother. Then that despicable Manson girl tried to shoot President Ford, right here in Sacramento. What was her name? Stinky?"

"Squeaky," Jenny said quietly. "Squeaky Fromme."

"Then George Moscone. The *mayor* of San Francisco." Mrs. Stallworth was stricken and somehow ecstatic. "Is there no end to the savagery? Why do people assault our way of life? Listen to me, girls. We need to pray." Her eyes lit again upon Lo. "Do you believe? Are you a believer?"

Lo nodded.

"You must believe you can make a difference, or you won't make a difference. Do you know who said that?" Mrs. Stallworth turned down the TV and dropped to her knees, right on the plush carpeting. She closed her eyes and held her hands out on either side and after a moment the girls joined her. "Let us pray for the safety of our president and his beautiful family. Please don't let the forces of darkness strike down this loyal servant of the American way." It was awkward to hear Mrs. Stallworth speak this way, but comforting, too. It bound them together.

Lo knew her mother prayed every night, but she had never actually seen it. Prayer was a private conversation, or maybe a silent form of begging.

When Mrs. Stallworth was done, she hugged her daughter. Then she hugged Lo, and wiped her eyes. "I'll call Lucia," she said. "She can make something nice. Lo, is your mother home?"

"Not yet."

"Then you must stay! I won't have you returning to an empty home at a time like this. It's out of the question. I need to make a few more phone calls. If Lucia needs me, I'll be in my bedroom."

The girls stared at the TV, at the news men disbursing their sober panic.

"Do you think he'll die?" Lo said.

"No. *Stable condition* means he's okay." Jenny dug at the straps of her bra. "My mom's totally in love with Nancy Reagan, in case you hadn't noticed."

"Were they really friends?"

Jenny flipped her eyes with an easy contempt; Lorena waited for a clarification. "They lived around here when he was governor. My mom was gonna sell them a new house, supposedly.

Why not a castle, my dad said. Nancy was her big-deal client. Did you know that she has her own personal astrologer?"

Lorena couldn't quite track all these facts and what they had to do with each other. "So they did spend time together?"

"That's different from being friends." Jenny was staring at the screen, her profile a blade. "I doubt Nancy would even know who my mom is at this point."

Lucia poked her head into the den and took note of Lo, frowningly.

Lo thought about calling her mother at the hospital, though her mother wasn't allowed to talk during a shift. It had to be an emergency. Did this qualify as an emergency? She feared that Mrs. Stallworth would insist on speaking to her mother, and that her mother would get confused.

Mr. Stallworth arrived home with Glen. Mrs. Stallworth hugged her son and, after a moment's hesitation, her husband, who spoke to her quietly. They looked like a TV couple, gravely considering what sort of life insurance policy to purchase. Then he glanced up and spotted Lo outside the den and she tried to dampen the electricity firing through her.

At dinner, everyone watched the little portable TV on the kitchen counter. The bullet had been removed. Reagan was resting comfortably. The shooter was identified as a young man from Colorado named John Hinckley. He told the FBI his motive: he hoped to win the attention of a young movie actress named Jodie Foster.

"I don't understand how he got away with it," Lorena said.

"The criminal mind can get away with anything," Mrs. Stallworth said.

"Yeah, but what kind of sicko shoots the president to get a chick?" Glen sneered. "She's barely legal."

"His brain was poisoned by luuuust." Jenny stretched the word into a breathy innuendo.

"It wasn't his brain, dude—"

From Mr. Stallworth's place came the scrape of cutlery, so sharp that Lorena flinched. "Enough," he snapped. He got up and shut off the TV.

Mrs. Stallworth looked briefly forsaken. Then she smiled and said, "Your father is right. We can talk about something more pleasant."

"HAVE YOU BEEN picking up on all the weird vibes?" Jenny said later.

The question flopped around in Lorena's gut.

"It's because my mom paid like a grand to go to some fundraiser at Nancy's house. They had this big stupid argument. Then my dad didn't even vote for Reagan. Like it all matters so much."

Lorena tried to imagine $1,000 in one place. She couldn't do it.

"Who'd *your* mom vote for?" Jenny asked.

"She likes Reagan," Lo said carefully. "Because he talks about his faith." The politics in their home was of a different sort. Lo had papers. Her mother and brother did not. For as long as she could remember, Lo had known what this meant: that they might disappear into custody at any moment.

"My mom just wanted Nancy to be First Lady so she could get more mileage out of her connection." Jenny scowled but her eyes looked sad. "They've got this whole routine down. Like everything's so fucking honky-dory."

DOWNSTAIRS, LUCIA REMOVED the dishes from around Mrs. Stallworth, who stood entranced by the TV on the counter.

"Earth to Mom," Jenny called out, from the bottom of the stairs.

Mrs. Stallworth looked up and produced a smile. "I'll be driving you home," she announced to Lo. "Mr. Stallworth felt—we both felt—it would be best if you got home, given the situation." She finished her wine and waved her purse.

The moment they'd rounded the corner, Mrs. Stallworth pulled a pack of Virginia Slims from her purse and punched in the cigarette lighter. "I shouldn't be doing this. I quit years ago. A Russian hypnotized me. There was a whole group of us in a little theater. The man wore a tuxedo with tails!" She dipped her head and lit up with a practiced air. The man on the radio droned on about executive authority. He played audio of the assassination attempt, the hollow popping like firecrackers. "What that family must be going through."

"Is it true you were friends with her? Mrs. Reagan?" Lo asked shyly.

Mrs. Stallworth hummed, her teeth lavender with wine.

"Jenny loves this story for some reason. You probably know that the governor is supposed to move into a mansion when he takes office? But the Reagans inherited a tinderbox. The wiring was from the 1920s, if you can imagine. Shall I turn on Broadway? Yes? Look at these new homes. Nice. This whole block used to be slums." Mrs. Stallworth blew smoke out the window. "Anyway, they rented that delicious Spanish Tudor on Forty-Fifth and M Street, which made us practically neighbors. I shouldn't even tell you this—you'll think me *mad*—but I used to slow down when I drove by, hoping to catch her out front. Once, I nearly peeked in the windows, to see how she decorated her rooms. Isn't that positively ghoulish?"

Mrs. Stallworth flicked away her cigarette and shook out another. "Then the most wonderful thing happened: Shelby, my regional manager, told me he had an anonymous client looking for something in Gold River. An older home with classical bones. *Classical*—that was the word. You can imagine how I felt when Nancy appeared at that first showing! We hit it off right away. She could walk into any house on earth and tell you where everything should go."

Lo nodded along. She knew that Nancy Reagan wasn't really friends with Mrs. Stallworth, but she found herself rooting for the possibility.

"Oh, she saw how the press was going to portray her!" Mrs. Stallworth added, with a sudden vehemence. "She joked about it. *Marie Antoinette, they'll call me!* Her only crime was looking out for her family. People forget that—it was all for her family." Mrs. Stallworth peered through her windshield. They had passed from South Oak Park into Fruitridge Pocket. "Have I gotten us lost?"

"It's just a few more blocks," Lo said.

Mrs. Stallworth took in an auto body shop, a storefront church hunched in shadow. "I haven't been to this part of the city in a while. It used to have a few nice lots. I suppose the government snatched those up for projects."

"Did Mrs. Reagan buy a house from you?" Lo asked.

Mrs. Stallworth twirled her cigarette like a tiny wand. "Oh, no. In the end they bought an acre over in Carmichael and built themselves. If you want it done right, do it yourself. That was her feeling." She saw no reason to dwell on ensuing events: the party she attended in Mrs. Reagan's private garden, Marcus's abominable reaction, the buzz of informing her mother that she had lunched with the First Lady of California.

They pulled up to Lo's building. "Isn't this nice?" Mrs. Stallworth peered at the vinyl siding. "Is your mom home yet, do you suppose? Perhaps I should come in and say hello to her. That would be nice. I do worry about you, Lorena. Am I being silly? A girl your age, so much on her own. And now this. I don't mean to imply that your mother . . . She just seems to work an awful lot. You do know what I mean, don't you?"

Lo nodded. "I'm grateful. You've been so kind."

"Perhaps I shouldn't say this. It's rather dramatic. But I feel you've been brought into our life, Lorena." Mrs. Stallworth turned to Lo. She looked like a medieval queen, regal and forlorn. "All I've ever wanted is for my family to be happy. That's why we get along. You understand. You appreciate what we've built." Mrs. Stallworth reached out and stroked Lo's cheek with the back of her hand.

There was something in the gesture that made Lorena think about Jenny, the way her hand took possession, with an ease that was almost innocent, and so different from Mr. Stallworth, who, for all his gruffness, appeared frightened.

Mrs. Stallworth turned away to toss her cigarette onto the street. Then she was dabbing at her eyes. "I'm sorry. It's just this shooting that's got me off-kilter. I have this dreadful feeling that the fates are turning against us."

MANY YEARS LATER, when she thought back to this era of her life, Lorena Saenz would recall this moment, the cool brush of Rosemary Stallworth's hand across her cheek, her dire invocation of the fates, those unseen forces that governed distant events.

The First Lady of the United States believed in unseen forces, too. Jenny had been right about that. Nancy Reagan knew others mocked her for relying on astrological guidance. But she trusted the ancient bodies that loomed over the earth. They had guided her to Ronnie, and guided him to the presidency.

Even now, with her husband laid out under a surgeon's blade, a sacral truth was taking shape: the shooting had been an act of Providence. She held this notion close, like an amulet, in the grim wash of those hours. All around her, staffers marveled at Ronnie's vitality: how he had insisted on walking into the ER under his own power, then cursed at the doctor who cut off his $1,000 suit. "I hope you're all Republicans," he told the OR team, with a wink, just before they put him under and pried open his chest.

When at last word arrived that he would pull through, cheers erupted. Nancy found herself revolted by the jubilation. Radio transmissions crackled with their Secret Service code names, *Rawhide* and *Rainbow*, as if they were characters in some twisted fairytale Western. She marched outside and ordered her body man to back off. She needed a moment alone, just her and the stars. She stared into the blurry vault of heaven and vowed that her husband's blood would serve a higher good.

The shooting had tugged at the unseen threads of the universe, and set into motion a chain of events that would lead the First Lady of the United States to intervene in the life of the young woman standing on the cracked steps of an apartment building in Sacramento.

Lorena Saenz waved goodbye to Mrs. Stallworth. The hall light was out, so she proceeded in darkness past the bickering Fajardos and the irate prophecies of the AM preacher who serenaded the widow Gomez. Tony had installed a deadbolt before he left for basic training, to keep them safe he said, but the rod always jammed. As she worked her key back and forth, images from the TV tumbled through her mind: the panicked crowd, the vanished president, the men lying in shadows of blood.

THE GYM SMELLED of mildewed rubber mats and vinegar from countless homemade volcanos. The science fair exhibits were lined under rainbow bunting. *Why Coke Corrodes Your Teeth. It's a Potato—No, It's a Battery!* The girls presented a project called *Trusting the Stars: Is Astrology Destiny?* There was a large poster with lavish illustrations of the zodiac signs. There was a survey for the judges to fill out, and a mounted chart with quasi-scientific statements about the correlation between planetary configurations and personality.

Mrs. Stallworth arrived in a peach sweater set and hugged both girls. "Look at all this. So professional. You'll win. I'm certain. Lorena, I hope we won't stop seeing you." She looked down at Lo and they both felt the crush of their unexpected affection for one another. Then she strode off to make her rounds, sleek and pristine, the way Jenny would someday look.

"Is your dad coming?" Lorena said.

"As if," Jenny said.

She knew there was almost no chance she would ever see him again.

Miss Catalis paused before their display and delivered her standard pep talk. She had approved the project with a blank expression, knowing Lorena had acquiesced.

She had hoped the opposite would happen, of course, that Lorena would discover she was just as powerful as Jenny Stallworth, more so in the ways that mattered. Miss Catalis believed in her own version of the fates, that certain students could be rescued by the grace of an eighth-grade science project.

But Lo knew it would take more than that; she wanted to understand the world she wished to enter, and the people who lived there. She thought of her dinners at the Stallworth home. She followed President Reagan's recovery and envisioned the First Lady hosting a reception, to which Mrs. Stallworth would be invited. She pondered what Mr. Stallworth did all day. Did he have an office at a college? A giant cabinet with a million plastic canisters, a scorpion thrashing inside each? She read the book he loaned her and imagined riding her bike to their house to return it to him.

These fantasies played like movie clips against the dull backdrop of her daily regimen: extra credit assignments, chores, the part-time jobs her mother arranged through church. At school, she hung out with her everyday friends, bookish Mexican girls who spouted the wishful gossip of geeks. They avoided directly addressing Lorena's adoration of Jenny Stallworth, disguising their envy in gentle mockery. Privately, they longed to know what the inside of the Stallworth house looked like, secrets Lorena refused to surrender.

Sometimes, late at night, besieged by restless impulse, she seized the scorpion paperweight she had taken from Mr. Stallworth's desk and wrapped it in a thin blanket and pressed it against herself till she felt a twinge. She did this while Graciela snored softly in the next room, while the characters in her favorite telenovela, *Los Ricos También Lloran*, sang of the pleasures and tortures of love. It was disgusting. She did it only once. Until she did it again.

LORENA KNEW ANY invitation would have to come from Jenny. Their collaboration was over now, a small failure amid the essential failure of middle school. Still, she found herself slowing down as she passed the Stallworth home, hoping someone might appear, Rosemary or even Glen. After science class, she waited in the bathroom behind the portables, just in case. But Jenny didn't show up there anymore.

Then, one day, she did.

"There you are," Jenny said. "I was looking for you."

"Yeah?" Lo made herself look busy at the sinks.

"We should hang this afternoon."

"Okay."

"Is your mom around?"

"No, she's working late."

"We can do it at your house then."

Lo tried to conjure an image of Jenny Stallworth inside the apartment she shared with her mother. "It's kind of far, though."

"Not a prob," Jenny said. "I know where it is."

Lo didn't understand how this could be true. But there she was when Lo arrived home, in full makeup and skintight Calvin Kleins. A few of the corner guys were eyeing her, spitting through their teeth. Lo hurried them inside.

Jenny flitted around, taking in the paneling, the daybed where her mom slept beneath the blanched portrait of sad blond Jesus, while Lo rushed into the bathroom and ripped down the dingy bras and compression stockings hung from the shower rod, then darted through the kitchen, shoving the pot of beans left out for dinner into the fridge. She and her mother kept the apartment scrubbed, but it still smelled of fry grease.

"There's really nobody here." Jenny pulled a lighter and a hard pack of Virginia Slims from her pencil case.

"Where'd you get those?"

"My mom stashes them around the house."

"Won't she notice if they're gone?"

"She forgets. That's kind of her thing."

"Maybe we should go out on the patio?"

Lorena puffed at one of her mom's Trues, while Jenny sought to perfect what she called the French inhale, jutting out her jaw and pulling the smoke into her nostrils. Lorena could see what she was after: a gestural elegance that derived from her mother. "I'm getting a head rush," Jenny said. "Shit. It kind of stinks out here, right?"

"That's the Campbell's plant."

"Like, the soup?" Jenny made her gagging noise. "*Mmm mmm* gross."

Lo could see how lame her room looked: the stucco, the twin bed with its dark rayon bedspread. Worst of all was the little study center she had made at her desk, color-coded by subject. Nerd Central, Tony called it. Jenny barely registered any of it. She flung herself down on the bed and asked for a Coke. When Lorena returned with two cups of cola, Jenny was holding a tiny bottle in her palm, which she displayed like a game-show model. "Chivas Regal," she announced.

"I didn't know they made that size," Lorena said.

"They give these out on flights. Aren't they just, like, too cute? Wait, have you ever been on a plane?"

"Not yet."

Jenny shrugged. "Have you gotten wasted at least?"

"More like buzzed. On beer."

"This is better than beer."

"Okay, but just a little. I'm a lightweight."

She was borrowing words from her brother.

Jenny poured herself most of the bottle. "My parents are such assholes," she said. "I know you think they're, like, this perfect couple."

"Did something happen?" Lo said.

"You know why they got married? My mom was knocked up. It's like they don't think we can do math."

"Does she know you're here?"

"She thinks I'm at Young Life. Making some business plan with God. What a joke. Why did *your* parents split?"

"My dad just wanted to move out."

"C'mon. There's always something else."

Lorena remembered her father appearing in the middle of the night and her mother—her gentle mother—rushing at him, punching, cursing in Spanish, Tony stepping between them, her dad knocking Tony across the room, a neighbor threatening to call 911, her mother wailing, *No! No policia!* Then someone was setting her down on the mattress she shared with Tony and telling her to go to sleep, it was just a bad dream, though she could hear her brother howling in the next room. *I'm gonna kill him, Mama.*

"Are they fighting or something?" Lo said.

"*We don't fight, Jennifer. We discuss.* What fucking bullshit." She flung the mini bottle and it tinkled across the linoleum. Jenny got up to check out the framed photo of Tony in his navel dress, the one Lo's mother kissed every night before bed. "He doesn't look like a thug. He looks like a chihuahua in a sailor suit."

"Don't let the uniform fool you."

"Yeah, but, like, what did he *do* that was so bad?"

"He got busted once for stealing a car," Lorena said quietly.

"No *way*."

"It was more like a joyride."

"That's it?" Jenny was staring at her. "I thought he was this big-shit gangbanger."

Lorena had been warned not to speak of Tony's life on the streets, which had caused so much strife already. But she felt a perverse impulse to defend his infamy. "There was one other thing."

"What?"

"He pulled a gun on a guy." Her voice dropped. "He was at this gang initiation thing and some dude got in his face. He had to defend himself. That's how it works around here."

Jenny's pale smirk was gone. "Holy shit. What gang was it?"

"They're called the Latin Kings. They do this thing where they initiate members by beating them up. It's stupid."

"He's a Latin King?"

"Not anymore. He was just hanging out with the wrong people. That's why he joined the navy." This last part was true.

But the rest was something Lorena had improvised, a tale woven out of bullshit and bravado. Tony was the one who'd been beaten up at the "initiation." And it wasn't the Latin Kings, just a bunch of wannabes from the neighborhood. Tony bragged about how he'd fought off three guys, but his face told the story: a split lip, a swollen cheek. The beating had become a bit of neighborhood lore, cited to stave off boredom. It was only after this humiliation that Tony had pledged to get himself a gun.

Lorena was worried her friend would press her for more details. But Jenny suddenly announced that she was bored and dug a cassette of Blondie out of her backpack and lit another cig and French inhaled and began flinging herself around, singing, *One way or another, I'm gonna find ya, I'm gonna get ya, get ya, get ya.* "Are you wasted yet? I'm wasted as shit. C'mon, Lo. Loosen *up*. You're living the dream. You could have a guy over here every day and your mom wouldn't know shit." Then, as if she had just thought of it: "Hey, we should totally do that."

Which was how Peter Stinson wound up at the apartment, an actual tenth grader, tall, sneering, his hair gelled into a frosted blond wedge. "You're the best," Jenny said, as she led him into Lorena's room.

Where else could Jenny Stallworth behave this way? Not at home. Not with her real friends. Lo knew she was being used. But she was using Jenny, too, remaining close to her family. It was what people did. Her father used her mother for sex. Her mother used her father to reach the United States. Pastor Jorge at church used his parishioners to fund his little storefront. They used him to keep their faith in Jesus Christ alive. She had used Tony's delinquency to enthrall Jenny. There was no shame in any of it. Lo told herself this each time Jenny came over.

TOWARD THE END of the school year, Miss Catalis asked Lorena to stay after class. She had just sent out the notice for parent/teacher meetings and wanted to make sure Graciela Saenz would show up this time.

"I'll remind her," Lorena said.

"Good. Because certain parents, if they're not familiar with how things work, they can worry about having to see official people." Miss Catalis had her gradebook in front of her, all her prim little notes about who deserved what.

"She just works a lot."

"I'll schedule whatever time works best."

Lorena glared at Miss Catalis, then made her face go blank before her teacher could look up. She knew that it was her role to be grateful for this extra concern, but she found herself annoyed, as if she were being singled out for extra homework.

THEY TOOK THE bus to school together, her mother in church clothes, everything cotton, the colors not too bright, a little mascara. Lorena offered to translate, but it wasn't necessary because Miss Catalis spoke Spanish. She was made to wait in the hallway outside.

"Look who it is!"

Lo looked up to find Mrs. Stallworth beaming at her. A pair of slender hands stretched toward her and Lo was gathered into a quick, expensive-smelling hug. She thought about Mr. Stallworth, how he had gazed upon her breasts, and a joyous shame ripped through her.

"What are you doing here? A little damage control? I'm *kidding*, my dear! Lo! You're so serious. It's been too long since you came over. You and Jenny haven't had a fight, have you? I hope not. She can be so moody these days. Why don't you come over for the party? Glen's graduating next month. He's heading off to St. Mary's."

That wasn't really how it worked. They both knew that. But Lo nodded.

Then the door opened and Lo's mother appeared and Mrs. Stallworth nearly pounced on her. "I'm Rosemary Stallworth. Jennifer is my daughter. Our daughters worked on the science fair together. We absolutely love your Lorena. Such a gift!"

Mrs. Saenz smiled up at this tall immaculate woman; the silver rim on the crown of her left incisor peeked out. "Yes, yes. She love you very much also."

Lo felt embarrassed, then ashamed of her embarrassment, then furious at her mother and her teeth. She was relieved when Mrs. Stallworth hurried off.

They returned to the bus stop. According to her mother, Miss Catalis said that Lo scored the highest in her class on the standardized tests but that she seemed distracted this term. "If you want to be in the special classes, the AP, you have to be a top student. This woman is trying to help you, Lorena." Her mother sucked her cigarette and blew the smoke through her bangs. The streetlights showed the cracked skin around her fingernails. Her body was a dull reminder of the labor it did. "I know you're becoming a woman. I was your age once. Don't think some boy is going to give you a future. Use your brain, *mija*."

Lo stared straight ahead. She'd heard her mom say this to Tony a hundred times. He had absorbed her lectures in mulish silence and stared past her. By the end of his eighth grade, he had started smoking weed, hanging out with a bunch of clowns who called themselves a gang.

The bus driver was listening to the radio. The president was speaking in that soothing way he had, purring the word *opportunity* over and over.

"And stop stealing my cigarettes. You understand?" Mrs. Saenz grabbed her daughter's chin and stared into her eyes. "I give you liberties because you've never been dumb. Don't start now."

SCHOOL ENDED AND Lorena took the job her mom had arranged, washing dishes at a retirement home for two hundred a week, under the table. One evening, she returned home to find a note from her mother. *Jennifer called*, she wrote, in careful script. *Nice manners.* Lorena waited a whole day to call back. Jenny talked about Glen's graduation party, which was epic: pony keg,

broken arm, the cops. It emerged, rather indirectly, that Rosemary had hoped to see Lorena there. "Anyway, we're having a
little pool party, if you wanna come."

Lo rode her bike over and spent ten minutes in the shade of
a cedar, dabbing away sweat. Inside her backpack was a swimsuit, an extra outfit (carefully selected), mascara, lip balm, and
the book she'd borrowed from Mr. Stallworth. It had been a
couple of months since she'd been in the Stallworth home. She
had starved herself the entire time. Her curves had become pro-
nounced, womanly. She found a consignment store where, if she
hunted patiently, she could find clothes with the right labels,
that flattered her new figure. The transformation sent Mrs.
Stallworth into a rapture.

"Look at you! Ravishing! I'd kill for all that hair."

She insisted the girls come along for a pedicure. "A little gift
for surviving middle school! Don't give me that look, Jennifer.
Let me spoil you two a little."

"We had a plan."

"What plan? Lie in the sun and fry like an egg?"

They went to a place in the fancy downtown mall where
Asian women buffed their feet with pumice stone. "Isn't this
nice?" Mrs. Stallworth kept saying. They had tea and sand-
wiches at a Russian tea room, then little desserts called patis-
series, each of which had a thousand calories. Lorena could feel
herself sinking again into the world of the Stallworths, the cool
leafiness of the Fabulous Forties, a world without the drumbeat
of duty, where time itself was a luxury.

***

THE MOMENT THEY got home, Jenny pulled Lo into her room.
"She's like this all the time now."

"Like what?"

"*That*. Frantic. Clingy. Wait till cocktail hour."

"What happens then?"

Clothes spilled from Jenny's closet onto the carpet. A bowl of macaroni and cheese sat congealing on her desk. "This place is kind of a sty, huh? We had to let Lucia go last week." Jenny locked her door and peeled off her top.

"What about your dad?" Lo said.

"What about him? He's a robot basically." Jenny began imitating her father's crisply modulated voice. "Hello children! I am your paternal unit! Please don't express emotion. It is non-empirical data. I must now depart for my fieldwork. Scorpions are my only true friends."

Lo laughed. "He's not that bad."

"He's not your dad," Jenny said. "Come on. Get into your suit. Ro doesn't like to go outside. She's terrified of skin cancer."

"Are you going to change, too?"

Jenny nodded, then sat on her bed in her fancy bra and watched Lo undress.

"What are you now?"

"I don't know. 34C."

"C? You're a *C*." Jenny's face collapsed. Within a year, she was going to be the prettiest girl in their class but all she could think about was her flat chest. "I don't get it. You can fix everything else. Braces. Contacts. But if you want a decent set of tits, it's like a federal offense. Wait. You're not going to wear that, right? You can't. Borrow one of mine. You'll be pouring out of it."

Out by the pool, Jenny rubbed in Coppertone and let the sun broil her. Lo stayed in the shade, so she wouldn't get too dark. Glen turned up with two friends, younger boys who stood behind him like jumpy lieutenants.

"Who's your friend?" one of the boys said to Jenny.

"That's Lo." Glen nodded, his dominion on display. "Scorpion Girl. My dad put one on her hand and she didn't even flinch. No lie. Look at you, little Lo. You've grown a couple of cups since the last time we saw you."

"Pig," Jenny said.

Glen jumped into the pool in his soccer shorts and splashed the girls and his lieutenants—they were both named Trent—followed. They leered at Lo's chest. The pool, with its soft magnifying water, was like a staging ground for desire. But Lo knew her face wasn't right. She looked too much like Lucia, who'd been fired. Jenny hated her body but she knew how to flirt, how to be needy and a little hateful at the same time.

Glen fired up the grill and made hot dogs. Mrs. Stallworth let them eat around the pool, why not, it was summer. She had to visit a sick friend, but whoever wanted to could stay over. She liked having a full house. She stood and stared at her children, smiling with a glassy intensity that made everyone a little nervous.

She's lonely, Lo thought. Her mother was lonely, too. But her loneliness had seeped into her, taken its place within her private cabinet of disappointments, while Mrs. Stallworth flaunted hers like a goblet of wine. If she spilled enough, everyone would have to look and she would no longer be alone.

IT WAS NO secret where the wine coolers were. Glen hauled them out the moment his mom drove off. Lo sipped hers carefully. Glen said they should play a game. It was called Pimps and Hos. They sat around on the patio making up rules. The object of the game was to get the girls naked. This was the object of every game ever devised by teenage boys.

Glen ran to the cabana and came back with a snorkeling mask, which the boys took turns using. It was a strange sensation. Lo's body was being viewed but not touched, like the photos in magazines. She sat on the pool steps in her bikini bottoms, one hand in front of her breasts, the other grasping her wine cooler. Nobody was worried about Mrs. Stallworth coming home. They would hear her.

She wondered if she would see Mr. Stallworth and what he would do if he caught them. She imagined him standing by the edge of the pool, staring down at her body. Everyone else had somehow disappeared; it wasn't clear what he was going to do next. The wine cooler tasted like cough syrup. She couldn't let go of it. She felt like she was watching a movie of herself, one of those horror ones where the ugly girl gets killed first. She eventually discerned that she had become drunk. She stood and wobbled toward the patio. One of the boys whistled and the other called out for her to dance and began singing "La Cucaracha."

"Fucked up," Glen said, laughing.

Jenny tapped on the bathroom door. "You okay?"

Lo kept herself from throwing up. At least there was that. She told Jenny she should be getting home. She had church the next morning and an afternoon shift. "Wait for my mom," Jenny said. "She'll drive you. You don't want to ride your bike all fucked up."

They went into her room and Jenny locked the door.

"You don't have to stay here," Lo said. "Go hang out. They're waiting for you." She lay down on the carpet, which spun.

"It's okay. I don't even like those guys. They think they're hot shit. That one dude, Trent—he's a fag anyway."

"What do you mean?"

"It's just something I heard." Jenny flung off her towel and wiggled out of her bikini; the stark white of her skin shone against her tan like a second suit. Then she threw on a T-shirt and pulled a bottle of Absolut from beneath her bed. "This mixes with orange juice. You can hardly taste it." She went to the kitchen and returned with a giant plastic mug. "Don't look at me like that. It's mostly ice."

A car pulled up outside and Lorena edged toward the window. Down below, Mr. Stallworth emerged from his Jeep and began heaving camping gear from the back. The flare of his triceps made her gut hop. "That's your dad," she said. "You should put that stuff away."

"Don't stress. He won't come upstairs. He stays in his little lair."

Lorena wanted to ask what that meant, but Jenny said, rather abruptly, "What do you think of Peter Stinson, anyway? He's kind of a dick, right? I gave him head, like, a month ago. He kind of made me. His crotch smelled like old laundry. Is that gross? Do you think I'm a slut?"

"Of course not."

"We're not hanging out anymore. By the way. He's fucking some slut from Roseville now." Jenny took another glug from her giant mug. "I'm telling you cuz you know how to keep your mouth shut. If you say anything, I'll tell everyone you were the one who sucked him off." Jenny started laughing, then she was sort of crying.

"Are you okay?"

"Of course I'm okay. I *wanted* to do it. I was fine with it. It was so nothing." She closed her eyes. Within a minute, she was asleep.

Lo got up to get a towel, just in case. There was a small window, through which she could see down onto the pool. The boys were still out there, pale naked bodies flickering in the blue water. Glen had the scuba mask on and he kept dipping his head underwater to look at his friends. Lo knew then—without wanting to—what his secret was.

She slumped down onto the carpeting and stared at the glint of the Absolut bottle. The Stallworths were careless. Sloppy. They could afford to be. That was the thrill they imparted. She felt liberated among them, from the confines of her discretion, the prison of careful habits she had constructed at her mother's behest. The risk of being found out was the heart of the whole thing. That was what Lo would decide in the end, though the end was still a long way off.

▬▬▬▬▬▬▬

HER DECISION TO go down to the basement that night had little to do with her mind. It resided in her body, which was a month from turning fourteen, which yearned without precedent and thus without restraint, which kept her up at night, a tender riot, a fumbling shame; she imagined Mr. Stallworth's hands and the particular way his lips and tongue formed the word *empirical*.

Mr. Stallworth was unpacking camping gear, all manner of which lay strewn about the office, so that when Lorena appeared in the doorway she was able to admire the efficiency of his movements for a few moments. At last, he looked up.

"Lorena?" The lower half of his face was masked in whiskers that had grown beyond stubble but not yet into beard. "You've grown up a little, haven't you?"

She blushed fiercely. Her outfit consisted of a thin halter top, denim cutoffs, and mascara; she'd had to steady her hands to apply it a few minutes earlier.

"What are you doing here this late? It's past eleven."

"I'm staying over."

"Where's Jenny?"

"Asleep. I just wanted to return your book."

"My book? Of course." He set down the portable stove he'd been disassembling. "What did you think?"

"Yours was better."

"The romantic babble of a young man," he muttered.

"It's not babbling," Lorena said.

"Tell you what. You can borrow my copy, if you'd like. I'll trade it for the one you've been lugging around." He went to his bookshelf and pulled out *Prince of the Desert Night*. "I'm sorry

I didn't make it to the science fair, by the way. I heard you two did great," he said, more softly. "Just put the book on my desk. I'm sorry about the smell in here. I've been on something of an expedition."

"Where were you?"

"The Chocolate Mountains."

"Where are those?"

"Near Joshua Tree."

Lorena shrugged.

"I can show you on a map. Let me get this place aired out and maybe we can take a look tomorrow."

Lorena nodded but didn't move. She'd been waiting so long to see him. The alcohol in her system helped blur things. "I don't mind the mess."

Mr. Stallworth squinted and grinned. "I'll take you at your word then."

He went to his backpack and pulled out a laminated topographical map of California and opened it on his desk. She came and stood next to him. The map had a scattering of notations, all set down in his cramped, meticulous script. "The Chocolates are down here, a couple of hours past Fresno. High desert. Pretty terrain."

"And the spots you've marked, the Xs, those are campsites?"

"Right."

"How long were you camping?"

"Not quite a week."

"What's it like out there?" Lorena said.

Mr. Stallworth cocked his head and scratched at his beautiful neck. "Honest," he said. "The wilderness doesn't lie the way we do. Plants and animals deal in truth."

"I'd like to go out there again."

"You'd like it."

Neither one of them had moved toward the other but now their flanks were brushing. The scent of him, an animal ripeness, rose up around her. She should have been disgusted. She imagined running her fingers through his hair. She imagined them snagging.

"Were you gathering specimens?"

"This was more of a planning trip."

"What are you planning?" she said.

"Top-secret stuff."

"I really would like—"

"I know," he said. "I've had a feeling about you."

She felt her hip beginning to tremble. Then, somehow, they were facing each other and his hand was on her cheek and he was lifting her chin with his thumb, very gently, so that she had no choice but to look directly into his eyes.

"I think you should leave before things get complicated."

"Complicated?" The trembling was awful. She didn't want it to stop.

"Animals don't lie," he said quietly. "And we're both animals."

LO STUMBLED UPSTAIRS. Mr. Stallworth had touched her. He had confirmed the thing between them, but only vaguely, as if that thing were happening by accident and you didn't get to have feelings about it. Even his expression had been a puzzling blend of benevolence and something sharper—impatience or maybe disdain. She knew she should go home.

She went to fetch her backpack and found that Jenny had thrown up a little in her sleep, which meant she had to clean that up and get her friend into bed and pour the rest of the Absolut down the bathroom sink and stash the bottle at the bottom of the kitchen garbage. The backyard was a mess, too, so she cleaned that up, her body antsy and confused, half waiting for him to appear again. But it was Mrs. Stallworth who thumped into the house as she was finishing up. The zip of her purse in the foyer, keys cast into the crystal bowl, a soft grunt as she toed off her heels.

"Oh, hello! You decided to stay. How nice."

"Jenny's asleep," Lo said quickly.

"Of course she is. You're up late though, aren't you? Keep me company. We'll have some tea. Do you drink tea, Lo?" Before Lo could say anything, Mrs. Stallworth weaved toward the kitchen. "Who did all this cleaning up? It must have been my little elf. You should have left it for Lucia. That's her *job*. It's how she makes a living for her family. We all have our roles to play. Did you call your mother, Lo? Does she know you're here? I wouldn't want her to think you'd been kidnapped."

Mrs. Stallworth got out a fancy wooden box of tea bags and dropped one in a mug, then filled the kettle, though she appeared to lose interest and never actually turned on the burner. "Your mother is a labor nurse," Mrs. Stallworth continued. "That must be such a blessing. To help bring new lives into the world. I would have liked to become a baby nurse. I suppose I never took college seriously enough. I got distracted."

"By what?"

"Boys. Social duties. I grew up in a certain milieu. Do you know what I mean by *milieu*?" Mrs. Stallworth went to the fridge and pulled out a bottle of pink wine. "We had money. I'm not going to apologize. The president is right. Prosperity breeds aspiration. I saw this myself, when I visited San Miguel for a service project. That was one of the great adventures of my life. Do you know that village? Which part are you from again?"

"My mom is Honduran."

"That's right. I so enjoyed meeting her! She's a bit shy, isn't she? Still, it must have taken great courage for her to come to America. And great hope, too."

Lorena worried that Mrs. Stallworth would start asking questions about her family history, which she knew only in fragments: that her father had left El Salvador for Honduras and met her mother, that they married young, that her mother's parents disapproved. That her father had crossed the border with Tony and her mother had followed, seven months pregnant, so Lo could be born in America. It was supposed to be a story of triumph. But her early memories didn't feel triumphant. They involved adults yelling, a mood of sullen accusation, crowded rooms in which something indispensable—a key or a document or a pack of cigarettes—had always been lost.

Mrs. Stallworth poured her wine into the mug with the tea bag. "The important thing is you're here now. You get to make your own way. Don't let anyone else drive the bus. That's my advice. The bus is officially yours. Sit, Lo. Oh my. I was going to have tea, wasn't I? I don't even like tea. It's just something I always think I'm *going* to like. What a silly." Mrs. Stallworth wore a scoop-neck blouse trimmed in lace, from which her throat rose like a mottled stem. It was an odd outfit for visiting a sick friend.

"Jenny said you fired Lucia," Lo said suddenly.

Mrs. Stallworth looked at her with no great concern. "That's more of a provisional situation. Jennifer knows better than to discuss family matters. It's gauche. Shall I drink this rosé? Wait a second. We were talking about something interesting. What were we talking about? Oh, San Miguel. Can you keep a secret, Lo? I fell for a man down there, a married man." She put a finger to her lips. "We were mad for each other. Jesus Armas. Chuy. We were going to run off together. To the Sierra Madres. Catch the train in Chihuahua City. What did they call it? The Chicken Train! I believe it transported actual chickens. Chuy had a cousin with a ranch near the Copper Canyon. We had provisions stashed in the basement rectory of the church we were rebuilding. It was all terribly romantic. Can you imagine? I would have lasted a grand total of two minutes on the Chicken Train. But we clung to the idea. Everyone is entitled to a getaway plan."

"What happened?"

"We got caught. That was the point, I guess. What a scandal! I walked around like Hester what's-her-name. Pastor Tom had me shipped home a month early. Such is the power of the forbidden. *We dream in our waking moments and walk in our dreams.* Is that the line? Something like that." Mrs. Stallworth fished the tea bag out of her mug and drained her wine, then eyed the bottle, a little accusingly. "I don't have to tell you how it is to be young. Glen is already dating. Whatever it's called these days. You and Jenny will have suitors soon enough. Don't look so embarrassed, Lo. It's perfectly natural. The body matures. The rest is chemistry."

Mrs. Stallworth chattered on in her bright oblivious way. Lorena felt guilty, but also a sort of jumbled gratitude. Her own mother never discussed any of this with her. The closest she had come was leaving a stack of pads on the toilet tank, the bulky kind from the maternity ward. The rest of her instruction had come from the Bible and bits of lore picked up in church basements and laundromats. Young ladies should behave in ways that were *decent* and *honorable*. This meant doing well in school, respecting elders, stifling urges. In this way, God might consent to forgive you.

"The most important thing is to make good decisions. Don't let boys decide for you. They can't think straight at your age. At any age, really. They just keep telling you how beautiful you are until they get what they want."

"Is that what happened with Mr. Stallworth?" Lo said.

Mrs. Stallworth sat back. Lo had meant this question to be amusing but she could see at once that it had been wildly inappropriate. Mrs. Stallworth released a short sharp laugh. "You're a funny little bird, Lo. I can't quite figure whether you don't know anything, or whether you know it all. Neither one keeps you safe. That's the point I was making. Or was I just being a boring old fool?"

It was difficult to resist Mrs. Stallworth when she exposed her doubts so openly. "I'm not bored," she said. "I like listening to your stories."

Mrs. Stallworth examined Lo, searching for signs of sarcasm. "How sweet you are, Lo. I've always seen it. This is what I mean. We've got to stick together, us girls. We have to look out for each other."

LO SPENT JUNE racking dishes and staring into mirrors at the broadness of her nose. She wanted to call Jenny but it was against the rules. Her mother dragged her to church; nagged her to eat. Lorena biked to the pet shop in Oak Park to see if they had scorpions, but it was just smudged cells of puppies and bleating parakeets.

In July, her brother, Tony, returned home for the first time in six months, buzz cut and draped in camouflage. Graciela had flown into a panic when he first joined, certain he would be deported. But Tony assured her that the navy had a special program for guys like him, with a green card at the end of the rainbow. The recruiter had explained it all.

He wound up stationed at a base called China Lake, down in the Mojave. It didn't make sense to Lorena. What was a naval base doing in the middle of a desert? Tony said China Lake was where they assigned all the advanced weapons personnel. His work was *Top Secret*.

Tony the Hero, strutting around the July Fourth picnic at Rinconada Park in his white tunic and polished boots, saluting all the *viejo*s while Graciela beamed. Tony showing the little *vatos* how to take apart a rifle in thirty seconds, talking calibers and muzzle burn, blast radius, how pussy can't resist a uniform. Tony who had turned his life around. He escorted his mother to church in full service dress and kissed her on the forehead. But when she was gone, he prowled the corners with his old crew and glowered at Lorena. Tony was the same person who'd left for basic a year ago: a bully on the sly.

A few days after the Fourth, able to stand it no longer, Lorena called the Stallworths. She got Rosemary, who promised to have Jenny call her back. Lorena knew this would never happen, but the next weekend—under orders, no doubt—Jenny did call. There was her voice, sort of friendly, sort of bored, her inflection soaring at the end of every sentence. Maybe Lo wanted to come over for, like, a swim or whatever. They would have the place to themselves. Lo stared through the window at the blistered paint of the dumpster, the sulfurous spatters of fireworks on the pavement. "Cool," she said.

Tony emerged from the room they had shared, which he had commandeered. "Who the fuck is that?"

Lo covered the receiver. "None of your business."

"I need the phone."

"Who's that?" Jenny said.

"Nobody," Lo said. "My brother."

"The Latin King? I thought he was in the navy."

"He's on leave."

"Does he still look like a chihuahua?" Jenny said.

Tony, now aware he was being talked about, hollered, "Off the phone. *Now.*"

"Oooh, an angry chihuahua! I'd spank his little butt if he yapped at me like that."

"I'd like to see that," Lorena whispered, curling away from Tony. "Maybe I'll bring him."

Jenny let out a squeal. "I totally dare you."

The line went dead and Lorena turned to find Tony grinning, his thumb on the hook switch. "I warned you."

Lorena went into the bathroom to comb out her hair and put on some makeup but Tony planted himself in the doorframe. "Don't you got work today? Ma doesn't want you skipping work."

"It's my day off."

"Look at you. Putting on your whore paint. You got some kind of hot date? I'm serious, *gordita*. Where you going?"

"*Nowhere.*"

"I'm not fucking around."

"To a friend's."

"What friend?"

"You don't know her."

"Bullshit. Is it that little Vargas slut? What's her name? Where's she live?" Tony wasn't going to let up until he got an answer. With a pride that was almost vengeance, Lorena murmured, "The Fabulous Forties."

"Bullshit," Tony said. "Seriously? You hanging with some richie rich now? Some *guera*?"

Lorena knew it was best to ignore Tony, let him work off his tedium. But she kept thinking about how excited Jenny would be to meet Tony, and how small he would seem in the realm of the Stallworths. "You can drive me over if you don't believe me."

"Fuck that," he said.

But a few minutes later he was insisting on it. Tony drove the Mercury Bobcat he'd borrowed from one of his burnout friends. It had chrome hubs and a busted muffler that roared.

"Ma says you've been fucking up in school," Tony said.

"You're one to talk."

"Starting to get an attitude, too." Tony had a beer jammed between his legs. His right hand rested lightly atop the steering wheel, which was composed of welded chain links. "Don't fucking smirk."

"I'm not smirking."

"You grew some titties and lost a few pounds and you're big shit now? A big-shit ninth grader. Just because mom won't crack down on you don't mean I won't."

"Right," Lo said. "You're in the navy, so you get to be my dad now."

Tony slammed the brakes. Right in the middle of the Alhambra. "What did you just say to me?" He swung just to watch her flinch. "Look at me, *gordita*."

She wouldn't.

Tony swiped at his nose then reached down and pulled something out of his waistband and tossed it onto the seat next to her.

She glanced down at a small nicked pistol. "What the hell?"

"Don't back talk me, Lorena. I'll fucking end you."

Lo stared out the window. So Tony was doing coke again. Maybe he'd never stopped. "You're acting crazy," she said quietly. "You're gonna get busted again."

Tony snorted. "That's registered. I own that shit." He gunned the engine.

Lo had messed up. But asking Tony to drop her off on the corner would only infuriate him. He whistled when he caught sight of the mansion. "That's some *Masterpiece Theater* shit right there."

Mr. Stallworth's Jeep gleamed in the driveway and Tony's eyes locked onto it.

"Thanks for the ride," she said.

He grabbed her arm. "Hold up. Don't just fucking jump out of the car." The engine's idling felt out of place, lewd.

The front door opened and Jenny stepped onto the porch in a leopard print one-piece that rode up her slender hips. She looked down at the rumbling car and waved.

"Let go of me," Lo muttered to Tony.

"You're not going to introduce me to your little friend?"

"*Please.*"

He released her arm and snatched up the gun and tucked it into his waistband. Then he got out of the car and waved at Jenny, who was still squinting. "She's a pretty little *flaca*, ain't she?"

Lo got out of the car and walked around to where Tony was. "Please," she said again, and her voice was quavering.

"Okay. Calm down. I'm not going to mess with your rich bitch friend. She's a fucking little kid. No tits and braces on her teeth. Shit." Tony snapped into his military posture and swung his boots together so they smacked. He had tucked in his shirt and now offered a crisp salute to Jenny, who had ventured down the stairs to investigate. She stood canted against the railing, her legs radiant with tanning oil.

"Hey," she sang out to Lo.

"Hey," Lo said, then, to Tony, "Thanks again."

"Are you Lo's brother?" Jenny called out.

"Correct."

"You're in the navy?"

"Right again."

"Lo told me about you."

"Don't believe everything you hear." He glanced at Lorena. "You going to introduce us?"

"This is my brother, Tony."

Jenny descended to the sidewalk. She was trying to figure out if she should shake hands with Tony, what it would mean if she touched him. He wasn't tall or handsome or rich or suave. He was nineteen, though.

"You're, like, launching missiles from a submarine."

"Not quite. Advanced munitions."

"How old are you?" Jenny said.

"How old are *you*?"

"Old enough." She folded her arms across her chest. "And you're back on leave or whatever."

"What are you doing hanging around with my sister?" Tony said.

Jenny smiled carefully to avoid showing her braces. "Did you go to Sac High? Maybe you knew my brother, Glen?"

Tony shook his head like it didn't really matter. "You shouldn't be walking around in a bathing suit."

"Why not?"

"You got neighbors. They might talk."

"It's summer," Jenny said. "We have a pool."

All three of them were sweating. Lo had moved to the steps. She feared Tony would walk up on Jenny, the way he did with the younger girls in their building. But the neighborhood held him in check, the size of the homes, the grand trees and lawns shimmering with money. Next door, some old lady was watering her roses.

"You're welcome to come inside if you want to cool off," Jenny said.

Tony took a few seconds to mull this offer. Then he glanced at Mr. Stallworth's Jeep, the rear door of which was ajar. He strolled over and leaned against it in a way that showed the faint outline of his pistol. "Nice ride."

"That's my dad's."

"I thought he was at work," Lo said.

"What do you care?" Jenny said. She was playing to Tony now.

"He wouldn't want some stranger touching his car," Lo said softly.

Tony laughed. "Some stranger. Lorena. Always the good girl." He ran his finger along the roll bar, like the supermodel in the TV commercial, and recited taglines in a mocking falsetto: "*Going off-road turns me on. Why drive when you can Jeep? Danger is my compass.*"

Jenny laughed like it wasn't that funny but whatever.

The old lady from next door was watching them now, her eyes shifting apprehensively from Tony to the exhaust belching from the Bobcat's tail pipe.

"What's that in your belt?" Jenny said.

"What's what?"

"That bulge?"

"Listen to that mouth. What do you know about bulges?"

"More than you think."

"That so?" Tony let his eyes roam over her body and Jenny reddened. An awkward desire jellied the air between them—sudden, racking, almost hostile.

Then the front door swung open and Mr. Stallworth appeared at the top of the stairs. An oversized backpack hung from one thick arm. He looked down the stairs at his daughter, half naked, then spotted Lo on the curb and his face took on an agitation that made her take a step backwards. She had come over hoping to see him. In a way, his reaction confirmed this; he had been waiting for her, too.

"Get some clothes on," he snapped at Jenny.

Mr. Stallworth couldn't see Tony, who was off to his left in the driveway. But Tony saw him and sauntered back toward his car.

Mr. Stallworth's eyes shifted from his daughter to Lo to the rattling car parked in front of his house. Then he spotted the young man—a Mexican, he assumed, by the looks of him, with sweat glazing his forehead—and hurried down the steps.

"Have fun with your little *guera*," Tony muttered to Lo. He swung into the driver's seat and slammed the door and gunned the engine.

Mr. Stallworth arrived at the bottom of the stairs just as Tony peeled away from the curb. He was darker than the last time Lorena had seen him. Golden hairs shone on his forearms and the backs of his hands. "Who the hell was that?"

"Lo's brother," Jenny chirped. "He's in the navy."

Mr. Stallworth wheeled around and ordered his daughter inside, then trained his gaze on the skid marks Tony had left on the street. "What kind of person drives like that? Is he training to be a getaway driver?"

Lo stared miserably at the chipped remnants of her first and only pedicure. "He was just dropping me off. I'm sorry."

Mr. Stallworth stalked toward his Jeep, then turned and waited for Lo to look him in the eye. She could feel the heat of his scorn, his disappointment. "Tell your brother to show some respect."

"**HE HAD A** *gun*," Jenny gushed. "Right in his waistband."

"He just wants people to think that," Lo said.

"I, like, *saw* it."

"That was a bowie knife."

"Whatever," Jenny said. "He's too short, anyway. He's got one of those Napoleon complexes."

They were in her room. Lo had put her swimsuit on at home, so she wouldn't have to take her clothes off in front of Jenny.

"Is that why he joined a gang?"

"He's not really doing that anymore."

"That's where he must have gotten the gun," Jenny decided. "Thank God my dad didn't see it. He would have gone mental."

They went out to the pool to lay out. That was the phrase she used: lay out. It sounded European. Lorena could hear Mr. Stallworth in the garage. He had pulled the Jeep in to load it up. She told Jenny she was going to the bathroom.

"What are you doing here?" Mr. Stallworth said.

"I wanted to apologize for my brother."

"You did so already."

"I just felt bad."

"It's fine."

"I've still got your book," Lorena said, as if she'd just thought of it. "Should I bring it back?"

"Fine. I really do need to get on the road now."

"Another top-secret mission?"

Mr. Stallworth bristled. "What's that supposed to mean?"

"Nothing. We were just joking last time."

"I don't remember that," Mr. Stallworth said curtly.

Lorena began to tear up. He was being so cold to her, because he knew now what kind of family she came from, which she couldn't help. All she wanted was to be close to him, to talk about scorpions, but he wouldn't look at her. He kept pushing her away, kept leaving. She wiped at her eyes, furiously.

"Please," Mr. Stallworth said.

She turned, hoping to slip away before the humiliation grew worse, but he was upon her with a swiftness that was stunning, drawing her into an embrace, his hands moving across her back. The rough pads of his fingers almost stung. His mouth made the shushing sound parents used to comfort children. She smelled licorice on his breath, the sweet and bitter of it. Then that same mouth bent down to brush against the hollow of her throat, leaving an imprint there. She pressed against him. The instant she did this, he shoved her away.

"No," he murmured, more to himself than her. "Not that."

"Did I do something?"

"You need to leave. Now."

In the bathroom, she sat on the toilet and traced the patch of skin his mouth had moistened. She closed her eyes, eager to conjure that mouth. Lorena could sense what they were up to, the skirting of a sacred border; she would need courage to cross over, to touch what lay beyond.

LO RETURNED TO the Stallworth home a few weeks later, at the invitation of Rosemary. "We've got this new VCR and she wants to have a girls' movie night," Jenny said. "I could just barf." Lorena expected a group, but it was just the three of them.

"Here she is," Mrs. Stallworth said, when Lorena arrived. "Our little scholar! Marcus mentioned that you might have a book of his. He said to leave it on his desk." While Jenny and her mom argued over what to watch, Lo ducked down to the basement.

She was surprised to find a laminated map on his desk, which she took to be the same one he had used to show her the Chocolate Mountains. But this map covered a much larger area, all the way down to Mexico, and it was blanketed in notations. There were four red *X*s and beneath each were two numbers in parentheses, carried out to the third decimal point and followed by the letters *N* and *W*. Coordinates. Latitude and longitude.

Beneath each coordinate was another notation—*5 gal*; *3 gal*—which might have stood for gasoline, or water. A neat, dotted line connected the *X*s and extended south from Death Valley to something called the Coachella Canal, then east to the Colorado River and into southern Arizona. The only name Lorena recognized was Yuma, where long ago her father and Tony had crossed into the United States. In the lower left-hand corner of the map, Mr. Stallworth had printed three words, in letters so tiny she had to lean close to read them: *The Scorpion Escapes.*

Lorena stared hard at this odd phrase. Her eyes tracked back to the red *X*s and the coordinates beneath them. Was this the secret mission Mr. Stallworth had joked about? She needed more information, something to explain the map, his behavior, to bring him closer. Her mother would have warned her not to be a meddler (*No seas metiche, mija!*). But her mother wasn't around.

His desk drawers contained office supplies. Playing cards. A bridge manual. Three boxes of Good & Plenty. A Spanish/English pocket dictionary. There was a sofa in the corner. The cushions smelled of him, the deodorant he sometimes wore and, more faintly, his body odor. She spied the pale corner of a bedsheet. Was he sleeping in his office now?

She moved on to the file cabinet behind his desk, from which he had drawn the laminated map. Both drawers were locked. Lorena hesitated a moment, then took a paperclip from his desk. Tony had showed her how to jimmy locks one afternoon long ago, back in the days when he took pride in corrupting her.

The top drawer contained file upon file of meticulous field reports. But in the bottom drawer, stashed way in back, Lorena found a cardboard box filled with a confounding array: three pairs of rubber gloves, a razor blade, a Xerox copy of a manual entitled "Police Forensics." Beneath the box were two folders. The first was marked "Family." It contained school photos of Glen and Jenny, the whole family posing atop the groomed snow of a ski resort, a wedding portrait showing both of them smiling, unbearably young and clearly terrified.

The second folder was marked "confiscated." It contained two pornographic magazines of a sort Lo had never seen before. There was no brand name on the front. The models were young men, not much older than Glen, clearly amateurs. They lay about in awkward postures of seduction, regarding the camera with expressions meant to project a flagrant ennui. Lorena could hear Jenny mocking these guys, their ridiculous dangling cocks. Then she realized that the magazines had, most likely, belonged to Glen. Beneath them was a single blurry Polaroid of a young naked girl sitting on the steps of a swimming pool, her face turned away from the lens, her breasts floating in the blue. It took Lo a few seconds to recognize herself.

Then Jenny was calling out her name; the photo slipped from her fingers. She picked it up and set everything back in order and her damp hands shook.

"WHERE *WERE* YOU?" Jenny said. "We're watching *Mommie Dearest*. Joan Crawford beats her daughter with a wire hanger. It's totally choice."

"Why not *Chariots of Fire*?" Mrs. Stallworth said. "It's supposed to be stirring."

"I'm fine with either," Lo said quietly.

Jenny snorted. "Such a diplomat."

They watched *Mommie Dearest*. "They always turn the mother into a villain," Mrs. Stallworth said.

"Sometimes the mother *is* a villain," Jenny said.

Mrs. Stallworth looked at her daughter for several seconds. Onscreen, Joan Crawford was berating her spineless husband.

"It must be so satisfying to know so much at such a young age."

"I didn't say that."

"I can assure you, my dear, that a time will come when the world informs you of how little you know."

"A lecture? Really? In the middle of the movie?"

"Not a lecture," Mrs. Stallworth said. "A prediction."

WHEN THE MOVIE was over, Lorena quietly excused herself and slipped back downstairs. She stared at the map on Mr. Stallworth's desk, trying to decide if he had left it out for her to find or whether it had been an oversight. She grabbed a pen and copied the coordinates from the map onto a piece of paper, which she stuffed into her pocket. It was an action—like snooping through his drawers—she would not have been able to explain or justify in the moment. Her behavior felt guided by animal instinct. Perhaps she was something like a scorpion herself, groping in the dark at perils she could only vaguely sense, aglow with an alarm that would become visible only after it was too late.

IN EARLY AUGUST, Tony showed up at home again. He told their mom he'd been granted a longer furlough, based on merit. He no longer bragged about missile technology or green cards. The moment Graciela left for work, he turned mean. It didn't take

Lorena long to figure out that he'd gotten the boot. So now she had that secret to keep, too.

A week later, Jenny Stallworth called to invite her over. Lorena knew she should stay away from the Stallworths. But she felt a part of their dramas now. She could no more resist them than cast away her own shadow.

Jenny had gotten her braces off and there were her teeth, bleached white and straight as any model's. She had her father's eyes. Jenny was obsessed with the new Blondie video. She mimicked the lead singer with a practiced fervor, the haughty sway of rebellion cushioned by money, a blondie twirling in her blondie world. In a few weeks, high school would start, and Jenny would be absorbed into a caste of older girls and her dealings with Lo would be quietly expunged from the record.

She took some vodka from the cabinet and mixed it with Sprite and they went out to the pool, which had begun to lose its blue sheen. Jenny smoked Virginia Slims and swigged her Sprite. "I'll tell you one thing that's weirding me out. Mommy Dearest and the Robot have gotten all lovey dovey recently."

"What do you mean?"

"The other night I caught them, like, necking right outside my room." She shuddered.

"That's good, right?"

"They can't stand each other for a decade and all of a sudden it's like *The Newlywed Game* around here. It's fucking creepazoid."

BY THE TIME her mother returned, Jenny was sprawled on her back, snoring through her pretty new mouth. Lo listened to Mrs. Stallworth pour herself a drink, then snap on the TV. Lo wanted to wander into the den, to see what the alcohol might shake loose. Was it true Rosemary and her husband were in love again? Did she know anything of the strange items hidden away in his office?

Footsteps sounded on the stairs, then stopped in front of Jenny's door. Mrs. Stallworth's face slid into view. Lo heard her name whispered, tenderly, drunkenly. She kept her eyes shut and waited for the door to click.

Later that night, the Jeep pulled into the driveway. The whine of hinges sounded. Half a minute later, the whir of running water from the basement. Even in darkness, she could feel the opulence of the Stallworth home, the lush carpet into which her bare feet sank, the fluted silhouette of the spindles that moonlight cast across her body as she descended to the first floor. She stalked past the kitchen, the den, the room where Glen slept amid his trophies and rancid laundry. Downstairs, light seeped from under the door of the bathroom across from Mr. Stallworth's office. The sink was on full blast.

Her toe caught the edge of the door and it swung open. Mr. Stallworth was facing away from her, shirtless. His back was broad, swathed in muscle and dark hairs. It rippled as he hunched over the sink, frantically rinsing something. The air smelled of gasoline. His horn-rimmed glasses rested atop the toilet tank, a brown smear on the left lens. A plump black duffel had been wedged between the toilet and the sink. She could have gone back upstairs. She still had time. Then Mr. Stallworth glanced behind him and noticed the door. He tensed and turned to peer into the dim hallway.

"Who's there?"

"Me." Lorena edged into the light.

Mr. Stallworth's pupils were enormous. Blood dripped off his wrist, making little red fangs on the scalloped bowl of the sink.

"You're bleeding," Lo said faintly.

"What are *you* doing here?" Mr. Stallworth grabbed a towel and wrapped his hand. "Didn't I tell you to stay away from me?

We had that discussion." He sidled toward her, his wounded hand cocked like a club. Then he seemed to catch himself, and his eyes—soft and stunned without glasses—blinked. "Go to bed, Lorena," he said. "Please. This is none of your business."

"What isn't?"

He shut the door and she stood in the dark hallway, listening to the faucet turn on and off, the toilet flush.

Just as suddenly as the door had closed, it opened again and Mr. Stallworth appeared, looking more orderly, his shirt and glasses back on, a thicker towel draped over his injured arm in the manner of a French waiter.

"I'm sorry about that, Lorena. You startled me. You shouldn't be skulking around this house. It isn't your place."

"What happened?"

Mr. Stallworth offered a faint laugh. "I cut my hand, that's all."

"How?"

"The door to my Jeep. There's a ragged bit of metal and it sliced into my palm."

"Where were you?"

Mr. Stallworth took a deep breath through his nose. "Please, Lorena. I've had a pretty long night."

"Shouldn't you maybe go to the emergency room?"

"I appreciate your concern, but you need to respect certain boundaries." He was speaking now in the modulated way his daughter mimicked. "I have tried to be patient with you. I have tolerated your advances, and your . . . pool parties. But my patience is not inexhaustible. I don't like that you stay over without being invited. I realize Mrs. Stallworth makes exceptions for you. She fears you may not have a secure home life. Your mother, as I understand it . . ." He pinned her with a cold appraisal. "My wife is a sensitive woman, Lorena. That is why I love her so deeply. But she can be taken advantage of."

Lo's head had begun to reel. "You want me to leave?"

Mr. Stallworth looked about impatiently. "I'm going to forget we had this little chat," he said finally. "I suggest you do the same."

He brushed past Lo and a chill swept through her: Mr. Stallworth was in the midst of something illicit. She dimly recalled the way her father had lashed out at her mom when he'd been caught in a lie, his ruthless tone of injury. It occurred to her suddenly where the photo of her in the swimming pool had come from. Glen hadn't taken it. He had.

IN THE KITCHEN, she dialed her house. "What's wrong, *mija*?" her mother said, in groggy Spanish.

For a piercing moment, Lo wanted to tell her everything. But where did everything end? She had wandered too far away already, into another life. "Is Tony there?" Lo started to lose control of her breathing. She put her hand over the receiver and plunged a thumbnail into her thigh.

"What happened, Lorena?"

"Nothing. I'm fine. Jenny got sick, that's all. I need a ride home."

"At this hour?"

"Can you please just get Tony?"

After a minute, Tony came on the line. "What the fuck?"

"I need a favor."

"That's what you get for trusting a rich little bitch."

"She's sick."

"Bullshit, *gordita*. You did something. I can hear it in your voice."

"I just need a ride."

"You owe me, you little slut."

SHE SLIPPED OUT the kitchen door, locking it behind her, and walked to the front of the house, where she stood in the shadows at the bottom of the front steps. A minute later, she heard the kitchen door open. Mr. Stallworth looked like a dad you might order from a catalogue: freshly showered, chinos, a thin wool sweater. "There's no need for you to go." He strode toward her. "You've misunderstood me."

"It's alright. I called my brother," she said. "He's coming."

"There's been a misunderstanding."

He reached her and stood breathing. Moonlight put a blue tint on his face. "Please, Lorena. Don't make this into a production. There's no need to get people upset. I cut myself and panicked a little. It was stupid. The remarks I made—disregard them. Come inside." Mr. Stallworth raised his eyebrows, as if to usher her back into the realm of reasonable behavior.

"My brother is on his way," Lorena repeated.

"Don't be afraid of me, Lorena. I don't want that." Mr. Stallworth took another step forward, then stumbled so that he was suddenly on his knees. "Please, Lorena." His voice cracked on the middle syllable of her name and she could hear, for the first time, a beseeching tone beneath his fatherly composure. A white bandage spanned his left palm. "I'm trying to do the right thing. For all of us." He winced, like the hero in an action movie who's just taken a bullet. "You've got a sharp enough mind to see it."

His right hand moved forward cautiously until his palm was touching hers. His fingers slipped between hers and slid slowly down the length of each. "In another life," he whispered. He had started making small undulations, so that she could feel the power in his hands. She thought of the mating dance he had described, and knelt down, perhaps to kiss him, but he turned away.

"I need to know more about you. Whether I can trust you."

"You can trust me," Lo said. "I'm a friend of Jenny's."

"That's what I mean."

Behind them something creaked—the house settling, some distant static—and he loosened his grip. Lorena swayed back. She had stumbled into the territory between desire and suspicion. Or had she been dragged there?

"It doesn't matter," Mr. Stallworth said, as if she had spoken her thoughts aloud. He bowed his head and his hands reached up to sculpt the air around her until his arms looped around her waist. He held the pads of flesh above her hips and pressed his face against her belly and exhaled. She felt the warmth of his breath travel through her jeans and swimsuit. The Stallworth home rose behind him like a rampart, its majestic windows smudged with yellow light from the old-fashioned streetlamps.

Mr. Stallworth let out a muffled sob. He was still kneeling, pressing his nose against her mons pubis. His hair, showered and combed, quivered in the light. She could see now into the tiny box at the center of him, which contained his helplessness. Lo expected to feel desire or pity or alarm. But the sensation that coursed through her was vindication. "I'm the one you want," she said.

This was what she had been chasing, the realization that kept eluding her, scurrying into the shadows. She wasn't just some charity case summoned to gaze upon the golden lives of the Stallworth family. Mr. Stallworth desired her. He was on his knees, shaking now, awaiting her blessing. "You don't really love Mrs. Stallworth at all," she concluded, in quiet amazement.

The words bit into him.

Lorena began to run her fingers through his hair.

He sobbed out a muddy phrase and pressed his mouth against the place where her legs joined.

"What?"

He spoke the words again: *Find me.*

"You're right here," Lo said.

From down the street came a burst of noise, the corroded flatulence of Tony's Mercury. Mr. Stallworth flinched. He tried to pull away from her, but Lo curled her fingers so that her nails bit into his scalp. He barked in pain and twisted away. Headlights scrolled across them as they staggered apart, Lo toward the sidewalk, Mr. Stallworth toward the stairs.

Tony leaped from the car. "What the fuck?" he yelled. "What the fuck's going on here?"

"Nothing," Lo said. "Calm down."

"It didn't look like nothing."

Tony bounded toward Mr. Stallworth, who was leaning against the bannister.

"He was waiting with me. To make sure nothing happened. Mr. Stallworth, this is my brother, Tony."

Mr. Stallworth rose to his full height and nodded down at Tony.

"Were you stepping up on my sister?" Tony said.

"What?"

"Jesus, Tony. Calm down. He dropped his keys. We were looking for them."

"What are you accusing me of, young man?"

Tony squinted at Mr. Stallworth: the Izod sweater, the chinos, the hair freshly combed but mussed.

"Jenny got sick," Lo said. "She threw up. He was trying to be a gentleman."

Tony cocked his head. "Cuz this neighborhood's so fucking scary. Fucking three in the morning. You kick a girl out of your house?"

"Nobody kicked anyone out—she insisted on leaving."

Tony glowered at Mr. Stallworth and spit on the ground. "Rich fucking assholes."

"You had better watch your mouth," Mr. Stallworth said.

"Why? You gonna fucking do something, Dad?"

Lo stepped in front of Tony. "Stop it."

Tony reached into his waistband and drew out his small gun. "Or what? Or *what*? You'll call the cops?"

Mr. Stallworth shrank back at the sight of the weapon.

"Yeah, that's what I thought." Tony smiled his coked-up smile. "I *am* the fucking cops."

In the car, she let Tony run down a little. He talked about how the world looked at someone like her, how men thought and behaved. "You think you know it all. But you don't know shit."

"He wasn't doing anything," she said quietly. "He's a professor."

"A professor." Tony smirked.

"What if he calls the cops?"

"He ain't calling shit. He's a fucking punk."

"You got it all wrong."

"No, I don't," Tony said simply. "And you can't lie to save a fucking ant." He lit up a cigarette and gunned through a red light.

Lo wanted to thank him. She might have even said the words. He had come when she called, thinking to rescue her. But the way he had done so was savage, out of control. She understood now that there was nothing she could do to rescue her brother. He was doomed—not by the drugs, but whatever hidden demons prompted them.

"Stay away from those people, *gordita*. It's the fancy ones that'll fuck you up."

THE GIRLS HAD no classes together that fall. From time to time, Jenny appeared in the halls, across the quad, amid her flock, all of them dabbing lip balm on with their pinkies and balancing like cranes.

Lo watched from her quiet glade of regret. There was no appeal, no moment of cruel dismissal. Their friendship was over. It was almost nothing personal.

But what was there to regret, exactly? Had she been too timid in their midst, or too daring? Had she allowed the Stallworths to use her? Or had she wanted to be used? Was it possible two opposing things could be true at once?

Tony stuck around for another few weeks. Then he got into some kind of hassle with a guy, probably his dealer. He told their mother he had to report back to the base, though he drove down to Fresno where his friend had a cousin who had gotten him a job at an oil change place. Lo knew this but said nothing.

In September, Lo turned fourteen. Her face remained plain, her nose too broad, but her body continued to swell with curves. With Tony gone, the boys around the building whistled at her.

Some nights, a vision of Mr. Stallworth would come unbidden, the shape of his shoulders as he knelt before her and breathed; she would lie in a state of delighted torment, whispering *find me*. She thought of Mrs. Stallworth, too, her drunken affection and silly stories. Late one night, Lorena dug out the notebook marked "Science Fair," the one filled with idiotic astrology facts and flowery quotes about scorpions. She tore out the pages and dumped them in her trash can, along with the paperweight she had taken from Mr. Stallworth's desk, the tiny scorpion in its amber coffin. After a few moments, she retrieved the paperweight.

IT WAS LATE October when word began to spread of a tragedy involving Jenny Stallworth. She had been abducted. That was the word kids kept murmuring, in hushed tones, savoring the hard consonants: *abducted*. As if to confirm this account, Jenny went missing from school. Then the story changed. It wasn't Jenny who'd been abducted but her father. He'd vanished into the desert. Beamed up by aliens. Dragged off by Big Foot. Kidnapped by burnouts. Nobody knew anything, which meant everything was possible.

Lo went to the library and scoured the *Sacramento Bee*. The story was true, confirmed by a single column of type on page 17A. Marcus Stallworth, age 41, an adjunct professor of zoology, had been reported missing by his wife on Monday, October 26. Four days later, a sheriff's deputy had found his Jeep Laredo at the end of a dirt road south of Death Valley. His belongings had been rifled through. There was blood on the upholstery of his vehicle and what the police characterized as "signs of a struggle." The investigation was proceeding as a case of foul play.

Lo thought about the blood drops on the bathroom sink, the forensic manual, the laminated map. She thought about his "top secret" plan. For a moment, it seemed clear to her what had happened. Then that moment passed and she thought about Jenny and Mrs. Stallworth and what they must be going through.

Jenny appeared in school the next week, brightly dressed but hollow-eyed. Lo wanted to say something and couldn't imagine doing so. It was only chance that brought them together, for a few moments, in the little alcove outside the attendance office.

"I'm really sorry," Lo whispered.

"Thanks," Jenny replied without looking up.

"I'm sure they'll find him," Lo said.

"How would you know?" Jenny said quietly. "How in the fuck would you know?"

A day later, two police officers showed up on the doorstep of Lorena Saenz. The next era of her life had begun.

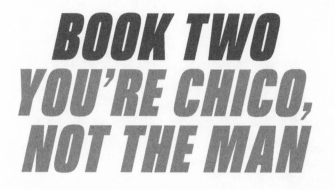

BOOK TWO
YOU'RE CHICO,
NOT THE MAN

THEY ARRIVED AT DUSK ON a Wednesday. The Mexican gentleman introduced himself as Officer Pedro Guerrero. He was short and slight, and he spoke English with a soft barrio accent. With him was an older white detective named Douglas Jolley, whom Lorena assumed to be the one in charge.

This was true. Jolley worked Homicide and had spent the previous week looking into Marcus Stallworth's disappearance. Guerrero was technically a patrolman and had been put on the case only a day before.

Guerrero had grown up in Fruitridge, just a few blocks from Lorena and Antonio Saenz. His grandfather had come to the United States from Morelia, Mexico, joining his siblings in the fields of the Central Valley. He eventually wound up in trouble with the law and returned to Mexico, leaving his wife to join relatives in Sacramento.

Guerrero had a quick mind and a nervous temper. He had always been small, and he learned to use impulsiveness to compensate. He might have wound up on the other side of the law but for his cousin Fernando, who crashed his eighteenth birthday party in a sharkskin suit, with a tooled leather holster strapped under his arm.

Nando Reyes sat his little *primo* down and explained, somewhat drunkenly, that, with a bit of cunning, Guerrero could attend the police academy and earn himself a real salary and a pension and get his ass out of Fruitridge before he turned into a *gamberro* himself.

The year before, Guerrero had gotten a girl pregnant and agreed to take a job in the orchard where her father worked. Then the girl announced that she had lost the baby. He'd been hanging around the neighborhood ever since, running errands for men he knew better than to trust, restless for calamity.

"I heard what you been up to." Nando smacked his nephew in the back of the head—hard. "The streets got ears, P. Listen to me. God gave you one chance, and that girl gave you a second one. Don't waste it."

Guerrero didn't much like the academy—too many dumb jocks—but he took to police work. He started out in traffic. It took him three years to get bumped up to community policing; that's how it was if you were Mexican. Eventually, the brass figured out that they needed patrol officers who could speak Spanish and thereby convey the rules and customs of American law enforcement to the immigrants populating Sacramento's south side.

Guerrero reveled in the power of his new position; the badge and the gun put muscle behind his moods. He earned a reputation as a hard-ass on this beat and a hothead around the station. But his sergeant, Maurice Hooks, recognized Guerrero's knack for investigation. He understood the rhythms of criminal logic, with its nimble dance between guile and disguise. He knew how to read perps, the subtle ways they gave themselves up. Guerrero enjoyed shooting the shit with the sweet dumb crooks and schemers who intuited, as he did, that the world was a fallen place in which men were obliged to find their advantages.

When Hooks finally made captain—the first Black man to do so in department history—he put Guerrero in plainclothes, as part of the Street Crimes Unit. That had been three years ago. Guerrero had passed the exam for detective but was still awaiting promotion. In the meantime, Hooks had been kicked over to Homicide and taken Guerrero with him, unofficially, to serve as a translator for his detectives, none of whom spoke Spanish.

Guerrero had started going bald just after high school. Although he was thirty-one, the wrinkles around his eyes and the dark patches under them made him appear a decade older. His teeth were small and sharp and he had a habit of dipping his chin in apology before he spoke.

Now he stood in the doorway of the Seanz apartment, dwarfed by Jolley's pasty bulk. "Is this the residence of Graciela Seanz?" he asked in Spanish.

The girl looked at Guerrero, then at Jolley. She was plainly terrified.

"We're police officers," Guerrero said in English.

"Is something wrong?" Lo said.

"Not at all," Guerrero said. "We just have a few questions for Lorena Saenz." He dipped his chin. "Is that you? Are you Lorena Saenz?"

GUERRERO HAD BEEN put on the Stallworth case owing to an unlikely series of phone calls. The first had been placed a day earlier by the office of the First Lady of the United States. Mrs. Reagan had just finished a formal luncheon at the White House, where she entertained the First Lady of Indonesia. She sat, stiffly smiling, for the photo session that followed the meal. Denise, her chief of staff, used the minutes before her next event to call an old friend, Shelby Rhodes, a realtor in Sacramento. The Reagans would be visiting California for Christmas and she wanted advice about luxury dude ranches.

Rhodes sounded flustered. He had just learned that the husband of a former employee, Rosemary Stallworth, had been abducted. Denise remembered Rosemary Stallworth for her elegance and for her peculiar habit of bowing slightly before the First Lady. She suspected Mrs. Reagan would appreciate this morsel of gossip, which she shared on the way back to the residence upstairs. "They found his car in the desert," Denise reported. "There was blood all over the place."

The First Lady's large beautiful face looked stricken. She peered through the peach curtains of her sitting room, at the eerie tufts of fog that lay upon the East Lawn. "Who would have done such a thing?"

"The police have no clue."

"A family man," the First Lady said. "A brilliant scientist. Snatched from his car in broad daylight." She sounded like a news anchor sharing the lurid details from behind an empty console. Then her voice dropped to a whisper. "What sort of country are we becoming?" As her fists clenched, she realized that she was still holding the gift she had received at the luncheon and held proudly for the official photos, a tiny compass that glowed in the dark. In a moment of uncharacteristic pique, she considered hurling the device against the wall.

She was the First Lady of the United States. She had a schedule to abide. But the story stuck with her: the ransacked Jeep, spattered with the blood of an innocent. Her husband had run for governor to restore law and order to the great state of California. The violence of those years—the Manson murders, the uprisings in Berkeley and Watts—had registered as evidence of a moral decadence that threatened to rend the nation.

She recalled the somber baritone of the Secret Service agent who told her about the attempted assassination of her own husband, the depraved calm he hoped to impart. The name of the hospital, the droning reassurances of her staff, the sirens and handkerchiefs. Ronnie grinning gamely from his gurney, a scimitar of crimson seeping through the gauze dressing on his ribs. They had come to the White House to heal America. Hadn't that been the whole point? Of all the rallies and speeches and glad-handing? And then some madman had gunned him down in broad daylight. The phrase gnawed at her. *In broad daylight.*

"Mrs. Reagan?" Denise said. "Are you okay?"

Within the hour, a called had been placed by a staffer in the Office of the President to the Federal Bureau of Investigation, where an assistant to the director reached out to the Office of the US Attorney for the Eastern District of California, who dispatched his chief deputy to inquire about the status of the Marcus Stallworth case. These sorts of communiques were not uncommon, the ghostly currents of political power run through the grid of law enforcement. But the prosecutor now made an uncommon request: that the sheriff in Barstow allow the investigation to be handled by the police in Sacramento, where the case had originated. The First Lady was of the opinion that a larger department would be better equipped to make sure justice was done.

INSIDE JENNY STALLWORTH, an insidious notion had taken shape: that Lorena Saenz had something to do with her father's disappearance. She knew it didn't make much sense, but seeing Lorena again, even for a moment, had filled her with a senseless rage, Lorena who was forever kissing up to her parents, the innocent ghetto girl who bragged about her thug brother. She

phoned the police on her own and, because there was now official heat on the case, the call was routed to Captain Hooks.

"Would you like me to send an officer out?"

"It's probably nothing," Jenny said nervously.

"Okay," he said. "No officer. What's up?"

Jenny issued a thin sigh, then began speaking quickly. She
mentioned Lorena and the science project they'd worked on
and the fact that she, this girl Lorena, had an older brother in
the Latin Kings. The guy, Tony, had a record. He'd come over to
their house and been "really aggressive."

"How so?"

"Just, like, he was checking out my dad's Jeep and saying
what a great car it was and saying stuff to me, too, like trying to
flirt or whatever. The thing that made me think of it is . . . he had
a gun."

"A gun?"

"Like, tucked into his waist."

"Did Tony meet your father?"

"No. He burned rubber when my dad showed up. You can still
see the skid marks on our street."

Hooks waited for Jenny to continue.

"I'm not saying it's anything. It's probably nothing. I never
even told my mom because I knew she'd freak out. Especially
about the gun."

"You did the right thing," Hooks said. "If you think of anything else—anything—just call." It took him no time at all to run
a check on Antonio Saenz. That was why he put Guerrero on
the case.

FOR AN INVESTIGATOR like Guerrero, it was difficult to read over
Antonio Saenz's file and not regard him as a suspect. This was
how police work shaped the mind. There was evidence, which

was often incomplete and therefore ambiguous. And there were the broader mechanisms of crime, most of which ran contrary the prevailing cultural myths, which attempted to divide the population into villains and victims.

Guerrero knew that vile intentions lurked within everyone, muffled under layers of moral training, fear, and vanity. Most crimes were merely the revelation of this secret self, abruptly activated and turned on the world. It was the guys like him, Pedro Guerrero, who had to make decisions about who might do what, about history and character and violent possibility. Which leads to pursue and which to abandon. Hooks had put him on the case with an implicit mandate: figure out if Antonio Saenz had anything to do with the disappearance of Marcus Stallworth.

Saenz was nineteen years old, undocumented, unemployed, a high school dropout. He had come to the States from Honduras at age four, crossing illegally with his father. His mother had joined them later, though the couple soon split. Mom worked custodial at Mercy, the swing shift. By the time he was a junior, Saenz had missed enough classes to get himself tossed and was running with known delinquents. He was careful when it came to cops, more so because of his mom. There was no telling how many times Saenz had fed an officer a fake name, or flashed a phony Social Security card. Guerrero recognized the pattern from his own youth. There were different rules for kids without papers, you covered for them.

Records did show that Saenz had been party to at least two crimes as a seventeen-year-old: an assault and an alleged vehicular theft. No charges filed in either case, but the kid clearly got spooked. Within five months, he had earned his GED and weaseled his way into the navy. Eleven months later, he got booted for drug use.

Seanz had become more reckless of late, whether because of his drug use or because he'd figured out that police this far north didn't always coordinate with INS. He'd been cited for possession of pot, then disorderly, after getting into a hassle with a local cocaine dealer. Two weeks before the Stallworth disappearance, Saenz had moved to Fresno, where he had been pulled over for speeding. A search of his vehicle uncovered two unlicensed firearms and a knife. Guerrero spoke to the uniformed officer who arrested him. The consensus view was that Saenz was one lucky punk. The coke dealer echoed this verdict, in more profane terms.

Jolley wanted to drive to Fresno immediately, but Guerrero argued that they needed to interview the sister first. Best to work in concentric circles.

"If she knows anything, she warns her brother. Then we're fucked."

"If he runs, that tells us what we need to know."

Jolley scowled. He wasn't going to argue. It was bad enough he'd been paired with Guerrero, the section's little spic translator.

And so they showed up on Lorena's doorstep together. Guerrero knew she would be scared and would probably allow them in and answer their questions if it meant keeping her mother out of it. He also knew that she would be more inclined to speak candidly if he portrayed himself as her protector in this initial interview.

THEY SAT AT the small table just outside the kitchen. Guerrero recognized the salted chemical smell of fried hot dogs. A stack of text books sat before Lorena, a sheet with equations behind them.

"I guess you're wondering why we're here," Jolley said.

Lorena nodded.

"Do you have any idea?"

The girl shrugged miserably. "Is it about my mom?" she said softly.

"Your mom?" Jolley said.

"No," Guerrero said quickly. "You don't have to worry about that, Lorena. This is something else."

Jolley glared at Guerrero. It was all part of the script. "I'm sure you've heard about the disappearance of Marcus Stallworth by now," Jolley said.

Lorena sat back. Her eyes grew cloudy. Some part of her had been waiting for the police to arrive. "Did they find—"

"No, no," Guerrero said gently. He noticed the base of her throat pulsing.

"It's an ongoing investigation." This was Jolley. "We just need you to answer a few questions. Then we'll be done. Can you do that? How well did you know the Stallworths?"

"I mean, not like—Jenny and me did a project for school. In spring. I went over there a few times. And she came over once or twice."

"What's a few times?" Jolley said.

"Six? I just, I had dinner there a couple of times. Mrs. Stallworth was, she would invite me, and we talked to Mr. Stallworth, for, like, to get help on our project. We didn't hang out in school or anything."

"What did you think of the Stallworths?"

"Think of them?"

Jolley looked up from his notepad. "Yes," he said slowly. "You were a frequent guest in their home, were you not? I'm asking what you observed. What can you tell us about how they interacted? A man has disappeared."

Lorena took a gulp of air. "They seemed happy. They had, you know, they spent time together. As a family." She looked at Guerrero. "I didn't really know them that well."

"Okay," Guerrero said. "Okay."

Lorena was almost crying now. "It's so sad. I tried to tell Jenny how sorry I was. She wouldn't even look at me."

"Why wouldn't she look at you?" Jolley said.

"I don't know." Her cheeks were wet now. "We weren't that good friends, I guess."

Guerrero handed her a tissue. "Let's give her a few seconds here, Doug. Okay? This has come as a big shock to everyone. We didn't come here to upset you, Lorena. It's just our job to figure out what happened. You understand you're not in any trouble, right?"

Lorena nodded. She glanced down at the worksheet and Guerrero followed her eyes. He noticed a little paperweight near her elbow, a lump of amber with some kind of insect suspended inside it.

"Did your families ever spend time together?"

"It wasn't really like that." Lorena glanced at Guerrero. "It's pretty far between our houses." There was an awkward moment, so familiar in American life, when the unspoken fact of class rudely presents itself.

"Just one more question." Guerrero seemed to be asking Jolley for permission. "Did you spend time with Mr. Stallworth himself?"

Again, Guerrero saw the pulsing in her smooth neck.

"A few times. To get help with our project. For the science fair. He was gone most of the time."

"Gone?"

"At work."

"Wait a sec," Jolley said. "You just said the family spent all this time together. Now you're saying dad was gone all the time. Which is it?"

Guerrero held up his hand. "I think she meant—"

"No," Jolley snapped. "I'd like Miss Saenz to explain this."

"He just worked, you know, like a lot of dads. So when I came over, after school, he usually wasn't around. Or, you know, he

went on these trips. To collect scorpions. That's what he studied. He took us with him one time."

"He took you on a *work* trip?" Jolley said.

"No. Like a family trip. Camping. He took us out and showed
us the scorpions. He lit them up with a special lamp."

"Us?"

"Me and Jenny and Glen. Jenny's brother."

"And where was this expedition?" Jolley said.

"Down south. I don't know where we were exactly. It was
kind of in the middle of nowhere."

"Could it have been Death Valley?" Guerrero said.

"I guess."

Jolley shook his head. "I don't get it. All of sudden he's taking
you on camping trips. Sounds like you *did* know Mr. Stallworth."

Lorena saw the stars overhead, pressing down. Mr. Stallworth stood behind her in black silence. She thought about the
map in his office, the numbers written on the slip of paper
tucked into her old science notebook. Then she heard her
mother's voice: *Nos puede destruir*. Talking to a cop, *any* cop,
can destroy us.

"He was being a good dad." Lorena's voice caught on the
word *dad*.

Jolley started to speak, but Guerrero touched his arm.

"Okay," Jolley said. "That's enough. We're all done here.
We're just trying to cover our bases. Thank you for bearing with
us, Miss Saenz. I know it's a difficult subject." He got up and
yawned elaborately.

Lorena seemed uncertain whether she should get up, too.
Guerrero saw her eyes dart to the paperweight. He realized
what it was: a scorpion.

"Did Mr. Stallworth give you that?" he asked suddenly.

Lorena couldn't quite meet his eyes. She nodded.

"Was he in the habit of giving you gifts?"

"No. It was just something, like, from a gift shop."

Jolley reached over and snatched the object, like the oaf he was. He held it up to the light and made a noise of disgust. "These things don't creep you out?"

"Kind of," the girl said.

"This little sucker looks pretty unhappy. It's like he's screaming, *Get me outta here!*" Jolley was trying to joke around; Lorena looked stricken.

"We'll get out of your hair," Guerrero said.

Jolley set the paperweight down and smiled formally.

Lorena glanced at Guerrero. "Do you have any idea, I mean—"

"We're trying," he said. "If you can think of anything that might help." He placed one of his cards atop her stack of books.

EVERY MURDER INVESTIGATION was a kind of story. You had a dead body, or a missing one, and you had to reconstruct the life of that body as it traveled through its final days and hours. In most cases, this wasn't that hard. There was a corpse, a crime scene, a weapon, blood, prints, fibers, witnesses, motive, and means. A dispute, a plan executed or gone wrong. The event created its own small family of misfortune.

The case of Marcus Stallworth offered almost no guidance. The facts as Guerrero had inherited them were as follows:

On Friday, October 23, Stallworth left home for the university, where he spent the morning in his office. Around noon, he got into his Jeep and drove south, intending to camp in the Mojave National Preserve for the night, to observe scorpions and collect samples. On Sunday, October 25, at 9:23 p.m., Rosemary Stallworth placed a call to the Sacramento Police to report that her husband had not returned home. It wasn't like him to show up late without calling, though she allowed that he might have gotten tired on the drive back and stopped at a motel. When her husband failed to appear the next morning, Mrs. Stallworth filed a missing person report.

A uniformed officer headed out to take an initial statement. It was immediately apparent—from the size and location of the Stallworth home, from the very manner of Rosemary herself—that this matter would be treated with the utmost gravity. The officer who met with Rosemary certainly understood. He spoke to his supervisor, and within the hour the case was reassigned to Jolley, a seasoned homicide detective. This was merely an abundance of caution, the phrase Jolley used with Mrs. Stallworth. She seemed relieved to be dealing with a professional, however ill-fitting his suit.

Jolley compiled a basic profile of the missing man. Stallworth had grown up in Elkhart, Indiana, in a strict, religious home. Both his parents were deceased. He had studied biology at a small college outside Philadelphia, where he and Rosemary Upton met and married. They spent a short time in Tucson, his graduate years, then moved to Sacramento. He received a doctorate in zoology from CSU-Sacramento and later accepted a position as a researcher. He was in exceptional health according to his physician and had no known history of mental illness or substance abuse.

In contrast to his wife, who was involved in numerous civic organizations, Stallworth had few social obligations. He played bridge occasionally and took part in a discussion group on science and skepticism. Once a month, sometimes twice, he drove down to the Mojave to do fieldwork. On occasion, he picked up hitchhikers, a practice of which his wife vehemently disapproved.

His salary at the university was modest. Rosemary had supplemented their income by working as a realtor for a few years, but the family's underlying wealth derived from her family, a subject she was reluctant to discuss. Marcus Stallworth had purchased a term life-insurance policy six years earlier, on the advice of his accountant.

In the absence of any physical evidence, Jolley was left to consider the unspoken possibility: Stallworth had disappeared himself. A man hits forty, the marriage goes stale, kids mostly grown, maybe he finds a new flame. Figures he can duck a nasty divorce, nab his wife an insurance payout, and start a new story. It happened more than people realized. Jolley even called his old pal Ricky Stark, who handled missing persons down in Yuma and served as a liaison to the Border Patrol. Gringo runaways loved Mexico.

But the interviews argued against this. Marcus Stallworth was a quiet man, an introvert dedicated to his work and family. Mrs. Stallworth had been so distraught it was difficult to ask her much. She had described them as very much in love, particularly in the preceding months, an assessment confirmed by her children.

A DAY LATER, on the afternoon of Tuesday, October 27, a hydraulic engineer dispatched to check the water level at an agricultural reservoir outside the small community of Calico spotted an abandoned Jeep at the end of a dirt road off the Mojave Freeway. The next morning, a pair of deputies from the Barstow Sheriff's office found the alleged victim's Laredo, ransacked, the blood stains, an empty wallet. They ran the license plate and up popped Marcus Stallworth, missing person.

The crime scene report sent up from Barstow was seven pages in its entirety. The photos showed skid marks indicating that Stallworth's Jeep had swerved before coming to rest, at an angle, near the terminus of a dirt road. Both doors hung open. Blood had dripped onto the front passenger seat and the sandy soil outside that door. Clothes and dehydrated food packets were strewn about the back of the Jeep, along with several dozen small clear plastic canisters, which the deputies characterized as "possible drug paraphernalia." (It was later determined that Stallworth used these to collect scorpion samples.) Outside the vehicle, the empty wallet lay near the rear right wheel. The blood tested as O-positive, Stallworth's type. The only fingerprints on the wallet belonged to Stallworth. Curiously, none of his three credit cards had been used.

It was unclear how the alleged assailant, or assailants, had returned to the main road; there were no clear tracks to work from. Deputies canvassed the nearby gas stations, a couple of farm stands, a truck stop with a restaurant and shower facilities. No one remembered having seen a man matching Marcus Stallworth's description.

Rosemary Stallworth had buckled at the news that her husband's abandoned vehicle had been located, and crumpled at the sight of the wallet. She cursed him, quietly, for his habit of picking up hitchhikers. She expressed concern about what to tell her teenage children.

With the indications of foul play came a new consideration, one Hooks was careful to impress upon Guerrero: the Stallworths were "a prominent family." That was the phrase he used. This meant the investigation, if not conducted with discretion ("the utmost motherfucking discretion" was how he put it) could trigger a media frenzy. Americans were acutely attuned to sagas of abduction and captivity, thanks to the Iran hostage crisis. Sixty-six diplomats had been held by militants for more than a year and released into US custody only upon the inauguration of Ronald Reagan—who was himself, three months later, shot in broad daylight.

THE MORNING AFTER his interview with Lorena, Guerrero drove six hours down to Barstow. A deputy named Fuentes led him to the impound lot, where they found Stallworth's Jeep amid the dusty beaters abandoned by the freeway. "Please don't tell me they left my central piece of evidence exposed to the elements," Guerrero said.

Fuentes shrugged. "It's an impound lot, not a valet service."

"Has it rained down here?"

"Not since 1974."

Guerrero pulled on his gloves and inspected the interior of the Jeep. He tweezed hairs and stray fibers, shined a penlight under the seats, fingered the tires for irregularities in the tread. He took out his portable print kit and spent two hours dusting. Guerrero found a new print on the roll bar, two in fact, smudged and partial but there, right next to each other. They probably belonged to Stallworth, but he could check them against the FBI database just in case.

"You take this shit serious," Fuentes said, on the drive out to site where the Jeep had been found. "Nando said you'd be like that."

"How you know Nando?"

"Used to work in Fresno. He's big shit up there."

"You got that half right," Guerrero said.

They turned north onto a dirt road.

"Who uses this?"

"Agricultural hydrologists. It's a federal access route, officially."

"There a reservoir around here?"

"More like a well. It's called an on-site gauge. Basically, a hole in the ground that allows these guys to measure the level of the aquifer." Up ahead, yellow crime tape had been wound around a scattering of plastic poles.

Guerrero could see at once that the Barstow deputies had made a mess of the site, tromped all around the vehicle, driven over the tread marks. He had a photo of the squiggled tread on the hiking boot Stallworth was thought to have been wearing, but there was no sign of any such tread in the fine soil of the road. *No visible sole*, he jotted in his notebook. Guerrero stared out at the pointless scrub. He kicked a stone in frustration and leaped back when a creature scuttled from beneath it.

"Woke the little fucker up," Fuentes said.

Guerrero watched the scorpion scrabble across the sand and into a little dip a few yards from where the vehicle had been found. Guerrero cocked his head. He scanned the photos in the original report. He could see the same little trench leading from the rear of the vehicle into the desert. Actually, it wasn't quite a trench, more like a shallow declivity, as if an object had been dragged through the sand.

He pointed it out to Fuentes.

"Yeah, okay. I see it."

"It's like someone tried to erase their footsteps."

"Maybe." Fuentes didn't sound convinced. "Or maybe our photog didn't realize his bag was dragging on the ground."

Guerrero followed the path for a few yards. It dissolved into nothing, another dead end. He trudged back to the car. Fuentes was leaning against the driver's side door, smoking.

"What do you make of all this?"

Fuentes shrugged. "He picked up the wrong drifter. Or messed with some lot rat and got dusted by her pimp. Then the perps panicked, drove out here, left the vehicle."

"And they left no prints on the car, no blood, no tread? Because, what, they wore gloves and used their helicopter to get back to town?"

"Maybe. If you just killed some guy, yeah, you put on gloves. This is happening at night probably, at some truck stop off I-5.

Maybe there's a hacksaw involved in the proceedings. Or a bonfire. Or maybe they just dump the body in the desert. It's a pile
of bones within a week. Mean land down here. The Mojave
don't forgive."

"Sounds like you got it all figured out," Guerrero said softly.

"You're missing the point." Fuentes flicked his cigarette and
spit. "Nobody knows *shit*. The guy is gone. The rest is guessing."

Guerrero saw another lazy Mexican waiting for some rich white
asshole to draw a sombrero on his head. "I don't like guessing."

BACK IN SACRAMENTO, Guerrero drove to the university to meet
with the man described as Marcus Stallworth's closest friend, a
fastidious and aged herpetologist named Joseph Tennyson.
They sat in an overheated office that smelled of menthol rub
and wood shavings. Tennyson spoke of Stallworth as a dedicated researcher who admired the animals he worked with for
their stark beauty and resilience. "I stress this because those of
us who work with the reptilian and arachnidous phyla are
sometimes viewed as sinister." Tennyson had clipped on a tie
for the interview, at which he now tugged. Behind him, in a
terrarium whose ancient lightbulb faintly buzzed, a serpent the
color of corn silk lay coiled like rope.

Guerrero asked if Stallworth had ever talked to him about
professional or personal conflicts.

"Heavens no. That's not the sort of man he was."

"He got along with everyone?"

"'Get along' isn't quite right." Tennyson frowned dryly. "Marcus enjoyed—or rather, let us hope, *enjoys*—the solitary aspects
of his work. When pressed to do so, he taught an introductory
section of animal biology. But he staunchly avoided the sorts of
feuds that animate academia."

"Was he well-regarded in his field?"

Tennyson stared at Guerrero, his eyes milky with glaucoma. "I must tell you, young man, that the dominant motive for investigating the natural world today involves what are called commercial applications. Extracting venom to brew a cure for arthritis. Grinding blossoms into perfume. This sort of thing. Marcus was something of an anachronism. He was most interested in the creatures themselves. *Sociobiology* is the fancy term, the idea that we might learn something about human nature from observing the social customs and discourse of the animal kingdom—in his case, an order of arachnids that have inhabited the earth for 450 million years."

"Does he have tenure?"

Tennyson shook his head. "Nor did he seek it. Such an ambition would have required him to attend departmental meetings and serve on thesis committees, duties that did not suit his temperament. He is officially a research fellow with a contract renewed annually. His family had the means to allow him to do this work, as I understand it."

"Is that something he ever talked about? His finances?"

Tennyson frowned again. "I'm merely making a deduction."

"Do you have any reason to believe Marcus was unhappy at home?"

"Again, we didn't—that isn't the sort of thing we talked about. Marcus is a private person. The only time he mentioned his family was some years ago. On a camping trip. He loved to camp, you know."

"What did he say?"

"Not very much. His parents passed away when he was quite young. He mentioned that. I got the feeling his childhood was difficult. He said how happy he was to have escaped into a normal family."

"What did he mean by 'a normal family'?"

"I don't know exactly. As I say, he wasn't someone . . ." The old man trailed off. "One thing. I don't know that I should say this either. But I had the feeling that there was some part of him that was, was—I guess the phrase I would use is *out of reach*. I just had that feeling. And that it was mixed up with his life as a boy. Some agitation there. You're going to ask me why I say that. But I can't tell you." The old man peered at the badge clipped to Guerrero's belt, to remind himself that he was duty-bound to share such intimate impressions.

"Did you sense that he was struggling recently?"

"Quite the contrary. Marcus seemed energized. For some years, he's been researching the phenomenon of parasitic mating habits. He took on a second project this summer. Something a bit unusual for him."

"About?"

Tennyson cast a wry smile at his guest. "It has to do with the mechanisms and utility of fluorescence in the exoskeleton of scorpions. I can't imagine this subject has kept you up at night. Nor how it might be relevant to your investigation. But it is of considerable interest among scorpiologists."

"When was the last time you spoke to him?"

"We were supposed to meet on Monday, that Monday—" Tennyson turned abruptly and discharged a cough into a ragged handkerchief. It took a few seconds to discern that the old man was upset.

"Professor?"

Tennyson gathered himself and turned to face Guerrero. The scalp beneath his wispy hair was pink as a blister. "Marcus has a calling. It is hard for those outside of this calling to understand. Go among the animals and learn their ways and you shall know yourself."

"Who said that?"

"I did, young man."

GUERRERO DECIDED TO swing by the Stallworth home on his way back to the office. Jolley had visited earlier in the week to introduce himself to Rosemary Stallworth. But something in the old man's words convinced Guerrero that he should meet the wife in person. The Stallworth home was the only mint-green mansion he had ever seen.

Rosemary answered the door and took a half step back. Her expression was one of solicitude tinged with suspicion, an old and familiar mask donned by the rich for the benefit of strangers.

"Officer Pedro Guerrero, ma'am." He held up his badge. "I work with Detective Jolley."

Rosemary raised a hand to her mouth. "Is it—do you know anything new?"

"No, ma'am. I'm sorry."

"What happened to Detective Jolley?"

The tone of this question affirmed something they both understood: Rosemary Stallworth expected to deal with a white officer.

"He's working on something else right now."

"Something *else*?"

"Another aspect of the case. I'm sorry to drop by unannounced. I had a few more questions."

Despite the careful burnishing of makeup, Mrs. Stallworth looked drawn. "I must say, and I mean no offense, but I don't understand why they keep sending new people. I spoke to the one in uniform, then a sheriff, and then Detective Jolley at some length. It's been a week now." Rosemary Stallworth struggled to control her voice. "I have children—I have to *tell* them something." She had refused to move out of the doorway.

"I'm very sorry, ma'am. I know it's confusing. We all have different roles."

Mrs. Stallworth led him into a living room bright with lace and throw pillows. She ripped a Kleenex from a pewter box and pinched her nose silently, then seated herself on a crushed velvet couch.

"I've been trying to piece together the details of your husband's biography," Guerrero said tentatively. "Part of what we have to consider involves family history, relatives with whom he might have had issues—"

Mrs. Stallworth issued violent little shakes of her head. "My husband has no contact with his family. None. He was practically an orphan when we met. There was an aunt whom he mentioned once or twice. She didn't even come to our wedding. I never met anyone else. Once he left Indiana, that was it."

"Where does she live now? The aunt?"

"I've no idea."

"What about your family?"

"*My* family? What have they got to do with anything?"

"These are questions we have to ask, ma'am."

"My husband has been abducted, Officer. Do you think my family is responsible for that in some way? Is that what you're insinuating?"

"Not at all."

The polite smile remained pasted to Rosemary Stallworth's face, but any trace of good will drained from her eyes. "I'll thank you to leave my family out of it. Both my parents and my children."

Guerrero stared down at his notepad. He was unaccustomed to dealing with witnesses this self-possessed.

Had she chosen to speak candidly, Rosemary Stallworth would have conceded that her parents had disapproved of Marcus, rather forcefully. They represented the merger of two Main Line families with considerable fortunes. Their daughter's decision to marry Stallworth had been a crushing disappointment.

He was from a troubled family, and they believed that character was inherited as well as instilled. They also continued to provide an allowance to Rosemary, which subsidized the pittance Marcus earned as an academic.

"I realize this is a trying time—"

"Do you?"

"You told Detective Jolley that you and your husband had been happy in recent months," Guerrero continued quietly. "Have there been periods of unhappiness in the marriage?"

Mrs. Stallworth was glaring at him now. "It seems to me you came here to discuss my marriage. Is that right?"

"It's hard to find a man unless we know as much about him as we can."

Mrs. Stallworth's mouth curled, as if at some private joke. "Are you married, Officer? No, I didn't imagine so. No one who is would ask such a thing. Of course, we've struggled. Marcus and I have been together for nearly twenty years. We are, as you may have already deduced, distinct in our temperaments. Marcus is a quiet man, a scientist. I am more outgoing. But we love each other very much. And if the next question in your little notebook is whether we ever cheated on one another, or rather, whether he ever cheated on me, I can only tell you that Marcus is an orderly man. He likes things neat, not messy. You can ask around about that."

"I understand—"

"I'm not sure you do." Her cheeks flared. "Marcus and I are not some couple from a dime-store mystery. We are pillars of this community. We have two children." She spoke haltingly, in brittle syllables. "There was blood all over the seats of my husband's Jeep, Mr. Gonzales. Blood on the sand. I am not a stupid woman. Someone shed my husband's blood. I suggest you focus your investigative efforts on finding that person, or people. Along with my husband."

Guerrero dipped his chin.

Before he could say anything more, a man stepped into the room and stood at the end of the sofa where Guerrero sat. He wore a waxed moustache and a tailored suit with comically large shoulder pads. His cheeks and forehead showed the orange tinge of a tanning bed.

"This is Mr. Van Dyke," Rosemary Stallworth announced.

Royce Van Dyke produced a business card from his breast pocket, pungent with cologne.

"I wasn't aware that you had retained a private detective," Guerrero said.

"I wasn't aware I needed your permission."

"Hold up, let's just—" Van Dyke smoothed his absurd moustache. "My client wants to find her husband. Our job is to work together, amigo. We're on the same team."

That wasn't true. Private detectives got paid to prolong investigations, not shorten them. They tapped phones and witness-tampered and choreographed stakeouts, all so they could generate invoices.

"How long have you been under contract?" Guerrero asked Van Dyke.

"Do you have other questions for Mrs. Stallworth, Officer Guerrero?"

"So you're her lawyer now, too?"

Van Dyke kept his face impassive.

Guerrero had to figure out whether this dipshit had spoken to Antonio Saenz, to Lorena, whether he'd visited the scene of the disappearance. He had to tell Captain Hooks they had company, which would infuriate him.

Guerrero turned to Mrs. Stallworth. "If it's alright with you, ma'am, I'd like to take a quick look at your husband's office."

Rosemary turned to Mr. Van Dyke, who shrugged his assent.

"Be quick about it, please."

Van Dyke led him down the stairs.

"I assume you've already looked through his personal effects," Guerrero said.

"As did your partner. You read his report. There's nothing to see. The guy folded his underwear into perfect squares. A real Boy Scout."

Guerrero glanced around the office: a topographical map of California tacked to the wall behind his desk, an Ansel Adams print. The low bookshelf behind his desk was filled with scientific texts, a few volumes about bridge, *Futureshock*. On the desktop, a mechanical pencil nestled in the middle of a book.

"*Mechanisms of Fluorescence*," Van Dyke said. "A real barn burner."

His desk drawers contained two decks of cards, a bridge scoring pad, his children's annual school photos in two tidy stacks. The file cabinet contained scores of field reports. Behind these, in a hidden compartment, were tax documents, the deed to the house, and titles to the family's two vehicles. The only sign of habitation was a small bowl beneath the desk lamp half-filled with Good & Plenty.

"What do you think?" Guerrero said.

Van Dyke seated himself on the corner of the desk and canted his head theatrically. "Hitchhiker's Guide to Homicide. No clue how they kept the Jeep so clean. But I don't see a Mr. Hyde in this guy. I'm guessing, obviously."

"How do you know what the Jeep looks like?"

Van Dyke let Guerrero do the math. Who had he bribed down in Barstow?

"You gone visiting anywhere else?"

Van Dyke thumbed a bit of lint from his lapel. He was the sort of man who would eventually sport a gold-tipped cane.

"Don't make me put you under oath."

"I thought we were going to be friends."

"You been down to Fresno?"

"Should I put it on my dance card?"

Guerrero took a quick step toward Van Dyke, just to watch him flinch. "This is an open investigation. My captain won't hesitate to sign off on an obstruction warrant."

"Hooks? Don't be so sure."

"Stay away from my witnesses," Guerrero said.

Van Dyke saluted lazily. "I wasn't aware you had witnesses. I thought that was the whole problem."

GUERRERO NEEDED TO get to Antonio Saenz ASAP, so he called Nando down in Fresno. "If you can find the kid, please keep eyes on him. I'm heading down this afternoon."

"You cleared this with your captain?"

"Just about to," Guerrero said.

Hooks was out to lunch, so Guerrero checked his phone messages. One was from a reporter at the *Sacramento Bee*. Two days in, the investigation was getting away from him. He walked over to Jolley's desk and jingled his car keys irritably. "Let's go to Fresno."

Jolley poked at his carton of lo mein. "I'm off at five."

"We gotta get down there tonight," Guerrero said.

"Enjoy the scenery."

"No. We have to do it the same way as with the sister."

A couple of the other homicide detectives were watching them now. Jolley leaned back in his chair, savoring the moment. "I told you we should interview that punk two days ago. But, Officer Guerrero, in his boundless wisdom, drawing upon his many years of experience, advised against such a course of action. Does any of that ring a bell, little man?" Jolley discharged a snort. "So don't march your ass over here and start issuing orders."

Guerrero held up his hands. "You're right, Doug. I should have listened to you. I apologize."

Jolley tore open a packet of soy sauce with his teeth and dripped its entirety onto his noodles. "You might want to hear what the good widow Janet Shartle had to say this morning."

"The who?"

"Sweet old bird. Lives next to the Stallworths. Grows prize roses. Takes in shelter dogs. You know the type. She called while you were out at the university, talking to the snake man. Says she witnessed the incident the daughter disclosed to Hooks: a 'young gang-type individual' on the premises. It was her impression the cholo in question said something inappropriate to Jenny, who was dressed in a bikini that hardly covered her rear end. Then dad showed up and chased him off."

"Did she see whether Saenz had a gun?"

"Nope." Jolley chewed at his noodles with a leisurely and sullen pleasure. "But she did report getting 'a bad feeling' about the suspect. His car was so loud it made her dog upset. Woof woof. So she took down his license plate." He gestured with a chopstick to the report on his desk: a stolen vehicle report.

"Holy shit. Why'd she wait so long to call?"

"Said some snoopy reporter from the *Bee* jogged her memory. We'll get a lot less bullshit if we bring that along, don't you think?"

Guerrero smiled.

"I'm driving," Jolley said. "Your car smells like refried beans."

THEY FOUND ANTONIO Saenz at his place of employment, a dim storefront in an area of Fresno known as El Barrio Fortunata. No awning or signage, only a spider of duct tape that held the front window intact.

The shop offered an odd variety of goods and services. There was a barber's chair against the back wall, in which a *viejito* peacefully slept, the instruments of his trade floating in jars of luminous blue water. Next to this was a counter that advertised Western Union telegrams and passport photos. The rest of the room was filled with racks of candy, soda, chips, beer coolers, candles in glass cylinders decorated with saints. An old woman sat regarding them from behind a tray with homemade empanadas. The place smelled of sandalwood and garlic.

"Nice," Jolley said. "The local five and crime."

Guerrero had grown up with a *mercado* like this at the end of his block. The old couple held all the licenses. The real action was in the back, or downstairs. A sports book, some fencing, a little loansharking maybe—the other financial services industry.

"You gentlemen need a haircut?" the old man called out in Spanish.

"I wish." Guerrero touched at his thinning hair. He picked up an empanada and took a bite. "Did you make these, Grandma?" He laid a five down in front of her.

She looked at him without kindness. "Who you looking for, *joven*?"

Guerrero dipped his chin. "Antonio. Saenz."

The old woman picked up the five and shuffled over to an ancient register.

"Mind if we look around in back?"

The old woman didn't respond. Men in suits did what they were going to do.

Guerrero led Jolley through the door in back, down a narrow staircase, into a basement room with an empty desk and a jittery fluorescent light. In a display case, an array of knives, nunchucks, and three battered pistols lay atop crushed velvet. After a minute, two men entered. Both wore plaid flannel shirts buttoned just at the top, wife beaters tucked into Ben Davis jeans, and military flip belts.

"Cholo one and cholo two," Jolley muttered.

"Is one of you Antonio Saenz?" Guerrero said in Spanish.

"Who wants to know?" the older one asked. He sneered at the half-eaten empanada in Guerrero's hand. "You don't got to buy shit. Everybody knows you police, man."

Jolley pulled out his badge. "Let's speak English, okay? Detective Douglas Jolley, Sacramento Police Department. This is my colleague, Pedro Guerrero. Which one of you is Antonio Saenz?"

The younger man started to speak, then hesitated. He looked about sixteen: a wispy mustache, a smooth chin sprayed with zits.

"You ain't gotta say shit to them," the older man said.

"Shut up," Jolley said. "Nobody's talking to you. Beat it or I'll run a check on every pistol in this dump."

"Those guns ain't for sale," said the older man.

"Careful," Guerrero murmured in Spanish. "My friend's got a temper."

"He ain't the only one."

"How about if we speak fucking English, okay?" Jolley growled. "Like, pretend we're in the United States of America instead of some Tijuana whorehouse. And don't fucking glare at me."

"You still don't got to say shit," the older man muttered. He was already on his way out of the room.

"I know my rights," Antonio said. "I'm a veteran."

"Let's calm down and do this the nice way," Guerrero said. "We just have a few questions."

"About what?" Tony said.

"The Stallworth family."

Tony sneered. "Again?"

"What does that mean?" Jolley snapped.

"Your partner up there. Pike. He already came sniffing around."

The officers glanced at each other.

"Van Dyke?" Guerrero said suddenly.

"Whatever his name was."

"He told you he was a cop?" Guerrero said.

"He didn't have to tell me. I know cops."

"That man was a private detective," Guerrero said.

"Same difference. I'll tell you what I told him: I don't know shit about any Stallworths."

"You never met any of them?" Jolley said.

"My sister was friends with the girl. I met her for like three seconds."

"You never met her father, Marcus Stallworth?"

"Hell no. The girl was my *sister*'s rich bitch friend."

"How do you know they were wealthy?"

"I seen their house."

"So you've been to their home?"

"I dropped my sister off. The girl invited me inside, but I said no."

"You're aware that Mr. Stallworth has disappeared?" Guerrero said.

"I don't know nothing about that. I told the other guy. I don't know how I can help you officers."

Jolley took three quick steps toward Tony. "You could start by telling us the fucking truth," he snarled. "Remember, we've been out there gathering evidence. We know whether you been naughty or nice, whether you've been driving stolen cars, ingesting illegal drugs, stuff like that. So try not to mess this next question up, Mr. Seanz: Have you ever met Mr. Marcus Stallworth? Answer carefully. It's never a good idea to lie to officers of the law."

Antonio exhaled through his nose. "I told you everything I know."

"That's a *no*? You never touched him or his vehicle?"

"What? No. What the hell are you accusing me of?"

"What should I be accusing you of?" Jolley was seething.

"I'm not saying nothing else, man. You're crazy."

Guerrero stepped between the two of them and eased his partner back a few steps. "Let's take a time-out. Come on, Doug. Grab a smoke."

Jolley glared at Antonio. "I'll be back. Don't think this is over."

They listened to Jolley pound up the stairs. "I told you he's got a temper."

"So what, you're the good guy?" Antonio cast a dubious glance at Guerrero. "I got nothing to do with any of this. You're making a big fucking mistake."

"Okay. Let's just calm down."

"I don't have to tell you shit."

"No, you don't. At least for now. But you know how it works, Mr. Saenz. It doesn't look good if you're afraid to talk with us. Looks incriminating. We know about the stolen car you were driving, and why you left Fruitbridge. We can haul you into the station. Or call our pals at INS."

Tony stiffened.

"We're just trying to get background," Guerrero said tiredly. "If you got nothing to hide, what's the harm?"

"What more do you want me to say, man?"

"I want you to tell me, one more time, whether you've ever had any contact with Mr. Marcus Stallworth?"

Tony cast his eyes around the room, trying to decide what to say, or how much. "There was something fucked about that family," he murmured.

"What do you mean?"

Tony ground his fist into his temple.

Guerrero, who regarded Saenz as a suspect, interpreted this gesture as an act of calculated hesitation. But Tony himself was thinking of the Stallworth family, of the bad news they had absorbed. His impulse to elide the truth was, oddly, an act of mercy, carried out by a young man who knew what it was like to be abandoned, left fatherless.

"We can do this the hard way, if we have to," Guerrero said. "I'll come back down with a warrant. But that only makes more trouble. And not just for you, Antonio. Your mom—she certainly doesn't need that." Guerrero let the implication linger for a beat.

"Alright. Look. I didn't want to get into this because the guy, like you said, if something happened to him, I'm sorry for his family and everything. But when I picked up my little sister—she called me in the middle of the night, all freaked out—and when I pulled up I saw the guy, Stallworth, he was on his knees, like kneeling, and he had his arms around my little sister's waist."

"He was hugging her?"

"That's what it looked like to me."

"What did you do?"

"Got her the fuck out of there."

"You were upset?"

"Fuck yeah, I was upset."

"Did you have an altercation with Mr. Stallworth?"

"No no no. It wasn't like that. I just—that's my fucking little sister, man. She's fourteen. I wanted to get her out of there."

"I thought you were dropping off."

"No. Yeah. I did. That was another day."

"I'm sorry. I'm confused. You visited another time?"

"Yeah. Like, a month earlier or something. I dropped her off."

Guerrero waited for Antonio to go on, but he was done.

"What did your sister say? On the night Mr. Stallworth was hugging her?"

"She made up some bullshit about they were looking for the keys he dropped. I could tell something fucked-up had gone down."

"How?"

"She's my *sister*, okay?"

"He messed with her?"

"The world's a dark place."

"There you go." Guerrero sighed. He looked at Saenz for a long moment, not in the sly way of a cop who wants his suspect to keep talking, but with a genuine and reluctant sympathy. Antonio Saenz was saying too much, stumbling into the crosshairs, becoming a target.

"Why didn't you mention any of this before?"

"You don't speak ill of the dead. It ain't right."

Guerrero dipped his chin. How did the kid know that Marcus Stallworth was dead?

"Besides." Tony glowered. "That's my sister, okay? You got a sister? It's private shit. You say something to a cop, it becomes public."

"Some conversations are off the record."

"No such thing, bro. Come on. I was in the navy." He glanced at Guerrero's notebook. "She's just a kid. Smart as fuck, too. That little bitch is going somewhere. She doesn't need to get dragged into all this."

"What's this? Dragged into what?"

"Your investigation, man. This whole mess with the Stallings."

"Stallworths."

"Never mind my mother. She's evangelical."

"Do you think your sister had some sort of relationship with Mr. Stallworth?"

"I didn't say that. I just know what I saw. Sometimes guys like that get themselves into trouble."

"Trouble," Guerrero said. His chest was tingling. He waited for Antonio to make his next statement. But the kid, the suspect, was done talking.

THEY DROVE TO the substation where Nando was the lieutenant. It was a mile away, tucked among the brown neighborhoods that hugged the highway, with their strip malls and shitty prefabs. Jolley stayed in the car. He'd heard enough Spanish for one day. Guerrero was there to update his cousin and seek his counsel.

Nando swept Guerrero into his cramped office. EL GRAN QUESO read the sign over his desk. "You like?" he said. "Beats the shit out of busting into double-wides and hauling *borrachos* down to county." A few years ago, Nando had taken a bullet in the calf at a quinceañera he was working for off-duty cash—some drunk who'd clicked off his safety.

He was still Nando: loud, mocking, his big nose beaded with nic sweat. He walked now with a fat man's limp, pitched forward as if chasing a rolling coin. "I'm gonna get one of those golf carts and see if anybody can tell I'm Mexican." He laughed like anybody who didn't was missing out.

Young deputies kept sticking their heads in the door. Nando told them to fuck off. They talked family shit for a few minutes. Then Guerrero came to the point.

"I need you to shade the Saenz kid for a few days."

"You worried he's headed down to Acapulco?"

"I don't know. Maybe. He had some kind of altercation with the alleged victim. Told me the guy messed with his little sister. Like pervert stuff. Says he was protecting her honor."

"You think he's telling the truth?"

"If he is, there's your motive."

"And if he isn't?"

"He knows the family. Knows they have money. He's seen their house. Maybe he gets a big idea. Based on his priors, he was headed that way."

"Why not just rob the house?"

"He doesn't strike me as a brilliant criminal mind."

"So how does he get that Jeep so clean?"

"Maybe he gets help from his new business associate. I was hoping you could also send me whatever you've got on him."

Nando sat back and licked the tip of his pencil, like he was making a list.

"You want me to run this through the proper channels?" Guerrero said.

"I'm just giving you shit."

"I'll make sure everyone knows you're helping out."

Nando laughed. "You gonna take care of old Nando, *primo*? Funnel me some pesos from your big-city slush fund? Maybe I'll get that golf cart after all."

"This is serious," Guerrero said.

"Course it's serious. Some rich preppy got popped. That's a top-shelf life right there. Just remember your little punk-ass beaner has a life, too. How many detectives you figure would drive down from Sacramento if *he* disappeared?"

"I'm following the evidence."

"Okay. Hey. It's a big case, *primo*. Don't listen to me. I'm just thinking out loud. I been listening to Cesar Chavez tapes before bed."

Guerrero wanted to push back, but Nando didn't give you anything to push against. He laughed his big laugh, like when they were kids, packed six to a couch, sucking at popsicles and goofing on each other.

"Wait. Shit. *Beaner*'s a racist term, isn't it?"

HOOKS CALLED GUERRERO into his office the next morning.

"Should we wait for Jolley?" Guerrero said.

The captain was former military. Words offended him. "Talk."

Guerrero launched into his investigative summary.

Hooks rapped the dossier at the center of his desk. It was, Guerrero realized, his own case file. "Not what you know. What you *think*."

Guerrero said he didn't know what to think yet, there wasn't enough to go on.

Hooks grunted. "Guess."

"Saenz. There's history with Stallworth. He tells a buddy down in Fresno. They hatch a plan. Armed robbery. Kidnapping, maybe. But it goes south."

Hooks listened impassively. The gray ash on his cigarette crept toward his knuckles. He dropped the butt into his coffee cup and handed a manila folder to Guerrero. Inside was a report from an analyst with the FBI's Automated Fingerprint Identification System. It stated that the two partials lifted from the roll bar of Marcus Stallworth's Jeep, having undergone "computer enhancement," indicated a "definitive match" with Antonio Saenz.

There were two additional reports. The first was from a hematologist who had examined the Stallworth Jeep. Among his findings: a considerable volume of blood ("undetected by previous investigators") had soaked into the dark carpeting under the passenger seat. FBI serologists had then analyzed this blood and compared it to a sample taken from Antonio Saenz, which agents obtained, by subpoena, from the firm that conducted drug tests for the navy. An analysis of blood serum proteins indicated a "significant statistical likelihood" of a match.

Guerrero sat stunned. "Wait, who the hell invited the feds in on this?"

Hooks held a finger to his lips.

"I did," a voice behind him said.

Chief Ellis stood in the doorway, his face sharp and shaven, like a pink hatchet. "It's a bit more complicated than it seems, Officer." He shut the door and glanced down at Hooks, who handed Guerrero an oversized sheet of slick, camera-ready paper.

"You read the *Bee*?" Ellis said.

Guerrero nodded unconvincingly.

"That's going to run Sunday. Front page of the local section."

The headline read WITHOUT A TRACE, with a little tagline underneath: POLICE FIND NO SIGN OF MISSING PROF – OR AN ASSAILANT. The story was blotter and bio stuff until the quotes at the end. One was from Janet Shartle, the elderly neighbor who recalled an altercation involving Mr. Stallworth and "a young Latino thug." The second was from Van Dyke, the private detective. "It's been two weeks. The family still knows nothing. They want Marcus back. If that's not possible, they deserve to know what happened to him. To live without closure is a kind of slow torture."

Hooks cleared his throat. "Any errors of fact?"

"How'd you get this?" Guerrero said.

Ellis checked his watch. "TV folks read the *Bee*. They'll pounce on this. Then, trust me, the feds will happily step in to save the day. You understand?"

"We're doing everything—"

The chief stared him into silence. "I'm asking for results, Guerrero. Hooks believes in you. I'll defer to him. But some people very high up want this matter resolved. Higher than any of us can see. You've got forty-eight hours before this goes to a federal task force, seventy-two at the outside."

The chief departed. Guerrero sat clenching his fists. "Your pal Van Dyke tampered with my suspect," he muttered finally.

"Why are you still here, Guerrero?"

"He portrayed himself as an officer of the law."

Hooks looked up slowly. "Quit whining. You guessed right. Go make the case."

GUERRERO EXPECTED THE girl, Jenny Stallworth, to be fragile. She'd looked that way as her mother led her into the family den and went over the "rules" of the interview. Jolley stood there nodding, producing gentle noises, smiling his white cop smile.

But the moment her mother left the room, Jenny's mouth became a little purse of insolence.

"We're here to ask you a few more questions," Jolley said. "If you're feeling overwhelmed, just let us know."

"I *tried* to tell her about Lorena's brother," she said quickly. "I told her, like, even before you guys showed up. She said I was being ridiculous, which is what she always says when she can't handle the truth."

"What did you tell her exactly?"

"That he'd driven over to our house in this, like, low-rider." Her eyes shifted to Guerrero. "And that he had a gun. That's the thing I remember."

"He showed it to you?"

"It was tucked in his belt. He was standing in a way you were supposed to *see* he had a gun. That was the whole point. He was this big weapons expert in the navy."

"Did you tell your mother or father about the gun?"

Jenny stared into her lap. "I didn't want them to freak out."

"Did you talk to Lorena?"

"Of course. I was, like, 'What's up with your brother carrying a gun?' She said it was just a knife. But that was bullshit." The girl looked up defiantly, to affirm her use of profanity. "Because she was the one who first told me about his gun. She said he was a member of the Latin Kings. I thought she was just bragging. But I guess she was telling the truth."

"Did Mr. Saenz ever threaten you?"

"No."

"What did he say to you?"

"Just dumb stuff, like, trying to flirt. Checking out my dad's Jeep."

"Did he interact with your father?"

"I wouldn't call it interaction. My dad came out and saw this kind of delinquent-looking sp—" Jenny caught herself. "This guy messing with his Jeep."

"What does 'messing' mean?" Guerrero said.

"Just, you know, gawking at it."

"Did he touch the vehicle?"

"I don't know. Maybe."

"Did your father speak to Mr. Saenz?"

Jenny nibbled at her thumbnail. "I've been trying to remember. He may have said something as he was coming down the stairs. He was pissed."

"That's why Mr. Saenz left in such a hurry?"

She nodded. "With the gun and the way he was dressed and everything. It was pretty obvious he didn't belong in the neighborhood. No offense."

"Is there anything else you remember about the incident? Anything else we should know?"

Jenny leaned forward. "I don't want this to sound mean. But Lorena had certain problems." She aimed what she believed to be a furtive glance at Guerrero.

He reached down and pressed a button on his beeper, causing it to shrill. "It's the captain," he whispered to Jolley. "What should I do, Doug?"

"Take it."

Guerrero hurried from the den.

"Sorry about that," Jolley said. "You were saying, about Lorena Saenz?"

"Yeah, you know, in terms of us being friends, it was more like something my mom pushed. She got the idea that Lorena had this rough life and it would help her to spend some time over here, like with her confidence. My mom is big into service work."

"So you two weren't really friends?"

"I mean, I liked her at first." Jenny's voice seemed to catch. Jolley watched as her pretty face twisted. "But she wasn't who she said she was."

"How so?"

"She acted all shy and meek. But she was always trying to find excuses to come over, eat dinner over here, whatever. It was like she had some idea that our family would adopt her or something. She kissed up to my mom constantly. But she was different in private." The girl's eyes darted about, searching for a place to land. "Like, if we were going swimming, she would undress in front of me. It was like her family didn't have any boundaries." Her voice had grown faint, almost wistful.

Guerrero, who was listening from the hallway, could barely hear her. There was a long pause. Jolley cleared his throat. "Are you okay?"

"I don't know. Yeah. I just got a creepy vibe from that family. Like, the minute Lo showed up in our life, something bad was going to happen."

"That's why you stopped being friends with her?"

"She was never really a friend to begin with."

The words stung Guerrero unexpectedly. He reminded himself that Jenny Stallworth was a terrified young girl. Her father was missing, almost certainly dead. She was using contempt to keep the pain at bay.

"Like I said, it was just something my mom wanted."

GUERRERO DROVE STRAIGHT from the Stallworths' to Lorena's workplace. Safe Harbor was one of those Medicaid facilities where working families stashed their dying, a converted elementary school with kid rooms and kid ceilings. Guerrero found the kitchen manager, who wrung his fat hands. His employees were underage or undocumented or both, which allowed him to pay in cash and skim the difference from the state subsidies. Guerrero's mom and aunts had been a part of the same scheme. The pine-scented industrial soap, the rubber aprons and veils of rancid steam—he remembered it all.

Lorena worked the loader, pulling dishes from the conveyor belt, slotting them into sickly green racks. The *jefe* whistled over the roar of the machines. Lorena looked up and spotted Guerrero. The plate she was holding began to shake, dripping pink strings onto the floor mats. He knew, then and there, that the girl was hiding something.

This was true, of course, given all that had transpired between herself and Mr. Stallworth. He had made her party to a secret history. (Or maybe she had forced her way into that history?) But cops meant danger, especially for her mother. She couldn't get dragged into it. She had spent the past week telling herself the police would figure out what happened without her. It was their job. What did she really *know*, after all?

The *jefe* curled his finger at Lorena. She set down the spray nozzle. In her periphery, she could see sunlight slanting though the rear screen door. For a second, she imagined running. Then she returned to herself and walked calmly toward Guerrero.

The *jefe* led them through the dining hall. It was three in the afternoon, snack time. A scattering of residents sat gazing at bowls of gray pudding. They wound up in the art room, with its paper roses and watery landscapes, which fluttered against their thumbtacks.

"Did you find him?" Lorena said. "Mr. Stallworth."

"We're still working on it, Lorena. To be honest—can I be honest? I don't think we're going to figure this one out. I shouldn't tell you that. It's not very professional. We're kind of grasping for straws." Guerrero pulled out his notebook and flipped through it a bit distractedly. "Hey, first thing's first. Your boss won't give you a hard time about this. We had a little talk. And you don't have to worry about your mother, either. Okay? Okay. We're just doing this thing called due diligence. You know what that is, right? It's like dotting your *I*'s or crossing your *T*'s. We're trying to help this family, the Stallworths. You know that, right?"

"Of course," Lorena said softly. Her hairnet itched.

"I need you to tell me if there's anything else you forgot to mention the last time we talked?"

"I don't think so."

"Anything about your relationship to Mr. Stallworth?"

Her head shook.

"Did you like him?"

"Did I like him?" Lo was taking little sips of air, trying to settle her eyes on some object that wasn't his notebook.

"It's a pretty simple question."

"I didn't think about him that much."

The spot at the base of her throat pulsed.

"I know this is upsetting to think about."

"May I use the bathroom?" Lo whispered.

"Of course," Guerrero said.

Lorena hurried to the bathroom, where she threw up. She washed her mouth out and tried to calm herself by staring hard into the mirror. It was kid level. All she could see was her neck and chest. Was there any way she could make him stop? Did she have the right to a lawyer? She couldn't stop thinking about her mother, who had come to America for her and Tony, to give them a future—the phrase had become an incantation chanted over the minutes of her life. Tony had messed that up. But she wouldn't. She would become a nurse. Or even a scientist. She took a deep breath and decided she was being silly. Acting like a kid. She had nothing to do with any of this, really. She just had to answer a few questions and it would be over.

When she returned to the art room, Guerrero stood, like a gentleman.

"You okay?"

"Yeah. No. I'm okay."

"It's weird talking to a cop. I get it. I wasn't always a cop, you know." He watched Lorena attempt a smile. "We're almost done."

"I'm so sorry all this happened," Lorena said. "But I barely knew Mr. Stallworth. Me and Jenny were friends. That's all."

"I hear you. Just a few more quick questions. Okay? Did your family ever meet the Stallworths?"

"No. Like I said, I was just friends with Jenny."

"Right. I got that. But I figured, if you went camping with the Stallworths, maybe your mom wanted to meet them?"

"You're not going to talk to my mom, are you?"

"I don't think so," Guerrero said. "I'm just trying to tie up the loose ends, remember? If we can get through these questions, I'll be on my way."

"My mom met Mrs. Stallworth one time at my school, for about five seconds. At parent-teacher conference night."

"How about your brother?"

"He's in the navy."

Guerrero looked puzzled. "Are you sure about that, Lorena? The navy says Tony was discharged—" He flipped through his notebook. "Yeah. Discharged in August. Did Tony ever meet the Stallworths? Maybe dropping you off or something?"

"What does Tony have to do with this?"

"Like I said: loose ends. Can you just answer the question?" He sounded bored, a little impatient.

"I don't think so. I can't really remember."

Guerrero tilted his head to one side and fixed his eyes on Lorena. "I'm starting to get the feeling that maybe you're not taking this real seriously."

"I am. I swear."

"So your brother never met Jenny Stallworth or her father? That's what you're telling me?" Guerrero's voice dipped abruptly, as if someone might overhear them. "I'm trying to keep you out of this, Lorena. You and your mom."

"Out of what?"

"Can I give you a little advice?" Guerrero said, this time in Spanish. "Just please relax and answer the question. Then I can cross you off my little list and we'll be done. But don't lie. Because if you do that, then I have to ask you more questions and it looks like you have something to hide and it gets more complicated. But you don't have anything to hide. Not that I can see." He smiled in the way that was both official and a little more than that.

"He met Jenny one time," Lorena said. "He was back on leave and he dropped me off at their house."

"He came inside?"

"No."

"He met Mr. Stallworth?"

"No. He just dropped me off."

"Did he pick you up, too?"

"No."

"He never picked you up from the Stallworth home? Think, Lorena. Late one night. He didn't come and pick you up?"

Lorena felt a cold thump. Tony, all coked up, his stupid gun. Tony who had caught Mr. Stallworth embracing her. "You think Tony had something to do with this," she said suddenly. "You're asking all this because you think—oh my God." She began hyperventilating.

"Calm down, Lorena. We don't think anything. That's not how it works. We're trying to figure out what happened to Marcus Stallworth. A man has disappeared, a husband and a father. Do you understand? He may have been murdered."

"No," she said. Then again, more loudly: "*No*. He wasn't murdered," Lorena said defiantly. "He left. He ran away."

Guerrero sat back in astonishment. And waited.

SHE HAD DAMMED the truth within her for two weeks. Now that dam gave way. She recounted how Mr. Stallworth had behaved toward her, how he had waited outside the tent and led her away from the camp, how he had spoken to her and later touched her. His maps. The secret compartment in the file cabinet. The forensics manual. The night she had found him bleeding. How he tried to keep her from leaving.

From time to time, Lorena would seize up. But Guerrero wasn't afraid of the silences. He treated them as ellipses, a rest period, a chance for the witness to be summoned further toward the truth. He went to get them some water and when he sat down again, it was next to her, so she wouldn't have to look at him.

"Did you tell anyone else about this relationship?"

Lorena shook her head. "It wasn't a relationship."

"Tony?"

"Of course not."

"Why not?"

Lorena started to say something about his temper, then stopped herself. "It's not something—we're not that close."

"He would have been angry, no? An older man messing with his little sister."

"He didn't know anything about it."

"Did he or did he not come to pick you up at the Stallworths'? On the night you were just describing?"

Lorena fell silent.

"We can get phone records, Lorena."

She nodded.

"That's a yes."

"Uh-huh."

"And there was an altercation of some kind?"

"No."

"No? Tony wasn't angry? He didn't have words with Mr. Stallworth?"

"He came to get me because Jenny got sick. That's all. Maybe he thought—I don't know what he thought. It doesn't matter. Mr. Stallworth had a whole plan to leave. That's what I'm telling you. He didn't love his wife."

"He told you that?"

"Not exactly. But Jenny . . ." Lorena felt her cheeks start to burn. "She said her parents kind of hated each other. The affection was just an act."

"Did he love you?" Guerrero said seriously.

"No." She couldn't describe what had passed between them. It wasn't love, exactly. But it didn't feel like a crush either. Mr. Stallworth had recognized her ambitions, her yearnings. He had breathed himself into her. She had glowed under his secret gaze.

Guerrero sat back but kept his eyes locked on Lorena. "Why didn't you tell me any of this before?"

"I didn't want to get anyone in trouble."

"Anyone like who?"

"I figured you'd find him. The police would find him. And no one would get into trouble."

"You keep mentioning trouble. Why would you get into trouble?"

"Not me. My mom."

"Okay. You're worried about your mom. I get it. But listen, Lorena. I have to tell you this. You have to listen. This is a homicide investigation. A criminal matter." Guerrero spoke slowly, as if to underline the words. "If you don't want anyone to get into trouble, you need to tell the truth. Right now. No more games. No more stories."

"You don't believe me," Lorena said.

Guerrero sighed and set his notebook down and rubbed his eyes. "I don't have beliefs," he said. "That's not how it works. I just need you to tell me what happened between your brother and Mr. Stallworth. I know they met on two occasions. You were present on both occasions. You are what we call a 'material witness.' That's the legal term. We can do this right here or I can call your mom and she can bring you down to the police station to give a sworn statement. She'll have to give a sworn statement, too. You understand what I'm telling you?"

THIS WAS HOW Lorena Saenz became a witness for the prosecution. She confirmed to Officer Pedro Guerrero that her brother had met Mr. Marcus Stallworth twice. On the first occasion, he had admired Mr. Stallworth's Jeep. He had fled the scene when Stallworth appeared. On the second occasion he had come to pick her up in the middle of the night and, by her own account, had caught Stallworth behaving in an inappropriate manner. Yes, Tony had been angry. Yes, he had threatened Stallworth.

Guerrero asked if Tony had been carrying a weapon. Lorena said she wasn't sure. Guerrero reminded her that withholding information from the police was a crime. Lorena began to cry. Maybe he had a gun but he would never use it.

"*Maybe* he had a gun?"

"It was dark."

"Come on, Lorena."

"He was just trying to scare Mr. Stallworth."

"With a gun?"

"That's how he is. He acts tough."

"He threatened to kill Mr. Stallworth?"

"No," Lorena said. "That's not how it was."

"How was it?"

"He was looking out for me." Lorena began to cry even harder. "He was right."

"About what?"

"I told him he was crazy. But he was right."

"Have you talked to him since he left town?"

Lorena shook her head. Tears dripped off her chin. "Tony didn't do anything," she said. "Mr. Stallworth ran away. He had a plan. I can prove it."

"How would you prove it, Lorena?"

"He had a giant map with his route all drawn out. You just have to follow the *X*'s with the coordinates next to them. I wrote them down."

"The coordinates?"

She nodded frantically. "He's going to Yuma, Arizona."

"Okay. I hear you, Lorena. I'm listening. Let's get you some Kleenex, okay?" Guerrero got up and grabbed some paper towels from a dispenser near the door. He sat down and took a deep breath. "I realize this is scary. But let's think about this. Mr. Stallworth was a field researcher, right? He made a lot of trips into the desert. And he had maps in his office. I've seen them."

"There were those other things, too. The police manual. And rubber gloves."

"You saw these things yourself?"

She nodded.

"He showed them to you?"

Lorena said nothing.

"So you snuck into his office and found all this incriminating stuff just lying around?"

"It was locked in his file cabinet."

"And you just happened to have the key?"

Lorena closed her eyes. Her neck pulsed again. "He forgot; he must have forgotten to lock it."

Her lies had become so transparent that Guerrero felt bad for her. "It's going to be okay," he said quietly.

"He told me to find him." Lorena sobbed. "I'm telling you the *truth*."

Guerrero watched the girl shudder. He set another paper towel down in front her. "You're not in trouble. We're trying to help the Stallworth family, okay? That's all we're doing."

GUERRERO KNEW IT was wrong to feel jubilant. But police work had its own narcotic lure. There were bad guys, or guys who did bad things. Sin made its mess in the world. His job was to detect its origins and to punish its authors. He was a kind of custodian—of motive and action.

He stared at Lorena Saenz, this poor kid who'd just given up her brother. He knew where she lived, and how. He knew her prospects. It was impossible to overstate the power Marcus Stallworth must have assumed in her mind. He was exactly the sort of man she would fall for: handsome, wealthy, devoted to family. A kind of superhero. Maybe Mr. Stallworth had been flattered by her attentions. Maybe he had encouraged her somehow. As a consequence, she had brought her brother into the orbit of this man and thereby, in all likelihood, contributed to his murder. Now she was stuck trying to protect her family.

The rule was simple: a witness who lies once will keep lying as the facts demand. She had denied that Tony ever met Stallworth. Then admitted to one meeting. Then a second. Then the altercation. Then the gun. Maybe Tony himself had cooked up this story about Stallworth's secret getaway plan and fed it to his little sister. It had the feel of something hastily conjured, adolescent.

"What's going to happen?" she said.

Guerrero wanted to offer her a reassuring response, the neat and necessary clichés of police work, about evidence and justice. Then he could lead Lorena back to her filthy dishes and steam. He had done his job, gained her trust, extracted the truth. But the nervy and improvised intimacy he had established between them suddenly felt more like manipulation. His mind drifted back to those gray bowls of pudding; the image soured his stomach. He had used her innocence to make his case. And though he couldn't see it yet, that innocence would be turned against both of them.

"I need to check out what you've told me," Guerrero said finally. "You're not in any trouble. Neither is your mother. And Tony's not in any trouble either. Not if he didn't do anything. Okay, Lorena? I'm making a personal promise here. But don't talk about any of this with anyone. Understand? No one. We'll know if you do."

"I'm telling the truth," Lorena said.

"I know you are."

"I can prove it," she said again.

Guerrero stood and Lorena tried to do the same. But she wobbled and fell against the table between them and he reached to steady her, a brief hand upon the body he had ushered into ruin. He wanted to whisper that it was all going to be okay. Instead, he asked her to please stop crying.

GUERRERO GOT HIMSELF patched through to Hooks, who listened to his report in silence. Guerrero assumed the next step would be an arrest warrant. Dangle a plea offer, get Seanz to name accomplices.

"Not yet," Hooks said.

"What if he drives down to Mexico?"

"Slow down," Hooks said. "The little fuck is presumed innocent. You jack him, he gets a lawyer and suddenly we've got the ACLU up our ass."

"What about the story in the *Bee*?"

"You're not listening, Guerrero. This is big. We're being tracked. You go too fast, you fuck it up. We need everything proper. Find another way."

"What does that mean?"

But Hooks had hung up.

Back at the station, Jolley was waiting for him. "Where the hell you been? They found a witness who saw Stallworth the day he went missing, between three and four in the p.m. Some fast-cash hut south of Fresno. Witness says he came in wearing a ball cap. Real twitchy, like he was in a hurry. Cashed a money order for five thousand smackeroos."

"Who's *they*?"

Jolley handed him the report, an embossed FBI logo on every page.

"They're going to take this fucking case from us," Guerrero muttered.

"The feds are involved because someone wants them involved. That's how it works downtown. You're Chico, my friend. Not the Man. Try not to get your feelings hurt." Jolley began to the whistle the theme from *Chico and the Man*. It had been a hit sitcom back when Guerrero worked in Oak Park, the hokey tale of a smiley Mexican mechanic and his racist-but-sweet-hearted old boss. Jolley laughed and patted his fat cop gut. *Chico*, he sang, *don't be discouraged. The man, he ain't so hard to understand.*

GUERRERO CALLED NANDO'S house from a pay phone—a little advance warning. A girl answered, one of his daughters or his new girlfriend. Nando was busy, she said. "Just wake him up, honey."

"Really?" Nando said. "It's the Sabbath, *primo*."

"I need to talk to our little friend again. I'm heading down."

"Monday?"

"Right now."

"Don't do that," Nando said.

"Too late," Guerrero said. "I already did."

He could see the whole thing playing out. The feds swooping in, a press conference for the TV crews in a marble lobby, a quick thanks to the local police for their assistance. The drive should have taken three hours. He made it in barely two. Nando answered the door in his robe.

"Christ," he said. "You're one dumb fucking mule. What did I tell you? Calm down. Listen. You're not the only one keeping tabs on Saenz. The Bureau called the boss man down here a few days ago. Capital *B*."

"Why didn't you tell me?"

"Because I figured you'd race down here and fuck up your career."

"Hooks told me to come down."

"I doubt that."

"He implied it. He wouldn't let me get a warrant. But he told me to find another way. Those were his words."

Nando shook his head. "Good old Hooks. That's one crafty bastard. You see what's happening?"

Guerrero didn't.

"The *Bee* publishes on Sunday. The TV stations blow it up. So now everyone's watching, and what happens? Sacramento's finest make the case. That's the play, primo. Hooks is under orders to back off from the feds. So he tells you to back off. But he *knows* you. He knows you're gonna barrel through that red light. If you get Saenz to confess, he's the hero for putting you on it. If you mess it up, you're the dumbass who defied a direct order. They always find a way to put the risk onto a brown man."

"Hooks is Black."

"Not since he made captain." Nando hobbled to the kitchen to make them mugs of instant coffee.

"What's Saenz been up to?"

"Hold on. Lemme check the Batphone." Nando held a banana to his ear. "Nothing. Just scratching his nuts."

"What about his friends?"

"The kids he invites over for slumber parties?"

"This coffee is crap."

"Don't leave a tip."

"His business partner. What's his story?"

"Victor Peña. He was running around town yapping about being Latin Kings a few years ago. Then some real banger stomped him. The end. No record to speak of. He and your guy were pals in the navy. They've got that little business going in surplus weapons."

"Legal?"

"Permits and everything. They prefer the term *private brokers*. Very classy."

Guerrero told Nando about the money order. "You know that place?"

"Bank of choice for Fresno's finest narcotic retailers. Sounds like Stallworth had a helluva weekend planned."

Guerrero gulped at his crap coffee. "They must have grabbed him and forced him to buy a money order. Maybe it's a down payment on the ransom? Then things go bad."

"Grabbed him from *where*? His house? The college up there? You're making shit up."

"The blood in that Jeep. The prints I lifted. Am I making that up?"

Nando was shaking his head. "You got the man's Jeep, his wallet, his credit cards. Why make him buy a money order?"

"They wanted cash. No way to trace that."

"Why run the risk? He could walk in and call the cops."

Guerrero hated this about Nando, the way he picked at your logic, as if he were loosening a hastily knotted shoelace for the pleasure of watching you trip.

"Unless there's someone, like, waiting in the parking lot with a loaded gun. Stallworth's scared shitless. Maybe he takes too long. Tries to run."

"You got a bunch of circumstances, *primo*. That's a theory, not a crime."

"It is if I get him to cop," Guerrero said.

Nando lit up a cigarillo. Smoke billowed from his nostrils. "Feels like a setup to me, *primo.*"

THE SECOND AND final meeting between Officer Pedro Guerrero and Antonio Saenz lasted just five minutes. Guerrero entered the basement beneath the *mercado* from a door in the alley to which Nando's men had directed him. The suspect was downstairs, hunched over some kind of ledger.

"That you, *pendejo?*" Tony called out.

"Afraid not."

Tony glanced over his shoulder and saw Guerrero standing there in his wrinkled suit. The room smelled of silver polish. The display cases gleamed with weapons.

"You got a few minutes to talk?"

"We already talked."

It was never good when the police came around a second time. But Tony's perspective on the situation was considerably calmer than his sister's. He understood himself to be on the fringes of whatever had happened to Marcus Stallworth. Mostly, he was confused as to how Guerrero had found his way into the private showroom of his new business.

"I told you everything I know," Tony said politely.

"My partner—you remember him? He's got this idea in his head. That you know more than you're saying."

"He's wrong."

"That's what I think, too. But you can help me out, okay? Just tell me where you were two weekends ago? I'm talking about Friday, October 23, through that Sunday, October 25."

"Where I was?"

"The weekend before Halloween. I'm trying to rule you out, Antonio."

"Rule me out of what?"

Guerrero waited.

TONY KNEW WELL enough where he'd been that weekend, his second in Fresno. It began on Friday afternoon. He had the day off from his new gig at Quik Lube, but nowhere to go, so he showed up at the parking lot next door, where the staff sometimes gathered to drink after closing. This girl Trina, the niece of his shift manager Gonzo, showed up around dusk, already buzzed. She pulled a beer from the cooler, walked right up to Tony and asked him if he could pop the top. She wore a tight black tank top and mesh stockings; black liner slashed out from her eyelids like tiny scimitars. Gonzo told him to be careful. Trina shook her tits and laughed. "He can take care of himself."

Tony was transfixed as only the lonely can be. They shared a six-pack and later Trina took him to a motel room off the freeway, a kind of flophouse (Tony saw that in retrospect) where they had some rum and laughed and kissed and Trina undressed and whispered what she wanted in his ear then climbed onto him and Tony had to stop himself from announcing that he loved her. Then this guy came by, an old white hippie with fucked-up teeth and a bunch of rock cocaine. Tony and Trina began smoking and talking frantically. It all felt deep and hilarious till the rock was gone. Then panic set in and they called the same guy, Winnie was his name, and it went on like that, Tony running to a cash hut for more, Trina laughing, dragging him into the bathroom, her mouth eager to engulf him. Then everything went black.

Tony heard pounding and a door opened and beams of sun struck his eyes. A fat little maid recoiled at the sight of him. Blood from a cut on his scalp had dripped down his cheek and painted his naked torso. His wallet was gone. He missed his Saturday shift at Quik Lube, and got the shitcan and the girl, or

Winnie, or the both of them, charged a bunch of booze and ste-
reo equipment on his card, maxed it out. His license was gone,
too, his VA card, all that shit. Welcome to Fresno.

Tony had left Fruitridge because he had a problem. Now he
knew how easy it was to find that same problem in Fresno. He
called his friend Peña, who laughed for a full minute. "You got
rode, bro. Lemme know when you're ready to stop fucking up."
He had a new business, weapons, specialty shit, mail-order,
COD delivery, totally legit.

Peña sent him off on a run with two antique pistols. Tony got
pulled over. The cop found the guns, which were unregistered.
He got cuffed, marched off to county. Peña showed up a few
hours later, bailed him out, paid his fine, and threw in $500 for
the trouble. "That was just a test, little man. Needed to make
sure you weren't a snitch." Peña grinned. "Relax. Keep straight
and we'll make us a lot of money." Tony didn't have much in the
way of options.

THE COP, GUERRERO, was still waiting for an answer.

"I don't remember," Tony said.

"That's going to be a problem," Guerrero said.

"How's that?"

"My partner thinks you had something to do with the disappearance of Marcus Stallworth."

Tony looked aghast. "Bullshit," he said softly.

"Probably," Guerrero said. "But you know how it is with cops.
You got to unconvince them."

"I told you everything I know."

"Are there any people who can tell me where you were on
those particular days? Who can account for your whereabouts?
You need to think."

"You serious?"

"Did you, or did you not, threaten Marcus Stallworth with a gun?"

"*What?*"

"Did you conspire to rob or abduct him?"

"No."

"Did you visit physical harm upon him?"

The suspect's cheeks swirled with blood; his eyes were skittish.

"Do you have any knowledge of the events leading to the disappearance and/or death of Marcus Stallworth? If you help me out, Antonio, I can help you."

"Help me with what, man?"

"There's evidence now. Fingerprints. Blood. Yours."

Tony's mouth fell open. In his previous dealings with cops, he'd been guilty of something. Deep down, he'd accepted that any story he might tell would unravel. Now he was being told about evidence that couldn't possibly exist, proving he committed a crime he knew nothing about.

"Can you account for your whereabouts on the evening of Friday, October 23, or the next morning?"

"Hold up," Tony said.

"This wasn't your idea, Antonio. That's what I figure. Peña, maybe some other guys, got you in and now they're sticking you with it."

"There was no idea."

"Think about the big picture. Your family. Your mother."

"No. No no no." The kid was trying to hide his heaving now. "I been living straight. I don't know nothing about that sick fucking bastard."

"I'm trying to offer you a way out here," Guerrero replied patiently. "Maybe it's like you said. Maybe Mr. Stallworth deserved what he got."

"I never said that." Tony fell silent. He tilted his head back slightly, so no tears would come loose. He could see what this cop was up to now, what he'd been up to all along. "You're framing me up, bro."

Guerrero was operating on instinct. He knew the suspect was in a fragile state, having to decide in a matter of seconds how to navigate his guilt and where to invest his trust. "I'm trying to help you," Guerrero said again. "Believe me."

The suspect was trembling now.

Guerrero wanted to get closer to the kid, to establish some trust. But the distance between them kept growing. "I didn't do shit," Antonio Saenz murmured. "You know I didn't do shit. So arrest me or get the fuck out of here."

Officer Pedro Guerrero felt the weight of what he was about to do. It hovered before him like a blade. He stared at Saenz and thought, for a moment, about the kid he had been at eighteen, disrespected, helpless, ready to murder the world and call it an act of self-defense. He wanted to hug the kid, to squeeze the wickedness out of him, to forgive him for what he'd already done.

"You're under arrest," Guerrero said sadly. "You have the right to remain silent." He pulled a pair of cuffs from his back pocket and grabbed the suspect and bound his slender wrists. If you'd been watching the two men through a window, they would have looked, in their brief moment of struggle, like scorpions engaged in a promenade à deux.

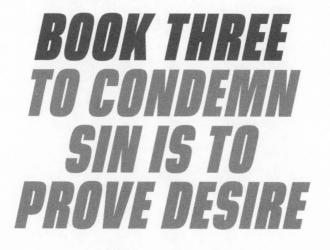

BOOK THREE
TO CONDEMN SIN IS TO PROVE DESIRE

BEING A DEAD MAN TO the world behind him and a fugitive in the one to come, Marcus Stallworth kept to the low scrub, traveling by night, into slaps of wind, retracing the path of missionaries and hermits.

On the third day, he rose at dusk and stared west across the Salton Basin, the silt flats stained rose by the sun's retreat. He could just make out the foothills of the San Jacintos, the loose rope of smog suspended over the interstate. Nearby, a pack of javelinas spit and cackled like fat on a grill. Joshua trees rose from ponds of shadow, their furred limbs pawing the sky.

He saw few signs of man here, the bleached rubble of aqueducts, fractured culverts, the architecture of a fever dream by which businessmen would soak parched soil into emerald farmland. The sun swung down, a red hammer upon the horizon. A Gambel's quail skittered in withered shrub and shrieked like a party streamer. Purple nimbostratus, lit orange at the edges, released gray threads of rain and creosote spores exploded, emitting a resinous perfume.

Stallworth packed his gear and chewed a breakfast of nuts and dried fruit and drank a quart of water while the sky stitched itself into an indigo quilt. He strapped on his headlamp and marched south. A shred of moon appeared, then the stars and planets. From time to time, he drew a black light from his pocket and swept the ground for scorpions. He couldn't help himself.

He knelt to greet them. Split tailed devils, slender and harmless; reddish-brown flat rocks. Theirs was a language of concealment and attack, the calm pulse of survival beneath abrupt motion. Just before dawn, Stallworth came upon a cove of cholla cacti. Scorpions—hundreds of them—had collected to lick the dew that gathered on the needles, just beneath their gaudy yellow blossoms. He lay down to sleep amid this assembly, his body like a giant ark, and woke dizzy and scorched by sun. A vulture wheeled above him. Its frail barking ripped the air, a song without color.

DISAPPEARING HADN'T BEEN easy. It took months to figure the staging and the route, to lay in supplies, to create a new legal identity and work the family accounts to arrange purchase of an RV, which awaited him in a used car lot outside Yuma. The real work lay in summoning his nerve. That had taken years.

To discern *why* Marcus Stallworth had settled upon this course requires an understanding of his childhood. He had been born out of wedlock, to a woman who was, at nineteen, already a devout drinker. The state of Indiana remanded him, at age five, to the custody of a foster parent who called herself an aunt, though she was unrelated to Stallworth by blood.

She raised him as a Christian Scientist, and the central tenets of her faith took root within him. Although he embraced the rigors of science in his schooling, he accepted that the material world was ultimately an illusion, and that his salvation would require a spiritual resurrection of the flesh. It was this belief that his aunt used, starting at the onset of his puberty, to justify certain rites of purification. He was, for instance, forced to present himself for inspection upon waking in the morning. If he had an erection, as he often did, his aunt would strike at it with a small crop while pressing herself against the bedframe in a silent and grimacing fury. The instrument left slender abrasions. Stallworth, who attended private school as a subsidy student, became accustomed to having his body acted upon as a form of penitence.

He escaped Elkhart by earning a scholarship to a small college outside Philadelphia, where, as an excruciatingly shy teaching assistant, he encountered Rosemary Upton, a sophomore enrolled in his section of Introduction to Zoology. The granddaughter of a major industrialist, she was elegant, loquacious, worldly, forthright in her pursuit, and aggressive in her affections. Whatever discretion he might have sought to impose upon their romance, her assurance overran.

Then came pregnancy, a marriage arranged in haste and carried out in a climate of anxious duty. Stallworth was presented as a respectable suitor: a budding man of science, handsome in a rented tux, eager to transcend the defects of his bloodline. They both knew what neither could acknowledge: that she had selected him as a means of defying her family.

Rosemary, woozy with nausea, threw her mother out of the vestibule for suggesting the ceremony be delayed. She wobbled to the altar, her eyes vindicated beneath the veil, as the men of her family, robber barons and quiet drunks in tails, glowered from the rosewood pews. A gaunt bishop murmured incantations, then oversaw their consecrating kiss, which tasted of lipstick and mouthwash.

His own illicit impulses had first expressed themselves with the teenage sister of a nanny. There were kisses, a moment of avid groping. Rosemary refused to cast him out, firing the nanny instead. "I won't be made a fool by my own family," she told him, later, in the darkness. The ambiguity of this statement settled over them like a dense fog.

There had been a second episode two years later, in Tucson, where they moved for his graduate work. This one involved a girl of fifteen, part of a private school study group he tutored. Marcus had panicked initially, and driven off with a hastily packed suitcase, before returning home chastened the next day.

Rosemary responded to the accusation by hiring a private investigator who specialized in "familial crisis management," and who gathered evidence that the young woman in question had engaged in several clandestine sexual encounters. Armed with this evidence, Rosemary confronted her parents, explaining that the girl had become "infatuated" with Marcus and "confused" as to the nature of their relationship. He alone recognized the ferocity of her defense as the most damning evidence of his guilt.

Her loyalty was revenge. She had trapped him within the habitat of his virtue. With the move to Sacramento came an implicit pledge: there would be *no more ugliness*. This was the phrase Rosemary had used; she nearly choked on it.

And so they put aside these episodes in favor of safer dramas: whether to ask her parents for money and how much, the accompanying fuss over each new home and suitable décor. Regret acted as their central theme. All marriages, he imagined, operated in this way. They were performances staged for the benefit of civilized society, in which two actors valiantly struggled to bear their secrets and hide their disappointments.

He had been able to exhaust himself when the kids were young. But as they grew older, they were no longer interested in riding on his shoulders or camping trips or the little experiments he set up on the floor of his office. He watched, helplessly, somewhat bitterly, as they withdrew into a world of music and movies and clothes, their round faces carved into angular masks, their bodies seized by the sullen riot of adolescence. They became vain, preoccupied with status. Because he had never known his own father, Stallworth could not see the ways in which his disappointment fueled their retreat.

He felt himself drifting into the perverse confusions that had prevailed early in the marriage, beginning to take note of bodies he had no right to regard. Then came the girl, Lorena. He had sensed, from the first night they met, that she possessed the precise qualities to which he was most susceptible: the curiosity of a scientific mind, a hunger for risk, the exquisite neediness of neglect. If he placed his trust in her, she would consent to anything. He could feel it.

And yet his own childhood presented him with another possibility: she had been dispatched as a temptation, a resurrection of the flesh by which he could prove, once and for all, that he had tamed his iniquity. This was why he had led her into the desert and shown her the scorpions and the stars. He wanted to believe he could be someone better. At night, images of her body swarmed him. He struck at himself. He gouged his eyeballs. He withdrew into the desert.

The problem was the girl, her persistence. She kept barging into his office, into *him*, a plump acolyte bent on damnation. He knew this was nonsense, a form of moral superstition that belonged in the Middle Ages. He was a scientist. She was just a lonely girl, tender and careless and blind. In darkness, she had trespassed upon his burrow.

This time, though, he was prepared. He called the private investigator in Tucson, who referred him to a trusted colleague in San Francisco, a Mr. Van Dyke. Stallworth explained that his work required him to travel into the desert alone and that he worried about his family, should something happen to him.

"Something like a disappearance?"

After a long silence, Stallworth replied, "I want to ensure my wife is given no cause for worry. She can be a fragile person. I need her to be strong for my children."

"Of course," Van Dyke clicked his tongue. "The world is a harrowing place. We cannot prevent the unforeseen, but a wise man plans for it." He briskly outlined terms and requisites: a floor plan of the house, keys, access to an escrow account for contingencies. "It is a sacred duty to serve as a guardian of secrets," Van Dyke observed, before hanging up. "For they are all that keep us from destroying ourselves."

In the end, Marcus banished himself before he could strike. That was what mattered. He found a way to protect his family, to spare them the mortification he was doomed to inflict. He drove south and dragged his pack along the sand, erasing each footstep. It was a kind of molting.

For all his calculated preparations, there came a moment when he could no longer deny what he was doing. He looked back at the abandoned Jeep and thought of the years when it seemed possible for him to live as the self others had made of him. He recalled the young father who worked at a university and returned home to a brittle but loving wife, to the squealing of two beautiful children. He had carried them on his back as they sang nonsense into his ears. A searing commenced at his temples; his vision blurred. He stood that way for a long time.

When at last he turned toward the desert, Marcus Stallworth knew the nature of his exile. It was because he was unfit to live another way.

HE'D STASHED HIS first cache of provisions in a cave at the base of the Bullion Mountains, fifty miles east of Barstow: five gallons of water, dehydrated meals, the starched khakis of a park ranger.

These were days of autumnal progress, beneath stratocumu-
lus whose gray undersides shaded jetties of volcanic rock. The
Marines used the Bullions for military exercises; its playas were
pocked with craters carved by artillery, which bloomed algae
after storms and bubbled like primordial cauldrons. From the
summits, he could see the hydraulic grooves worn by rain,
braids of shale that broadened into alluvial fans near the valley
floor. He zigzagged down these channels, onto vast aprons of
rock and dunes crowned by wigs of salt brush.

South of Eagle Mountain he turned west again toward the
Salton Sea, the faded beach resort now a reeking mirage. He set
up camp and climbed a hill of debris to survey his position. Sunlight flashed upon the water. From the north came a swarm of
migratory birds—cranes and cormorants, grebes and glossy
ibis—drawn by the dead fish floating on the surface. They
looped and keened, white notches against a lavender dawn. He
listened to the feathery *plish* as the birds impaled these car-
casses. The winds shifted and the stench burned his eyes.

Farther south, he saw signs of the sea's recession: a wasteland encrusted in salt. The pilings of a pier, the dainty udders of
a captain's wheel, bones leached of feather and scale. Appliances lay scattered about, half submerged and bleeding rust
into the saline sludge.

He came upon an entire dwelling whose rooms had been
pried apart by time, the intimacies of medicine cabinet and toilet bowl exposed. The kitchen table set for four, a carton of
milk, a box of cereal, a teaspoon resting delicately atop a plastic
honey bear. In the yard beyond, near a collapsing swing set,
stood a headless woman, her torso striated in salt. Stallworth
stood for a long time, gazing upon this macabre figure. It was a
sewing mannequin. But he saw something else: Lot's wife, frozen as she cast her gaze backward, toward home.

HE HAD COME to the Salton Sea on a scavenger hunt of sorts. For years, rumors had circulated among scorpiologists, of a species adapted to the extreme salinity of dried seabeds. He himself attended a conference in which a Lithuanian researcher claimed to have discovered a new variety of scorpion in the salt-rich fens that had once been the southern fringe of the Ural Sea.

The little Lithuanian was not a presenter at the conference, but an amateur collector with exaggerated credentials. His evidence did not consist of live specimens or lab data. Instead, he carried with him at all times a small antique box filled with cadavers. The Lithuanian haunted receptions and cocktail hours, an unkempt figure who thrust his "specimen case" at anyone who came near. On the last day of the conference, he cornered Stallworth in the lobby of the conference hotel.

"You are the ones interested in the behaviorials, is this right? Then I must tell you of my species!" The Lithuanian leaned in, as if to caress Stallworth's official laminated badge. His breath was bitter with old coffee. "I have observed for many months, Mar-cooze. They do not behaves as other scorpions do. The mature male travels with the juvenile female. He protects her. He hunts for her. Why? She is his mate! These female breeds just once, you see. And she kill him! I have seen with my own eye." The Lithuanian peered at him expectantly, pupils beaded with mania. "Do you understand?"

"I'm not sure that makes sense."

"Of course it do. Because of the salt content in the metabolisis, Mar-cooze. They have not fully adapted! The mature female makes crystals in the reproductive tract. She cannot breed again. Just one time. Tiny crystals. Like diamonds. I have seen them! Under the microscopes!"

Stallworth glanced around, and the Lithuanian glanced with him; they were now aligned against a vast confederation of skeptics. "You must see the specimens!" The little man took hold of his lanyard, like a leash.

There were half a dozen specimens, three of each gender, pinned like delicate broaches to black velvet. They were barely an inch in length, with slender pincers and thick tails. Their bodies were a chalky white, speckled with symmetrical markings like those on tribal masks. The Lithuanian pressed a magnifying glass into his hands. "Look closer." What he saw astonished him: the animal's exoskeletons were virtually translucent and beneath them, as the Lithuanian had promised, hundreds of white crystals.

"You see?" the Lithuanian cried.

"Why can't you produce a live specimen?"

"That is just it, Mar-cooze! He dies in captivity each time! It is months to find each one. That is how rare. Sometime more. But the minute you remove from the home of soil she stings. Every single time. They are like—" The Lithuanian tapped at his temple, searching for the right word. "*Outlaws.* Wanted dead and alive. Do you believe me now? You must believe."

YEARS LATER, HE came across an article in the *Journal of American Sociobiology*, citing the Cahuilla Indians, who had once inhabited the banks of the Salton. One of the central icons in their folklore was a scorpion known as the Pale God of Death. Its venom, ingested during purification rituals, was said to ignite the heart. Those who survived were cleansed of evil spirits.

Stallworth doubted there was any such species. But he went to investigate the reeking marshes anyway. He had allotted himself three weeks in the wild, figuring his disappearance would be long gone from the news by then. For two nights, he raked the salt beds and midden heaps. All he found were stick-like Diplocentridae, garish Superstitioniidae, a sluggish *Hadrurus obscurus*; they writhed in the grip of his forceps. At dawn, he returned to his camp, resigned to sleep away the heat of the day.

But he kept hearing a faint scrabbling. He aimed his light into the corner seams of the tent, where beads of condensation gathered. The creature illuminated by his beam was clearly of the family Buthidae, the genus *Centruroides*. Its morphology was similar to *sculpturatus*—the same slender pincers and thick tail. But the abdominal segmentation suggested an elongated digestive track, perhaps evolved to absorb brackish water. The exoskeleton was cream-colored and exquisitely thin, like vellum paper. Stallworth dug out his magnifying glasses. Enzymatic prisms—crystals—were clearly visible beneath the exoskeleton. His hands began to flutter.

In winter, scorpions sometimes congregated by the dozens. But this one, a male, was traveling solo. Its cephalothorax was marked by a rust-colored splotch in the shape of a hand mirror. He made a quick sketch of the specimen and bestowed it with a name—*Centruroides narcissus*—then set it down outside the tent, hoping it would lead him to its burrow. The creature refused to move. Then, without warning, it raised its tail and struck at its own eyes. It was dead within seconds.

ON THE NIGHT he was to depart the Salton Sea, Stallworth heard whoops in the distance, and spotted the flare of a bonfire. He shouldered his pack, intending to melt back into the desert, but turned toward the beach instead. Music pulsed from a boom box. He dimly recognized the tinny wail of the singer. A peculiar rabble encircled the flames: witches, ghosts, a vampire with bloody fangs. It took a moment for the situation to register: Halloween.

Teenagers, drunk on pint bottles of flavored wine. The girls danced in tattered costumes designed to reveal their bodies while the boys dashed about in dizzy orbits, summoning the courage to tackle them. He thought of his own children, the pool parties they had begun to host, their coy postures and mocking banter. They believed, with a faith no warning could undo, that beauty would keep them safe from the perils of desire.

A clown in a fright wig pulled a plank from the fire and held it aloft. He let out a whoop and set the rotting remains of a sloop on fire. A curtain of flames rippled across the oiled surface of the water. Stallworth was so transfixed that he failed to notice one of the girls turn away from the group and jog up the beach, toward the structure behind which he crouched—a dilapidated lifeguard's stand. He scuttled back into the shadows, stumbling in his haste.

The girl ducked behind the stand and squatted. He listened to the hiss of her urination. She stood. Suddenly, she turned toward the place where he lay pressed to the ground. "That you, Royal?" Her flashlight swept the darkness in a wobbly arc. "Royal? I ain't playing with you." The beam passed over his pack then doubled back. "Okay. Be like that." She began to advance on him. He could hear the slap of her sandals. He needed to snatch his pack and steal away. But she was too close now.

"Royal?"

He rose up, expecting the girl to scream and flee at the sight of him. But she merely stared, sad and unsurprised. There was something in her, a feral courage he associated with the poverty of his boyhood. The hair on his arms tingled.

"Who the fuck are you?" Grease paint whiskers traced her cheeks. She looked to be a hard nineteen beneath the makeup, with scabs on her elbows and a round belly. He couldn't quite discern her race. *Half-breed. Mulatto.* Those were the words that popped into his head. A hundred yards off, the fire raged; her comrades whooped. The moon had slipped behind clouds. "Who the fuck are you?" she said again.

"A ranger," he said. His voice was husky with disuse. "With the Park Service."

"What kind of ranger hanging round here at this hour?"

Stallworth kept his head bowed. "I'm conducting surveys."

"Surveys?" She aimed her light at his pack. "That your equipment? You come from Salton City? You part of that government project? You gonna restore the lake?"

He nodded.

"You lie. There ain't nothing to restore. It's dying. You can't undo what God done. You one hairy-ass ranger. The Lone Ranger."

He could smell the wine on her breath, the cloying spray she used to tame her hair, which sat atop her head like whorled yarn. "How come I ain't seen you before?" She blinked slowly. "You got a badge?" She aimed the light at his face.

"Please don't do that," he said.

"Why you hiding your face away?"

"I'm warning you."

"Warning me what?"

He took a step backwards and was shocked when she followed. Whatever she had experienced in life had relieved her of caution. "What kind of ranger come round here? Ain't nothing to ranger *for*." She regarded him glassily. "I think you out here for some other reason. Spying on little girls. Sneaking up on us like some kind of Chester. I met guys like you. They come through Bombay Beach. It ain't so special."

He began to wonder how long it would take before the others took notice of her absence. She was close enough that he might snatch her light.

"I could scream," the girl said. "My boyfriend'll cut your ass. All I got to do is scream." She took another step toward him and his hands shot out and took hold of her throat. It happened so quickly they were both choked of sound. She tried to twist away but his hands clamped down. Behind them, the fire threw up a blanket of sparks and the music rolled across the reeking barrens. He recognized the song, a clatter of gongs and synthesizers, the distant fragile wailing of a girl with a heart of glass. It had emanated once from his daughter's room.

He released the girl with a furious shove and lunged for his pack.

The girl coughed and sank to her knees and vomited quietly. She seemed not to understand entirely what had happened.

Stallworth dug into the lining sewed inside his shorts and withdrew a $100 bill. "There's been a misunderstanding," he said.

He set the bill down on the ground in front of her, as if it were a saucer of milk for a kitten.

The girl stared at the money dazedly. "Royal got a gun," she rasped. She touched her belly absently. Royal, he realized, was the father of her child.

"You ain't no kind of man anyway. Running away from what you are." She wretched again. "I know what you are and so do God. He got eyes everywhere. You gonna get found. Everyone get found."

All around them, like a hidden constellation, scorpions had absorbed this commotion through the fine hairs on their fore-limbs, and frozen. The girl was still on her knees. She looked squarely at Marcus Stallworth. Her mascara left streaks that bled across her whiskers. "You a dead man now." She said this softly, without contempt, as she knelt in the darkness.

BEFORE MAPPING HIS route, Stallworth had read about William David Bradshaw, the first white man to traverse the Mojave. In 1862, with civil war raging in the east, Bradshaw set out to es-tablish a route from California to the gold fields of La Paz, in the central Arizona Territory. He managed to befriend the Ca-huilla chief Cabezon, who shared the location of springs and watering holes. All along the Bradshaw Trail, ancient tribes had carved geoglyphs into the desert floor; tribute to the gods of cloud and rain.

Stallworth's course was the inverse. To minimize the risk of detection, he had to skirt any source of water. This was why he had been so careful to lay in supplies. Five gallons of water awaited him, in an arroyo two miles east of Bombay Beach. But now he had made an error, had come out of hiding and assaulted a local girl. So he turned south toward his next cache, buried fifty miles away, beneath the Algodones Dunes. The journey took three nights, his tongue swollen by the end, such that he had to gulp for air. Wind had glued his contact lenses to his eyeballs. He had to steady himself against a cottonwood to read the figures on his compass.

When at last he located the supplies, he poured two quarts of water down his throat. He stripped off his clothes, intending to burn the rancid garments, then lay down, too bloated to move. A new sun nicked the horizon. He thought of his son, as a new-born, the drowsy euphoria that followed his dawn feedings. Glen would spit up, almost joyfully, then his mouth would curl into a pink smile. The memory pierced him and he clung to it and stabbed it deeper, repeating his son's name until the sound of it was gibberish. He needed those memories gone, pummeled out of him by privation.

THE EARTH WAS shuddering when he awoke. High above, a squadron of jets chalked the sky. He grabbed his binoculars and tracked them as they dipped down and leveled out. Their bomb bays disgorged dark tassels of ordinance. Stallworth knew there was an abandoned gunnery range on the southern fringe of the Chocolate Mountains. He had been careful to bypass the area. But events far beyond his ken had conspired against him.

With the election of Ronald Reagan, policy toward the Soviet Union shifted. The president's advisors recommended a massive military buildup. Imperial pride compelled the Soviets to keep pace and eventually bankrupted the Kremlin, triggering the collapse of Communism. Marcus Stallworth was witnessing the first consequences of this policy: the revival of bombing runs on long-dormant ranges.

He felt no immediate sense of alarm, for he had stashed a final cache in the Little Picacho Wilderness, a habitat under the protection of the federal government. He turned away from the valley floor, and toward the high desert, scrambling up steep ravines onto slender outcroppings of brittlebush. The air cooled and the sandy soil gave way to burnt orange cobbles. At the summit of each ridge, ramps of polished stone rose into spires. A westerly wind buffeted the mountains and turned the air sodden. The mist thickened. Stallworth opened his mouth and waited for the clouds to release rain. They merely loitered. The sky had begun to play tricks on him.

The terrain was too jagged to traverse by night and so he lay fidgety in his nylon tent, listening to the thin shriek of jets and the deep distant tremolo of their payload striking. When the noise faded, Stallworth stepped outside to breathe in the night. Stars pierced darkness, so vast and luminous that the vault of the universe appeared to swoop down into the earth. The exertions of his ascent, the lack of food and water and sleep, had left him light-headed, so that he honestly believed for a time that he was floating in space. Another plane streaked overhead, this one close enough that he could hear the munitions whistling in the darkness. Then, a most curious sensation: he was cartwheeling through the air. It was as if the wish of every child—to be released from the grip of gravity—had been absurdly and violently granted.

STALLWORTH'S BODY TRAVELED several yards before landing. He had no idea what had happened. Nor did he ever ascertain the source of this cataclysm, which had been conceived and executed by personnel at the China Lake Naval Base, one hundred miles to the north. The Logistics Unit at the base had worked for months to map out targets. Among the young "data engineers" assigned to the project was a scowling private who spent the weeks before his expulsion from the navy tapping coordinates into a computer terminal. His name was Antonio Saenz.

STALLWORTH WOKE IN agony, pinned against a berm of sand by some celestial hemorrhage, his eyes singed, his ears ringing. It took him several minutes to locate the rational explanation: a bomb had detonated near him. He touched at his cracked ribs, then conducted a ginger inventory of his other injuries—burns, abrasions—and waited for his senses to return. The earth around him lay convulsed. His pack and tent were gone, all his careful provisions.

Perhaps the time had come for him to perish. He lay for a time savoring the prospect. Then, with a wince, he rose. Humans loved to pretend they were the engineers of their own fate. An entire catalogue of myth had been manufactured to prop up this fragile deception. But people were no different than any other creature. When slammed against mortality, survival overruled every other impulse.

He staggered for hours in this spectral state, through box canyons and crags of loose shale. Bombs had blasted out sockets of rock, leaving craters etched in black powder. Every time he breathed, his ribs gored him.

South of Picacho Peak, Stallworth reached the maze of caverns where he had buried his final cache—likewise demolished by the munitions. At the mouth of each cave lay creatures who had sought shelter from the holocaust. He came upon a pair of burros, then a herd of desert bighorn, the ewes plump with their unborn. The sand beneath was crimson. Spotted bats sucked indelicately at the congealed blood. A wild pony had been crushed and its wheezing snout peeked from amid the fractured stone, one panicked eyeball recalling *Guernica*.

Stallworth sat for a long time. He thought—and tried not to think—about his daughter's infatuation with ponies. Her mother had nurtured this interest; she shared her daughter's passion for the accoutrements of dressage. There was a period when she had strutted the sidelines of Glen's soccer games in jodhpurs. In the end, Jenny's fixation lasted until the precise moment the equestrian coach ordered her to muck a stable. Still, for years, any time she received a gift of any size, someone, usually her older brother, would mutter, "Is it a pony?"

Daylight was rolling into shadow. Stallworth lay down for a moment. When he opened his eyes again it was dawn. In fact, he could open only one eye. The other had sustained what he assumed to be an abraded cornea. Burns along his forearms had begun to blister. He had to get off the mountain, away from the rampaging jets. He figured the distance to Yuma at thirty miles, the nearest road half that span. Then a small motel—or better, a truck stop—where he could clean his wounds. But he needed sustenance to get there. There were no cacti here, only clumps of creosote. His compass was gone, but he still had a knife. He heard the faint snorts of the dying beast nearby. As he drew out the blade and whetted it against a rock, the phrase crept back into his mind. *Is it a pony?*

HIS ORIGINAL PLAN had been to head due south, to Yuma, where he could take refuge in the RV he had purchased and consider his options. But his condition would invite too many questions. His wounded eye had shut altogether. The flesh around his ribs had swollen. His burns had begun to putrefy.

So he turned west, toward the barren flank of Fort Yuma Indian Reservation. If he continued south, he would eventually cross the border into Sonora, where an American with cash could find a quiet place to recuperate. He hobbled on, through heat that bent the air into waves. Night hoisted a dizzy scrum of stars. The blue lights of a city rose before him, then reeled away. Scorpions floated across the sand.

He kept falling and it hurt every time. An empty highway stretched from nothing into nothing. At some point, he heard cattle lowing in the dusk. Cattle meant water, vegetation. Night fell but he tumbled on. He felt something sting the meat of his calf, then a dozen more stings across his lower body. Had he stepped into a nest of fire ants? Bark scorpions? Vines coiled around his limbs and waist, like something out of a fairy tale.

IT WAS BARBED wire. Stallworth had walked into a fence that ran along the northern edge of a small ranch; then he had collapsed from exhaustion. A young caballero found him the next morning and liberated him with a pair of pliers. The cowboy spoke some words in Spanish, then slung Stallworth over the back of his horse. When he woke again, someone was spooning a sweet gruel into his mouth.

"What is it?" he croaked.

"Pinole," a soft voice said. "Corn gruel. Eat."

"Thank you." He felt the cool lip of a clay jug pressed to his mouth and guzzled. His ribs ached. He sucked at the pinole until he felt his bowels loosen. "I'm sorry," he sobbed.

"Don't feel bad." The voice addressing him was young, female, oddly formal. "You're hurt pretty serious, sir."

The view offered by his working eye was of a small room with low wooden beams. The furniture was sparse: chair, bedside table. The girl tending to him was a few years older than his daughter. A bone-white bonnet, knotted beneath her chin, framed her plain brown face. She set down an empty bowl and took up a bucket and a sponge.

"Where am I?"

"Father Ammon says to clean you up. Expect it to sting a fair bit."

"Father who?"

"Can you lift yourself, sir?"

The girl nudged him up on his side and cleaned the mess beneath. She dabbed alcohol on his wounds and tweezed bits of fabric from them.

Stallworth focused on the room's sole decorative element, a painting that showed a young man kneeling in a clearing. He wore a shabby waistcoat and clutched a golden box to his chest. A robed angel hovered over him. Owing to some quirk of the artist's brush, the angel bore an expression that was more ominous than beatific.

The girl continued her ministrations, without pity or comment. When she came upon the dark swell of his ribs, her face twisted. "Don't fret none," she said quietly. "To the Lord, you're just another broken vessel."

STALLWORTH WAS GIVEN a bell, told to ring when in need. The girl and three older women tended to him, sponging and dressing his wounds. From time to time, unsure as to his whereabouts, he attempted to rise from the bed. Pain stabbed him back down.

At some point, an older gentleman appeared in the chair next to the bed. He looked vaguely like Abraham Lincoln, with a chinstrap beard and deeply creased cheeks the color of butcher paper. His trousers had been handstitched at the seams. He wasn't Mexican, but Stallworth couldn't say precisely what he was.

"Evening," the man said, in genteel English. "Hoped you might be well enough to talk a bit now."

Stallworth nodded.

"Not so much pain anymore? That's good, friend. Good. You're carrying a couple cracked ribs at least. Second-degree burns, if I'm judging right. But one thing at a time. We can start with introductions. My name is Ammon Taylor." Taylor smiled shyly and held out a long thin hand.

Stallworth reached carefully to take it.

"Your name, sir?"

"Dennis. David."

"David Dennis?"

"Right."

"You know why I'm asking, Mr. Dennis?" The man paused. "Because you didn't have much in the way of possessions when my tenant found you. What he tells me. I know Josiah to be a man of faith."

"Where am I? In custody?"

Taylor expelled a whinnying laugh. "Custody? Heavens no. Why would you be in custody, Mr. Dennis?"

"I don't know," Stallworth said. "I'm a little confused."

"As am I, Mr. Dennis. We don't get many unannounced visitors around here. Especially an American in your condition."

Taylor picked a bit of straw off his pant leg. "That tells me you might be mixed up in some sort trouble. Is that the case?"

"No," Stallworth said. "I was robbed."

Taylor looked at him steadily. "You had nearly $5,000 in cash on your person, Mr. Dennis. I highly doubt you were robbed."

"My car," Stallworth said. "That's what they wanted."

"I see. And these injuries?"

"I resisted."

Taylor studied his face again. "You've sustained serious burns, Mr. Dennis. Did these robbers burn you? I must ask you to be forthright. There is a good deal of illegal activity in this area, given our proximity to the border. The smuggling of drugs and other contraband. None of this is my concern. But you are on my property now, and thus, in the eyes of the law, I am *harboring* you. That is the term of art, I believe. If you have done something wrong, or someone is looking for you, I must ask that you not involve me or my family."

"No one is looking for me," Stallworth said. "I was hiking and got robbed."

"And burned."

"I live in Tempe. I was on my way to Joshua Tree. The national park. They steered me off the road. Three of them. Mexicans."

"Mexicans."

"They took everything I had. My wallet, all my gear, the car."

"But not your cash?"

"I had that sewed into the lining of my—" Stallworth realized, with a start, that he was wearing a long cotton nightgown. Someone had removed his shorts. Of course. How else would Taylor have found the cash? This meant he probably also had in his possession the passport Stallworth had purchased more than a year earlier, from a company that advertised in the back of *Soldier of Fortune* magazine. The name on that passport was . . . Tennyson. Not Dennis. His name was David *Tennyson*.

"My name is David Tennyson," he said slowly.

"I see."

"I live in Tempe, Arizona. I was on my way to Joshua Tree National Park to hike. I was robbed."

"You mentioned that," Taylor said. "May I ask your social security number, Mr. Tennyson?"

"My what?"

Taylor drew out an antique silver pocket watch and began to wind the stem. "How about your home address?" After a pause, Taylor continued. "I understand. You've absorbed numerous injuries. It is not my intention to put any further strain on you. You can explain it all to the police."

Stallworth closed his eyes. "Have you called them?"

For half a minute, the only sound was the click of the watch stem. "I am not in the habit of contacting government agencies," the old man said. "I do have a phone you may use for this purpose. Surely you have family you wish to contact, as well. And if the ribs don't heal up, we'll have to get you to a hospital on the other side."

"The other side?"

"You're in Mexico, friend."

Stallworth sat up a little. His mind felt gummed, groggy. "You gave me something, didn't you?"

"For the pain. Certainly."

"Where am I, Mr. Taylor? Where exactly?"

"As I told you, you're on my property."

"How far am I from the border?"

"Right that way yonder, a few miles. You can see for yourself once you're well enough." Taylor nodded at the room's only window, which was the size and shape of an old-fashioned cathedral radio, with tiny wooden shutters.

Stallworth nodded. He needed time to think. And a clear mind. "You've been extremely kind, Mr. Taylor. I should have said that right from the start."

"The Lord brings us them that are in need." Taylor rose from his chair and held his hand just above Stallworth's head, as if uncertain whether to bless him.

"Your daughter, too. I haven't had a chance to thank her."

Taylor smiled stiffly. "Why don't you get some more rest now, Mr. Tennyson? Then, when you feel well enough, you can tell me who you really are."

STALLWORTH KNEW ENOUGH about religious sects to recognize the markings of one—the antiquated clothing, the austere furnishings. But he couldn't figure why an aging American was living on a ranch in Mexico. Was he missionary? A Mennonite? Didn't the Mennonites speak Dutch? Or was it German?

One of the older women brought him supper. They all wore the same long dresses, as shapeless as habits. She made little puffs as she peeled away the stained gauze of his dressing.

"Thank you," he said. "I'm sorry to trouble you like this."

She shook her head.

"I'm David Tennyson. Perhaps you knew that. Are you allowed to talk to me?"

"It's no trouble," she muttered, without much conviction. The woman put a tray down with a watery bowl of stew.

Stallworth took a few mouthfuls, then set the spoon down. "It's delicious, but I don't feel well this evening."

The woman nodded doubtfully and took the tray away.

Stallworth closed his eyes and waited until the middle of the night. His ribs were aching again, but his head had cleared. He rose from the bed and hobbled to the door. It was bolted from the outside. The drawer in the end table contained an old Bible. Nothing metal, nothing sharp.

He limped to the window and quietly unlatched the shutters. No lights anywhere, just a dull bulb of moon overhead. The breeze smelled of manure and hay. He could hear the distant nickering of horses, the pitter of wind through leafless branches. As his eyes adjusted, a small courtyard came into view, beyond which lay an expanse of pasture. The window was too small for him to climb through.

When Taylor returned the next day, he had combed his hair and shaved his cheeks. "We keep the Sabbath," he explained, in his courtly fashion. He sat down in the chair next to the bed and placed a small drawstring pouch on the floor. Then he took a minute to appraise Stallworth's condition. "I understand your appetite has been inconsistent. You must eat to recover. Perhaps you're concerned about pain medicine?"

"Why am I being locked in this room?" Stallworth said.

Taylor smiled, again, in that way that was not quite a smile. "Have you thought about our conversation? I'm reluctant to call you Mr. Tennyson, as I'm not certain that's your real name. We also know that you're involved in some extra-legal activity. The particulars are not my concern. The laws of man bare our imperfections. But the deeds of man—which might bring harm to my family—those *are* my concern."

"I don't understand what you want from me."

"A true accounting of how you came to be on my property to start with."

"I told you yesterday."

Taylor sat up in his chair and laid his palms upon his thighs. The expression etched upon his face was that of a biblical judge, firm in its rectitude and pained by it. "When word of your arrival reached me, I had a choice. I could have left you to die or delivered you, as it were, into the hands of the Romans. I brought you into my home instead. Do you know why? Because I believe God has sent you here. But I can't discern the wherefores unless you tell me the truth."

"You wouldn't believe me if I did."

"Only one way to know for sure, friend."

"I'm not your friend," Stallworth whispered.

Taylor smiled, authentically now, his teeth tarnished and worn. "You're a believer. No believer can live as a fugitive from the Lord."

Stallworth felt his eyes start to blur. He had grown up among such men, absorbing their pieties and pompous cadences. They loved God because he granted them the power to act without moral hindrance. That is what Stallworth sensed in Ammon Taylor: a sovereign whose dominion cloaked itself in humility.

His aunt had remitted him to the care of such men, when the burdens of custody depleted her. They beat him for perceived impertinence, in a barren courtyard not unlike the one outside his room.

"What are you running from?" Taylor said, more gently.

"Nothing."

He felt a hand laid gingerly upon his ribs, just above the cracked bones.

"Please don't touch me," he said quietly.

"It's time now, son. Release your burden."

Stallworth wanted to recoil from this stranger's touch, his unctuous plea. But all he could do was twist his mouth. It was true what Taylor said. He believed in God. Not the God Rosemary worshipped, who dressed the family for church, who insisted on everything clean and pretty. But the God of his youth, who flogged the sinful, then cast his love upon them. Taylor's voice was a benign hum. *Let me alone,* Stallworth said. That was what he meant to say. His tongue couldn't shape the words. What greater threat did the fallen face than mercy?

HE DIDN'T TELL Taylor everything, only that he had left his family back in Arizona and he hoped to start over again.

"What does 'family' mean?"

"A wife. Two boys. Young men, one in high school, one in college."

"They figure you're dead. That's how you made it look."

"A son would rather lose a father than be abandoned by one," Stallworth said curtly. "That's my own experience."

"When did you leave?"

"Mid-October."

"What have you been doing since?"

"Hiking."

Taylor whistled. *"Into the wilderness, where for forty days the devil tempted him."* He produced a pipe from his vest pocket and slid it into the corner of his mouth.

"My wife would have used the kids as pawns in a divorce."

"What about all this?" Taylor nodded at the bandages that decorated his arms. "You threw yourself off a cliff?"

"That's the part I don't expect you'll believe."

But Taylor didn't look surprised by any of it. He clicked at his pipe for a minute, then caught himself and tucked it away. "No wonder you were reluctant to speak. I won't ask for your name. Better for both of us. Rest easy, friend. I've no intention of turning you in. You're precisely where you were meant to be. We'll talk more when you're feeling stronger." He rose from his chair, then paused and tapped at his temple. "Almost forgot. We found a couple of other personal items in the lining of your clothing." He handed the drawstring bag to Stallworth.

The first item was his contact lens case. The second was the plastic canister containing the pale corpse of the scorpion he had found inside his tent. The third was the Polaroid of Lorenza Saenz sitting naked on the steps of his own swimming pool, her brown breasts half submerged in glowing blue. Stallworth looked up to find Taylor staring down at him from the doorway, impassively.

"I don't know who she is," Stallworth blurted.

"That makes her a stranger to us both, I suppose." Taylor gave a small bow and shut the door. Then came the sound of the bolt being thrown.

HE'D FOUND THE photo in his daughter's room, tucked away on her astrology shelf. Jenny had snapped the pic with some vague plan to use it as leverage, should Lorena try to narc about the secret parties at her apartment. The arrival of adolescence had done this to the children, made them calculating. Rosemary didn't want to know about it. She clung to a vision of their family that was, if not chaste, at least well-mannered.

Stallworth tried to ignore their defiance. But when the house was empty, he wandered into their rooms, searched their closets and drawers. He told himself he was checking for drugs. He reached into the dark recesses of the cupboard under their bathroom sink and found the pornographic magazines and his pulse went rabbity with dread. No one said anything. Still, it was there when they gathered around the table for meals, or edged past one another in the hallways. His children had been infected.

And now there was this photo of Lorena. She had taken off her clothes in his own backyard—a flagrant display. What he noticed in the image, what he fed upon, wasn't the naked body but the acute shame that registered in her posture, the way her skin bunched at the hips as she leaned over to conceal her breasts in the iridescence of the pool. He should have thrown the photo away. He should have burned it. Instead, he slipped it into his passport.

He crumpled the photo in his fist, then flattened it out again and returned it to the bag, with the dead specimen. Then he opened the drawer beside the bed. To fit the bag inside, he had

to remove the Bible, which wasn't a Bible at all. The gold lettering on the cover read *An Historical Account of the New Prophets
of the Church of Jesus Christ and the Latter Day Saints in the
State of Mexico, 1874–1961.*

The volume's spine issued a soft crack; its pages threw up
spores of must. The smell brought Stallworth back to the damp
church basements of his boyhood, the verses he was to recite
while Elder Rennert stood over his shoulder. He remembered the
menacing clang of steel rulers struck against wheezing radiators.

The prose of this strange history aped the King James Bible:
*thee*s and *thine*s, elaborate genealogical compendia, soaring
odes to the hardships endured as Mormons settled the Western
Territories. In 1875, Brigham Young called for a mission to Mexico and several hundred Mormons migrated to Chihuahua and
Sonora. These numbers swelled in 1882, when Congress passed
a ban on plural marriage.

The narrative was a garish conflation of the Old Testament,
the American colonial saga, and frontier mythology. All the elements were there: a chosen people targeted by imperial perse-
cutions, an exile through the desert, a promised land where
savage armies lurked.

He read until dark and woke to find Taylor staring at him.
The room was frigid with desert dawn. Taylor was dressed in
overalls and work boots. He nodded at the book, which lay open
on the bed. "Wondered when you might open that. It represents
many years of labor on the part of my father."

"He wrote this? Was he a historian?"

"Of sorts. He served as bishop for the Mexicali Ward. That
was before the Quorum of Seventy turned against him. He
wanted to make sure the real story got told. There's almost
nothing written about the transmigration."

"The transmigration?"

Taylor squinted. He had the smell of coffee and bacon on
him. "My grandfather Hiram Taylor settled this ranch in 1873.

Defended it, too. There's arrows in this lumber older than me. Lost an eye and part of his right hand to the Cucapá." Taylor nodded at the book. "My father wrote down everything he could remember, just as it happened. But the Quorum changed what they saw fit and flowered up the language. They sent us that. It's a fairy-tale book."

"Did your father object?"

"It was his doing. A man from the Quorum flew down here in a private plane. Said he wanted make sure every missionary got a copy of my father's account. They shook on it. That's how the earthly realm operates, friend. If you got the power, you get to make the story." A fly had begun to circle the room lazily and Taylor reached out and snatched it from the air. He shook his fist until the buzzing ceased.

"Most of us don't enjoy that privilege. We have to live with the story we're handed. That's why people run off to Mexico. They want a new story. You're like that, aren't you? For days, I've been asking myself: Why would the Lord send such a man to me? What is his purpose? Then I saw that photo of the young girl—"

"It doesn't belong to me."

Taylor closed his eyes and inhaled through his nose. "I've been patient, friend. But I cannot help those who traffic in deceit. The photo is yours. What a man keeps is what a man harbors. Don't insult my intelligence further. You are preventing us from understanding one another." Taylor opened his fist and cast away the fly. "I am of an age where such storms have settled. But they are perfectly natural and necessary within the proper marital arrangement. It is the disfigurement of such arrangements that confounds us. My grandfather settled this land because he had been denied the right to make a family as he saw fit. Do you understand?"

Stallworth nodded.

"No. You don't. I can see it. You think plural marriage is an aberration. As if man were born to lie with one woman for life.

As if Abraham had never taken Hagar into his tent. As if Solomon had never ruled Zion. But why shouldn't man live like a king? By his labors fortunes are built, by his urges orchards replenished. The government cannot regulate such things. To condemn sin is to prove desire, friend. No honest man would turn away from a girl in the heat of her blossom."

Taylor rose from his chair and went to the window and threw open the cathedral doors; Stallworth's cell was drenched in a brightness that made his wounded eye throb. He blinked violently. Outside, sheep bleated, a tractor squalled. Taylor stepped into the path of the sun. "You will remain here as my guest. When you feel well enough, I can show you around."

"I appreciate your kindness," Stallworth said. "But I need to continue my journey. Obviously, I would want to pay you for your kindness."

Taylor showed his ruined teeth. "You still don't understand, do you? You are here by God's will. He knows your heart. He answered your prayers."

THE YOUNG ONE arrived the next morning, bearing his breakfast. His stomach grumbled at the fragrance of smoked meat. "Father Ammon says to try a bit of solid food today." She set the tray on his lap—a bowl of pinole studded with chunks of glistening bacon. He played the fatty meat between his teeth; his jaw ached with the pleasure.

The girl shyly grinned.

He had been studying her, too. She referred to Taylor as "Father Ammon" but her nose was too wide, her face too round, to be his daughter.

"May I ask your name?"

"Alma."

"Thank you for your kindness, Alma. I should have said that before."

"You've thanked me many times, sir."

"Have I?"

She nodded.

"You're his wife, aren't you?"

"Of course."

"There are four of you in all?"

"Five. Eliza passed a year ago."

"Do you mind if I ask how long you've been married?"

"We wed three summers ago. I was fifteen years of age. If that was your next question." The girl smiled down at him. Her teeth were snaggled but healthy.

Her grandparents had immigrated from Utah at the turn of the century. They traveled in the same party as Hiram Taylor but had established a ranch farther west, outside Morelos. She was honored when her father informed her that Ammon Taylor had asked for her hand in marriage. "Everyone knows Father Ammon," she explained. "He's the last of the Taylors. Without them, there would be no mission in Mexico."

"You're a Mexican citizen?"

She laughed softly. "The kingdoms of the earth are not the kingdoms of heaven." She swept the room as she spoke, a little carelessly.

"Why are you talking to me?" Stallworth said.

"Why wouldn't I talk to you?"

"The others don't."

"They wish to protect Father Ammon." Alma set the broom aside. "He says we're not to ask your name."

"You want to know my name?"

"It would be nice to have something to call you."

"Call me Mr. Tennyson."

"Is that your real name?"

"You don't trust me?"

"Your passport is a fake."

"How do you know that?"

The girl held a finger to her lips and smiled into it. "I have to go. I'm glad you enjoyed your breakfast, Mr. Tennyson. Father Ammon will be gladdened, too."

"Wait. Why do you call him Father? Is he a priest?"

Alma paused in the doorway. She regarded him curiously, as if the question had never before occurred to her. "*Father* is a term of honor."

A DOCTOR CAME to examine him. He carried a scuffed kit and muttered so quickly that the patient, despite efforts to polish his high school Spanish, didn't understand a word. The doctor walked his fingertips along the ribs in question and aimed a tiny flashlight into Stallworth's injured eye. Both were mending. Taylor took notes on a small pad, then walked the doctor out. He returned a few minutes later with a pair of Ace bandages and a steel-tipped cane. "It's about time you got on your feet."

Stallworth looked at him incredulously.

"You don't intend to be an invalid for the rest of your life, do you, friend?" Taylor approached the bed and hoisted Stallworth into a sitting position and wrapped the bandages around his torso. Stallworth smelled the pipe smoke and liniment on the old man's garments. Taylor knelt down and took hold of Stallworth's feet and gently slipped them into huaraches. "The fallen must learn to rise again," he whispered.

Stallworth grasped the cane and found that he could walk slowly, with little pain, if he kept his upper body rigid. He teetered through the door and into the courtyard and let the sun warm his cheeks. He sucked at the cool air. Wisps of cirrus drifted across the blue above. In some faint but persistent manner, he began to consider whether he might yet emerge from all this a better person.

Taylor smiled. "You feel that, do you?"

THE NEXT TIME he came, the old man brought him a shirt and dungarees and commenced a brief tour. The stalls around the courtyard had been the stables once, and his own cabin the tack room. They proceeded up a dirt path with Taylor at his elbow. It was like being escorted stiffly into the past. There was an old barn, canted to one side, and an antique red tractor. There was a hog pen with a mud-caked sow, a chicken coop, a grain silo, a smokehouse. A pair of sullen mules lounged in the shade of an empty stable. Beyond the barn a few bony cows nibbled at stubbled pasture.

They rounded a bend and Stallworth gasped. Before him was a cement wall, twenty feet high and crowned with shards of twinkling glass. It appeared to be a work of incremental effort, with distinct strata.

"What is the expression? Tall fences make good neighbors?" Taylor laughed.

The main house of the compound was on a small mesa. It turned out to be something closer to a sprawling cabin, the wood covered with overlapping plates of metal siding, like an armadillo. A couple of women, wives presumably, peered at them through slender window slots. Smoke trickled from a tin chimney nailed into the roof.

Taylor led him to the back porch, where they could survey the crop fields—carrots, peas, radishes—all wreathed in shining tubes. "Drip irrigation," Taylor said. "It's how the Hebrews turned the desert green." A series of low shacks flanked the main house. This was where his "tenants" lived. He used the term with a proprietary delight, as if they, too, had been coaxed 176

from the soil using drip irrigation. To the east, Stallworth spied scrawny orchards, where tenants in smocks weaved between rows with stepladders and baskets. It was the same wherever you went: the human engine of harvest.

Taylor led Stallworth to the meeting house, a two-story structure whose most striking architectural element was an elevated widow's walk that served as an observation tower. "I imagine you regard this degree of caution as excessive," Taylor said. "But we are not in America. We do not enjoy the virtues of plenitude here. This is a different geography." Taylor's tone had tightened in a way Stallworth recognized. It was how he had spoken to his own children, in the face of their complaints and demands, their innocent and corrosive privilege.

"Let me show you one more thing."

They came to a small outcropping of log cabins. In the front yard of one, a matron slapped balls of dough into tortillas and set them onto a griddle hung over a cook fire. She bowed as Taylor passed. "This is where my grandfather lived with his family." Several beams had been gouged with arrows and hatchets.

"He was attacked?"

"The Lord blessed him with twenty-one children. Five survived."

He brought his fingers to his mouth and produced an ear-splitting whistle. A small buggy appeared. "This has been quite a constitutional for a man still recuperating. I expect you'll want to rest." Taylor helped ease Stallworth into the passenger seat. "Let us be gladdened by your progress."

He felt like a prize calf being shipped to market.

THE NEXT MORNING, Stallworth woke to find a giant aluminum tub next to his bed, which a tenant filled with buckets of steaming water. When the tub was full, the tenant departed and Alma appeared, bearing a towel crowned with a cake of soap, a straight razor, and a mirror.

"I gather it's time for a bath." His hair had grown sodden and tangled.

Alma smiled and began matter-of-factly unwrapping him. She eased his nightshirt off so that he lay exposed to the cool morning air. "Hurry now. The water won't hold heat for long."

Alma turned away and busied herself with the shaving equipment. Stallworth stepped into the water and nearly howled. He recalled the pleasures of bath time, Jenny dipping a toe and squealing, "Owie! Too owie!"

"Can you get in on your own?" Alma said.

Stallworth lowered himself, breathing hard. The raised perimeters of his wounds turned an angry pink; he jabbed the worst of them with his thumbnail until it wept fluid. Why had he survived? He should have been annihilated, his mortal shell blown apart and the spirit within damned to its appropriate depth.

A hand brushed his shoulder. "May I wash you?" The girl didn't wait for him to answer. She dipped the soap in the water and slid it across his shoulder blade.

"You don't have to do that," he said.

"I don't expect you'll be able to clean your own back." Alma took up a small brush and scrubbed while he sat very still. The pleasure was excruciating. She circled his back and came up to his neck and ran her fingers behind his ears. She lifted his arms and steam rose in white spirals. The air smelled of lavender. She began to wash his chest.

"Does Father Ammon know you're here?"

"Of course."

"He doesn't consider this immodest?"

"Was Mary immodest when she anointed him with spikenard?"

Stallworth tried to recall the episode; Jesus reclining like a pasha, Judas smirking from the doorway. "I'm not sure that's an appropriate comparison."

"We don't really know who we are," Alma said brightly. "That's why so many get lost." She tapped at the back of his neck and poured water over his head. She worked up a lather with the soap then let her fingers slither down to his scalp. The room had grown foggy. She placed a washcloth over his eyes so they wouldn't sting and rinsed his hair. He heard the bark of a chair and felt his feet lifted from the water and set upon her lap. She began to cut away the dead skin and callous. She clipped his mangled toenails.

Then she set down her tools and lathered his calves. He could feel his body roused from the long slumber of injury. The instrument of his desire swelled from the murky bath. The girl carried on, humming. Then she drew in a breath and her hands fell still. They had come to an invisible boundary, toward which they had been, in some half-realized fashion, wandering. The girl leaned over him and he felt the washcloth lifted from his eyes. There was her face, round and red with shame. She smiled; her long snaggled teeth lent her a wolfish beauty. He closed his eyes and felt the washcloth laid gently across his midsection. "I'm sorry," he said.

"Why would you be sorry?" The girl spoke in genuine astonishment.

She carried on, washing his thighs, then took up a brush and a bottle of peppermint oil and began to yank at the snarls in his hair. She combed out his beard and snipped at the edges, dark curls gathering in her palm. She pressed his forehead, so the back of his skull balanced on the rim of the tub. "Be still," she said. The blade ran across the exposed skin of his throat, the whiskers shorn with a tender scrape. When she was done with his neck, she shaved the tops of his cheeks.

At a certain point, she let out a soft gasp.

Stallworth opened his eyes. Alma was leaning back on her haunches and staring at his face intently, almost fearfully.

"What is it?"

"You look so much alike."

"Alike who?"

The girl reached for the small hand mirror behind her, which she held up for him to inspect. The figure staring back at Marcus Stallworth appeared plucked from antiquity: hair parted down the middle and fallen to the shoulders, his beard trimmed to reveal his cheeks, and neatly tapered beneath his chin. The bruising was nearly gone, with just a trace of purple beneath his left eye. His face had been restored.

Alma set down the mirror and unfastened the top button of her dress. Then, with a preternatural calm, she reached inside and drew out a small silver locket, which she flicked open with her thumbnail. She leaned close and gestured for Stallworth to take hold of the locket. The metal backing was still warm from where it had nestled. They were inches apart now. The lavender steam gave way briefly, thrillingly, to the pungency of her body. He took in the pink of her tongue, the exquisite pulsation of the veins at her temple.

"Do you see?"

Stallworth had to stanch his foul yearning, so he could focus on the picture: a younger Father Taylor in tidy notch collar. The resemblance struck him as plausible but rudimentary. He nodded. Perhaps this was why Taylor looked upon him as some variety of deliverance. As the girl gently withdrew, he spied the straight razor that lay on the stool beside her. He might have reached out and seized it.

"Do you like it?" She meant his hair and beard.

"Very much," he said. The water around him had cooled by now. It was milky with soap and filth and dark drifting whiskers.

He made as if to stand and she glanced at the length of his body, lingering for a tense moment, then looked directly into his eyes. "I am glad of it. You're to take supper with us tonight."

"Supper?"

"Father Ammon likes for everyone to dress proper on the Sabbath."

HE FOUND HIMSELF escorted into the plain rooms of the main house and seated at one end of a table laid with food. The walls were covered with aging wallpaper and sepia prints of assorted Taylor forebears, emaciated men and women in formal dress who appeared to be surveying the food below them with grave longing.

Stallworth wore the clothes that had been presented to him that afternoon, a stiff cotton frock, buttoned jacket, dark woolen trousers. His feet had been tucked into tooled leather shoes. Ammon Taylor sat opposite him, on a throne of carved oak, in an identical costume. Four wives sat between them, two on either side.

He recognized all of them. They had fed and bathed him and emptied his chamber pot. But he had never been introduced to the older three. Earlier, Taylor had detained each of them as they bustled from the kitchen with platters of cornbread and sauerkraut. He named them in turn—Sariah, Emmeline, Martha. They curtsied and looked past Stallworth as he thanked them for their kindnesses. Now they sat, somber and erect, like statues wrapped in organdy.

"Heavenly Father," Taylor began, "in thy name we offer thanks for the food before us and those who toiled in its preparation. We pray for the safety of those not with us, and for patience in abiding those who have yet to find a path to the light. We offer thanks for the recovery of our visitor, who comes among us now as a friend. You have asked us to pray always in the name of thy son, Jesus Christ. Amen."

Alma ladled a mountain of stew onto Taylor's plate, then did the same for Stallworth. To the women she doled out a watery portion that might have fit in a teacup. Their plates were filled out with hunks of cornbread and vegetables. It was a flagrant display of inequity, one Stallworth recognized from the church suppers of his boyhood. They didn't have enough meat—that much was clear.

The greater curiosity was the absence of any progeny. Stallworth had assumed Ammon's marriages would have yielded several children, perhaps even grandchildren. But the only residents of the property, aside from the tenants, appeared to be the patriarch and his wives. The women ate in silence, while Taylor told the meandering story of his grandfather, who had fooled Pancho Villa into releasing his nephew in exchange for the deed to a silver mine that belonged to the federal government. Villa, Taylor insisted, was a drunk who won fame by the savagery of his men.

"Did you fight in the war of Vietnam?" Taylor asked him.

Stallworth shook his head.

"May I ask why not?"

"I was a college student." That was only part of the truth; Rosemary's family had arranged a deferment.

"College," Taylor said. The word evidently left a sour taste in his mouth.

Suddenly, the wife at Taylor's right hand spoke. "Where do you come from, sir?" she demanded.

"Arizona."

"And what is your business here?"

"My business?"

"You heard me. Do you know my son?" The woman's hair was yanked back in a bun; her cheeks blazed in the flickering of the oil lamps.

Taylor set his hand upon hers. "Sariah," he said sharply.

"Justin Taylor. That's his name. Answer me."

Stallworth shook his head.

"You best hope that's the truth." She rose abruptly, still glaring at Stallworth. It appeared for a moment that she might lunge at him. Then she tucked her face away and hurried from the room.

After the meal, Taylor led him into a small front parlor. "You mustn't blame Sariah. Our boy got himself into some trouble up that way."

"Why would she think I had something to do with it?"

"Grief clouds the mind. It's a known fact." Taylor pulled a sack of tobacco from his desk and began to stoke his pipe. "You continue to heal, which I take as encouraging."

Alma appeared with two mugs on a little silver tray.

"Thank you, my dearest." Taylor looked at the girl fondly. "Drink up, friend. A little sweetness to consecrate our Sabbath." The drink was delicious, hot milk with sugar and cinnamon.

"You've been very kind. Your whole family. It's more than I deserve."

"*Now therefore ye are no more a stranger, but a fellow citizen with the saints, and of the household of God.* Do you know the verse? Paul's Second Epistle to the Ephesians."

"I'm afraid I don't qualify as a fellow citizen with the saints."

"We shall let God judge that."

"If I may ask," Stallworth said, "do you have other children?"

Taylor smiled stiffly and took a pull from his pipe. Smoke curled from his nostrils. "They have gone north for a time. To make their fortunes, you might say, among the Chaldeans. You are a father, so I expect you are familiar with this pattern."

For a piercing moment, Stallworth saw his children: beautiful and haughty in their designer clothes, their muscles and makeup. "I'm sorry," he said, though he knew these weren't the right words.

"Sorry for what?" Taylor replied. He removed his pipe and directed it at Stallworth with a wink. "I have everything a man might want. For even if Our Father in Heaven seized this land from beneath my feet, even if he took every pillar and post, every beast and grain of millet from my storehouse, every soul who dwells here, even if he sent plague to ravage my body, as he did to Job, still I would be blessed beyond reckoning. Do you understand?"

Stallworth nodded. He was starting to see the situation—the Taylor ranch was a failing concern, the relic of a life his children had rejected, pious and outdated, like the words he had been made to recite on Sundays. Perhaps the pity registered on his face, for Taylor when he spoke next did so without a trace of kindness.

"I have asked several times why you came among us, friend. Now I will ask you a final time. *Gird up your loins like a man; I will question you and you shall declare to me.* Who are you?"

"I've told you what I can," Stallworth said.

"No," Taylor said. "You have let the poison of deceit issue from your tongue."

"Let me go then. Take what you want of my money and be rid of me."

Taylor shook his head. "That money never belonged to you. It belonged to your wife."

Stallworth felt punched of breath.

"It will be best for you to return to your room now. You do not look well. But bear these words with you. If you attempt to leave this property, or cause any disruption, I will alert the authorities, Mr. Stallworth."

"What?"

"The days of your running are over, friend."

THE REST OF the evening returned to him in fragments: the night air chilling his ears, a spray of stars overhead, the complaints of a donkey slapped with a switch, a jostling that flared through his ribs; his body laid to rest on his sagging manger bed. Then a tug on his belt, the pants stripped from his body.

The sensations began to swirl. A soft body pressed against his, then carefully wriggled beneath; the plain brown face of the girl stared up at him intently. Was this Lorena? Had she come to him? The warmth of her skin poured out across his and a shy hand took hold of him and his craving lurched awake. Her knees fanned wide and she guided him to the slick notch of her womanhood. There was no boundary. She let out startled breaths of cinnamon and milk; pain shot through his ribs. The damp collision of hips. Her feet clinched around his calves.

Now it was morning. The light of it hammered at his temples. He felt certain he had had a wet dream. The agitation of his bath yesterday, the girl's provocations. It made sense. He reached down and ran his fingers through his hairs then sniffed at them. The aroma marked what they had done.

STALLWORTH SPENT THE day in mystified agitation. What were Taylor's intentions? Extortion? The pursuit of ransom? And how did Alma's nocturnal visit fit into this plan? He deduced that the scorpion specimen must have been the crucial clue. How many scorpiologists went missing any given month?

But the explosion that sent him pinwheeling through the air had blasted a clue from his memory: the tiny, ten-digit phone number secreted on the last page of his passport. It was this number that Ammon Taylor had called five days earlier, reaching the offices of Royce Van Dyke in San Francisco.

Taylor left a message with the answering service mentioning David Tennyson. Van Dyke called back less than a minute later.

"A client of yours has wound up on my property," Taylor explained. "I want his real name. It shan't be hard to find, now that I know he's from Northern California."

"The less you know, the better," Van Dyke said breezily. "Trust me on that."

Taylor fell silent and let the pause gather weight. Van Dyke did not strike him as a man to be trusted. "Each day he remains here, my family bears a risk. I wish to know the precise nature of that risk. My next call will be to the police."

Van Dyke confessed, then tendered an initial offer, which Taylor did not dignify with a response. Eventually, the two men reached an accord: $2,500 per week for the medical care provided to Marcus Stallworth, another $2,500 for discretion. "Aim him south and I'll double your stake for doing the Lord's work," Van Dyke pledged.

"You would do well not to mock God," Taylor replied sternly. The phone line cracked and hissed, as if the call were emanating from the distant past.

Van Dyke smirked at the old man's preening piety. But when he glanced down at his own hand, the one scratching out terms, he found it trembling.

ALMA RETURNED LATE in the night, wearing a cape of muslin, rain damp and clasped at the throat with a plastic brooch.

"What the hell did you do? You drugged me."

She looked at him, almost amused. "I did not."

"What are you doing here?"

"You're angry?"

"Of course I'm angry."

"You didn't appear angry last night." The girl set down her lantern and removed her bonnet and cloak. She fished the clips from her hair and it fell unbound. "You were provided nothing but a Sabbath meal," Alma continued quietly. "Then you were provided a bed and a woman to lie with. I was that woman. You desired me and took what you wanted. Do you deny it?"

The girl sat in the chair and peeled away her stockings. She had left her shoes near the door. He could see one of them, rimed in red mud. Behind her was the portrait of Joseph Smith, enthralled by the angel he had dreamed up in a fever.

"How does Father Taylor know who I am?"

"That is none of my affair."

She stood and began to unbutton her dress.

"Please don't," he whispered.

"Don't what?"

"Does your husband know where you are?"

"Does your wife?"

The girl let her dress drop, revealing the thin undergarment beneath. "You are no longer in America, or Mexico, or any other place where the laws are made by men."

"I'm being held against my will," Stallworth said.

"You were spared. Then sent to us. That was the work of the Lord, not the devil. Father Ammon saw it at once." Alma stepped toward the bed and the lantern showed the outlines of her body. *"Adam fell that men might be, and men are, that they might have joy.* Do you believe that? Would God create desire without design?"

Alma had rehearsed these words. He saw her standing before a looking glass, arranging her face around them, her husband seated behind her listening, nodding.

"I can secure more money. Tell Father Ammon. Tell him I'm willing."

"Money?" The girl's face soured. "You think this is about money?"

"Why won't he grant me freedom?"

"The question is whether you wish to deny your own nature. Do you, Mr. Stallworth? Do you wish to deny?"

He tried to look her in the eye but neither of them could bear it. The girl had begun to shiver; the shadow of her body quivered on the wall.

"No," he said finally.

"Good," she replied, and climbed into bed with him.

FOR FIVE CONSECUTIVE nights, Alma returned. She stood by his bed and removed her garments and pulled him into her body with a silent writhing that registered pleasure and apprehension. As he approached climax, her palms pressed him deeper; more than once he had to entreat her to release him. Afterwards, she tilted her hips toward the ceiling, remaining in this posture to the count of one hundred.

Ammon Taylor needed an heir. That much was obvious. His only son had decamped for Arizona or Utah, a wayward soul. His two daughters had married into other clans. Stallworth thought of the Old Testament, its blood-soaked poetry, which redounded, in the end, to patrimony, the endless begats, the senseless slaughter of the Middle Ages, the twisted lore of kingship and kingdom. By some strange logic, he had abdicated his throne only to assume the role of royal stud.

This was how his mind operated when he wished to step back and negotiate with his dilemma. The rest of his day was a quilt of impatience and dread. He took short walks around the courtyard and peered at the walls of the compound, soaring up through the November drizzle like a futile gesture, a fortress locked from the outside.

Inside Alma, he surrendered to sensation: heat and delight, the soft thrashing. With the lamp doused, he could barely see her face. She was neither a coquette nor a courtesan, just a girl devoted to the duties of the cult.

In the minutes after Alma departed, he worried his options. He could attempt an escape and take his chances, but he was without money or any sensible plan, still not fully recovered from cracked ribs. He could stay on and curry Ammon Taylor's favor. He tried once to threaten Alma with disclosure.

"You've defiled me," she replied calmly. "He'll kill us both."

"But didn't Father Taylor—didn't he send you?"

For a fleeting moment, the girl hesitated. Then she stared at him in pity, as though he were a child who had failed to grasp the simplest lesson. "God sent me here. Just as he sent you. Our course is set."

ON THE FOLLOWING Sabbath eve, he was invited to bathe in the main house and he managed to pocket a straight razor. He stashed the razor in his bedside drawer, beside the plastic canister that contained the corpse of *Centruroides narcissus*. His gaze lingered on the pale corpse, the scythed stinger still lodged in its own eye. He felt a shiver of recognition.

The girl, Alma, had arrived in his bed later than usual and plainly exhausted. After their coupling, he curled away from her and evidently fell asleep, for he was shocked to find her still beside him as dawn broke.

Voices rose suddenly from the hallway, two men whispering fiercely in English. Stallworth thought of the blade inside his bedside drawer. The girl woke in a panic. The door burst open and Ammon Taylor's face appeared, lit from below by a lantern. Taylor stared at him severely, taking in the roil of bedsheets, the scent of their congress, before alighting on Alma. Her eyes were squeezed shut, as if she might vanish altogether.

It all happened in an instant: Taylor's face stamped with wrath, Stallworth lunging for his razor, the tiny black eye of a pistol, its deafening report. A wet thud punched the breath from his body and replaced it with a frantic gurgling, his vision clouding as a second man (short, balding, chin dipped) raised a black baton and sent a tiny bolt of lightning into the ear of Ammon Taylor. Then, as Taylor fell, a third figure became visible, squatting impossibly in the shadows of the hallway: Lorena Saenz.

**BOOK FOUR
OFFICIALLY
CONFIRMED
MAYHEM**

THE HOURS FOLLOWING THE ARREST of Antonio Saenz for the murder of Marcus Stallworth were chaotic for all those bound by the events.

Pedro Guerrero drove the suspect to the Fresno Police Department, where he was photographed, fingerprinted, and placed in a holding cell. Guerrero called Hooks to inform him of the arrest. The captain had left for the day—it was by then nearly 8 p.m.—but dispatch patched the call through to his home. "Tell me you got a confession."

"He confessed to threatening the victim," Guerrero replied. "With a gun."

Hooks spent some time breathing into the phone. "That's not a confession."

"He was a flight risk, sir."

"Zip it. Unless you want to explain to the FBI why you decided to disobey a direct order from your superior. Would you like to do that, Guerrero? Does that sound like a fun Saturday evening?"

"No, sir."

Hooks was grinning broadly. A tumbler of scotch awaited him, to which he now added a third finger. He happened to be stark naked. In a few minutes, after the profound pleasure of phoning the FBI's deputy director to inform him of the arrest, he would settle into a hot bath drawn by his lover, a young escort named Drew, who was already in the tub.

"Jolley will inform the family," Hooks said. "Apparently, you offended the victim's wife. Remand the suspect to Fresno. And keep your mouth shut. This is going to be a shitstorm by tomorrow."

JOLLEY DROVE TO the Stallworth home and informed Rosemary that a suspect had been arrested for the murder of her husband.

The color seeped from her face. "What are you talking about?"

"A suspect, ma'am."

"A suspect?" She reached for the arm of the sofa.

Fearing a collapse, Jolley hastened to her side, but she flinched his hand away and seated herself. "But how do you know—have you found . . ."

"In these cases, the victim is not generally recovered until the assailant makes a full confession."

"I don't understand. Has he confessed or not?"

"He has confessed to certain facts."

"To killing my husband?"

"I realize this is a lot to absorb."

"Then you don't really know, do you?" Mrs. Stallworth said sharply. She shook her head, as if to dispel the whole unpleasantness. "I appreciate the work you and your colleagues have done. But until such a time as my husband is located, I would prefer to be left alone."

"That's not how the system works," Jolley said helplessly. "It's a felony charge. There's likely to be a court case. State court, or even federal."

"Federal?" She touched at her hair, which had been carefully arranged.

"The young man in custody is named Antonio Saenz. He's the older brother of one of your daughter's classmates. Lorena."

"Lorena?" Mrs. Stallworth spoke the name in tender bafflement. "That's absurd. She's just a poor little Mexican girl."

"Antonio Saenz attempted to rob Mr. Stallworth. There's a good deal of physical evidence, I'm afraid. Fingerprints. Blood."

"But it's all just *speculation*. This is senseless. I'll need to consult my attorney." Mrs. Stallworth went to the phone. "I'm sorry. I think that would be the best thing."

"I'd like to leave a police detail," Jolley said. "To make sure you're not disturbed."

"Disturbed?"

"There may be reporters outside your home. Television crews."

Rosemary Stallworth was so aghast at this notion that she seemed incapable of speech. She fixed Jolley with a withering stare. "I have children. In high school. This is completely unacceptable. I was very explicit about that."

Jolley stood awkwardly and let himself out of the house while Mrs. Stallworth dialed her attorney.

In his brief report of this conversation, Jolley noted that the victim's spouse was quite evidently in shock. What he did not report, and would never learn, is that Rosemary Stallworth knew who Antonio Saenz was. She had seen him through her bedroom window, on the same night Lorena found her husband bleeding and fled.

Rosemary did not witness their embrace under the streetlamps. Nor did she hear the ardent words that passed between them. It was only the noise of Tony's car that roused her. She saw Marcus on his hands and knees and Lorena standing over him. She saw the young man bound from his car and watched Lorena trying to calm him down, Marcus shrinking back, like the coward he was. She knew the young man was trying to protect his sister. She could see it on his face. And in some stubbornly hushed part of herself, she knew why.

The next morning, when she confronted him, Marcus would say only that it was a misunderstanding, that she wasn't to worry. He swore that he loved her and that things would get better between them, as they did in the weeks before his disappearance. To mention any of this to the police, Rosemary knew, would be to open a new front in the investigation, one that could only lead to ruin. And so she sent the fat officer called Jolley away. Within twenty-four hours, her hair had turned the color of ash.

THE PHONE RANG, as Lorena knew it would. The clock radio read 3:17 a.m. It had been twelve hours since Pedro Guerrero had interviewed her. She listened to the groan of the sleeper sofa, her mother padding to the phone. A better daughter would have gotten there first.

Graciela had the receiver pressed to her chest, as if to stanch a wound. "Tony's in jail," she moaned. "He won't say why. He wants to talk to you, *mija*. Make him tell you what's happening."

She took phone. "Tony?"

"Don't tell mom shit. I don't want her worrying." He was speaking quick and quiet, in English.

"Where are you?"

"Fresno. Listen. They think I did something to your rich asshole friend Mr. Stallworth. It's going to be fine. I didn't do nothing. This is what the cops do. They throw shit against the wall."

"You're under arrest?"

"They needed to hang it on someone."

"Hang what?"

"His murder."

She began to cry, as quietly as she could manage.

Her mother was staring at her. "What is it, *mija*?"

Lorena covered the receiver. "He's okay," she said. "It's just a misunderstanding." The word she used was *desorden*: disorder.

She saw Tony marching around the neighborhood in his navy whites, a boy still starved for the regard of his father. He couldn't be a killer. Or maybe she was being naïve. Maybe something in him had grown more dangerous than she had been able to admit. She was left with no good choice: either her brother had been party to murder or she had been party to his false arrest.

"Calm the fuck down and listen," Tony snarled. "I'm going to get a lawyer to straighten this out. That's how it works. But the public defenders are for shit, okay? They work for the state. So you gotta call Peña, my partner."

"Your partner?"

"Peña. Victor Peña." He gave her Peña's beeper. "Get him on the phone, *gordita*. Tell him what happened. I'm at county lockup. Not jail. That's the city. *County lockup*." A recorded voice informed them they had half a minute left to talk. "Call Peña until you get him. Tell him I need a real lawyer. And don't say shit to Mama."

"Wait. What if Stallworth's not dead?" Lorena said. "What if he just ran away?"

"What the fuck are you talking about?"

"He wanted to leave. His family."

"How do you know?"

The recorded voice came back on, announcing that the call would terminate in ten seconds.

"I told you those rich assholes were trouble," Tony said miserably.

"But he's alive," Lorena said. "I'm almost sure."

"Then fucking find him, you little bitch. You got me into this mess. Get me out of it." Tony was trying to sound hard, but his voice kept cracking. "Tell Mama I love her," he said. Then the line went dead.

LORENA FELT HER mother gently pry the receiver from her hand and hang it up. "What did Antonio do?"

"Nothing."

"Why is he in jail, *mija*?"

"Like I said, it's a misunderstanding."

"What's the *charge*? Don't hide the truth from me. It will come out anyway."

"It has to do with that family, the Stallworths. The father disappeared and they think Tony might know something."

"They don't arrest young men for knowing things. They arrest them for doing things."

Graciela Saenz handed her daughter a paper towel and told her to blow. In a few hours, she would pack a lunch and head off to her first shift, mopping floors and emptying waste bins on the maternity ward at Mercy, where young mothers limped the bright hallways with their pink bundles of hope, their perfect little somethings, stunned with gratitude. Then she would take a bus to Roseville, where she worked in a halfway house for seniors with dementia. These jobs allowed her to cover rent and groceries, to make tithes to her church and send money to her family in Honduras. There was a little besides, which she put away in the hospital's credit union for her children. She wanted them to go to college—both of them, eventually—to have possibilities larger than her own. She had seen the dashing new president delivering a speech on television, and though she hadn't understood most of the words, she could feel him invoking this radiant and fragile dream.

Her daughter stood quaking. She had begun to dress in clothes that clung to her curves, to squander the precious gift of her intelligence. Graciela felt a sudden urge to slap the girl, to rouse her from the foolish spell of her hormones.

"He's got a lawyer, mama. They're going to figure it out."

Graciela went to fetch her cigarettes. She was already thinking about deportation, how Tony's idiocy had flushed them, once again, from the shadows into a bright realm of panic. "He was always weak," she murmured, through a shroud of smoke. "Like his father. God can't save a coward."

These were the most damning words Lorena would ever hear her mother utter.

GRACIELA SAENZ WAS ashamed to have made such a statement. It arose from the part of herself she kept a secret from the world. For Graciela wasn't merely the person her children perceived, a weary and vigilant mother. She, too, had been passionate in her youth, impulsive, drawn to risk. She had married a man her parents didn't trust, then followed him to America.

Graciela was pregnant with Lorena when her husband declared that the child would be born in America. He would travel first, with their son, and join his uncles in the fields of California. She didn't want to let the boy go, but her husband insisted the trip would be too arduous for a pregnant woman with a child. He sent for her five months later.

For a brief time, it was as he promised: a decent life. But the humiliations her husband absorbed on the journey north had changed him. He began to stay out late; there were other women, drunken disputes. She would have made her peace with all of it, for the children, but Antonio Sr. now blamed her for the move to America, her Honduran pride, her demands.

She could see the changes in Tony, as well. When she tucked him in at night, he clung to her, then wiped away her kisses.

After her husband left, Graciela joined a church, where she vaguely hoped she might find another man. In a sense, she did. Her devotion to Jesus Christ allowed her to come to terms with her own suffering, which she could see, in more forgiving moments, as a kind of fatal innocence.

She moved into the basement of a cousin's apartment in Sacramento. Late at night, after the kids were in bed, this cousin had played records, mushy romantic ballads mostly, but also more raucous norteño songs that allowed the women to dance. Graciela loved to dance.

Her favorite band was Los Tigres del Norte. They played *corridos*, story songs about immigrants driven to drastic measures. Her favorite was an old hit, "Contraband and Betrayal," about Emilio and Camelia, a pair of lovers who sneak across the border to make a big drug deal. The moment they have the cash in hand, Emilio announces that he is leaving Camelia for another woman. So she shoots him dead and disappears with their fortune. The police find only a dropped pistol.

Graciela worked hard, avoided drink, saved her money. Los Tigres marked her only vice. On her thirtieth birthday, she allowed her cousins to take her to a concert at the Sacramento county coliseum, where she took her place amid the couples dancing cumbia, twirling like bright bows to the jaunty growl of the bajo sexto.

As her children grew older, Graciela tucked away her devotion to Los Tigres. The music, with its tales of mayhem and drugs, was a bad influence. But there were moments when she couldn't help herself, when the kids were out of the apartment, and she would pull a battered cassette from beneath her mattress and slip it into the boom box they kept in their room, so that she could listen, again, to the story of Camelia, and let the music lift her body into a kind of illicit grace.

She knew it was wrong to root for a woman who sold narcotics and committed murder and got away with it. But she knew, also, that nestled within the obedience of her circumstance was the spirit of an outlaw. Tony had inherited that spirit.

ON THE MORNING of Sunday, November 5, Sacramento chief of police Robert Ellis called a press conference to announce the arrest of a suspect for the murder of Marcus Stallworth. Privately, law enforcement officials referred to such events as FTPs. They were designed to Fuck the Press. The editors at the *Sacramento Bee* faced a particularly awkward circumstance: a few hours before the press conference they had printed a front-page story suggesting that police had been unable to crack the case.

Chief Ellis made no reference to the *Bee*'s report. He merely emphasized that local investigators had worked "around the clock" in close coordination with federal agents and the FBI's crime lab. The suspect, Antonio Saenz, was nineteen years of age. He was an illegal alien. He had "a troubled history" that included gang violence and drug use. He had been discharged from the navy for the latter. His lengthy record included pending charges for grand theft auto and possession of unlicensed weapons. He had apparently attempted to rob Marcus Stallworth, who had resisted. The suspect's fingerprints had been found on the vehicle, his blood inside.

Reporters clamored for more information. Where was the body? Why had the vehicle been abandoned in Death Valley? Had the suspect acted alone? A reporter from the *Bee* asked why, given the preponderance of evidence against Saenz, police had taken more than two weeks to arrest him.

Chief Ellis stood before a bristle of bulky microphones and a bank of television cameras, staring down the reporter. He outlined the unprecedented challenges law enforcement faced: the absence of a body, a crime scene that had lay degrading in the desert heat for four days, and a perpetrator, or perpetrators, who had acted with considerable "criminal acumen." It was only the use of new scientific methods, pioneered by the FBI, that had allowed police to link Saenz to the crime.

Above all, the chief said, his department had remained cognizant of due process. They had exercised an abundance of caution. Antonio Saenz, he reminded the assembled, was a suspect, not a convict. It was up to the judicial system now to adjudicate his guilt. Regardless of that outcome, one family had suffered a devastating loss. He asked the press, by its use of discretion, not to compound that pain.

Reporters continued to yell questions. How had Stallworth been murdered? Had Saenz confessed? Shown any remorse? Did he know where the body was?

Chief Ellis took no questions. But before stepping away from the microphone, he quoted the book of Ecclesiastes: *Do not let your spirit rush to be angry, for anger abides in the hearts of fools.*

This odd declaration, which never appeared in the subsequent news coverage, lingered in the mind of Pedro Guerrero, who was one of the dozen officers standing behind the chief. If one were tracking the inner life of the aspiring detective, the man responsible for the arrest of Antonio Saenz, this was the moment at which he began to lose faith in his own work.

BY ALL ACCOUNTS, Chief Ellis had turned in a virtuoso performance. He had cast the most powerful spell known in the world of journalism, the spell of Officially Confirmed Mayhem. The reporters disgorged themselves from the press conference. But they couldn't bring themselves to leave the lobby of police headquarters just yet. They gathered in a scrum of orgiastic glee, one that disguised itself in solemn murmurings. The Tabloid Process had begun, the process by which the Fourth Estate took possession of a private misfortune and began to tell a larger, more lurid story to the public.

Reporters and cameramen fanned out across Oak Park and Fruitridge and sped down to Fresno and Barstow. They ransacked the available police records for photos, relics, visuals to entice the viewer. They pressed their "law enforcement sources" for background info, something more to go on. They interviewed anyone with an inkling of a connection to the culprit or the victim: the elderly neighbor who had seen Antonio Saenz in front of the Stallworth home, the university secretary who described Stallworth as "a gentle soul," the pastor who praised his "dedication as a father."

What made the case difficult for law enforcement—namely, its many unanswered questions—supplied news organizations the ideal blueprint for a serialized saga. *A new detail unearthed by our team!* Paradoxically, this slow drip of clues deepened the mystery and the horror. Truth, in its confounding subtlety, receded; conjecture came to the fore.

One of the local television stations, noting his stint at the China Lake Naval Reserve, cited "law enforcement sources" who speculated that Saenz might have buried the body in nearby Death Valley National Park. The graphic accompanying this report read THE DEATH VALLEY KILLER? The question mark soon fell away.

A former friend from the "violence-plagued ghetto" where Saenz had grown up recalled how the suspect—a munitions expert in the navy—had taught neighborhood children how to break down and reassemble a rifle during a July Fourth picnic. Intrepid TV reporters dispatched from downtown offices stood in front of the shabby apartment house where the killer had lived, so that viewers came to understand Fruitridge not as a community of low-wage workers but a criminal habitat.

The default image in media reports was a photo taken of the suspect after his arrest on gun charges, just days after the alleged murder. He wore the bleary glower so common to mugshots, one eye half closed, the other glaring at the camera. A dark bruise mottled the flesh above his right eye, unmistakable evidence of his violent proclivities. The second image, which found its way into the hands of local media, was a photo of the homemade tattoo emblazoned upon the killer's slender shoulder, a blurry crown with five points, which was identified as the gang marking of the notorious Latin Kings. These images were presented to the public hundreds of times, often in tandem, until they became symbolic of the suspect himself: the iconography of the Death Valley Killer.

Footage soon emerged of the "arsenal" Saenz had amassed in the basement of a Fresno grocery store. One carefully shadowed informant spoke of his connection to the Kings. Another cited his addiction to crack cocaine, a virulent new form of the drug with the potential to trigger psychotic episodes. Self-styled criminologists, citing his record as a juvenile, branded him a "career criminal," and speculated about the possibility that the assailant had stalked his victim. An expert on gang warfare hinted at the possibility of torture. These reports inevitably referred to the killer as an illegal, neglecting to mention that Saenz had been brought to America by his father at age four.

The story exuded a racial and economic paranoia so reflexive as to be virtually invisible to its intended audience. The key phrases—*gang-related, drug-fueled, cholo culture, suburban tranquility*—became a kind of code. Residents of the Fabulous Forties sighed wearily when interviewed about the case and harkened back to an era in which they and their children could walk the streets free from the terror of abduction. By some quirk of actuarial fate, Marcus Stallworth's murder marked the three thousandth homicide in California that year, a grisly milestone that rendered the story a proxy for the larger wave of violent crime that had engulfed the state.

All of this happened within the span of three days.

AMONG THOSE TRACKING the coverage was the First Lady of the United States. She had asked to be informed of any developments in the case and was among the first people to learn about the arrest of Antonio Saenz. She immediately went to her desk and composed a handwritten note of condolence to the widow:

Dear Rosemary,

I was stunned and saddened to learn of your husband's disappearance. Please know that Ronnie and I are praying for your family. It breaks my heart to think of the suffering caused by the dark souls of certain men. If there is anything we can do to lessen your burden, please don't hesitate to reach out.

Most sincerely,
Nancy

The First Lady considered adding her last name but decided not to. She knelt beside her bed and prayed for the victims of violent crime. Then she got into bed next to her husband, who was sleeping, his famous hair peacefully mussed against the pillow. She stared at him for a time, then went to the small balcony overlooking the East Lawn and tried to make out the relative position of the planets. The lights from the roof of the White House reduced them to smudges.

She came back inside and called down to her assistant. She wanted more information about the suspect. A teletype arrived within the hour. She took down Antonio Saenz's date and time of birth and approximate location (San Pedro Sula, Honduras) and sent these along to her astrologer. The chart returned to her the next day showed an astral formation known as a Yod at its center, which, in his case—he was a Scorpio with Mars as his rising planet—indicated restlessness, instability, and the risk of harm to others. The First Lady was sufficiently alarmed as to order a copy of the chart transmitted to the director of the FBI.

The chart had revealed precisely what she expected, what she might have learned from watching even a few minutes of the local television coverage. The suspect had been fated to transgress.

SHORTLY AFTER JOLLEY departed, Rosemary Stallworth called her children home and told them about the arrest of Antonio Saenz, and the police *speculation*—this was the word she used—that their father was gone. Both remained silent for a long time.

"That's bullshit," Glen said. "They didn't even look for him."

Jenny couldn't stop thinking about Tony, the way he'd looked her up and down, the lewd bulge of his gun. She had dared Lorena to bring him by. "I knew it was him," she said quietly. "That fucking thug." Then she burst into tears.

The next morning, the family woke to find TV vans lining the street in front of their home. Rosemary unplugged the phone. The crowd showed deference to the grieving family; they were allowed to come and go without being filmed or harassed. Reporters resigned themselves to canvassing neighbors and conducting stand-ups on the sidewalk. One especially aggressive columnist from the *Bee* approached the home. He was roundly booed before he could make it halfway up the stairs.

Rosemary could see what lay in store. Vultures with notebooks and cameras stalking her, snooping into the history of her family, ripping loose gossip to set before their readers like a feast of shame. She summoned her children to the den and told them to pack for a short trip and booked three rooms at the Hyatt Regency in Monterey.

It took only a few hours for reporters to track down the address of the apartment in Fruitridge where Antonio Saenz had grown up, and where his sister and mother still lived. On Monday morning, Graciela Saenz walked outside and into a phalanx of glamorous strangers. The men wore suits and ties; the women were impeccably made-up, their hair ironed straight and blown out. They looked to her like movie stars, and not just because of the cameras trained on them. Then the movie stars did something curious: they began to surge toward her and to push microphones into her face.

Señora Saenz! they called out. *Graciela!*

Most of the stations had hired stringers from Spanish language radio stations, in the hopes of coaxing a few words from the mother of the Death Valley Killer. They began to yell questions about her son, if she thought he was innocent, if she'd spoken to him, how he was going to plead.

It wasn't just the reporters who wanted answers. Dozens of her neighbors had gathered, lured by the scent of some trouble that did not belong to them. They were friends, acquaintances, children she had watched grow and on occasion fed. Their faces shone with a shy malice, and their eyes would not meet hers. She thought of the coyotes that had prowled the outskirts of her village when she was a girl.

Graciela Saenz carried a sack lunch in one hand and her Bible in the other. In her rush to retreat from the horde, an apple escaped from her lunch and rolled into the gutter. One of the young stringers, sensing opportunity, plucked up the fruit and ran toward Ms. Saenz. It was this young man who captured the only words spoken by the Death Valley Killer's mother before she scuttled back inside. *¿Por qué está pasando esto?* she whispered. *Why is this happening?*

GRACIELA SAENZ UNDERSTOOD now that her son had been charged with a serious crime. She was petrified that the police would arrive and discover she had no papers. This would lead to a detention cell and deportation. She didn't say any of this to her daughter; she didn't need to.

Graciela called Pastor Jorge, who devised a plan: the church van would pick them up in an hour and drive them to the basement of the church, which would serve as a legal sanctuary. Lorena told her mother this plan was crazy but Graciela clung to the idea that church property was impervious to the laws of the secular world. Lorena didn't know whether this was true; she doubted it. But she also didn't know what the police would do. She hadn't even told her mother about the cops who had come to see her. She still had the card Guerrero had left with her, tucked under her mattress.

For now, she needed to calm her mother down, so she went along with the getaway plan. She ducked into the van and hauled her backpack down into the basement, which smelled of menthol cigarettes and moldy hymnals. Only after her mother left for work did she sneak into the church office and dial Guerrero's number. The phone rang nine times before she heard a woman asking who was on the line.

Lorena paused for several seconds then gave her name.

"Please hold," the woman said.

Guerrero's voice came on the line. "Lorena?"

They could both hear her breathing.

"You lied to me."

"I know everything feels crazy right now."

"I told you the truth and you ignored me."

"This is a police investigation, Lorena. I'm directed by the facts." Guerrero began droning in the way officials did when they wished to silence someone who was not an official. It was a way of becoming nonhuman.

"I'm calling about my mother," Lorena said. "You promised she wouldn't get in trouble."

"Let's take one thing at a time. This has to do with your brother."

"You *promised*," Lorena said.

"Is she in trouble?"

"She's scared to death. There were a million cameras outside the house."

"Okay. Calm down. Let me explain what's going to happen."

But she didn't want any more of his explanations. "I want you to swear that my mother won't get in trouble. She had nothing to do with any of this."

"Your mother isn't the target of this investigation. But she may be called to testify. That's how it works."

"He's alive—I told you."

"I heard everything you said, Lorena. But your brother's blood is all over Marcus Stallworth's car. Okay? His fingerprints. They didn't get there by accident." Guerrero could hear the pinch of cruelty in his tone. He had become the father of this tragedy, charged with bearing the bad news to all parties. "Look, I'm sorry it went this way. I'll try to take care of you and your mom. But we have to follow the facts, Lorena."

He expected the girl to knuckle under, to accept him as her protector.

"You're the one who started all this," she said softly, as if she had been reading his mind all along. "You're not sorry. But you're going to be."

AT SCHOOL, SHE moved about in the shadow of her infamy. Her classmates had seen the reports on television. Wherever she went, kids elbowed one another and quickly looked away. Her teachers, clearly stunned to see her in class, made elaborate efforts to pretend nothing was out of the ordinary. She saw two of the girls she sat with at lunch and they nodded at her, as if from the far side of an ocean. A boy from church, a gangly sophomore, grasped her hand and announced that his family was praying for hers. There was no sign of Jenny Stallworth whatsoever.

Just before lunch she was called out of class and led down to a dinky office where the guidance counselor, Mr. Olney, began to speak with her about her options. He was an enormous man with a high-pitched voice that seemed to be apologizing for his bulk. "You can certainly remain in school. But it's also possible for you to work from home if you prefer. That would be easy to arrange. Just until things get back to normal. Really, it's up to you." Olney brushed a crumb off his tie, which was decorated with a cartoon turtle famous for his guileless idiocy. "We don't want to see this situation affect your academic performance."

He prattled on about the logistics—work packets, take-home tests—and presented her with documents for her mother to sign. "Do you have any questions?"

Lorena shook her head. "Can I leave now?"

"Of course." Olney paused a moment and looked at Lorena. His hands, which were pink and puffy and damp, seemed to want to reach toward her. "Everybody knows you had nothing to do with all this."

ON HER WAY across the parking lot she heard a familiar voice call out her name. She turned to find Miss Catalis striding toward her. Without a word of warning she wrapped Lorena in a hug. It was an act of presumption that registered as a display of concern. She had no choice but to accept it.

Miss Catalis stepped back to take her in, still holding her by the elbows. She looked as she always did: earnest, imploring, her lipstick beginning to flake. "My God. Are you okay?"

"I'm fine."

Miss Catalis shook her head and hugged her again. Her sweater stank of formaldehyde. Lorena wanted to ask what she was doing at the high school in the first place. "I saw your mother on TV this morning. She looked . . . Jesus, they've staked out your house, haven't they? Is there anyone to help you out?"

"We have some friends from church."

"Church," Miss Catalis said. "That's good. But I meant someone, like, a legal representative. To help explain the process. There are groups that can advise you, Lorena. I have a friend who works at Legal Aid. Let me give you her number." Her eyes glistened with pity.

Lorena wanted no part of it. This was what the official world did: it sent spies who offered help as a means of sneaking past your defenses. They couldn't be trusted. Her mother had tried to teach her that, but the lesson hadn't stuck. "My brother has a lawyer," she said.

"I just feel so terrible about all this. I keep thinking about Jennifer and her family. About both of you. I can't help feeling that I'm responsible."

Lorena could hear the self-regard in this comment, the condescension adults often mistook for compassion. She had to restrain herself from pushing Miss Catalis away.

It was she and Mr. Stallworth who had started all this, on that car ride home months ago. His arm had brushed the skin of her belly. A spark had been lit. That had been the beginning. Without her, Tony would have never visited the Stallworth home, never become a suspect. Those were the facts.

"You have such potential, Lorena. I don't want anything to get in the way of that. Do you understand what I'm telling you? You can always talk to me. You're not alone." Miss Catalis stared at Lorena, squeezed her elbows. She smelled like something dead.

"You have nothing to do with any of this," Lorena murmured.

Miss Catalis released her grip and took a step backward. She knew she had been rebuked, and this pleased Lorena.

FOLLOWING HIS ARREST, Antonio Saenz was remanded into custody and processed. These were the prevailing verbs, ones that eased a person (son, teenager, veteran) into an abstraction (suspect). Fingerprints. Mug shot. The surrender of clothing and property. Issuance of a cement-colored jumpsuit. Hours spent on benches in municipal buildings. You couldn't even take a shit in private. The officer who accompanied him walked with a limp and wore a fat man's grin.

Nando saw the precarious nature of the situation: a patrol officer—at the prodding of his superiors, but driven by his own ambitions—had jumped ahead of the facts and arrested the suspect for murder without a body. Now they were all committed to the same theory of the case. He understood his given role: to trot out his magic Chicano bullshit and try to extract a confession from the suspect, or some stray filament of incrimination.

But another part of him was quietly rooting for Antonio. He couldn't help himself. The alleged murderer was so obviously a *child*. His jumpsuit swam on him, and from within it he exuded a homely, pimpled truculence, a befuddled loneliness, that was instantly familiar. Antonio reminded him of his own cousin, Pedro.

THE SUSPECT REFUSED to say anything. He just kept asking to make his phone call. "*Tranquilo, hombre,*" Nando said. "*Tranquilo.*"

Tony *was* calm. He had done nothing wrong. Yelled at Stallworth, maybe threatened him a little. That was it. The asshole who arrested him had lied. Cops did it all the time. Peña had warned him. The key was not to let them get under your skin. Ask for your phone call. Ask for your lawyer.

Nando led Tony to a holding cell and, an hour later, escorted him to a small room with a pay phone. It was one in the morning. Tony called Peña at home; no answer. He hung up and closed his eyes and his forehead came to rest against the concrete wall.

"Nobody home, huh?" Nando said. "Saturday Night Fever." He began whistling the Bee Gees song. "Okay. Look. I'll make you a deal. You listening? I'm gonna let you make another call. I don't got to do that. But I want something from you. I want you to tell me what you're thinking right now."

After a few moments, Tony said, "I'm thinking how corny you are."

Nando let out a whoop. "You're a sharp one, *joven*. The fuck you doing in lockup?"

Tony's second call was the one his mother received, in which he directed his sister to contact his partner, Victor Peña. Peña, in turn, left a message with the attorney he employed for legal troubles. A few hours later, Nando escorted Tony to a tiny interview room. Inside was a man in a rumpled polyester three-piece. His thinning silver hair had been trimmed into a patchy crew cut. "Good morning, Mr. Saenz. My name is Stanley Gill. Stan."

"You're my lawyer?"

"In the matter of your bail hearing, yes. That will be this morning. You know what a bail hearing is?"

"Are you my lawyer or not? I'm entitled to a lawyer."

"That you are, Mr. Saenz. It's a constitutional right. But I'm a private attorney. I haven't been assigned by the court. Mr. Peña retained me on your behalf. For me to become your attorney of record would require us to come to an agreement regarding fees and expenses. That's something we can discuss later."

"Peña promised to take care of this shit."

"Let's focus on what we can control, Mr. Saenz." He glanced down at the two-page intake document that constituted his case file. "My apologies, Mr. Saenz. I'm playing catch-up. It's Sunday morning. I keep telling the police to refrain from making arrests over the weekend, but they never listen. That was a joke." Gill pulled out a pack of cigarettes. "You mind? Want one? So you were navy, huh? And now you're here. Christ. Okay, let's start with the basics. You've been arrested under what are called 'exigent circumstances.' Just means the police didn't obtain a warrant. The state is claiming you were a flight risk and also that you might have destroyed evidence. So the first thing we can do is file a habeas writ. That's a motion to go before a judge to argue that your detention is unlawful."

"That gets me out?"

"No. But it's good to get on the record." Gill made a note on his pad. "Now then. Do you mind telling me if you committed this alleged murder?"

"Hell no."

"Did you have anything whatsoever to do with the alleged crime?"

"No."

"Please keep in mind that whatever you tell me is confidential, Mr. Saenz. I can't speak about it to anyone else."

"You don't believe me?"

"Belief doesn't enter into it, Mr. Saenz. My job is to prepare a defense. I need to know as much as possible about the case the prosecution is building. They're not going to tell me what they've got. You have to do that. I only know what's in the news reports."

"News reports?"

Gill fell silent. "Okay," he said. "Listen. This is a serious accusation. There's going to be a lot of media coverage, TV cameras, all that. If I were a betting man, I'd say the FBI is involved."

"I'm not scared."

"I get that. But I need you to recognize what's going on here. The state is going to have to produce a complaint within the next day or two. We'll know more about the charges at that point. Until then, you're my only source. You need to tell me everything you know about Marcus Stallworth."

Tony confessed to what little he knew. His primary concern was that his mother would be dragged into this mess and turned over to INS.

Gill sucked at his cigarettes and scribbled a note from time to time. He didn't make a promising portrait, with his smudged bifocals and frayed cuffs. But Gill was a shrewd and seasoned lawyer, a legend among the criminal element of greater Fresno. He'd been a prosperous defense attorney in Glendale for years, specializing in public corruption, but a drinking problem and a nasty divorce led to a few bad decisions, which led to him being disbarred. A decade ago, he'd been reinstated and moved to Fresno to rep clients such as Victor Peña, whose business interests brought them to the attention of the police.

Gill had worked both sides of the criminal justice system. He knew one set of rules prevailed for the rich and another for the poor. He'd watched the chief of police trumpet Tony's arrest on TV. Clearly, the cops had needed to make an arrest. The problem was they didn't have a body. The Latin term was *corpus delicti*. There was always a chance the corpse would be located. But without it, the prosecution was in real trouble— unless Saenz confessed.

Stan Gill had three decades of experience with the police. He knew that cops hid their hunches behind a bearing of assurance, and that they often steered big investigations toward an intended result without recognizing they were doing so. They gave credence to statements that supported their charge, ignored ones that didn't, and presented scientific evidence as ironclad when it was often something more like educated speculation. He also understood that the inner workings of any police investigation—the blind spots, the missed opportunities, the unconscious collusion—only came to light at trial. This was why the state worked with the defense to plead cases out: to serve justice in the eyes of the public, without exposing its underside.

Gill knew Antonio Saenz would be denied bail but also that he had far more leverage than he realized, so long as he kept his mouth shut. As Tony was cuffed, Gill set a hand on his shoulder. "Don't speak to *anyone* from the state, Mr. Saenz."

These were the last words of counsel Stan Gill would offer the defendant.

LIKE MOST VETERAN cops in Fresno, Nando Reyes knew Stanley Gill. He had been deposed by Gill, more than once, and the experience always left him shaken. Gill could pinpoint places where an official declaration of fact gave way to guesswork, where a reasonable assumption, if exposed to sustained scrutiny, could be recast as reasonable doubt. Gill was precisely the sort of defense attorney that Antonio Saenz would need. That was the whole problem.

When Guerrero called to see how the bail hearing had gone, he naturally asked about Stanley Gill. Nando could have feigned ignorance, or dodged the question. He could have told a version of the truth, that Gill was a *borracho* who had been disbarred down in SoCal and come to Fresno as damaged goods. But he knew that anything short of the truth would be a betrayal. "He's not the guy I'd want at the other table," Nando muttered. "He's old but crafty as shit."

"How the fuck did Saenz land a private attorney? His partner must have put up the money."

"That'd be my guess."

"Time to talk to Peña, then. He's next on my list anyway."

Nando knew exactly what Guerrero meant. His cousin would interview Victor Peña in a manner that made it clear he was a person of interest in the investigation. Peña would almost certainly retain Gill, making it impossible for him to represent Saenz. With any luck, a judge would disqualify Gill altogether.

It was the right play, and Nando was proud of his cousin for recognizing it so quickly. But he felt a twinge of remorse, too. Antonio Saenz deserved a fighting chance. An advocate like Stan Gill gave him one.

GUERRERO SHOWED UP at Peña's apartment a few hours later. Peña refused to be interviewed until his attorney, Stanley Gill, was present. Gill, who had just met with Saenz, understood at once what the police were up to. He scowled at Guerrero, then disqualified himself from representing either man.

When Peña finally sat for an interview, he told Guerrero that he knew Saenz from the navy. He'd spent a little time trying to help the kid adjust to military life. Peña felt sorry for him because he was so clearly in over his head. He was always looking for someone to impress, "one of those guys where the tougher they try to act, the more you see how scared they are." He hadn't been surprised when he heard Saenz got the boot.

They reconnected a few days before Halloween. Saenz had just been fired from a job at an oil change place. He had a bandage on his forehead. He reported having gotten into some trouble over the weekend. "There was some shit about a girl and her pimp who fed him drugs, then busted him up. That's what he told me. He wanted to get straight."

Peña had offered these details as evidence that Saenz was not a sophisticated criminal mind, but a naïve young man, more likely to get himself rolled by a couple of lowlifes than to plot a robbery or murder. Guerrero heard something else entirely: confirmation of the suspect's drug habit and the injuries he sustained on the weekend in question.

Guerrero interviewed three of the suspect's co-workers at Quik Lube. They remembered having beers with Saenz on Friday. His shift manager, Gonzo, reported that he failed to show up for work on Saturday and was fired on Monday. He, too, mentioned the bandage on Saenz's forehead. He did not mention that Saenz had departed the Friday gathering with his niece. He saw no reason to involve Trina. She had enough trouble with the law as it was.

In the twenty-four hours since his arrest, Antonio Saenz had lost the representation of a skilled attorney. Testimony from witnesses who might have provided him an alibi instead suggested his use of alcohol and drugs during the period of the alleged victim's abduction. He had disappeared for two days and resurfaced with a head wound.

This was all before he was loaded into a van and driven north to the Sacramento County Jail, where he emerged in shackles before a jostling of television cameras. Portable klieg lights illuminated the path from the van to the jail's prisoner entrance. This brief promenade—staged for the benefit of the assembled media and replayed hundreds of times over the next two days—provided television viewers their first look at the figure who had come to be known as the Death Valley Killer.

Graciela Saenz saw the footage the next morning, on a TV mounted in the hospital room she was cleaning on the Labor and Recovery ward. The TV had been left on but the sound was turned down, so that she heard none of the reporter's rapturous narration. All she saw was a brief shot of her son shuffling toward a gray building. He was surrounded by police officers. Lights washed down upon him and he blinked into the brightness, thin and terribly young, with a thick chain wound around his waist like a medieval belt.

Graciela was so stunned that she dropped the bundle of garbage in her arms. One of the bags split and its contents tumbled across the floor—disposable diapers, wipes streaked with baby shit, a pair of the temporary panties worn by new mothers, clotted with the dark purple of afterbirth. It was, in its own way, a kind of crime scene, the reeking peril of motherhood laid bare. For a moment, in the perfect silence of the room, Graciela Saenz wept, while behind her a baby suckled at the swollen pink bosom of his sleeping mother.

ACROSS THE COUNTRY, in the bedroom of the West Wing, the First Lady of the United States watched the same scene unfold on a video feed she had requested of her favorite Sacramento television station. She was troubled to discover that the suspect who had abducted Marcus Stallworth looked more like a child than a killer. She had to remind herself what he had done. The reporter noted that the alleged assailant had been a drug addict. That made sense to Mrs. Reagan. It was the drugs that had transformed this slip of a boy, this star-crossed Scorpio, into a murderer.

Lorena didn't see the footage of her brother's arrest until Monday evening. Her boss at the retirement facility called her into the break room and gestured at the TV. There was her brother shuffling toward a gray building amid the rampart of officers.

"That's why that cop was here before, huh?"

Tony's face emerged for an instant, his narrow jaw set in a grimace. It was an expression she had seen a thousand times, the look of a kid tucking his terror away behind a frail mask.

Tony had been a cruel older brother, quick to taunt, to pinch and punch. It often seemed to Lo that all she saw of her brother was the part of him that needed to hurt her. But that was just her selecting memories. He had fought on her behalf on the playground, in the courtyard. He had performed a boy's imitation of a father, all rage and no tenderness. Their mother had relied on him but she hadn't believed in him.

TWO DAYS AFTER his arrest, the case against Antonio Saenz was transferred from state to federal jurisdiction. This decision, which stunned legal observers, was based on a technicality: Marcus Stallworth's vehicle had been found on a federal access road; thus the alleged crime had been committed on federal land. The move signaled to all involved—the media and the defense in particular—that the full weight of the US government would be brought to bear in the service of justice.

Pedro Guerrero was livid. He paced for an hour in the break room, working up the nerve to confront Hooks. Jolley wanted no part of it.

"We made the case. Jolley and me. And now the feds, they're gonna march in like conquering heroes. It's bullshit. Excuse my language, Captain, but that's the truth."

Hooks understood Guerrero's beef. The case represented the apex of his career, his shot to make detective. Now it was being snatched away.

But Maurice Hooks—who had been required to change in a separate locker room for the first decade of his career, who had been called *boy* and *Uncle Tom* and worse, who had been pulled over and frisked by cops in a dozen jurisdictions, who had been shot at three times in the line of duty, who had concealed his desires to keep his badge—had no patience for self-pity. It was an indulgence, a gift the world handed white people. Guerrero would have to figure that out on his own.

"You did fine," Hooks said. "I'll remember."

"That's it?"

"That's it. Now get out before I start to regret giving you the shot."

THE UNITED STATES attorney for the Eastern District of California filed a criminal complaint against the defendant. This document was immediately presented to a grand jury, whose members ratified it as a true bill within the hour.

The complaint alleged that Antonio Saenz had engaged in a verbal altercation with Marcus Stallworth in late August of 1981, during which he had threatened Stallworth with a gun, demonstrating malice aforethought. Several weeks later, on or about October 23, Saenz again encountered the victim and attempted to rob him. Stallworth resisted and Saenz murdered him. He then abandoned the victim's Jeep in a remote location of the Mojave Desert and disposed of his body.

The defendant's fingerprints had been found on the roll bar of the Jeep. More significantly, the FBI's serology lab, using state-of-the-art technology, had discovered the blood of the assailant and his victim soaked into the carpeting below the front seats of both driver and passenger, a circumstance that suggested a sustained struggle.

Additional witnesses reported that Saenz was under the influence of drugs during the commission of the crime, and sustained a head wound consistent with an altercation. There was also evidence suggesting that Saenz had forced his victim to withdraw $5,000 cash from an "instant loan service" in Fresno, one notorious for its use by those engaged in the drug trade.

The complaint served a legal function: it initiated the criminal justice process. Just as important was its narrative function. By means of language—elegant, formal, indisputable—the murder obtained an official story. The magnitude of this story was signaled by the transfer of the case into federal jurisdiction, which the media interpreted as evidence that the Stallworth murder was a capital offense.

The suspect, having met with his newly assigned court-appointed lawyer for less than ten minutes, entered a plea of not guilty at his arraignment.

Afterwards, a spokesman for the US attorney issued a brief statement on the front steps of the courthouse. He characterized Antonio Saenz as a "profoundly deviant individual" who had yet to grasp the gravity of his situation. He suggested that the case represented the grisly alchemy of gang activity and drug addiction, plagues that too often transformed young American men into "soulless predators." He assured reporters that investigators were continuing to gather information, and that they expected to recover the remains of Marcus Stallworth with or without the defendant's assistance.

SAENZ'S ATTORNEY, a federal public defender named Holly Roy, did not address the press. She slipped out a side door. Her superiors had selected Roy because she was considered a skilled negotiator. The defense wanted the matter resolved, not litigated.

Cases of this sort were virtually impossible to win at trial. Prosecutors had too much invested in the outcome, which represented a referendum on their ability to protect the public. The state would devote unlimited resources to affirm that ability. The media, meanwhile, would spend the weeks preceding the trial profitably polluting any jury that might be empaneled.

In a sense, it was Antonio Saenz who had disappeared. He had been replaced in the public imagination by the Death Valley Killer, a hunter hopped up on cocaine and blood oaths, who sold weapons and stole cars and mutilated upstanding white professors.

The state's version of events had massive holes. But Roy knew that her office—with its meager budget and enormous caseload—stood little chance of rebutting the physical evidence, or her client's own self-incriminating testimony. This is not to suggest that Roy did not advocate for her client. She listened to his story and sent notes along to the public defender's investigative team. She read the reports made available to her. At Saenz's request, she ordered a polygraph test, which he passed. The lead prosecutor dismissed it: "Sociopaths always ace polygraphs."

THE DAY AFTER the arraignment, Roy was summoned to a private conference room in the federal courthouse. She was surprised to find her client slumped at a table under the watchful eye of a US marshal. Across from him, the prosecution team sat in dark blue suits. One of them offered an awkward greeting.

"What's this all about?" Roy said. "You can't just dragoon my client without consulting me."

"You *are* being consulted," said a friendly voice behind her.

She turned and saw the US attorney, flanked by a pair of aides. He was an extraordinarily stout man, famous within legal circles for his bright bow ties and ruthless affability. In a few years, the Attorney General would appoint him a deputy, and charge him with spearheading the War on Drugs.

He toddled into the room. "Mr. Saenz, my name is Cecil Stubbs. I run the office that's conducting the prosecution of your case." His voice was high and piping, his face cherubic. "You may recognize these gentlemen from court. They work for me. Your attorney did not call this meeting. She is no doubt skeptical of my having done so. I must apologize to you, Ms. Roy. It was not my intention to stage an ambush. I merely wanted a chance to speak candidly. Is that amenable to you, Mr. Saenz?"

"Say what you got to say."

"Ms. Roy?"

Roy glanced at her client. He looked even thinner than at the arraignment; he smelled of the ammoniac disinfectant she had come to associate with the incarcerated.

Stubbs gestured for her to sit. "It is my understanding, Mr. Saenz, that you have no intention of changing your plea."

"I didn't do anything," Tony muttered.

"Understood."

"Whatever you think you got, you wouldn't be here if it was solid."

Stubbs took this in with a nod. His pink brow furrowed. "I will beg to differ with you on that, Mr. Saenz. Please listen carefully to what I'm about to say. Ours is an adversarial system. But that doesn't mean we can't listen to one another. Ms. Roy, I know by your reputation that you will make known any objections to my little soliloquy." Stubbs proceeded to the head of the table. "The first thing I must tell you is that we have investigators combing the area near where Mr. Stallworth's car was found. His corpse, in whatever condition, will be recovered. Once it is recovered, the offer set out today will be considered null and void. We believe that you did not act alone, Mr. Saenz. But in the absence of cooperation, you will be considered to have acted alone and the state will seek the death penalty. This decision is based on the nature of the crime and the fact that the victim was tortured before his murder."

"You're making up more shit to scare me," Saenz said.

"No effort is being made to scare you, Mr. Saenz. I'm merely apprising you of the government's intentions."

"Just a moment," Roy said. "Before we go any further, I'd like to speak to my client in private."

"Of course." Stubbs nodded, but his eyes remained fixed on Saenz. "Let me say a quick word about the blood evidence, which may inform your discussion. You should realize that forensic serology has become far more sophisticated in the past decade. We are no longer limited to testing for type. Serologists in this case looked at specific biochemical markers, the enzymes found on the red cell membrane. They are called PGMs. These are more like fingerprints that trace to an individual, not a group of individuals. Ms. Roy will have a chance to scrutinize the work of the FBI's lab. She will be able to tell you that this evidence is virtually unassailable. Your blood is in that car. The blood of Marcus Stallworth is in that car. They are comingled."

"Bullshit," Tony Saenz murmured.

Stubbs grinned, as if he had been paid an unfortunate compliment. "I would like to mention one other factor. If I may, Ms. Roy? As you know, there is a good deal of television coverage of this case. There will be more if and when we move to trial. Inevitably, reporters will begin to investigate your life more broadly. They will want to offer some history of the defendant's family. This would be a natural line of inquiry in any such case. But it is likely to be more intense given that your sister is a prominent witness for the prosecution."

Tony looked up at Stubbs; his face went red. "What're you talking about?"

Roy set a hand on her client's elbow, but he jerked it away. She regarded Stubbs. "Stop trying to bait my client."

"Nobody's baiting anyone," Stubbs responded. "I'm attempting to provide your client with the information he needs to assess our offer. I would be negligent if I failed to do so. And if you discouraged me from doing so." He fixed his bright stare on Tony again. "You need to realize that questions about your mother's status as an illegal resident of this country will arise, as a natural extension of your status. I say this not as a threat. As Ms. Roy knows, my office has nothing to do with the decisions made by the Immigration and Naturalization Service. Nor is it my intent to make race or ethnicity the subject of this case. Justice is blind to such considerations. But these are aspects of the indictment that are likely to excite public interest, particularly as it is presented in the media." Stubbs paused, a jolly man beleaguered by regret. "It is not only your actions for which you will be held accountable, Mr. Saenz. Your loved ones will be impacted by the decision you make."

Tony turned away from Stubbs and shook his head. He was struggling to abide by Stan Gill's advice, to muzzle his fear and keep himself quiet.

Roy didn't know quite how to respond. She felt obligated to defend her client from what was clearly an event staged to intimidate him. And yet she could not dispute what Stubbs had said. It was a delicate situation.

Stubbs motioned to one of his aides, who handed him a folder. "I won't keep you another minute. I simply wanted to convey to you the urgency of the situation from our perspective. Though you are not an American citizen, Mr. Saenz, we are extending to you the right to a trail by a jury of your peers. You are innocent until proven guilty. But given the gravity of the situation and—if I may be frank—my own feelings about capital punishment, I felt I should talk to you in person rather than relying on go-betweens." He studied the defendant a moment longer, then slid the folder across the table to Roy. "This is our final offer on a plea. You have a decision to make. I hope you will consult your conscience and heed your counsel."

Roy waited for the prosecutors to file out of the room, then nodded at the marshal, who posted himself outside the door.

The prosecution wanted full cooperation: a confession, accomplices, the location of the body. In exchange, they would reduce the charges to second-degree murder, kidnapping, and possession of a stolen vehicle. Maximum prison time twenty-two years; as little as thirteen, at the discretion of the judge. Roy was astonished at the offer. She had expected the prosecution to seek first-degree murder, life in prison.

She explained this to her client, that he could be out in a dozen years, that he was being given a chance. She didn't use that word but her tone made it clear.

"You think I did it," Tony said.

"I'm not saying that. But it's my job to represent your interests. I have to consider what it would mean to go to trial, what your chances would be, how to keep you—" Roy stopped herself short. She knew the word *alive* would alarm her client, so she settled on *safe*, though it was absurdly inadequate. Such was the trap Stubbs had set for her. She nearly snapped her pencil in consternation.

Neither one of them spoke for a minute. Tony refused to look up. His eyes had gone wet with rage. Roy sensed that she had lost his trust; or rather, that she had never had it in the first place. She was simply the stranger who pretended to be on his side. The good cop, the good lawyer.

"That shit he was saying—about my mom?"

"That's not a part of the case, Mr. Saenz."

"Is it true, though? They gonna deport her?"

"Not necessarily." What was she supposed to say? Was she supposed to lie? "They're giving you three days. Then this deal is off the table. You have to figure out what to do."

"*Me*? You're my fucking lawyer. You're supposed to help me."

"I'm trying to help you. I am. I need to see what evidence the state has. It's called a motion for discovery."

Tony sat there, sucking in his cheeks. Roy felt overrun by an unwelcome contempt. She wanted to ask this kid how the hell his blood wound up in the Jeep belonging to Marcus Stallworth, if he understood how easy it would be for society to end his life.

TONY'S BLOOD WAS not in the Stallworth Jeep. The "second sample" detected by the FBI's serology staff belonged to the alleged victim himself. It was the result of Stallworth's original effort to stage his disappearance, the night he had cut his palm too deeply and panicked and returned home, the night Lorena had found him in the bathroom downstairs and Stallworth had followed her outside and Tony had come upon them—the night in question.

The blood sample appeared chemically distinct to the FBI's blood experts because Stallworth had attempted to scrub it away the next morning with a cleanser that included bleach. The blood had then been trampled and scorched for the next ten weeks. The nature of the PGM markers—the enzymes found on the membranes of all those tiny red blood cells—had degraded.

Kathleen Blunt, the serologist charged with comparing these enzymes to the ones found in Tony's blood, knew none of this. Blunt was not a malign or incompetent person. But she was aware that her superiors were eager to find a relationship between the two samples. Nobody said this to her directly. Nobody had to. There was a particular climate that prevailed when the request was pressing.

The science of PGM markers was new and inexact. In just a few years, forensic serologists would turn to DNA testing, which provided a far more precise and durable genetic fingerprint.

PGM markers would be virtually forgotten in the annals of forensic investigation. But this was the method used in the case of Marcus Stallworth, and though the serologist could not establish a definitive match between the two samples, there was enough of an overlap in the enzyme cohort observed (67 percent) to merit her use of the phrase "significant statistical likelihood."

In fact, any two random blood samples would have showed an enzymatic overlap of 30 percent or so. Blunt had included these statistics in the initial draft of her report. But her supervisor—after consulting with the special agent in charge of the FBI's Sacramento office—deemed this contextual information immaterial to her ultimate conclusions.

Blunt would have detailed all this in court, if a skilled trial attorney had cross-examined her, someone like Stan Gill. Gill also would have questioned how the suspect could have engaged in a dispute violent enough to leave the blood of both participants' in the vehicle without also leaving behind additional physical evidence, such as fragments of skin or clothing or hairs.

Finally, Gill might have noted another curious discrepancy, one buried in the serologist's preliminary notes, and excluded from her final report. Both blood samples taken from the Stallworth Jeep were listed as O+. The blood drawn from Antonio Saenz for his naval drug test sample was listed only as type O.

His blood type was, in fact, O-.

WITH THE TRANSFER of the case to federal jurisdiction came a flurry of activity. Agents from the FBI and the US attorney's office formally took over the investigation and fanned out across Sacramento, Fresno, and Barstow. A retinue from the Army Corps of Engineers was on standby to hunt for and disinter the remains of Marcus Stallworth, should new information emerge.

US marshals transported Antonio Saenz to the federal lockup facility, and his public defender arranged for a meeting between the defendant and his family. This took some negotiation, because Graciela Saenz believed she would be deported the moment she left the church basement where she had sought refuge.

Eventually, Graciela submitted to a formal interview with a young FBI interrogator named Maria Diaz in the basement of the federal building. Graciela wept silently, brushing the tears away. Antonio had never been able to focus in school, she told Diaz. He had gotten in trouble as a teenager, but joining the navy had taught him discipline. He was a child who needed discipline, a follower, not a leader. She was unaware, until recently, that he had been discharged for drug use. She knew her daughter had visited the Stallworth home. She had met the mother, who reminded her of Nancy Reagan. She did remember Lorena calling late one night, perhaps in August, and that Tony had gone to pick her up. But she knew nothing else about the family.

"I'm sure I appear quite naïve to you," Graciela said. "Mothers always make themselves a little blind to keep their hairs from turning white. But I know my children. Antonio is like his father. He talks, but he's a coward. He might be able to fire a missile through the ocean, but he could not kill a man as the television describes." At the conclusion of the interview, she asked Diaz to pray with her.

GRACIELA JOINED HER daughter in the lobby. Tony, they learned, was being housed in the building right next door. A marshal escorted them to the federal lockup and led them into a small room with vending machines. Tony sat at a table bolted to the floor, in shackles. Graciela couldn't see his body inside his jumpsuit; plum-colored patches stood out beneath his eyes. The marshal moved to another table to allow the family privacy. The conversation was being videotaped anyway.

Graciela embraced her son. "You're not eating," she whispered, in Spanish. "I can feel your ribs."

"I'm eating," he murmured.

She turned to Lorena, hovering behind her. "Come hug your brother!"

Lorena came forward and the two exchanged a hesitant embrace. Graciela took notice. "What's going on here?" she said. "My God. I won't have the two of you fighting at a time like this. We have to stick together as a family."

Tony took his mother's hands in his own. "This whole thing is a mistake. The police messed up. We just have to be patient and the truth will come out. In the meantime, you need a lawyer. Don't talk to anyone until you get a lawyer. Cops will twist up what you say."

"I have to cooperate," Graciela said. "You know the situation."

Tony's mind flashed to the fat prosecutor, Stubbs, the threat he had issued. "That's *why* you need a lawyer," he said. "Talk to my public defender. She can tell you what to do. Holly Roy. She works on the third floor of this building. Otherwise, they're going to try to scare us into doing something stupid." He looked at Lorena. "Isn't that right, little sister?"

"I didn't do anything." Lorena protested. She was crying now, in the same unobtrusive way as her mother. "They showed up at our house, Tony. At my work."

"Who showed up?" Graciela said.

"The police," Tony snapped. "She talked to the fucking police."

Her mother turned and stared at Lorena, who was too ashamed to look up.

"Is that true, *mija*?"

"She's a witness for the fucking prosecution, Mama. How's that for the family sticking together?"

"I just told them the truth." But Lorena knew she had gone well beyond the truth with Jenny Stallworth. She had twirled her brother's crimes like a bright cape around her own dull life. She kept trying to apologize to Tony. The words choked her.

"Okay," Tony said. "Calm down. We'll get through this shit."

Graciela began to sway; the air in the room felt too close, too thin, as if she couldn't get enough of it to remain upright. Her eyes drifted to the vending machines, the bright lettering of the candy bars. Long ago, her children had pleaded with her to buy them something sweet from the machines in the basement of the hospital. They had visited her at work back then, to spend time on her lunch break, two bus rides and six more blocks, Antonio a grim little soldier, leading his sister by the hand through the bright chaos of the lobby. A bar of chocolate had been enough to make them happy back then. She should have relented more often.

Tony reached over to support her; she had apparently fainted. He tried to get up to get her some water from the fountain, but he was shackled to the table. Her son was shackled to a table. The big marshal brought a cup of water and Lorena wet a paper towel and Tony held it to his mother's brow. "I'm sorry, Mama. I should have told you about the navy. I messed that up. But the rest of this, about Stallworth, whatever you're hearing, it's a frame-up. The cops are trying to make a case. I swear to God."

Graciela kissed her son on the forehead. It was the first time in years. "You don't have to answer to me, *mijo*. You have to answer to God."

"He didn't do it," Lorena said. She had settled on the other side of her mother, so that the three were pressed together on the tiny bench, fused into a single unit of misery. "Mr. Stallworth ran away. He planned it all out."

"How do you know this?" Graciela said.

"I saw his maps," Lorena said.

"Then tell *that* to the goddamn police," Tony said, his voice rising again.

"I did tell them!"

Graciela set her hand on her son's arm. His wrists were bruised from the handcuffs and so so thin. She wanted to buy him something from the vending machine, anything he wanted, but she knew he wouldn't take it. It was too late.

"I told them everything," Lorena sobbed.

"Well, tell them again," Tony said, more quietly. "Make them believe, *hermanita*. Because it sure as fuck didn't stick the first time."

IN HER FIFTEEN years as a US resident, Graciela Saenz had been detained by the Immigration and Naturalization Service only once. It had happened in the hectic months after her husband left, when she took a job in a basement factory, attaching beaded eyes to plastic dolls. An INS officer walked in and calmly explained that everyone present was under arrest. This led to a bus ride and several hours in detention. She pleaded with every agent who passed by the cell. During her intake interview, she grew hysterical. She had a four-year-old at home, who was being watched by her brother, age eight. The children were expecting her home. They weren't safe without her.

"What kind of mother does that?" asked the agent, who was herself a mother.

"Have mercy on me," Graciela whispered. "I beg of you."

She was led back to her cell, where she kneeled in prayer. An hour later, with no explanation, she was sent home with a summons to appear in six months. It was as if the US government had taken a look at the state of her life and decided such ruin was beyond their jurisdiction. Or perhaps her prayers had been answered. "The *migra* don't care about your kids," her cousin told her. "They just get a list from the governor of which businesses to raid."

Still, the words of the woman agent haunted her: What kind of mother *was* she? Graciela was much more careful after that. She held out for jobs she knew to be safe, where she had a referral. She avoided public spaces where police might have reason to appear, abstained from parties and rides in cars. She began to feel, also, that she would have to take a tougher line with her children, especially Tony, who had no papers.

She wanted—perhaps needed—her children to succeed, to make lives that would transport them beyond the reach of calamity and justify the decision made to bring them to America. She needed them to be responsible, to get themselves to school and back, to keep their heads down and do the work. When Tony began to act out, she told herself it was because she had been too soft with him.

She could see now that it was just the opposite: she had been too hard on her children. She had stifled tenderness to instill obedience and her babies had turned away from her, into lives where she could no longer reach them.

Graciela understood, too, why the rest of her family had stayed in Honduras, with its poverty and corruption. At least there you had family, someone to look after the young ones, traditions that kept you bound together. America was a place where everyone wanted more and where everyone wound up apart.

THESE WERE HER thoughts as she rode the elevator down to the third floor of the federal building and watched her daughter explain their circumstance to the secretary at the public defender's office, who smiled and nodded, then sent them away with a business card.

Graciela believed Tony was innocent. But she accepted that she didn't know him well enough to say for sure. That was what troubled her most, beyond the legal risks—the distance between all of them, the enormity of the deception within her own family. Tony had tried to make something of himself, to recast his weakness into strength. Perhaps the pressure had been too much and, like a bomb, he had exploded.

And what of Lorena? She had always been a good child, quiet and serious. Her body had grown into womanhood too early, and the men of the neighborhood had taken note. She knew Lorena put on makeup at school, and tucked her hems, and walked in a different way. Graciela wasn't a fool.

That was why she had been happy to see Lorena make friends with the Stallworth girl. It meant she was spending time with a good family, coming out of her shell in a safe place. She had seemed more assured, watching her weight, cutting back on the hair spray. She returned home with fancy clothes from second-hand shops, which she washed and pressed herself.

But Graciela knew her daughter had been hiding things, too. There was a caginess about her now, one that traced back to her friendship with Jenny Stallworth. Her life had become more covert. There were clues left scattered about: missing cigarettes, borrowed cassette tapes, a notebook filled with long passages devoted to the wonders of scorpions, even an amulet with a tiny golden scorpion inside. When Graciela asked about this last item, Lorena blushed. "I got that for Tony. He's a Scorpio, right?"

THE TV CREWS had decamped at last, so they were able to return to the apartment, and Graciela ran to the market and made *baleadas* with fatty pork for supper, because those had been Lorena's favorite, in the days before she worried about zits and extra pounds. Neither of them ate. Before she could escape to her room, Graciela regarded her daughter. "Why didn't you tell me police had come here, *mija*?"

"I didn't want you to worry."

"They came to your work, too?"

"It was about Mr. Stallworth at first, not Tony."

"You said that man ran away. Why would you say such a thing?"

"I saw things in his office."

"What were you doing in his office?"

Lorena sighed at her own foolishness. "I got interested in scorpions. That's what he studies. I shouldn't have gone down there."

"It makes no sense," Graciela said. "Why would any man do such a thing?"

"Men leave their families all the time," Lorena murmured. For a moment neither of them spoke, then Lorena added, "I don't think the Stallworths were happy."

"What makes you say that?"

"Jenny used to say it all the time."

Graciela narrowed her eyes. "But somehow Tony got mixed up in all this. It makes me ask what else I don't know, Lorena."

The girl shifted in her seat. "Let's just do what he said, Mama. We can get a lawyer. The public defender will help us." She got up to fetch the card.

Graciela followed her daughter down the short hall to the room she had once shared with Tony. Her eyes settled on a shiny object that lay on the dresser, amid the pencil erasers and hair ties. It was the amulet she was going to give to Tony, the tiny scorpion lodged in its casket of amber. She remembered the saying her grandmother had uttered when she checked her shoes before church, flipping them over to make sure no scorpions had climbed inside: *El escorpión caza mientras el resto de nosotros soñamos. Por eso conoce todos los secretos del mundo.*

The scorpion hunts while the rest of us dream. That's why he knows all the secrets of the world.

AFTER BEING RELIEVED of his duty as Antonio Saenz's minder, Nando Reyes returned to his Fresno substation with no expectation that he would play any further role in the case. But a few days later, he received a strange call from one of his patrolmen. The officer had booked a local transient by the name of Winnifred Thoms into the Fresno jail for possession and attempted sale of a controlled substance. While awaiting transport, Winnie spotted a familiar face on the television hung overhead to keep prisoners pacified. He began boasting that he had recently partied with the young man being hailed as the Death Valley Killer. "That kid ain't hard enough to kick a kitten," he announced.

Nando knew the feds would want to interview Winnie. But he figured there was no harm in their having a preliminary chat. The two men had history, after all. Winnie had made himself useful in a couple of drug busts. He was a thief and a liar, like all addicts, but he also recognized the power Nando held and didn't dare bullshit him. This made him a useful informant.

Winnie was ebullient when a deputy pulled him out of lockup. "Told you motherfuckers they got the wrong guy," he crowed. The deputy led him to a private cell in back, where Nando was waiting.

"If it isn't Minnesota Fats."

"Winnifred. Good to have you back in our humble facility."

"I didn't do shit."

"You never do."

"What's going on, boss?"

"I wanna buy some coke."

"It's not a weight-loss product."

Nando winked. "I'm told your stash just got popped, anyway."

"It wasn't my shit, man. I got set up."

"Calm down. I just want to have a little parlay about Antonio Saenz."

"Who?"

"The Death Valley Killer."

Winnie perked up. "I can tell you a story about that, boss. But I'd like to know what my incentible is."

"Your incentible? Your incentible is that you're under arrest for possession and attempted sale. Given your lengthy record of coking up the youth of south Fresno, you're just the kind of degenerate who would make an ideal poster boy for our new anti-drug campaign. How's a five spot at Folsom sound?"

"Folsom?"

"Better yet: San Quentin. Get you some beachfront property. They love strung-out white boys up there."

Winnie wasn't smiling anymore.

"Just tell me everything you know about Saenz, Winnifred."

"I partied with him a few weeks back, down at the Vagabond. This girl Trina said she made a new friend who was looking for a good time. That's it. End of story."

Nando shook his head. "I don't think I made myself clear. This kid is on the TV with his own graphic, okay? He's charged with murder. That murder happened the same weekend you were gobbling narcotics with him. This county is crawling with FBI who believe he had help. Do the math here, Winnie. You're a person of interest now, okay? Take a deep breath and try again. And this time, don't leave anything out, not one fucking detail, or I'll toss your ass to the feds and let them decide which penitentiary would look best on your resume."

Winnie began raking at his wispy beard. "We messed that kid up a little. But that's it." The rest of the story poured out: how Trina called him for supplies, how they got him high, sent him out to get more cash, and rolled him.

"What's 'rolled' mean?"

"Fed him some rum and a lude, just enough to black him out."

"He didn't have any help?"

"Come on, man. Do I look like I thug people up?"

"He had a cut on his head."

"He hit it on the bed frame. That's what Trina told me. I was in the bathroom, but I did hear, like, a thump. He was bleeding all over the place. You know how head wounds are. I said, 'What the fuck, Trin?' She said, 'What a fucking lightweight.' We laughed about it for a while." Winnie paused. "I guess you had to be there."

"Then what?"

"We took his wallet and did a little shopping."

Nando had Winnie tell the whole story again: when Winnie showed up, what drugs they did, what time Saenz went out to get more cash, how long he was gone, when he blacked out, the room number, the layout of the room, where and how Saenz had fallen, everything they bought with his credit cards. He worked the details for two hours, feeding Winnie Pepsi and Pop-Tarts to keep him sharp. It was what you had to do with dopers, take them through the events again and again, to see what other details might bubble up from the mush of their memory banks.

At last, Nando shut his notebook.

"What happens now?" Winnie said.

"You keep your fucking mouth shut until someone asks you to open it."

"I mean about my legal situation."

Nando laughed. He bellowed out to his deputy in Spanish. "Okay, we made love for long enough. You can have this pubic hair back."

NANDO KNEW THE proper procedure would be to inform his supervisor, who would turn his notes over to the FBI. But he was now even more troubled by the case. As it had been presented, the suspect had abducted Stallworth on Friday, October 23, presumably in Sacramento. He had then driven Stallworth's vehicle south, stopping at a Fresno cash hut between 3:00 and 5:00 p.m., where he ordered Stallworth to withdraw $5,000. Sometime later—it remained unclear when—Saenz and Stallworth had a physical altercation. And still later, Saenz, acting alone or with others, disposed of the body and abandoned the vehicle outside Barstow.

Winnie's story blew up that timeline. Saenz would have had to abduct Stallworth and murder him, then spend the rest of the day and night partying. Either that, or he had tied Stallworth up, or stashed his body, before breezing over to that parking lot where he met Trina. Was Antonio Saenz a criminal of sufficient expertise to pull off any of this?

Winnie's story explained several other incriminating details. Such as why Saenz was reluctant to confess to Guerrero where he'd been on October 23 and 24, and why he had a cut on his head. It also clarified, possibly, why his own credit cards had been used for a buying spree, hours after his commission of a lethal robbery. There was always a chance that Winnie had been in on the scheme. But why would he draw attention to his involvement?

Nando tracked down the number for Trina's probation officer, which led him to Trina herself. She sat in an IHOP clawing at her wrists and reluctantly confirmed Winnie's account, right down to the quaalude and the theft. "Why do you care so much about that poor kid?" she asked at one point. "Did someone dust him or something?"

Then it was over to the Vagabond, where the manager owed him a few favors. He even called up the maid who was on duty that night. Like most of his staff, she was undocumented, and thus obliged to cooperate. She provided a positive ID of Antonio

Saenz and admitted to finding him in *rough shape* a couple of Saturdays ago. She led Nando to the room and let him inside. "They'd been drinking a lot and doing all that sort of thing," the woman explained. "The boy was lying here."

"Did it look like someone beat him up?"

"No. He hit his head. There, I think." She pointed to a spot on the bed frame with a large dent. Just below, the yellow shag carpet had streaks of brown. "The boy opened his eyes for a second when I came in, then went right back to sleep. I think maybe he had a concussion. I told the manager. He said to clean the room anyway."

"Did you?"

"Of course. It's my job. I just cleaned around him."

"He didn't get up?"

"He must have, eventually. I left at four and he was still in there, sleeping it off. They charge by the hour, you know."

That was the thing about motels like the Vagabond: the rooms were all, to some degree or another, crime scenes.

WOULD THE FBI ever interview Winnie and Trina? Nando doubted it. Agents pursued leads that helped them make the charge, not unmake it. Let the defense chase down the alibis, if they had the means. So he wrote up his notes and had a currier deliver them to Guerrero. He wanted his cousin to hear what he'd learned, firsthand: that Winnie's story had checked out, all of it, right down to the credit card receipts.

Guerrero called him the next morning. "What the fuck, Nando. Does anybody else know what you been up to?"

"Old habits."

"Look, it's the feds' party now. They got me typing up statements, then I go back to rescuing kittens."

"Something's off, man."

Guerrero glanced at the stack of interviews he'd just finished transcribing. A vision of Lorena's face reared up before him; its calm defiance infuriated him. "They got blood in the car. That's all Hooks wants to hear about. You want to make trouble, get yourself busted down to Traffic, go ahead. But keep me out of it."

Nando said nothing for a few seconds. Then, almost with regret, he murmured, "You made the arrest, *primo*. You're in it for life."

GUERRERO FULLY INTENDED to turn his handiwork over to Hooks. But he kept hearing the girl's implacable claim: *I can prove it*. He took one last spin through her statements, zeroing in on the story she'd told in the final interview, about finding Stallworth in the bathroom across from his office, covered in blood.

He swung by the Stallworth home the next morning, early. It was still unmistakable, but upon closer inspection, the mansion looked more ragged. The mint-green paint had cracked near the foundation, and the front lawn showed weeds. He rang the doorbell and saw a light flick on upstairs. After a minute, he heard footsteps and a meek voice asked, through the door, who was there. The accent was the same as his. Guerrero introduced himself as a police officer who'd been sent out to make sure everyone was doing okay.

"Can you hold your badge up to the peephole, please?"

She opened the door but not in a way that would allow him to enter.

"Is the señora here?" he asked in Spanish.

"Oh no. She and the children left a few days ago."

"Do you know where they went?"

"Out of town for a few days, to get away from all this. She said she would call."

"And you are?"

"Lucia."

"Lucia what?"

"Sanchez."

"May I come in, Lucia?"

She moved aside, apprehensively. Lucia was older than most domestics, perhaps in her fifties. She wore curlers and an elegant house robe that reached the floor, apparently on loan from her employer.

"I'm sorry, Officer. I get so scared."

"Of what?"

"I don't know. Maybe I'm being superstitious. But the boy who killed the señor, he found his way to this house, didn't he? They said on the TV that he might have friends in the gangs."

"Have you seen anyone suspicious?"

"I guess not." With the toe of her slipper she absently straightened the area rug Guerrero had trod upon. She had a manner he recognized from his own mother, a kind of borrowed grandiosity that derived from working for an upper-class family.

"Have any other police officers come by to talk to you?"

"To me? Why?"

"You work for the Stallworths, don't you?"

"Not really." Lucia shifted nervously. "I used to work for them. But I took some other jobs. Anyway, it's not important. Everything is okay here."

"I'd like to take a quick look downstairs," Guerrero said. "I promised I'd just do a sweep of the utilities. Do you know your way around down there?"

Lucia shook her head.

"You never went downstairs?"

"That was Mr. Stallworth's office."

"I'll just take a minute."

The bathroom was spotless, conspicuously so, and smelled of disinfectant. Guerrero shut the door and hung a towel across the window to darken the room, then sprayed luminol and oxidant on everything in sight. He couldn't see anything at first. But as his eyes adjusted, specks of blue appeared beneath the sink and toilet, and in the grooves of the tile at the base of the shower—the places hardest to reach. He sprayed in the hall outside the bathroom: more droplets. Working a hunch, he checked the utility closet down the hall. The pattern was unmistakable: spatters and streaks around the bucket and mop, ghosts of blood. He peeked into Mr. Stallworth's office and was stunned to find that it had been cleared out entirely, the desk, the file cabinet, everything.

LUCIA WAS WAITING at the top of the stairs. She had put on her day clothes and her day face: soft blue eye shadow, lipstick a few shades too bright, the same as his mom.

"All good," Guerrero said.

"Thank you, Officer. It was kind of you to come by." She glanced at the front door. But Guerrero walked into the living room. The family photos had vanished, and there was dust on the sill of the bay window.

"Do you know when the señora will be coming back?"

"Who can say? In such a situation."

"When's the last time you spoke to her, anyway?"

"A few days."

"Well, you can tell her everything is okay, Lucia. But listen: Do you have something to drink, maybe? The air is full of dust down there."

"Of course," Lucia said miserably.

Guerrero followed her into the kitchen.

"Is water okay? Or juice?"

"Coffee would be better, if you have it."

Her jaw bunched as she put on a kettle.

From overhead came the faint whine of bedsprings, then feet coming to rest, as gently as possible, on the floor. Lucia Sanchez had a guest. She glanced at Guerrero, then down at the floor, her cheeks flushing.

"That's just a cousin of mine. He needed a place to stay for the night."

"It's okay, Lucia. That can be our secret."

"I just don't like staying here alone. There's a tragedy hanging over this house, you know?" The kettle began to shriek and Lucia busied herself making him coffee. "I need to get off to work. I have another house to clean this morning."

"I'm sure Mrs. Stallworth would understand," Guerrero said. "I imagine she was a good employer."

"Of course. It's her I feel the worst for, the poor thing. Did you know her hair turned gray overnight? One day she had all that lovely blond hair, the next it was the color of ashes."

Lucia handed him his coffee. "Milk? Sugar?"

He shook his head.

"Can I ask you something, Officer? What will happen next? With the killer, I mean? On the TV, they said there would be a trial. And then if he was guilty, they would put him in the electric chair. He deserves it. I know that. But still." She curled away for a moment. "He's the same age as my son, you see."

"I don't think it will come to that. But I've been wrong before." He dipped his chin. "Why did you stop working for the Stallworths, anyway?"

"The kids were getting older. Maybe they wanted to cut back on expenses." She quickly amended herself. "I don't really know."

"You don't have to worry about talking to me," Guerrero said. "I'm not here to investigate anything. The FBI is doing all that now. I'm just curious. My mom did the same work, you know. She said when you found a good family you had to stick with them. Ride them like a donkey to the river."

Lucia laughed. "It's true. Some of my friends get stuck with the bad ones. Cheap. Or they expect you to work on the Lord's day. Or teach the little ones Spanish. Or the fathers have those busy hands. Thankfully, I'm an old lady now."

"You're still pretty enough to receive visitors." Guerrero rolled his eyes toward the ceiling and grinned. He wasn't much of a flirt, but Lucia didn't look displeased.

"They were a decent family, anyway. So good-looking! And such a home. All this light! They just ran short on money. I thought a professor would earn a lot. But I guess they don't pay so much to study those disgusting creatures."

"Scorpions?"

She made a face. "He would bring them home in little plastic cans. You could hear them rattling around in his pockets like maracas." Lucia shivered. "Mrs. Stallworth wouldn't let him bring them upstairs, thanks to God. He had a place for them, like an aquarium with sand. She made him get rid of that, too."

"Did they fight?"

"Oh no," Lucia said quickly. "Not that I saw. They were just very different. The señora was social, you see. She did a lot of volunteer work. She could have been working, too, you know. She used to sell houses. She sold a house to Nancy Reagan once."

"Imagine that."

"It was when Mrs. Reagan was the wife of the governor. The señora didn't like to brag about it. But they took a photo together. It's here somewhere."

"What was he like?"

"Very private. Quiet. Handsome, too, behind those big glasses."

"Did he treat you with respect?"

"Oh yes. He was a gentleman. He liked to speak Spanish to me."

"He spoke Spanish?"

"Not exactly. He was learning, I guess." She did an imitation of his gringo Spanish and they both laughed.

"I wouldn't figure they had any problems with money in a house like this."

"Oh, you can always see how it is. They cut back on the gardener, the pool man. The steak becomes hamburger meat. The flowers come from the garden. Then they don't need as many cleaning days. They almost took out another mortgage on the house a few years ago. Anyway, none of that matters now," Lucia said.

"Did you tell the investigators this?"

Lucia looked perplexed. "Like I said, I didn't work for the señora when all this happened."

"I guess not." Guerrero swirled his mug. "This was delicious. Thank you. I should let you get on with your day." Then, as if it had just occurred to him and was of no great importance, he asked, "Who cleaned out Mr. Stallworth's office anyway?"

"The officer with the pointy mustache. I don't know his name."

Guerrero had to conceal his alarm. "Van Dyke?"

"Yes, he was the one helping her manage things."

"But why get rid of everything?"

"It's haunted now, isn't it? The whole place. At least for her." Lucia whisked his mug off the counter and into the sink. Then she straightened up, as if she meant now, after all the small talk, to set the record straight. "I will tell you one thing, Officer Guerrero: they should never have let that girl into this house."

"Who?"

"The little sister. Lo, she called herself. She made friends with Jenny. That's how he targeted Mr. Stallworth in the first place. I never trusted her."

"Why not?"

"She had stars in her eyes. You could see it from the start. A girl like that, riding her bike all the way from Fruitridge. She was like a peasant walking into a palace."

"Dazzled?"

"It was more, you know, there's a certain kind of girl who makes trouble."

"What sort of trouble?"

"She used to look at the señor in a certain way. You know what I mean."

"Did the señor look back?"

"Of course not!" Lucia snapped. "Oh, you were joking, weren't you? I see. No, he stayed away from her. But she was always lurking around, kind of spying on him. She used to sneak downstairs to his office. One night, she convinced Glen and Jenny to swim naked in the pool. I saw it myself! I told Mrs. Stallworth, but she would always make excuses. 'Think about the life she's led, Lucia. She's got no father. Her mother is at work all the time. We can be a good influence.' The señora was like that—too trusting. Then, after Mr. Stallworth moved downstairs—"

"He moved downstairs?"

"Just for a few weeks over the summer. They made up. But it was something about that girl. I'm telling you, she brought a bad spirit into this house. I know that sounds like superstition, but now you see how it is, Officer. Look at what her brother did in the end. He ruined a whole family."

GUERRERO DROVE BACK to office and dug out the embossed business card of Royce Van Dyke; it still smelled of his cologne. He left three messages with the answering service. Van Dyke called back late in the day. "I'm sorry, Mr. Gutierrez. I've dealt with a lot of inquiries on this case, for obvious reasons—"

"It's Guerrero. Officer Guerrero."

"Of course. Congratulations are in order. I saw you on TV."

"Thanks. I figured I might check in on the Stallworths. Make sure they're okay."

"Not necessary. Rosemary took the kids out of town for a few days."

"Do the prosecutors know she left?"

Van Dyke exhaled loudly, impatiently. "Of course. I'm sure nobody blames her, given the situation. Anyway, your concern is noted, Officer. Now, if you don't mind—"

"Actually, I wanted to ask *you* something. Do you know who did the deep clean on the bathroom in the Stallworth basement?"

"What are you talking about?"

"I understand you also helped Rosemary straighten up the house. Did you dispose of items in his office, too?"

After a moment of hesitation, Van Dyke released a trill of laughter. "Would you like to put me under oath, Officer Guerrero?"

"I'm just trying to figure out the nature of your involvement with the Stallworth family."

"I might ask you the same thing," Van Dyke replied. "I thought you were calling out of concern for the victim's family. But I see now that you have some other agenda."

Guerrero envisioned him leaning back in a plush leather chair, smoothing his mustache. "Answer my questions, please."

"You just helped put a monster behind bars. You should be bucking for a promotion."

"Thanks for the career tip. But I've got a better idea. Why don't you come down to the station? I get the feeling you'd be more forthcoming in that setting."

"I assume you're acting at the direction of your superior officer," Van Dyke shot back. "Is that right?" His tone was almost mocking.

Guerrero paused.

"I'm happy to call Captain Hooks myself. Shall I? I imagine Maurice would be fascinated to know what you're up to."

Before Guerrero could muster a response, he heard a click, then a dial tone. He stared at the receiver. He felt sure Van Dyke was bluffing but he had no idea what the bluff meant.

PEDRO GUERRERO WAS not yet convinced of Antonio Saenz's innocence. To believe this, he would have had to ignore too much evidence. It would be more accurate to say that he was unnerved. Each new revelation chipped away at the Theory of the Case that had prevailed when he arrested Antonio Saenz. The testimony of those who had partied with Saenz. The verification of Lorena's claims. The darkening portrait of the Stallworth marriage itself. He knew blood never lied. And yet he had trouble assembling the facts of the case into a coherent narrative. There were too many gaps.

Had Guerrero been a homicide detective, had there been less institutional pressure for an arrest, had this been a different era, he might have been able to request a copy of the serology report from the FBI, might have found some way to root out the elisions and tricks of language that made probability sound like incontrovertible fact. He might even have discovered the glaring discrepancy between O+ and O-.

But Guerrero was living in Sacramento, in the fall of 1981, the season of the Death Valley Killer. He steered his beater Buick back to the station with a knot in his gut and only a vague sense of what to do next. He would compile his notes and present them to Hooks, maybe even Chief Ellis. They would want to know about the supplemental evidence. He could hear Nando in his ear. *You're driving in the wrong direction, primo.*

He cruised past the visitor parking lot, which was clogged with news vans. They spilled out onto Capitol Avenue, where reporters were stiffening their $100 haircuts with cans of Aqua Net, readying for their stand-ups. Inside the lobby of the admin building, a mob of reporters hurled questions at the public affairs staffers. Guerrero saw Jolley and Hooks huddled with a couple of Ellis's deputies, everyone wearing grins. Jolley spotted him and elbowed Hooks, who flashed a thumbs-up.

"What's going on, Doug?" Guerrero called out.

"You didn't hear yet, little man? Saenz pleaded out."

"What?"

"Sang like Tweety Bird. The chief's doing a presser in a few. Just wants to make these jackals sweat their balls a little." Jolley gestured at the reporters. "Hey, Guerrero, how about a smile? You arrested the little fuck. They're gonna put your face on a trading card."

IN FIVE DAYS of custody, Antonio Saenz had been booked into four different facilities. He had eaten almost nothing and barely slept. His first lawyer, the old guy Peña hired for him, had been replaced by a public defender he didn't trust. He grasped the basic situation; the cops had framed him. But he didn't understand why his sister had helped them, or how his blood had been found in the vehicle of a man he barely knew. There was the additional mystery of his sudden notoriety, the swarm of armed guards and TV cameras and reporters that jostled around him as he was marched to and from court. Such moments triggered an uncanny sensation: he was a boy again, being led away from home, into a life of certain doom.

Most of all, Tony felt a crushing sense of betrayal. The episode at the Vagabond Motel had been a wake-up call. To wind up in a place like that, with a ribbon of blood tracing his scalp, a hammering headache, his wallet gone, and only scattered memories of the preceding events—such a circumstance felt, to him, at age nineteen, like the culmination of every bad decision he had made in his brief life, all the times he had trusted the wrong people, taken the wrong drugs, lunged for joy and landed in despair.

This was why he had reached out to Peña; he needed help, a guy who understood his limitations, who didn't fuck around. He had taken a job that looked sketchy from the outside but was, for him, a first step on the path to getting right. Even the gun bust Peña had engineered was a vital lesson. Remain loyal and he'd bail you out.

What sleep Antonio managed was marred by dreams that caused him to wake in a sweat, his heart thudding. Surveillance cameras mounted in his cell had captured footage of him during these events, flailing, shrieking, *"Déjalo en paz!" Leave him alone!* Antonio couldn't remember what he had dreamed, but the panic was familiar. He had suffered the same night terrors as a child.

In this reduced state, the suspect was transported to a room on the top floor of the federal lockup and remanded to the custody of a baby-faced FBI agent, who rose from his seat and nodded at him amiably. "Mr. Saenz, my name is Joel Salcido." It took Tony a moment to recognize that the man meant to shake hands with him. "I won't say pleasure to meet you. We both know that would be bullshit." Salcido's smile was more like a wince. "Let's see if we can figure a way out of this mess."

TONY UNDERSTOOD WHAT was happening, that he was going to be questioned. But the room didn't look like an interrogation cell. Usually, they stuck you behind a table in the corner, facing away from the door. In this case, the table was in the middle of the room and his seat faced a full-length window that overlooked the capitol building. Sun beat down on the fancy columns of the portico, the beams disappearing into the black dome, as if captured.

Salcido didn't look much like a federal agent. He was Hispanic, for one thing, one of those pale Mexicans with eyes that had green in them, which meant Spanish blood. He wore a sweater vest, not a suit, and radiated the kind of eager goodwill that Tony recognized from the youth pastors in his mother's church, the guys who were always hauling out their Bibles to recruit some fresh souls.

"You FBI or what?"

"Special agent," Salcido said. "That's my official title."

"How come you don't got a partner? Someone to play bad cop?"

Salcido shrugged.

"I got a right to my attorney anyway."

"You certainly do, Mr. Saenz." Salcido opened the folder in front of him and scanned the top sheet. "Miss . . . Roy. I can have her up here in ten minutes, if that's how you want to do it." He gestured to the phone at his elbow, as if to tender the offer. "My guess is she's trying to plead you out. Which means keeping you quiet so you don't screw up the deal."

"You want the same thing," Tony said. "For me to say I did it, so everyone can call it a day."

Salcido stared at Tony. "I know you did a hitch in the navy. I served four years in the army. It's the same mentality: cover your ass. Maybe that's what the government is trying to do, sweep this case under the rug. I can promise you one thing, Mr. Saenz: I don't want you lying. That's not why I flew out here. That's not my job."

"What's your job?"

"To figure out how the hell we got here. But you got no reason to trust me, Mr. Saenz. And you do have the indisputable legal right to remain silent until you have a lawyer present. So if you want me to call Miss Roy, say the word." Salcido, who had studied drama as an undergraduate, who understood the gestural tools at his disposal, looked to the phone again and set his hand down on the receiver.

Tony didn't buy the gambit. He knew he was being sweet-talked; the naval recruiter had coaxed him into his office with the same pop psychology. At the same time, he couldn't quite dispute the logic. Miss Roy *had* ordered him to keep his mouth shut. "What do you want from me?"

"I want you to prove you're innocent of these charges, Mr. Saenz."

"How do I do that?"

"By telling me the whole story, start to finish."

ONCE SUSPECTS START talking, they keep talking. This is the cardinal rule of interrogation. It redounds to a basic human compulsion: to be seen, heard, understood, perhaps even forgiven. All Joel Salcido had to do was ask rudimentary questions. When had Saenz returned to Sacramento from the navy? Under what circumstances had he come into contact with Marcus Stallworth? Where was he the weekend of the alleged abduction?

Salcido knew the answers to these questions already. But he was listening for the hidden clues, the story beneath the story. It went this way for a couple of hours. Salcido listened, nodded, said "right, right, okay." Mostly, he let Saenz vent.

Eventually, the sun started to drop down over the capitol, dragging a curtain of orange light behind it. Salcido sat back and stretched. "Okay. That's enough for now. You hungry? Let's get some food. What do you want? Can't imagine you're getting takeout in federal lockup."

Tony shrugged. Salcido was working him. He knew it was bullshit. But he *was* starving.

Salcido picked up the phone. "Yeah, we're almost done in here. Can we get some *comida* sent up? No, get takeout. What's close by? Okay, hold on." He turned to Tony. "You like tamales, pupusas, that kind of thing? Sure. Thanks." Ten minutes later, a marshal showed up with a bag full of pupusas, refried beans, garlicky *yuca frita*. Salvadoran food.

This was the same food he had eaten as a kid, back when his father was still living with them, before he ran off to Florida, or wherever the fuck he was. It was no mistake. FBI analysts had worked up a full psychological profile on Antonio Saenz. They knew his father was a Salvadoran immigrant who had abandoned the family when Saenz was nine. It was the reason they had dispatched Special Agent Salcido. He had a touch with young Hispanic subjects, a way of disarming them, playing the harmless uncle until it was time to get real.

SALCIDO KNEW SMALL talk would only make the kid wary, so he excused himself and let Saenz eat in private. He watched, via close-circuit camera, as the kid stared at the food warily, nibbled at a sliver of yucca, then allowed himself a bite of the pupusa. They did the *chicharrón* just the way he liked it, with little chunks of charred pork fat. He took another bite and sucked Coke from a big Styrofoam cup.

By the time they started up again, the blood had rushed to his belly and the windows were throbbing with the soft purple of twilight. Salcido called in a marshal to clear away the food. "Just a few more questions."

"I already told you everything I know," Tony said.

"I know. But I'm still confused." Salcido picked up a folder from the stack in front of him. "I got this report that tells me your blood was in Marcus Stallworth's jeep, Antonio. Your fingerprints, too. Something's not adding up. Now, I listened to

every word you spoke. That's why I'm here. To listen. But sometimes there's a distance between what we say and what someone else hears. So I want you to take a deep breath and listen to
what I heard. Okay?"

Tony looked down and nodded drowsily.

"The first thing, we got to be honest about this. You had a
drug problem, okay. We can't just ignore that. As we sit here
today, looking at the evidence, Antonio, we can't ignore that."
Salcido spoke softly and swiftly, as if issuing a reluctant but necessary verdict. "I know something about addiction. It makes
good people into liars. And we know you were still doing drugs
in Sacramento, because we talked to some of your friends. I'm
not judging you. I would have done the same thing. I *have* done
the same thing. But we gotta stick to the facts. I don't know if
you were on drugs when you drove your sister to the Stallworths. I don't even know if you had a gun, like she says. But
you were pissed. I feel the same way when I drive through a
place like that, with Porsches all over the place. You were driving, what, a Pinto?"

"Bobcat."

"Right. The Bobcat with the busted muffler. I'm not telling
you anything you don't know, Antonio. Your own sister doesn't
want you to get out of the car. She's afraid you'll make a scene,
right? You start messing around with the Jeep in the driveway.
Then the dad appears. And what's your reaction? You scurry
back to your beater. But why? Why not say hello? Why not say,
'Hi, I'm Lorena's brother, Antonio. I was just admiring your
Jeep, sir.'" Salcido shook his head. "Because you know what he's
thinking. You can see it in his eyes. *What's this coked-up spic
doing in front of my house? Talking to my daughter?* He's thinking the same thing as Lorena: you don't belong here."

"You're just making shit up now."

"What am I making up? That you burned rubber out of there?
That you were driving a stolen vehicle? Am I making up that

you warned your sister not to hang out with the Stallworths? Am I making up that Lorena called you a couple of weeks later, in the middle of the night, freaked out? That she begged you to pick her up? That you drove to that same house and saw Marcus Stallworth hugging on her? Your sister—fourteen years old. A kid. A dumb, dreamy kid. This little Mexican girl—"

"We're not Mexican."

"Course you're not. But we're talking about Stallworth. When he looks at your sister, all he sees—you have to excuse me for saying it like this, Antonio, but if we're gonna be honest—all he sees is a set of young tits and an easy mark. Okay? You knew exactly what was going on. Hell, *you were the one who warned her.* So now you do what any decent brother would: you defend her. You threaten the sick fuck—those are your words, Antonio. I happen to agree with them."

"And that's all I did," Tony said. He peered out the window, at the dusk seeping away. Soon, it would be impossible to tell what time it was.

"I wish that were the case, Antonio. I do. But we both know there's more to it than that. Because of the fingerprints. The blood."

"My prints got there cuz I touched the Jeep. I told you."

"That tells me you admired that Jeep, Antonio. It was something he had that you might take from him. Like he took your sister."

"My sister says the perv faked the whole thing. That's why you can't find a body. There is no body."

"Right," Salcido said. He was thumbing through his file. "Claimed Stallworth didn't love his wife. That she saw maps down in his office. I read her interviews. But you know what's odd, Antonio? Aside from the fact that nobody else ever saw these magic maps. Lorena never mentioned any of this until her *third* interview. Doesn't that seem weird to you? Two whole interviews and those facts just slipped her mind."

"Maybe she didn't know you guys were going to set me up."

"So we somehow got *your* blood into *Stallworth's* jeep. How, Antonio?"

"You tell me," Tony snarled. "You got all the answers."

"Okay." Salcido nodded slowly. "I'll to give you two scenarios. You tell me which one sounds more likely. The first scenario— and I'm being serious now—the first scenario is that someone did frame you up. Maybe it's the cops. Maybe it's someone you did wrong. Here's how that would have to work. First, they'd have to get ahold of your blood. Second, they'd have to know Marcus Stallworth was someone you might target. Third, they'd have to kidnap Stallworth and spill some of his blood in the front seat of his Jeep and mix it up with your blood. Then they'd have to make him disappear into thin air. I don't know how many enemies you have, Antonio. But that's a lot of work. Not saying it's impossible, but that's the only way your blood is getting in that vehicle. Unless something else happened."

Salcido leaned across the table. He had that handsome face, which Tony wanted to punch; and yet, confusingly, he also wanted Salcido's approval.

"You're not going to like this, Antonio. But I want to set out another possibility, based on what you told me. Because my job is to make sense of the evidence. That's my only job. I want you to do what I did: listen. Don't interrupt. Just listen, okay?"

Outside, the sky had gone black, the clouds snuffed out. The room in which they sat felt too bright against the darkness, like the set of a play. Tony was suddenly so tired as to feel drugged.

"We know you left Sacramento because you were getting caught up in the same stuff as before, the drugs. You wind up in Fresno. Change of scenery, fresh start, you know some guys down there. But you get yourself in a little trouble right away. The girl, Trina, her dealer Winnie. Some booze. Some coke. This new rock stuff that feels like rocket fuel in your brain. We know you needed money for the drugs. We know you went to that quick cash hut. Things get pretty out of control. At some point, you black out. When you come to, it's the next morning. You're trying to remember what happened the night before, but it's spotty. You've lost some hours. You're bleeding from the head, which means something violent happened. Trina and Winnie the Pooh are nowhere to be found. But here's something you couldn't have known, Antonio: a witness saw Marcus Stallworth enter the exact same quick cash hut as you did, on the exact same day, October 23." Salcido tapped the folder in front of him. "Can you imagine the odds?"

"I never saw him," Tony said.

"You don't *remember* having seen him," Salcido replied calmly. "There's a difference, Tony. Now, I'm not suggesting that you drove up to Sacramento and grabbed Mr. Stallworth. I'm not even suggesting that you stalked him, hoping to nab that Jeep you liked so much. I've got colleagues who think you did that. They think you're a sociopath, frankly. That's not what I think. I think you were out of your mind on drugs and you saw this guy—this *sick fuck*, as you put it—and you told your new friends about him, his fancy Jeep and his big mansion, and I think they cooked up a plan to rob him."

"They knocked me out in the hotel room. I told you."

"You told me you *woke up* in the hotel room, Antonio. There's a big difference. Now listen to me. There's such a thing as a cocaine-induced psychosis. It's even got an abbreviation: CIP. It's what the brain doctors call a 'dissociative state.' That means you're awake, but you're not aware. You can't recall the events. It's like a bad trip and a blackout rolled into one. You understand?"

Tony managed a sneer.

"That's what I think happened. This guy, Winnie—you have no way of knowing what kinds of drugs he's feeding you. Isn't that right? You have no clue. We do know that you were wiped out for the rest of the weekend. They hatched the whole plan,

Antonio. And you were too cranked up to think straight. We know Stallworth got shook down for five grand. We've got paper on that. A few hours later, his Jeep winds up in Barstow, with your plasma and his in a puddle. Come on now, Antonio— do the math. These folks fed you drugs. They saw a big payday fall into their laps and they got you to do the dirty work. That's how you wind up with a gash on your skull. Maybe you and Stallworth got into it. Or maybe they set you up. I don't know about that. I do know that you got cold feet at some point, though."

"Oh yeah," Tony managed. "How's that?"

Salcido pulled a VHS tape from his stack of evidence. He got up and wheeled over a cart with a VCR machine and a TV. In went the tape, with a click. A grainy video popped onto the screen, taken from above, of an emaciated teenager on a narrow cot, thrashing in his sleep. His only discernible words were a repeated imploration, delivered in Spanish. *Déjalo en paz.* Leave him alone.

ANTONIO SAENZ HAD never seen himself on film before. Nobody he knew could afford a camcorder. He found it deeply upsetting, the way he kept flailing in the greenish dark, his limbs no thicker than twigs; his trembling voice. It made him question what else the cops had on him.

Salcido clicked off the TV and shoved the cart away. Rather than sitting down across from Tony, he went and stood by the window and rubbed his face with both hands. All this was done for dramatic effect. He wanted the suspect to recognize that he took no pleasure in presenting his theory of the case. It had been a professional obligation. "I don't guess you're reading the papers these days," Salcido said, without turning around. "They're writing some crazy stuff. That the murder was a gang

initiation thing. That you went on this big shopping spree afterwards, to celebrate. The worst stuff is about your family. The
Bee did a piece about how your parents snuck you and your sister across the border. Made them sound like real masterminds.
That puts pressure on the INS to do something. They haven't
found your dad yet, in case you were wondering. And Lorena—
they've been floating this theory that she tried to seduce Marcus Stallworth. Sells papers, I guess."

Salcido walked slowly back to the desk, where Tony sat mo-
tionless, staring at his lap. "They got a hundred soldiers looking
for that body, including six canine units." Salcido crouched
down and gently laid his hand on the shoulder of the Death Valley Killer. It felt as frail as driftwood. "They're going to find that
body, Antonio. And when they do, it's game over. They'll rip up
that plea deal and file this as a capital offense. They'll put your
mom on the next plane down to Honduras. It'll happen fast. I'm
not trying to scare you. I'm trying to tell you what comes next.
You got a decision to make."

They were seven hours into the session, the point at which
most suspects, even the innocent ones, signal a willingness to
cooperate. But Tony was no longer responsive.

"Okay," Salcido said. "Get some rest. We can finish up in the
morning."

JOEL SALCIDO WAS one of the FBI's most skilled interrogators,
but the methods he employed were standard practice. The
goal was to shift the dynamic from confrontation to collaboration, from denial of the crime to an explanation of its commission. This required patience, improvisation, and a willingness
to embellish the evidence. Bad guys broke the rules all the
time. Sometimes good guys had to break the rules to make
them stick.

But for Salcido, who was a devout Christian, there was something more profound vested in the process, a moral restoration commonly associated with faith. Confession allowed for forgiveness and healing. By his sins, the suspect had been cast out of the family of man. By his surrender, he rejoined that family. Salcido saw himself as an angel of mercy. Without his guidance and support, Antonio Saenz would remain incarcerated within his false denials. He would be put on trial and convicted and executed.

The public defender, Holly Roy, had raised no objection when the regional director of the FBI informed her boss that he was sending Salcido to Sacramento. Roy might have read the serology report more carefully, or interviewed additional witnesses. But she wasn't building a defense for Saenz. She was urging him to plead out. She, too, was trying to save his life.

IN HIS INTERVIEW notes, Salcido would describe the suspect as "catatonic" at the conclusion of Session One. In fact, Tony was experiencing a common somatic reaction among traumatized people. Unable to fight or flee, he had frozen. He returned to his cell under his own power but appeared oblivious to his surroundings. At the direction of a psychiatric consultant from the FBI, he was moved to a unit known as a rubber room, one with no sharp corners. In addition to hourly rounds, an officer monitored the video feed from his cell.

There was very little to see. Tony lay on his cot. The real action was inside his head. He was thinking about the journey north, from Honduras to America. The trip returned to him now in fragments: his mother instructing him to be brave, promising him that he would be able to eat apricots in California. He remembered struggling not to cry, his father's hand clamped onto his, jerking him up the massive steps of a bus, brown scrub through a smudged window, a shroud of cigarette smoke around his father, the noxious fumes of diesel exhaust and diarrhea.

Now, languishing in a cell from which there was no escape, drifting in and out of consciousness, other memories began to dart into his mind. He remembered sleeping on the olive-green benches of a large bus station, his father meeting another group of men, all of them riding into the desert on the bed of a pickup truck. There were two men in charge and they spoke a different kind of Spanish, city-quick and full of slang. Tony didn't understand them. He didn't understand most of what was happening.

He remembered sitting near a campfire, the adults discussing what to do when they reached the border. Tony imagined a wrought-iron gate, the kind that surrounded cemeteries, only much taller, and beyond, in the magical land called America, an endless grove of apricot trees, the fruits lit from within like orange bulbs.

Then it was night and he was alone. A few men were still awake, gathered around a small fire, drinking from pint bottles. His father's voice rang out, with its worrying belligerence. Instinctually, Tony stood and tottered toward the commotion. He found his father curled in the sand. The two men in charge were kicking him. Tony yelled at them to leave him alone, but they tossed him aside, and a third man grabbed him. "Calm down, little warrior," he murmured. "Your papa is a drunk. He's going to get us all killed." He remembered the damp thuds of the beating, his father's girlish yelps. Tony could do nothing but return to the fire. He was too far from home. The next morning, he woke to the face of a monster: the nose gashed and mottled purple. A split eyebrow clotted with blood. Tony knew better than to ask what had happened.

His father told him anyway. *Un maldito escorpión me picó.* A goddamn scorpion stung me.

They traveled the rest of the way as outcasts, walking a few hundred yards behind the main group. A tense silence prevailed.

It seemed to Tony that his father was never the same again. But the opposite was true, as well: Tony was never the same. He became a withdrawn person, quietly defiant, mistrustful. He felt he should have saved his father. At the same time, he wanted his father dead.

HIS MOTHER WOULD never understand him; she hadn't been there. She had sent him away, at age four, with a drunken maniac.

It couldn't be true, what Salcido said. It wasn't true.

But the longer he lay in the dark, the more confused he became. There was a wickedness within him. He understood that much. He could be led astray by others, those more assured than him. Could the drugs have blotted out his memories? Was he remembering the assault of his father or was the man bleeding onto the sand Marcus Stallworth? Had he been dragged away from his father, or from the body of the man he himself had slain?

According to the surveillance tape, at 2:22 a.m. Antonio Saenz rose from his bunk and stumbled to the toilet in his cell. He stuck his head so deep inside the bowl that the agent monitoring him worried he might be trying to drown himself. Instead, the suspect violently expelled the food he had devoured hours earlier.

AS FOR THE confession offered by Antonio Saenz, that was mostly the work of special agent Joel Salcido. Tony was in the room, of course. He consented to the statement and participated in its construction, mostly in an advisory role. But there was no dramatic moment of capitulation. The process was incremental.

Step one was Tony's admission that it was possible he had been involved in criminal activities he could no longer recall, owing to his drug use. From there, Salcido extrapolated. *Isn't it possible*, he would ask. Isn't it possible you saw Mr. Stallworth's jeep in the parking lot of the cash hut? Isn't it possible Winnie and Trina convinced you to take part in the armed robbery of Mr. Stallworth? Isn't it possible he resisted? Isn't it possible there was an altercation? Isn't it possible he wound up dead?

Salcido never said these things happened. Nor did he expect Tony to do so. It was only a matter of admitting to a set of possibilities. In this way, the suspect was eased from innocence into a provisional form of guilt.

Tony was never quite alone. Salcido was right there, ready to offer him options. If Tony didn't remember shooting Stallworth, or burying the body, then perhaps his companions had done so. Perhaps Tony had tried to stop them. (*Leave him alone!*) These were *mitigating circumstances*—that was the phrase Salcido used. And they would be taken into consideration by the government. But they were not part of the Interview Report itself, which is what Salcido called the confession.

The theory of the case that emerged from this process was that Tony had been in a drug-induced state during the commission of the crimes. His apparent amnesia solved two other crucial problems for the prosecution; it explained why the murderer could not provide investigators the location of the body, and it justified the government's remarkably lenient plea offer. Despite the Death Valley Killer's deplorable actions, despite the call in some quarters for the death penalty, it was technically impossible to charge him with premeditated murder.

Next, they had to prepare the document. Salcido went over the facts again. ("We have to get this as clear as we can, okay?") He had the statement typed up. In effect, Antonio Saenz confessed to participating in the murder of Marcus Stallworth, which had transpired in the commission of an armed robbery. The report included several small but obvious errors, by design. Tony's last named was misspelled twice, for instance. The company for which he worked was identified as Quick Lube rather than Quik Lube. This required the suspect to initial each of the corrections. A notary was brought in to witness the final reading of the Interview Report, which Tony signed at 11:47 a.m. on November 10, 1981.

The two men had spent more than twelve hours together. It was time for them to part ways.

"What happens now?" Tony said.

"Just hang tight," Salcido said. "The hard part is over." He nodded and a pair of US marshals, watching for this signal through a one-way mirror, entered the room with shackles cradled in their arms.

"I'm proud of you," Salcido said. "The truth is a tough path to walk." He stood up and took Tony's hand into his own and pumped it. His green eyes gleamed with the grace of their partnership. He had just saved a young man's life.

"Wait, where are you going?"

LORENA DIDN'T WANT to visit Rosemary Stallworth. She felt she had no choice. Officer Guerrero had brushed her off. The public defender had informed her that a plea was Tony's only hope, given the evidence. At night, she listened to her mother whispering to God. She heard Tony, too, his final snarling order, which she eventually recognized as a plea for remedy: *Make them believe, little sister.*

Lorena arrived in the Fabulous Forties wearing a baggy sweater, with her hair tucked under a baseball cap; she feared that reporters might be gathered outside the Stallworth home, like on TV, but the only person around was the old woman next door, stationed next to a bag of mulch. For more than an hour, she troweled her flowerbeds, until the borders were just so.

Rosemary's Cadillac was in the garage but only a few lights were on in the house. Lorena hurried up the front stairs and stood for a full minute, not quite brave enough to ring the doorbell. She was especially nervous about seeing Jenny, who she knew hated her, probably always had. She peered through the windows, checked the garage and kitchen doors, and proceeded to the backyard, keeping to the shadows along the house.

It was unclear to Lorena whether she was prepared to break in, or how she would do so. But she had come this far. The pool water had gone murky. The deck furniture lay scattered about in the dusk. A pile of towels no one had bothered to pick up sat on a chaise longue near the sliding glass door that let onto the sunroom; she had to resist the urge to fold them. She tugged at the handle to the sliding door, and nearly stumbled when it slid open. Her heart was beating wildly.

"Lorena?"

A familiar voice sounded out her name from behind. She turned and saw that the rumpled towels had somehow reassembled themselves into a terrycloth robe, which was loosely wrapped around a tall figure.

Lorena let out a brief shriek. "Mrs. Stallworth?"

"What in God's name—"

"I'm sorry. You scared me."

"*I* scared *you*?" Mrs. Stallworth sat up, somewhat groggily, and pulled the robe around herself. An empty wine glass sat beneath the lounge chair. "You were just breaking into my home, if I'm not mistaken."

"No," Lorena said. "I was trying—I rang the—but nobody—" She was suddenly gulping for air. "I just wanted to say, to tell you how sorry—" Her knees buckled. "To you, and Jenny, and Glen. In person, so you would—" Mrs. Stallworth was staring at her. Lorena started crying, couldn't stop herself. "I know Jenny hates me." She had made a terrible mistake. This had been terrible mistake. She buried her face in her hands. Mrs. Stallworth rose up, blotting out what remained of the sun.

Then Lorena felt herself drawn into an embrace, pressed against the robe and the long, bony body beneath, the smell of smoke mingled with face cream. "Oh, you poor lost lamb." They stood that way for a long time, swaying a little, and Lorena knew, without wanting to, that she had come for this, too.

"What's with the hat?" Mrs. Stallworth said at last. "It makes you look like a cat burglar."

"I just wanted to talk, I swear."

"Okay. Calm down now. I believe you." She eased Lorena away and pulled the cap off and watched her hair came tumbling down. "You've always had such a nice thick mane. I'm the one who could use this." Mrs. Stallworth seemed to consider putting the cap on then tossed it into the pool instead. Her hair was in disarray, frizzy, smooshed down on one side, its natural gray showing through as the dye washed out.

"Is Jenny here?" Lorena said.

"She and her brother are away for now." Rosemary had returned after Lucia informed her that the little Mexican cop had come snooping around.

"I mostly wanted to talk to you anyway," Lorena said.

Rosemary pulled a cigarette from the pocket of her robe. "Let me get my bearings. I'm a tad bleary from the sun. And I certainly didn't expect to see you." She sat on the edge of the deck and blew smoke out of the corner of her mouth.

"I didn't mean to surprise you."

Mrs. Stallworth let out a sharp, rueful laugh. "I imagine the irony of that comment eludes you. You did surprise me, Lorena. I was not informed, for instance, that your brother was a violent criminal. Nor that you brought him to our home. I only learned that a few weeks ago. I suppose there was a lot going on around here nobody saw fit to tell me about."

"That was a mistake," Lorena said. "I made a mistake. But my brother, he didn't—" She took a deep breath. "This may sound crazy, but I believe Mr. Stallworth is still alive. I think he wanted to disappear, that he made a plan." Before she could stop herself, Lorena confessed to all that she had seen in his office and bathroom. She didn't mention that Mr. Stallworth had touched her, or said things to her, but there was something in the precision of her knowledge about him, in the timbre of her voice, that affirmed their intimacy.

When she had run out of disclosures, she fell silent and glanced at Mrs. Stallworth, whose face hovered inscrutably in the dense blue of dusk.

"What are you asking me, Lorena?"

"Asking?"

"What is it you imagine I'm going to do with this . . . *information*?"

"You could tell the police. They'll listen to you. Mr. Stallworth could be in Arizona right now. That's where you used to live, right?"

"Are you suggesting that the police go digging around in our past, as if we were the criminals? Do you have any idea how deluded you sound?" She brought her fist down onto the deck and Lorena tensed. Just as suddenly as she'd erupted, Mrs. Stallworth seemed to gather herself. She straightened up and let out a long sigh. "I would like more than anything in the world to believe you, Lorena. Because that would mean Marcus was alive."

"He could be. You said it yourself. Everyone has their own getaway plan."

Mrs. Stallworth flicked her cigarette into the pool. "Please don't twist my words. Fathers and husbands don't just disappear."

"Mine did," Lorena said quietly.

Rosemary stared at Lorena with an expression that seemed to fluctuate between pity and wrath. "Your family and mine are nothing alike. I suspect that's why you chose to spend so much time here. I don't think you understand the nature of what's happened. Maybe, because you're young, because you grew up in a certain milieu, it hasn't sunk in yet: your brother is charged with killing my husband, the father of my children. Knowing this, as, on some level, you must, the very idea that you would show up on this property, that I would find you, by all indications, attempting to break into my home, that you are, even now, portraying yourself as if you were a victim in all this, speaks to a kind of criminal depravity."

"I'm telling you the truth."

"That truth just happens to include a trove of evidence the police never discovered. And just happens to exonerate your brother." Mrs. Stallworth's voice was a gentle snarl. She stood and reached out to steady herself against the cabana. "You know, when you first came into this home, I felt we had received a blessing. My children mock me for saying such things. They think I'm hopelessly naïve. But I choose to think the best of people. My parents raised me that way. I can remember watching you and Jenny lay out by this pool over the summer. It feels like a long time ago, now. I thought to myself: Now isn't that lovely? This young girl from Fruitridge, so studious and respectful, but so much on her own in the world. I was delighted we could give you a little support. And I could see how much more confident you became. It was quite striking. But I suppose Lucia was right, in the end. She tried to warn me. A girl like that, she said, with no father and a mother who works till all hours. When you take in a stray, you never know what else comes in the door. That was how she put it."

Mrs. Stallworth began to advance on Lorena, the tiny ember of her cigarette flaring. "Jennifer eventually admitted to everything: that she had been visiting your apartment, the drinking you two did, the older guys, the skinny dipping. She tried to protect you at first. We all did. But I can see now what you were up to, that you needed a certain kind of regard. Even Marcus tried to give you that, in his own way. He sensed how lonely you were, a girl in your circumstances; he understood how much you needed a father in your life. He was sensitive to such needs, because of his own history. Need makes people do ugly things, Lorena. And then they tell themselves a story about it."

Lorena felt a cool prickling along her skin. "A story?"

"You were attracted to my husband. It's only natural. His looks have made him a target in the past. You're not the first young woman to get confused. But I won't have you spreading lies about my family. You pursued Marcus. You were the one who made the plan, Lorena. Lost all that weight, got those nice clothes, learned to style your hair. Jenny and Lucia saw what was happening. But as I said, I can be a little slow to face the truth. We see what we want to see."

"That's not what happened." The prickling had become a kind of numbness, as if Mrs. Stallworth's voice were a serum that had seeped in and was creeping along her limbs.

"So you weren't attracted to my husband? You didn't seek him out?"

Mrs. Stallworth had closed the distance between them. The sun was setting behind her, casting a molten light upon the surface of the pool. For a moment, she appeared poised to reach out and seize Lorena by the neck.

"I never imagined that you would try to break up this family, nor that you would endanger us. But now you have gone so far as to desecrate the memory of a man who wanted nothing more than to give you a little attention."

"It was more than attention," Lorena said.

Mrs. Stallworth's hand shot out and slapped at Lorena, grazing her cheek. "There was a time when I considered you—" Her voice broke and she stared down at her own hand, as if it had acted without her permission. "I'm going to do you a favor now," she whispered. "I'm going to give you ten seconds to leave this property before I summon the police. I'm sure my children would not approve. But as you know, strays have always been my weakness."

ROSEMARY DID NOT contact the police. Instead, she phoned her travel agent and bought three plane tickets to Philadelphia. She told her mother that she refused to subject her children to any further harassment by police or press. By the time they landed, the next morning, Antonio Saenz had confessed to the murder of Marcus Stallworth.

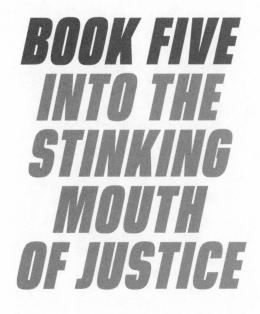

BOOK FIVE
INTO THE STINKING MOUTH OF JUSTICE

AT DAWN ON FRIDAY, NOVEMBER 13, Lorena Saenz stepped off the shoulder of Route 66 and left civilization behind. Her exact point of departure was a barren stretch of road just past the town of Siberia and on the way to Bagdad. More precisely, it was 12.38 miles due north of the spot on the map where, by her reckoning, Marcus Stallworth had camped some two weeks earlier.

Lorena walked south all morning, through prairies of caked powder and scrub, with a compass in one hand, a pedometer in the other, and a steel-framed backpack borrowed from Lisa Catalis, her eighth-grade science teacher. She had just crossed an access road when she encountered a barbed-wire fence, affixed with a sign that promised trespassers will be prosecuted.

She tore through the barbs and aimed for the distant crags of the Bullion Mountains. No more than a hundred steps later, a siren yelped from the access road behind her. She figured she'd been caught trespassing. Then a gravelly voice was booming in the air around her. "Come on back, Lorena."

She turned to find a cop standing next to a Fresno Police squad car. He had a radio pressed to his mouth and his voice was being amplified by speakers on the roof of the vehicle. It was just the two of them, faced off under the blue dome of morning. The cop was fat, with a thick mustache and an oddly jovial expression. "Yeah, I'm talking to you, muchacha. You see any other Lorenas around here?"

ON A TYPICAL Tuesday, at this hour, Lorena would have been dragging herself into third period, taking a seat near the back of the room and watching Mrs. Bunn slash algebraic formulas onto the blackboard. At some point, a boy would fart or burp or stick a spit-moistened fingertip into the ear of a girl he liked and therefore bullied, and Mrs. Bunn would turn for a moment and cast a withering glance in the general direction of the culprit and do nothing, because this sort of behavior was expected of boys in ninth grade. But Lorena had not seen a typical morning for weeks.

Miss Roy, the public defender, had called their home three days earlier to inform them that Tony had signed a confession. Her mother tried to visit him but was told he was "in transit." When he did finally call, Tony told his mother that he didn't remember committing the crimes of which he was accused, that it was possible he had done so under the influence of drugs, but he didn't think so. He said he was being set up and also that he was trying to protect her. His speech was jumbled and halting. Graciela instructed him to pray to Jesus to clear his mind and lead him to the truth. She told him she loved him no matter what and that she should have been kinder to him when he was a boy and wept in silence. She knew Tony would not abide the sound of her crying.

Lorena didn't believe the confession. The FBI had preyed upon the weakness of his mind. Tony had been right: it was the fancy ones who fucked you up. The police helped them do so. Her mind flashed to Officer Guerrero, his ratty face and fake kindness. It was on her now, to save Tony, to make the cops pay. What she needed was a plan, and a little bit of help.

LORENA RETURNED TO Sutter Junior High and stationed herself outside Miss Catalis's classroom just before the end of seventh period and waited for the bell that would send her students tumbling into their heedless afternoons of Little League and Atari. She hid behind a book as they clamored past.

Miss Catalis sat at her desk, while a bespectacled girl assailed her about mitochondria. Lorena knew that she might have been this girl last year, had she made different choices, the goody-goody lingering after class, wringing a little extra kindness from an earnest teacher. The girl blathered on, shifting from one foot to the other and picking at her forehead, until Miss Catalis noticed Lorena in the doorway and gasped.

"I can come back," Lorena murmured.

"No. Please. We were just finishing up." She paddled her hands in an antic gesture of beckoning.

The girl stared at Lorena blankly, a bit resentfully, and attempted to show Miss Catalis her diagram of a mitochondrion. "It's terrific, Rachel. Let's talk more tomorrow."

On her way out, Rachel looked at Lorena again, squinting this time until her eyes went wide and she scooted into the hallway, eager to find someone, anyone, to whom she could brag that she had spotted the sister of the Death Valley Killer, that she was *talking to Miss Catalis right now.*

Everyone knew Lorena Saenz and Jenny Stallworth had met in Miss Catalis's class, and that this meeting had led to the murder of Marcus Stallworth, because the girls had been mortal enemies. Lorena had been jealous of Jenny's wealth and beauty and popularity. Miss Catalis had forced them to work together anyway.

"Sorry about that," Miss Catalis called out. "Come *in*." She marched over and hugged Lorena, then shut the door. "I heard about your brother. Oh, Lorena. How are you? How's your mother?"

"She's okay. I've just been trying to focus on my schoolwork, you know."

"Of course."

"That's why I came. I need a little help on an assignment. I thought of you because of our navigation unit from last year. If you have the coordinates of a place, like, would it be possible to find it?"

Miss Catalis leaned back. "What class is this for?"

"Geography."

"Wouldn't you be taking biology as a freshman?"

"This is a special project. For Western Civ."

"You're doing a section on cartography or something?"

"Right."

Miss Catalis cocked her head. "How detailed are the coordinates? How many decimal points?"

"Three," Lorena said.

Miss Catalis whistled. "And this place you want to find, is it a village or something?"

"No, a campsite."

"A *campsite*?" Miss Catalis frowned. "This is for a cartography unit?"

"It's more like an ancient settlement."

"I'm a bit confused, Lorena."

"We're supposed to find this encampment used by the Pima Indians," Lorena said quickly. "It's for extra credit. But it's way out in the desert, so there's no roads or anything."

"Are there any changes in elevation, at least?"

"I don't think so."

Miss Catalis produced a soft popping noise, the one she made when you got an answer wrong in class. "It's possible," she said reluctantly. "But you'd need the right equipment. And you'd have to get pretty lucky."

Lorena could feel her chin quivering at this blunt appraisal.

Suddenly, Miss Catalis was studying her in a manner that made Lorena want to flee the room. "Wait a second," she said slowly. "This isn't really about an assignment, is it? This is about your brother."

LORENA KNEW HER best shot at getting help was to avoid any mention of her true intention. Miss Catalis was a teacher, part of the official world, and, as her mother had often reminded her, *when you tell one official, you're telling every official.* But Miss Catalis had deduced the truth—a portion of it, anyway.

So Lorena came up with a story. She told Miss Catalis that Tony had an alibi, that he had gone camping on the weekend of Mr. Stallworth's disappearance, had even left behind a baseball cap, but the police didn't believe him.

"Didn't believe him?"

"They said they had all the evidence they needed."

From the hallway came the squeak of a custodial cart. "Let's continue this conversation somewhere else," Miss Catalis said.

Her apartment was a garden-level studio shared with two nervy parakeets. The bookshelves were crammed with used textbooks and science-fiction novels. Hanging on the wall above her kitchen table was a framed quote—COURAGE IS FOUND IN UNLIKELY PLACES—by someone named J. R. R. Tolkien. Miss Catalis set out a plate of vanilla cookies, the stale kind Lorena associated with church functions.

"I know you want to help your brother. I get it. But the public defender's office has investigators. This is their job."

"They told me the case is over. He did a plea bargain."

"And you still think he's innocent." Miss Catalis nodded to herself, then stared directly at the young woman across from her. "I want you to listen to me, Lorena. Tony is in jail because of his actions, not yours. You don't have to take this on. It's not your job to save your brother."

Lorena's face fell into her hands. "I thought you were the one person who would understand."

"I *do* understand," Miss Catalis said. "Let me think."

"I'm just asking for a little help with navigation. It'd be, like, a hike in the desert. I won't even tell anyone we talked."

THEY STRUCK A deal. Miss Catalis would help Lorena, as long as she promised to wait for the weekend, when they could travel together. In the meantime, she laid out the steps they would have to take. This was years before GPS existed, back when the best a hiker could do was to get ahold of a compass with adjustable declination, to correct for difference between true north and magnetic north.

First, they would need to head to the map room of the central library to get detailed topographical maps of San Bernardino County. They would need to mark a spot due north of Tony's campsite and walk due south, checking the compass every dozen steps, to stay on the same longitude. "There's no guarantee," Miss Catalis warned. "But we can give it a shot."

Before she departed, Lorena confessed that she'd never gone on a serious hike before, and asked, shyly, if she could borrow the high-tech compass and the pedometer and backpack, so she could practice during the week.

Catalis agreed. "I know you're eager. Just wait till Saturday."

Lorena met her eye and nodded.

The moment she got home, Lorena Saenz marched into her mother's room and grabbed $300 cash from the emergency fund stashed in a shoebox at the back of the closet. She bought supplies at an army surplus store and left a note for her mother, explaining that she was staying over at a friend's house so they could study for a big test. She suffered no hesitation in buying a bus ticket, or traveling alone. Her mother had put her on Greyhounds before, to visit her cousins in San Jose. She knew how to take care of herself, how to deflect adults who might ask questions. From Fresno, she traveled on to Barstow. At first light, she hired a taxi to drive her out to Siberia, which was little more than a service station and convenience store called Last Chance Gas. "This ain't exactly Grand Central," the cabbie said. "You sure you want to get out here?" She told him she was meeting her dad.

LISA CATALIS WAS no dope. She had been teaching middle school long enough to recognize when a kid became a bad bet. It didn't matter how smart they were. The brain of a fourteen-year-old had the impulse control of a fourteen-year-old. This is why she dropped by the Saenz apartment the next morning, before school. Her next call was to the police. She was eventually patched through to officer Pedro Guerrero.

Miss Catalis introduced herself and explained the bizarre request her former student had made of her. "Her story didn't make any sense. She had these specific coordinates, supposedly from her brother."

Guerrero was incensed and quietly impressed at Lorena's audacity. "Where are you located, Miss Catalis? I'd like to get a little more information."

They met at a Sambo's near the middle school. Catalis recognized him, vaguely, though she couldn't say how. In fact, she had seen him among the officers lined up behind the chief of police, when he announced the arrest of Antonio Saenz.

He wrote down everything Lisa Catalis could tell him: what Lorena was wearing, the color of the backpack she had borrowed, the spot along Route 66 that she was most likely to have taken off from, which Miss Catalis had calculated herself, the moment she discovered that Lorena had gone missing.

"I should have called last night," she said. "I could see how upset she was." Lisa Catalis poked at her tea bag miserably. "I know this sounds silly, but I was the one who paired them up, her and Jenny Stallworth. For the science fair. I thought it would do them both some good. Shows what I know."

"I wouldn't take all that on, ma'am," Guerrero said. "You're just a teacher trying to do right by your students. That's what I see."

"Thank you." Catalis had begun to cry a little.

"It's okay," Guerrero said. "You go ahead and let it out. The world's a crazy place. It deserves more tears than it gets." He handed her a few napkins.

"I'm sorry."

"Nothing to be sorry for, ma'am."

"Lisa."

"Okay. Lisa."

"It just eats at me."

"What's that?"

"I don't know. I see all these kids come in to my classroom every year. And you know some of them are going to be fine. They've got parents to help them with their homework, money for tutors, a trust fund for college. And then you've got the other ones, where you know the support isn't there. When you get a girl like Lorena, where you can see they've got a real mind, you just want to make sure you do your part to help them."

Guerrero thought of Lorena as he had first encountered her, hunched behind the stack of books on her kitchen table. At the same time, annoyingly, he found that he was staring at Miss Catalis, deciding she was pretty.

"What?" she said.

"I don't know. I just wish they had teachers like you when I went to Sutter."

"You were a Sutter Miner?"

"About a million years ago."

"And what kind of student were you?"

Guerrero summoned his Sutter days. Petty theft, cut classes, flailing fights. "More like Antonio Saenz than Lorena, let's put it that way."

"But you did alright for yourself."

"Yeah, I got lucky. Point is, a good teacher can make all the difference." Against his inclinations, and with a terrified lurching of the heart, Guerrero set his hand lightly on the forearm of Lisa Catalis. "Try not to beat yourself up for seeing Lorena."

IT WAS GUERRERO who called Nando, and Nando who drove out to the access road that offered the best chance to intercept Lorena. He didn't hold out much hope. But he clambered onto the hood of his squad car anyway and surveyed with his binoculars, until he spotted an animal ripping its way through the barbed-wire fence to his east. Upon closer inspection, the animal was wearing jeans and tennis shoes.

Nando clicked on his bullhorn, hollered her name, watched Lorena go stiff. He limped down to the fence with his wire cutters, letting out little grunts and chattering all the while. "You're not in any trouble. It's just we can't have minors wandering around alone out here."

Lorena could feel sweat soaking her shirt; it stuck to her back. She had to struggle to steady her voice. "Am I under arrest?"

The cop smiled. "Heck no. You are a runaway under California state law, though. Why don't we have a little talk in my car? It's nice and cool."

"I don't really have a choice, do I?"

"Not really."

"How do you know my name?" she said suddenly. But then she understood: Miss Catalis had narked to the cops.

"You're pretty famous in some circles. Pedro Guerrero is a big fan. Doesn't look like the feeling is mutual."

"He arrested my brother."

"I warned him not to, if that counts for anything. Seriously, let's go sit in my car. I got pastries and everything."

They sat in the front seat of the squad car, with its cigarillo stink.

"What now?"

"We sit tight and stuff our faces." Nando reached into the cooler between them, and removed a waxed paper bag. "Usually, I'd eat all of these myself, which is how I keep such a lovely figure. I got *conchas, orejas, cuernos.* Those are the best. Come on, now. You been walking all morning. I know you're hungry." He held out the pastry, its custard shining like a giant yolk. "Okay, you change your mind, you know where these are." Nando ate two *conchas,* tearing them into chunks, which he dunked into a thermos of coffee.

Lorena observed him out of the corner of her eye. She could hear Tony's voice in her head: a pig eating like a pig. Something about his appetite, the shamelessness of it maybe, revolted her. "Why'd you say that thing?" she asked.

"What thing?"

"About telling Guerrero not to arrest my brother?"

Nando squinted through the windshield, then put his pointer finger to his lips. "That one was off the record, muchacha. You know what that means?"

"I'm not dumb."

"*Claro que sí,*" Nando muttered amiably.

"Mr. Stallworth is still alive," Lorena said. "He ran away. I can prove it."

"That's our job, no?"

"Then you should do your job."

Nando let out a gale of laughter. "Walked right into that one. *Pow.* I'm gonna need a smoke to restore my dignity."

Lorena stared into the nothingness of the Mojave, while Nando turtled his way out of the squad car and shambled around, puffing at his rancid cigarillo.

"What happened to your leg anyway?" Lorena said, when he had settled back into the driver's seat.

"Broke it attempting a triple axel. Olympic trials. 1976."

Silence.

"Tough crowd," Nando said.

"I just mean—they still let you be a police officer."

"What do you think they do to old cops, take us out and shoot us?"

"What if you have to chase a suspect?"

"You planning on making a getaway?"

"He's not dead," Lorena repeated. "I can prove it."

PEDRO GUERRERO HAD every intention of driving Lorena Saenz back to Sacramento. She was (just for starters) a minor who had fled into the desert alone. She was also the sister of the Death Valley Killer, and a material witness in his case, which remained at the center of a media frenzy.

But there was a reason he had instructed Nando to stay put rather than transporting the girl back to Barstow or Fresno. And that reason, though he couldn't quite admit it to himself, was that he knew Lorena might be right, that Marcus Stallworth was out there, somewhere. It was a long shot, but he could no longer ignore his misgivings. Lorena deserved the chance to test her theory of the case, though this would involve venturing into a desert he had no idea how to navigate, which meant relying on the dubious expertise of a fourteen-year-old girl. None of these thoughts was particularly welcome. He pulled up to Nando's squad car in a state of irritability.

"Fancy meeting you here," Nando called through his window.

"Hi, Lorena," Guerrero said.

Lorena glared straight ahead.

"Looks like you two are hitting it off, so I'm going to use the restroom, such as it is. You can thank me later for driving all the way out here."

"Thank you," Guerrero whispered. "I owe you."

He poked his head through car window. "You know I got to bring you home, right?"

Her black hair was pulled back in a ponytail; her jeans looked as if they'd been run through a cheese grater.

"Gather up everything you brought. I'll give you a minute."

She gave no indication of having heard him.

"It's nothing personal, Lorena. I'm just trying to do my job here."

"Stop lying to me," Lorena said quietly. It was an audacious thing to say to a police officer, but she was past caring what Guerrero thought.

"What do you want from me?"

"You know what I want."

"No, I don't."

"We're 5.7 miles from the spot Mr. Stallworth marked on his map. That's two hours. We could make it back before dark."

"We'll have an officer check it out."

Lorena closed her eyes. An afterimage of the sun pulsed red. "You must really think I'm an idiot," she said slowly. "Every single thing I've told you—you ignored all of it. Because you *wanted* to bust my brother."

"I can't ignore evidence."

"That's what you're doing right now."

"Something you think might be true isn't evidence. It's conjecture."

Lorena flung open the passenger-side door and grabbed her backpack from the back seat. For a second, it looked as if she might make a run for it. She lugged the pack over to Guerrero's car. "You can take me home, but I'm gonna come back here. And when I find what I know I'm going to find, I'm going to go to every newspaper and TV station in California and tell them what you did."

"I can see things are going well here," observed Nando, who had just returned.

"Miss Saenz believes we're engaged in a massive cover-up," Guerrero said. "She thinks we're trying to bury evidence that could compromise the case."

Nando looked away.

"Can I remind you of the situation?" Guerrero said. "We got a minor wandering around alone in the desert—"

"I'm not wandering," Lorena said.

"—her mother already has one kid in custody."

Nando held up a finger. "Lorena, would you mind returning to my car? Just for a minute, honey. Thank you." When she had closed the door, he led Guerrero away from the vehicle. "Whatever you want to do here, *primo*, that's what I want to do."

"We gotta get her back to her mother, right?"

"Of course."

"But. There's a *but* in your voice."

"Let's put it this way: if you were charged with murder and I thought there was some way to clear you and the cops were blowing me off, I'd probably do what she did."

"Blowing her off? Who drove back to the Stallworth residence and tested for blood in the basement? Who interviewed the maid? That shit could get me fired." Guerrero was shouting at his cousin now.

"Okay. No one's accusing you, *primo*. But look at the pattern here. You been confirming her leads, one by one." Nando licked an errant pastry flake from his mustache. "Tell me this: Have you told Hooks about any of this? How about the interview notes I sent? Does he know where you are right now?"

"What's your point?"

"We're already off the reservation. That's my point."

"You want me to go out there with her, don't you?"

"Would you rather she comes down here alone next week?"

"She wouldn't be alone. One of her teachers helped her plan this little escapade."

"Oh shit. Now you got a teacher mixed up in it. If something bad happens, his career goes down the tubes."

"*Her* career."

"I'd take her myself if I weren't such a fucking cripple. Then again, my career ain't riding on it."

"What's that mean?"

Nando held up his hands, like it was a stickup. "You wanna walk away, I ain't gonna judge you."

Guerrero felt a pressure building in his chest. He recalled the sensation from his criminal days. Every available choice struck him as a betrayal.

"There's nothing out there anyway," he said, half to himself.

"Probably not."

"And we tell her mother what?"

Nando made his hand into a phone. "This is officer Fernando Reyes, ma'am. Your daughter has joined the Major Crimes Unit. Turns out she's got a real nose for police work. But don't worry. She'll be home before *The Waltons* starts."

"What if we find something?" Guerrero said glumly.

"Then you made the right call."

GUERRERO INSISTED ON carrying the backpack. He was trying to be chivalrous, but Jesus it was heavy. Nando had lent him a pair of sneakers, which were better than his loafers but too large. He did a lot of stumbling, which Lorena enjoyed. They made a strange couple: a thin, balding man in a button-down shirt and rayon pants, with a gun tucked in the leather holster looped around his waist, walking beside a teenage girl in torn clothing, who bent to inspect a compass every five steps.

Guerrero had his shoulder unit radio switched on, but a mile into their hike, Nando's chatter turned to static and they were alone. They did not speak, aside from necessary communications. Guerrero questioned Lorena's compulsive inspection of the compass. Lorena replied that any deviation in direction would render their mission pointless. She did this in the proprietary manner that Guerrero recalled from his own school years. It was the way smart girls always talked, their hedge against what really mattered, which was being pretty.

At one point, Lorena confessed that she needed to go to the bathroom. Guerrero stood with his eyes closed, cursing silently, while the girl dashed behind a distant creosote bush. She had brought toilet paper, naturally. All the while, the sun inched across the sky and the northern edge of the Bullion Mountains loomed larger, until they stood in the shadow of a wrinkled ridge. Lorena consulted her pedometer. "We should start looking."

The goal was to detect any sign of human disruption, meaning footprints, trash, a campfire. They walked outward in concentric circles, marking their progress with little yellow flags that Lorena had purchased from the army surplus store. Lorena suggested they split up, to cover more ground.

"No can do," Guerrero said. "I'm responsible for you."

"What do you think is going to happen to me?"

"You could get lost, for one thing."

"That's why I bought the flares."

LORENA WAS OUT of flags by four. They had covered what felt to Guerrero like a square mile, venturing up into the craggy foothills, walking east and west, tracing ridges and plunging down into arroyos. "We have to go," he said, gently. "There's no way we're going to be able to find my car in the dark."

"Go ahead," Lorena said.

"You know I can't do that."

"I got everything I need." She reached into her backpack and began pulling out packages of dried fruit and beef jerky, canteens, a tarp for ground cover.

"Put that stuff back, Lorena. Come on now. It's time. Your mother needs you."

"Don't talk about my mother."

"Okay. Calm down."

But Lorena couldn't calm down. There was something about Guerrero speaking about her mother, thinking he had the right, as if it were his intention now to protect her, this man who had ruined her brother's life and sent her into the desert to chase a ghost. She kept getting angrier and angrier, until she was throwing camping supplies directly at Guerrero. Flashlight. Snakebite kit. Water bottle. "I have what I need," she shrieked. "I don't need you. I don't *need* you." The louder her voice became, the more violent her sense of assurance. She didn't need Guerrero or Tony or Mr. Stallworth or her own goddamn father, wherever that asshole was. She needed to get away from all of them. Suddenly she was running into the Bullion Mountains, leaving behind the stupid yellow flags they had planted, racing past giant boulders and outcroppings of the same hopeless hue.

Guerrero stood aghast, watching her recede. He told himself she would return. Then he realized he had no basis for making this judgment, aside from the vague intuition that human beings tended to cluster in the wilderness.

It took him ten minutes to catch up to her. They were soaked through and panting by then. Every time Guerrero came within fifty yards, Lorena would zig, or zag, or duck behind a boulder, and Guerrero would quietly consider pulling out his gun and shooting her in the leg. Sunset painted an auburn glaze on the horizon.

"Please," Guerrero said. "I don't want to have to arrest you."

He could see that Lorena was out of gas, but one final burst of adrenaline drove her forward. Then she was on the ground, her shoulder throbbing. She was sure he had tackled her. But Guerrero was ten yards behind her. She glanced back and saw a ring of stones; the one she had tripped over kicked loose, the rest forming a perfect circle around the remains of a fire.

"Officer Guerrero," she croaked.

Anyone could build a fire, Guerrero said. But Lorena knew. He had been here. She ran her fingers through the ashes as Guerrero stood there, threatening her. She began to look around for a place where Mr. Stallworth would have stashed supplies; her eyes alighted on a crevice at the base of a ledge.

"Where're you going?"

Lorena angled her body inside. She turned on her flashlight and swept the ground. There, at the very back of the burrow, lodged like a tonsil, was a freshly turned mound. She began digging with her fingers, scooping away the sandy soil, until her fingertips felt the soil give way to a rustling. She could hear Guerrero wheezing angrily behind her.

He stuck his head into the cave. "This is an animal's den."

Lorena aimed her flashlight at what she'd unearthed. There, stacked and crisply folded, wrapped in a clear plastic sheath, as if they had come straight from a laundry service, were the blood-stained garments in which Marcus Stallworth had disappeared nineteen days earlier.

▓▓▓▓▓▓▓▓▓▓▓▓

ALTHOUGH PEDRO GUERRERO was raised in the church, he had never considered the hand of the divine particularly reliable, especially during investigations. And yet he could summon no earthly explanation for what had transpired, the manner in which his pursuit of Lorena led her directly to the campfire and from there to the clothes—a blue Brooks Brothers oxford, pleated chinos, a Hanes undershirt, all flecked with brown spots—which matched, at least in its basic elements, the outfit described by Stallworth's wife and colleagues.

They spent the next hour scouring the area. Guerrero pulled on a pair of disposable gloves and dusted the stones around the fire pit for prints, then the plastic garment bag. He came up empty; whoever made camp had been wearing gloves, too. He sifted the ashes of the fire and recovered the charred remains of an MRE package. Lorena found what could have been the impression of a sleeping body on the floor of the cave and Guerrero tweezed two human hairs. Together, they managed to locate a dozen partial shoe prints, all the same waffle tread. It was nearly dark by the time they finished.

Lorena wanted to start back. But Guerrero knew they were too tired. They needed food and rest and daylight. He retrieved the backpack and they built a small fire, foraging twigs and dried branches, and guzzled from the canteens and gobbled dried fruit and jerky. They unfurled the tarp and stared up at the sky as it edged from violet into black and the stars one by one came lit.

"What's going to happen now?" Lorena said.

In the movies, Guerrero would say just the right thing here. But they weren't living in the movies. They were living in the world, with its human frailties and protocols, its bewildered pauses.

"I'm not sure," Guerrero said.

"But Tony's gonna go free though."

"We have to do some tests."

"Tests?"

"The blood spots, the hair. We have to see if they match with Mr. Stallworth."

"What are you talking about?"

"To establish that the clothes belonged to Mr. Stallworth."

"Who else would they belong to?"

"That's the point. We don't know yet."

"But Mr. Stallworth—he was here. Just like it said on the maps. We found his clothes. He made a fire."

"You saw those maps, Lorena. The police didn't."

The stars above her went blurry. She had been a fool to trust a cop.

"I'm sorry," Guerrero said. "It's going to take time." He wanted to be straight with Lorena, to convey how difficult it would be to undo the process by which her brother had been deemed a murderer. "We need *proof*, Lorena. Like there's proof against Tony."

Lorena wiped her nose on her sleeve, so Guerrero wouldn't know how upset she was. But he could hear her ragged hiccups over the crackling of their puny fire. It was down to embers.

"Your brother signed a plea deal. He confessed."

"He didn't mean it," Lorena sobbed. "He told my mom."

"He cut a deal—a good deal. He could be out in a decade."

The girl began to shake; Guerrero considered touching her shoulder; his hand hovered in the thin air.

"He's going to die in there," she said softly. "You're going to let him die."

"Let me explain something. If I tell my captain, if I go to him and say, 'Hey, I found these bloody clothes in the desert. The killer's little sister led me to them. They belong to Marcus Stall-worth.' You know what he's gonna do? He's going to start asking how *you* knew the location of a dead man's clothes—"

"He's not dead—"

"I don't want him asking that, Lorena. And you don't, either. Then he's going to send the Army Corps of Engineers out here and they're going to dig around for months, until they find a body. And if they don't, that just means the Death Valley Killer was extra careful."

"Why'd you even let me come out here?"

Guerrero said nothing for a long time. "Because you may be right. But we're going to have to find Marcus Stallworth to prove it. Which means I need to know where he might have gone."

They lay in silence on opposite ends of the tarp, two warm-blooded creatures beneath a gathering assembly of stars. Guerrero collapsed, almost at once, into slumber. But Lorena was too angry to sleep. For a few joyous moments, she imagined bludgeoning Guerrero with one of the stones from the firepit. Bad rat. Dead rat. Then she remembered another one of Miss Catalis's hokey sayings: *Frustration is the fuel of science.* She needed to find a way around the obstacle Guerrero had set in her path.

Her mind drifted back to the last time she stared into the ashy depths of the galaxy. She had stood beside Mr. Stallworth then, close enough to smell him. All around them, delicate bristled hunters ventured out from their burrows, traversing the floor of the desert, attuned to the vibrations of their pray. She had needed a special lamp to see them.

All at once, Lorena felt the adrenal surge that signaled an essential deduction. She nearly bolted upright. Lorena held almost no power in the world. She was a minor, the daughter of an undocumented worker and a man she could barely remember, the sister of an avowed killer. But she was in sole possession of the clues that might save her brother, and that gave her leverage over the cop who lay snuffling beside her. She was the only one who had seen the maps, who knew the coordinates. *Find me*, Mr. Stallworth had said. The lamp belonged to her.

IN THE MORNING, Guerrero discovered that he and the girl had curled into one another during the night, nestling against the chill of the desert. As he edged away, her arm reached out for him, for the animal warmth he provided. He laid his jacket over her and hurried into the dawn, bent like a crab, to gather kindling for a fire. There was a lancing pain behind his eyes that only caffeine would remedy.

He returned with an armful of nettled twigs and strafed forearms. Lorena was tending a small blaze in the shallow pit they'd dug. He assumed she was burning food wrappers, but as he drew closer he could see flames consuming the pale green topographical map she had consulted so faithfully during their hike out.

"What the hell are you doing? Jesus. How are we supposed to get back?"

"Head north. We'll hit Route 66 eventually."

"But why burn the goddamn—oh Jesus, they had the coordinates, didn't they?" He stared at the curled wisps of charcoal. "Destroying evidence is a crime, Lorena."

"They belonged to me."

"This isn't some kind of game."

Lorena stared at him, almost indifferently. "I'm coming with you."

Guerrero closed his eyes. A tiny anvil was being tossed, over and over, onto the soft tissue of his frontal lobe. "No, you're going home to your mama, and me and Nando are going to process the evidence."

"And if I don't give the coordinates to you? What are you going to do? Throw me in jail with Tony? Have the FBI interrogate me?"

"You have to let us do our job."

"We wouldn't be out here if it weren't for me," Lorena replied. "You wanted to give up. But I'm not going to give up. Because Tony is my brother. And I know Mr. Stallworth." She was speaking in a calm, methodical manner, bluffing at a kind of self-possession. And while Guerrero knew this, rationally, he also sensed that he was up against the indomitable will of an adolescent, that she would not give up, that it was not within her power to yield or surrender or trust.

"Do me a favor: shut up for a second." He reached down for his holster and strapped it around his waist for no good reason, pistol and all, and turned away from the little fire she had made and walked in little circles behind a clump of creosote muttering *fuck fuck fuck*, almost tenderly, and thinking, once again, about shooting Lorena in the leg, grazing the fleshy part of her thigh this time, though as he imagined this scene, he envisioned Lorena looking down at the wound and saying "missed me" in her quiet, unperturbed way, then taking his gun and calmly aiming it at his head and firing. That's how much his head hurt.

When he returned, she looked up grimly and handed him a collapsible tin cup full of instant oatmeal. "Face it, Officer Guerrero," she said. "We need each other."

IN THE DAYS after her arrival in Philadelphia, Rosemary Stallworth received two noteworthy phone calls. The first came from Royce Van Dyke. He had been a comfort during the early days of the investigation, a bit extravagant in his attention to wardrobe and grooming, but a steadying presence amid the parade of police personnel. Rosemary was pleased to hear his voice.

After inquiring as to how she and the children were settling in, Van Dyke announced that he had good news. Antonio Saenz had confessed to the FBI and entered into a plea agreement, which meant there would be no trial. "Even in our vulgar world," he intoned, "justice has a way of prevailing."

Rosemary felt her stomach unclench. "What a relief," she whispered. "To have that part of it all over, I mean."

Van Dyke hummed in accord. Beneath his veneer of professional calm, though, he was in a state. Over the past forty-eight hours, the status of the Stallworth case had swung from delicate to precarious. First, Ammon Taylor had contacted his office, demanding an additional $5,000—$3,000 more than remained in the escrow account. Then Officer Guerrero had called to grill him. Van Dyke enjoyed a certain latitude in his role as protector, owing to his influence over Captain Maurice Hooks, whom he had come to know from various erotic excursions. But the investigator was acutely aware of his legal vulnerability, should the precise nature of his relationship to Marcus Stallworth come to light. Guerrero had rattled him.

Thus, he was now in the unenviable position of having to request hush money from Rosemary, with a plausible explanation that did not involve disclosing that her husband was still alive. "There is one matter I wanted to mention before I let you go. In a case such as this there can be . . . aftershocks."

"Aftershocks?"

"Yes. Well." Van Dyke cleared his throat. "Because no body has been found, you see. At some point, there may be a need to identify."

It took a moment for Rosemary to divine his meaning. She let out a noise of distress.

"I'm sorry to bring this up, obviously."

A vision came upon her, of Marcus as he had been in the first days of their courtship, in the morning light of his dismal grad student flat. He was often in a state of arousal before he woke up, and sometimes she would reach down and take hold of him—or even pleasure him with her mouth—astonished at her own carnal daring. His body reacted with what she took to be assent, like a boy thrashing amid an ecstatic dream. For a few precious moments afterwards he lay limp and unguarded, and she could inspect his shy muscled body, the fine dark hairs that matted his chest and limbs, and the odd, filamentary scars scattered about his pelvis. Then he would curl away, violently, and they would both pretend not to hear his weeping. This was the part of his life she could never know, a fierce and terrible wound that was somehow always there between them, rattling like a loose secret.

Van Dyke was speaking to her again. "Of course, there are scenarios in which this is entirely unnecessary."

"You mean if his body is never recovered."

"I'm sorry to dwell on any of this, Rosemary. I am only observing that the full truth of what happened here remains unclear. Sometimes loose ends arise."

"Loose ends?" Rosemary sounded flustered.

"There are certain members of the law enforcement community," Van Dyke said carefully, "who seem to believe this case is more complicated than it is. I fear they may intend to dig into your past, and that of your husband."

Rosemary nearly dropped the phone. Her breathing seized up. She thought of the homely Mexican officer who had forced himself into her home, his cheap suit and impudent questions, his rank smell. Her mind flashed to the scene she had witnessed weeks before the disappearance: Marcus on his hands and knees, Lorena looming over him like some pubescent Circe. The girl had even returned, prowling about like a common criminal, casting brazen accusations into the air between them.

"Mrs. Stallworth?"

Rosemary knew she was meant to respond, but the pressure in her chest forbid it. She felt as if her ribs would crack if she so much as whispered.

"I fear I have alarmed you. That was not my intention. It's just that the police have a habit of frisking for secrets. And once one gets out, others are sure to follow. That's been my experience."

The pause lengthened. Van Dyke had been a vice detective in Tucson for a decade before his own desires forced him into another line of work. He now recognized the situation: Mrs. Stallworth was aware of her husband's illicit tendencies. He wondered, a bit more than idly, what else she knew.

"It is my job to protect you from such invasions. To insure that you—and your children, and your parents—are able to move on from this tragedy. That will require a bit more work than I anticipated, and thus additional expenses, but I will do so. I promise you that. Do you trust me?"

He could just make out her assent.

"Now listen to me," Van Dyke said, in his most reassuring tone. "I don't want you worrying about any of this, Rosemary. I want you to breathe easy."

Downstairs, her mother was pacing from room to room, berating her grandchildren with bright chatter. How delighted she had been to welcome her only daughter home, wreathed in the disgrace she had long predicted.

"Are we in agreement?" Van Dyke purred.

"Do what you have to do," she replied faintly. "Leave me out of it."

THE NEXT MORNING, Rosemary was prodded awake by a finger to her kidney. She had downed a Bloody Mary after the call with Van Dyke, and a Valium before bed, her second of the day. These were the general means by which she was managing reentry into the orbit of her parents.

"Get up, dear. You have a call from the White House."

Rosemary squinted at her mother, whose frown lines had been surgically ironed into a grimace.

"The *White House.*" Her mother held up the portable phone and stared at it reverently, as if the person from the White House might be nestled inside. "I promised them I would get you up. You've been sleeping long enough."

The woman on the phone—Denise was her name—explained that the First Lady remembered Rosemary fondly from their previous meetings and wished to offer moral support to "her favorite realtor" in precisely thirty-seven minutes.

Rosemary wanted to ask this Denise how she had secured the number to her parents' home, which was unlisted. Then she realized who she was speaking with. "I'd be honored. Of course." She took the call in the basement, which her father had converted into a faux British pub. "Stand by," a baronial voice said, then, a minute later, "Please hold for the First Lady."

The instant she heard Nancy's voice, she broke down. She watched her tears stain the felt of the lonesome snookers table. "I'm sorry."

"Nonsense," Nancy said. "You let it out."

"It's all been so awful."

"Of course it has."

"I don't know what to believe. Until they find . . . I mean—Marcus goes camping in the desert for days at a time. I'm sure I sound silly."

The First Lady had seen photos of the crime scene, the infamous blotches of commingled blood. She had read the killer's confession, the ghastly plea agreement to which he had affixed his childish signature. And yet she understood Rosemary. She had not accepted the truth until she saw her husband's wounds.

"It's not silly at all," the First Lady said. "We're praying for a miracle. Me and Ronnie both."

Rosemary paused to gather herself, while Nancy spoke to her in a low, soothing tone about the resilience of children. She could hear her mother, on the extension in the master bedroom, trying not to breathe, something she had been doing for most of her life. She knew her mother would dine on this conversation till the day she died—*they spoke for nearly an hour, just like old friends*; the thought exhausted her.

"You were wise to remove yourself from a toxic situation," the First Lady said.

"The police tromp around and ask question after question but they don't *tell* you anything. It's like they're just going through the motions. Half the time, I felt like *I* was the criminal." She shook loose a Virginia Slim and staggered to the window.

"It sickens me how victims of crime are treated in this country," the First Lady declared with a sudden bitterness. "It should sicken all of us. I promise you one thing: that animal will rot in his cell, plea bargain or no."

It took Rosemary a moment to decipher what the First Lady meant. She closed her eyes and saw her basement roiling with scorpions. How many times had she tried to banish those disgusting creatures from her home? Her cigarette had somehow come lit and she pulled smoke deep into her lungs, placing a hand over the receiver so her mother wouldn't hear her smoking. For a piercing moment, Rosemary Stallworth was fourteen again. She could see the glittering rebellion of her youth, could taste the sweet promise of each heedless decision.

"All I ever wanted was a happy family," she whispered.

"That's why I had to call," the First Lady whispered back. The two of them were bound together. They both understood the burdens of motherhood, the imposition of grace on a graceless world. Now they shared something even more elemental: evil had stalked their husbands. Nancy picked up a photo of the Stallworth family that had been sent along by FBI—such fine-looking children—and her voice caught. "I won't rest until justice is done here, Rosemary. You have my word."

IT WAS AFTER ten when Nando heard his cousin's voice break through the static on his shoulder. "What the fuck, *primo*?"

"We got caught out there in the dark."

"Is the girl okay?"

"Fine."

"You find anything?"

"Yeah," Guerrero said, after a pause. "Blast your damn siren already."

They emerged from the desert half an hour later. At a distance, the girl looked to be tugging Guerrero along, for he returned as he had departed, bent under the weight of the pack and sullen as a mule, his rayon shirt sopping. Only now he was bearing something in front of him, like a royal pillow.

THERE WERE THE obvious forensic tasks: blood, hair samples, the tread found around the fire. Checking in with those who had seen Marcus Stallworth on the morning of his disappearance. Beyond these, the decisions became thornier. The first was whether to inform Hooks of what they'd found. Guerrero felt they had no choice.

Nando shook his head. "You're thinking like an Indian, man. You gotta think like a chief. They held a fucking press conference. You were *there*. Remember all those cameras? That's the story now."

"Let me just see what he says."

"Remind me again who tricked you into arresting Tony Saenz?"

"It wasn't a trick."

They were in the front seat of his Buick. Guerrero had his cheek pressed against the A/C vent. Lorena was stashed in the squad car, supposedly eating the remains of Nando's pastries, though she was instead staring at them through the back window.

"If it was me," Nando said.

"It's not you—"

"But if it was, I'd see what I could document first. Better to seek forgiveness than permission. For now, let's get the girl home."

"About her," Guerrero said.

"What?"

He described Lorena's demand.

The more indignant his cousin got, the harder Nando had to work to keep from laughing. "She's just as hardheaded as you."

Guerrero wanted them both dead. He would have been fine with that.

After a minute, they heard a sharp rap from the direction of the squad car. Lorena was scowling at them through the back window. She certainly didn't see what was so funny. Nando tipped an imaginary cap in her direction. "What a fucking junkyard dog you turned out to be."

ON THE DRIVE back to Sacramento, Nando explained to Lorena that she would be charged with obstruction of justice if she withheld information from the police. Her mother would then have two children in custody, and her brother would be no closer to freedom. He presented these facts in the tone of cheery consolation he had perfected as a neighborhood cop, overseeing domestic disturbances. *Like it or not*, his manner said, *we're allies in this unhappy business.*

If she chose to cooperate, he would keep her updated on their progress. That was a promise. If she chose not to cooperate, he would book her into a holding cell and send a police car to her mother's place of employment. That was also a promise. Child Protective Services would need to initiate an investigation of parental negligence, which would naturally take account of her legal status.

Lorena's mother burst from their apartment upon her return. She wept to the point of choking, as the neighbors hung from their doorways. Lorena tried to wrestle free, but Graciela Saenz had no intention of letting go. She hadn't entirely believed her daughter would return at all. It was possible she would simply disappear, as Tony had, into a maze of police stations and prison cells. She thanked Jesus Christ. She thanked Nando, who explained that Lorena had hoped to visit her cousins in San Jose, but wound up on the wrong bus. "It happens more than you think, Señora."

When they went inside, Graciela insisted on making breakfast for Lorena. Nando followed them inside. He just needed to run a quick property inventory before he took off. While Graciela busied herself in the kitchen, he followed Lorena to her room and took possession of the maps she'd stashed under her bed.

One featured a dotted line that traced the route she believed Mr. Stallworth had taken: south through the Bullions to the Salton Sea, then south again and east toward Yuma. Nando stared at the final X on the map, a few miles north of the border. An American with enough cash could turn south right there and stroll into Mexico and vanish off the face of the earth.

BECAUSE HE HAD no interest in encountering the detectives who worked the day shift, especially Captain Hooks, Guerrero waited until after dark to wander back to the Homicide section. Jolley had left the Stallworth file on his desk, all of it, including the FBI's serology report. The lab was in Davis. The technician whose signature appeared at the bottom of the report was Kathleen Blunt.

He drove out there the next morning. Blunt wasn't hard to find. She was the only woman in the lab and the oldest tech by at least a decade. Her work station was dominated by racks of test tubes, filled with dark blood and sickly yellow plasma. "Special Agent Blunt?"

"Kathy will do just fine." She was peering intently into her microscope. "Who wants to know?"

"Officer Pedro Guerrero. Sacramento PD."

Blunt grunted.

"You wrote the serology report on the Marcus Stallworth case, correct?"

Blunt looked up and squinted at Guerrero's ID. The eye-guard of her device had left a pink welt across her forehead and flattened her wiry gray hair into a wedge. "If you say so."

Guerrero, taken aback by her brusqueness, said, "You did compile that report for the FBI, correct?"

Blunt cast a glance in either direction. "If you want to talk work product, let's go someplace quieter." She got up and walked to the back of the lab and turned down a long corridor, then ducked out a side door, to a little alcove littered with cigarette butts. "I'm going to smoke."

"Sure."

Blunt was wearing blue rubber gloves, which she saw no need to remove. "Some people throw a shit fit is why I mention it."

"I was hoping to get a little help with something," Guerrero said.

Blunt took a deep drag. "Help? Are you for real?" It was impossible to escape the impression that Blunt was mad about something.

"Yeah. I have a blood specimen that might be related to the investigation."

Blunt shook her head. "You can leave me out of it—"

"Guerrero. Pedro Guerrero."

"If you want to get Tilson to order me to run more tests, be my guest. But I'm in no mood to do the Sac PD any more favors." Blunt began shaking her head.

"Did I say something to offend you?"

"Don't take this wrong way. I know you're trying to get the bad guys. But I'm a scientist. And the way you all used my report—it doesn't sit right with me."

"Ma'am?"

"Do you even know what a PGM marker is? Are you aware that there are three such biochemical markers derived from the protein enzymes found on the red cell membrane? That while these markers can aid in the identification of forensic blood samples, their efficacy is limited, both by the condition of the samples in question and the inherent degradation of phospho- glucomutase when exposed to air and sun and sodium hypo- chlorite, which is the chemical agent in most cleaning products. Do you even have any idea of what I'm talking about, Officer Guerrero?"

"I think—I think you're telling me the results in this case weren't definitive."

Blunt set down her cigarette and did a slow clap. "Very good, detective. PGMs are a new tool. In conjunction with ABO typ- ing, they enhance our ability to interpret the blood evidence. But PGMs are not like fingerprints. There's statistical overlap from one sample to another. You can get to 70 percent accuracy, maybe, but you can't get 99 percent. To do that, we'd have to get inside the DNA, and we can't do that yet. PGMs aren't a micro- scope. They're spectacles. If you read my draft report, you'd know all this. But you couldn't do that. Because the boys in the Bureau did a little touch-up."

Guerrero closed his eyes. His head was spinning a little. "The report I read—it has your name at the bottom. Are you saying it's bogus?"

Blunt took a last drag of her cigarette and stomped on it. "Subject to misrepresentation. That would be more accurate. Anyway, it doesn't matter. If the suspect says he did it, he did it. You guys lucked out."

"Wait a second," Guerrero said.

"I did my part for the team. I'm through with that case." Blunt shook another cigarette from the pack. Her cheeks had flushed. Guerrero could see that she wasn't just angry; she was ashamed.

"Why'd you sign off on it?"

"Oh, please. Like you've never done something because the boss leaned on you. Spare me the saint routine. And what happens if I raise a stink? Do you think Tilson is going to come down here and say, 'Oh, Kathleen, thank you for your *nuanced* work! Thank you for showing such scientific *integrity!*' No, he's gonna find someone else to do what he needs done. That's how it works with you cops."

"But you're a cop, too, aren't you? A special agent?"

"I'm a serologist, Guerrero. The FBI rents my expertise. Senior tech. That's my official title. I've been running samples longer than most of the boys in there have been shaving their upper lips. That's why I'm the one who gets to teach them how to operate a centrifuge and clean up their work stations. It's loads of fun. The *senior* part was my little anniversary present three years ago, along with a 2 percent raise. You may have noticed that the Bureau doesn't have too many agents that look like me."

"What if I told you that the alleged victim in the Saenz case might still be alive?"

Blunt cocked her head. "I'd want to know your basis for such a claim."

Guerrero set down the paper bag he had with him and drew out the plastic sheath with its neatly folded contents. "I believe these may be the clothes in which Marcus Stallworth disappeared." He pointed to a dark spot on the cuff of the blue oxford. "That's his blood."

"Are you for real?"

"I don't know for sure. That's why I'm here."

"I'd say you should tell your boss before you do anything else, Officer."

"What if I told you that I'm not sure I can trust my boss on this case?" Guerrero looked at Blunt. "Would that make a difference?"

GUERRERO DIDN'T WANT to contact Rosemary Stallworth until he learned more. It would be unfair to lead her on in any way. But he did call on Joseph Tennyson, the professor who had been Stallworth's supervisor and friend. The old man looked at photos of the clothes retrieved from the desert and nodded his head. "I suppose this means you've found a body," Tennyson said.

"I can't say, actually."

"I shouldn't have been surprised when I saw the stories in the paper. But I must confess I was. Years ago, I served in the merchant marines. We wound up in the Battle of Wake Island. This was early in the war. I was a mechanic, thank God, so I got to stay aboard the ship. But I saw what happened to those who went ashore. I'm under no illusions as to what men are capable of doing to one another. I suppose I'd forgotten." Tennyson's head had begun to droop. He looked as if he had aged a decade since the last time they had spoken.

"Do you know if Professor Stallworth ever camped near the Salton Sea?"

Tennyson lifted his chin and his glaucous eyes widened. "Odd that you should ask. You see, I took a peek at the paper Marcus was drafting at the time of his . . . It wasn't entirely ethical, but I didn't want his contributions forgotten. He had become preoccupied of late by mechanisms of autofluorescence, as I mentioned. But for years, his central area of study was parasitic mating, which he believed to be most prevalent in habitats with high saline content."

Guerrero stared at the old man, a bit helplessly.

"The Salton Basin was one such locale," Tennyson clarified. "I should imagine he traveled there often."

GUERRERO PICKED UP Nando in Fresno the next morning. They drove down through Palm Desert on 111, along the flanks of the Salton. Guerrero spent four hours searching, fruitlessly, for the site where Marcus Stallworth might have stashed his supplies.

Nando checked in at the police substation on the east side of the sea, an unmarked shack that sat between the Lost Horizon Mobile Park and the Buckshot Deli. A hand-drawn sign on the door read IMPERIAL COUNTY SHERIFF and below that OUT TO LUNCH.

Nando stopped in at the Buckshot and asked the waitress where he might find the sheriff. She nodded to the last of the establishment's three booths, where a man, enormously fat and pink and bald, sat studying the photos in a firearms catalogue. He gestured to Nando without looking up. "Take a load off. You like corned beef hash? They do it good here."

Nando wedged himself into the booth. "I'm good for now."

"You change your mind, let me know." The man held out a hulking hand, the fingers stiff and gnarled, like petrified wood. "Jimbo Lugar."

"Fernando Reyes."

"Look at you, Ray. I thought I was a blimp. Shit."

He read Lugar instantly; his life had peaked as a high school football star—a lineman, to judge by his fingers—who had never adjusted himself to a world beyond the gridiron, and found in law enforcement a venue for easeful dominance. Most rural

deputies had lived some version of this drama. They were blunt
tyrants, pain machines. The world just kept handing them guns.

"That was a joke, hombre." Lugar grinned wide. "Us big boys
gotta stick together. What can I do you for?"

"Got a missing person might have camped around here a couple of weeks back. End of October, maybe."

"A runaway?"

"Sort of."

"How old was she?"

"He, actually. Caucasian. Early forties." Nando slid a photo of
Marcus Stallworth across the table.

"Handsome devil." Lugar squinted his eyes into fleshy slits.
"Wait. I seen this guy before."

"Might have been on TV," Nando said.

"That's it. Something about that Death Valley case. But the
killer turned out to be a little Mexican fella, am I right? One of
those gangbangers. FBI got him."

"Right. This is Marcus Stallworth. He was the alleged victim."

"Holy shit. You think the Death Valley Killer's been skulking
around here?"

"Doubt it. Just crossing names off my list. You had any reports of transients, guys who might have been camping on the
edge of town?"

"It's all edge around here, hombre."

"Maybe I could take a look at your blotter."

"You're looking at the blotter. All we get is domestics. Petty
theft. Burnouts doing burnout crime."

"No drifters?"

"Not unless you want to count the Ghost Ranger."

"The what?"

Lugar snickered. "There was a rumor going around about
some boogey man who attacked a girl on Halloween, down at
the boat ramp. Wore a ranger's outfit, supposedly."

"You interviewed the victim?"

"Angel Weems is not the sort to seek out officers of the law, if you catch my drift. Huffs paint. That's the budget dope in these parts. Couple of arrests for solicitation, too, up in Palm Desert. State shipped her down here a year ago to stay with her auntie, I guess it is."

"You didn't interview her, then?"

Lugar set his catalogue down and stared at Nando. "I *did* speak to Ms. Weems. She'd been wrung around the collar, alright. I'd lay odds her boyfriend did it. But he's already got a couple of priors. So they cooked up a story. The Ghost Ranger did it! Got the whole trailer park talking about it, like the monster in a fairy tale." Lugar yawned extravagantly. "You know how these young junkies are. Always setting fire to their dreams and having to blow them out."

"Okay," Nando said. "I got it now. And Weems lives in the trailer park over here, the Lost Horizon?"

"Naw, she's in the Oasis," Lugar said. "Couple miles north. The Oasis and the Lost Horizon. Jesus H. Christ. Welcome to the first seating of the apocalypse."

"Least you got plenty of guns for the End Times."

Lugar showed Nando his incisors. "Sorry not to be more helpful. We don't get drifters down here, Rays. The stink keeps 'em clear. Every now and again, some dumb wetback winds up staggering into town half dead. The coyotes get 'em up to Calexico and dump 'em in the desert and they head north. It's in the blood if you're a Mexican, I guess. No offense, obviously."

Nando laughed, a big hearty one. "None taken. Heck, I made it all the way to Fresno, right?" He picked up the photo of Marcus Stallworth and eased himself out of the booth. He took a few steps, then stopped and turned to look at Lugar, an island of mean in a kingdom of sand. "Thanks for the tip on the corned beef hash," he said, friendly as can be. "I was worried you'd be a stupid bigot, like everyone told me. But you're a real pro. This community is lucky to have you."

ANGEL WEEMS SAT in the dim light of her aunt's trailer, quietly relating her encounter with the Ghost Ranger. She wasn't exactly happy to have a uniformed officer on her property. But she looked appreciative that someone in an official capacity was listening to her, recording her words in a notebook.

She and some friends were having a Halloween party near the boat ramp. She left the group to go pee when she heard someone in the darkness. She thought it was her boyfriend Royal trying to scare her. "Then this dude step from the shadows, all messed up. I told him he shouldn't be creeping on girls, and he just starts choking me out." The girl's voice was soft and scratchy; slender bruises ringed her throat.

"What does 'all messed up' mean?"

"Tangled. Mangy beard. He had that desert burn white people get, where all the wrinkles look lit up because the rest of them is, like, red."

"Can you remember how tall he was?"

"Taller than Royal. Maybe six feet. Six-two. He was strong as shit, I know that."

"What about his hair and eyes?"

"Dark hair. Like practically black. His eyes looked, I don't know, spooky. And he had this giant backpack that was like a hundred pounds."

"He was wearing a backpack?"

"It was on the ground beside him." Angel glanced down at the peeling vinyl panels of the trailer floor. "I kept thinking this crazy thing. As he was choking me, I mean. You gonna think I'm crazy, Mr. Nando."

"What were you thinking?"

Angel cradled her belly with a dainty palm. "He's got a girl in there. A girl's *body*. I was trying to get his hands off me, you know? Trying to breathe. That was all I could think: 'I'm gonna end up in that fucking backpack.'" The girl's lips started quivering. "Everyone round here thinks I'm crazy. But I ain't crazy."

"I believe you," Nando said. "You're doing good."

Before he could say anything else, a scrawny boy burst through the door. The girl's younger brother, Nando figured.

"You been telling him?"

Angel nodded. "This Royal. My boyfriend. He was there, too."

"He just about kilt her! She couldn't barely breathe by the time I got to her."

"I told him."

"I was fixing to chase him, too. But he was out of there. Scurried away like one of those damn Scorpios."

"Scorpions."

Royal shook his head. "Did you tell him about the bill?"

"I was *getting* to that." Angel turned to Nando. "After he let me go, you know, he dropped me on the ground and he gave me a hundred, pulled it from his pocket like it was nothing. One of them real crisp ones, too, like, fresh from the bank."

"A $100 bill?"

"Mr. Ben Franklin," Royal said.

"Said we had a misunderstanding. What he called it. He was paying me off. Like, I choked you out, but here's some cash so we square now."

"Do you still have it?" Nando said.

"That was two weeks ago," Royal said.

"Hush up," Angel snapped. "You ain't done shit since you got here but run your yap." She turned back to Nando. "You can ask Mr. Wade at the Mini-Mart. He checked it for counterfeit. You believe that shit? I just got choked half to death and he thinks I'm fixing to pass a bill. People got no trust around here."

"Could you take me to the place where this happened?" Nando said.

"Why you so interested, anyway?" Royal said. "This motherfucker attack someone else?"

Nando looked at the boy. He couldn't have been more than fifteen. His clothes were bright and flimsy and three sizes too large. In a properly governed country he would have been in school at this hour, studying the periodic chart, learning how to solve for X. In a few months, he was going to be a father. "Lugar told me you've had some trouble with the law."

"Lugar. Shee-it."

"Why don't you wait outside for a minute, son. You can show me the way."

For a moment, Royal looked ready to object. Then he went out.

"Just one more question, Ms. Weems. Could you take a look at this picture?"

He handed her the photo of Marcus Stallworth.

She set it atop her belly and held it by the edges, like it was something of great value: a smiling white man in a polo shirt.

"Naw. This guy too clean-cut."

"Okay," Nando said. He took the picture back and turned to the folder he had set down on the counter behind him and drew out a second photo. In this one, snapped during a camping trip, Stallworth wore a sweat-stained safari shirt and a scruffy beard, and his hair was matted. He handed the picture to Angel.

The color drained from her cheeks. Her hand rose up slowly and paused before the bruised stem of her throat.

"It's okay," Nando said. "He's never coming back here. I promise." He gently withdrew the photo from her fingers. "You did good, Angel. I'm sorry the police didn't listen to you the first time around." He wanted to offer her something more before he took off, the assurance that she would be safe, that it was all going to be okay. But the world had taught Angel Weems too much already. She wouldn't wind up in a backpack. She would spend her life in rooms like this one, with particle board walls and cupboards sticky with flies.

THREE THOUSAND MILES from that trailer on the Salton Sea, in the salon of the East Wing of the White House, the First Lady of the United States was being fitted for the state dinner she had organized for Ferdinand and Imelda Marcos of the Philippines. Oscar de la Renta and Bill Blass had flown in for the occasion. The designers—who carefully kept clear of each other—presented Mrs. Reagan with four different gowns, each featuring discreet variations on the butterfly sleeves Mrs. Marcos had made famous. *Discreet* was the key word. She had no intention of copying Imelda, whose shoulder joins were as big as dinner plates.

They were on the final option now, and she was on the point of collapsing. She had consumed 210 calories at breakfast, and even though she hadn't eaten in the hours since, choosing instead to devour stick after stick of sugarless gum, she felt bloated. Oscar's tailor, a young Spaniard named Garland, or Garçon, or something, had just cinched the gown at the waist and was now marveling at her figure. ("You're like a lovely little wasp, aren't you?") His cologne dizzied her; every time she shifted her weight, she could feel the prick of the needles beneath her ribs.

They were still sore—her ribs. She had broken three of them the night after the assassination, having scaled the Bellini lounge chair in the Red Room, then pushed onto her tippy toes to reach a wedding photo she hoped to bring Ronnie in the hospital. Instead, she toppled over and landed on the carpet with a dull crack that sent arrows of agony through her torso. A stupid, clumsy accident.

Six months after the shooting that had nearly killed her husband, the First Lady remained unsteady on her feet. On July 4, she had stood on a dais, as fireworks bloomed over the mall. With each explosion came an image of Ronnie doubled over, blood at the corner of his mouth as he issued his immortal quip: "Honey, I forgot to duck." Had he ducked, the bullet would have struck his face, and now she was thinking about that.

At night, as he slept peacefully, her mind circled back to the same peculiar moment from their past. Back in 1957, young, dumb, drunk on love, they agreed to make a movie together. *Hellcats of the Navy* it was called, a slapdash romance featuring a daring submarine mission and an implausible love triangle. She played a dewy nurse lieutenant, while Ronnie was the skipper of the USS *Starfish*. They filmed down in San Diego, aboard an actual submarine.

On the first day of filming, Ronnie appeared on deck as Commander Casey Abbott. Real sailors scrambled around him, rushing to maneuver the vessel out of port while the tide was running. But someone had forgotten to untie one of the dock lines. The officer in charge noticed that the nylon rope was stretched thin as a pencil. If it snapped it would rip through anything in its path, including Commander Abbott. The officer began screaming: "All stop, goddamnit! ALL STOP!" The entire cast and crew of the film froze. Many took cover as the engines roared into reverse. The only person who remained oblivious to the commotion was Ronnie himself. He continued to run his lines—*Ahead one third, starboard back full!*—rocking back and forth in his gleaming gumboots, with his hands clasped behind his back.

She was haunted by this vision of her husband in his crisp uniform and artful makeup, barking out scripted commands. It was part of his charm, the fact that he refused to heed the dangers around him, the ropes ready to snap, the maniacs with guns. It fell to her to guard the glorious dream housed within his perishable body.

Her only reliable ally, amid the aides who orbited her husband like greedy moons, was her astrologer, Joan. She, too, recognized that Ronnie needed protection. This was why she had recommended the state dinners; they allowed him to perform his presidential duties from within the sanctum of the White House.

But now, as the First Lady stood in a fussy, hand-beaded evening dress, with sleeves that bulged around her shoulders like giant bells, the undertaking felt frivolous. *We're just going through the motions here,* she thought.

"Madame?" The little tailor was staring at her.

Apparently, she had spoken these words aloud. They had stayed with her from the moment Rosemary Stallworth uttered them.

She could sense a growing concern amid her staffers and the others involved in the fitting. But she ignored the biddings of decorum, for a grand notion was taking shape within her, one she had been groping toward for months: Ronnie needed to launch a new initiative, aimed at reforming a criminal justice system that coddled killers and neglected their victims.

All at once, she declared the fitting over—*All stop, goddammit!*—and ordered everyone out of her sight. Then she instructed Denise to call her astrologer.

Joan Quigley had a phone line dedicated exclusively to the First Lady. When it rang, in her Nob Hill aerie, the servants were under orders to summon her. She listened intently as the First Lady described the idea that had come to her in the midst of her fitting. A long silence ensued.

"How strange," Quigley said at last. She spoke in the crisp, well-bred manner of a headmistress. "I just drew a chart on this very subject. Your husband's dominant planet, as you know, is Mars. His ascendant is in Sagittarius, and the ruler of that ascendant is Jupiter. He fights fire with fire, Nancy. It's in his nature."

"That's right," Nancy said.

"He needs to address the nation about this."

"When?"

Quigley was precise in her declarations. "November 30 would be the ideal date. That's a Monday."

The First Lady glanced down at the calendar on her desk: it was November 17.

"And he should come here, to California, where the killing took place."

IT TOOK GUERRERO two days to secure a meeting with Captain Hooks. He arrived in Homicide bearing a cardboard evidence box.

"There he is," Jolley called out from the coffee machine, where he was yapping with two burly colleagues. "The man who shot Liberty Valance! Come say hello. You're gonna be working with these assholes soon enough."

Guerrero shrugged an apology. "Gotta go see the captain."

Jolley ambled over anyway and laid a meaty hand on Guerrero's shoulder and regarded him with an awful congratulatory kindness. "You deserve it." He thumped the lid of the box. "What's this, anyway? You know my birthday isn't till February."

"I like to think ahead," Guerrero said.

"Good work, Chico. I mean it."

"Thanks, Doug."

The captain grunted when Guerrero came in. "Ten minutes," he said. For the past two weeks, Hooks had been dealing with fallout from the Death Valley Killer.

"Can I close the door, sir?"

"Suit yourself."

Guerrero set the box down and removed the plastic package with the filthy, blood-stained garments he'd recovered, which he set gingerly on the edge of the desk. "These are the clothes Marcus Stallworth was wearing when he disappeared."

Hooks stared at Guerrero. "*What?*"

"Recovered from a campsite outside Barstow. Blood matches the samples from inside his vehicle." He handed Hooks the serology report.

"Outstanding work." Hooks smiled in earnest, a rare event. "We'll get the corps out there." He meant the Army Corps. He meant to search for the remains.

"You should have a look at a few other things first, Captain." Guerrero handed Hooks a folder labeled *Supplemental Material*: the first draft of the original serology report, written by Kathleen Blunt, with an affidavit clarifying her verdict on the sample, a write-up on the blood detected in the basement bathroom of the Stallworth residence, excerpts from the interviews conducted with Lorena Saenz, and the interviews conducted over the past week, with Winnie Thoms, Lucia Sanchez, and Angel Weems.

Hooks knew Guerrero had been up to something; he'd taken a few calls and made a few. But he hadn't anticipated anything like this. It was a record of his perseverance and his mistrust, a kind of dossier; Hooks felt the rebuke of it, the threat. He scanned the Blunt affidavit, then picked up his phone. "Tell Gary I need to push our four o'clock. No. No. Just tell him." He hung up and looked at Guerrero.

Then he began to flip through the reports, page after page. Outside the office, the day shift guys were grabbing their coats, shaking smokes loose, bickering about where to grab beers. A knock on the window startled Guerrero: Jolley's pasty face, his sweet idiotic salute.

Hooks kept reading. He ignored the rank aroma seeping from the garments on the edge of his desk. When he was finished, he closed his eyes and squeezed the bridge of his nose for a long time.

"I ever tell you about Jimmy Grinnell?" he said at last.

"Sir?"

"We worked down in Meadowview together, '71 to '74, couple of house Negroes working the Negro beat." Hooks's eyes were still closed, the thin purple lids pulsing. "Call comes across the scanner one day, dispute at a corner store near Scott Homes. By the time we arrive, there's a kid on the ground holding his guts. The first officer to respond is leaning against his unit, looking green as a Christmas tree. Jimmy knows the kid, played ball with his older brother. He's telling the kid to calm down, trying to stop the bleeding. EMS finally get there, cart him off to Mercy, but he's lost too much blood."

Guerrero had never heard Hooks utter more than a few words at a time. He spoke softly, deliberately, like a father who regards storytelling as a grim duty.

"So now it's an officer-involved fatality. The officer in question happens to be a rising star. Handsome white boy, real connected downtown. He interrupted an armed robbery in progress, suspect flashed a weapon, he shot first. Boom: self-defense. That's the official story. Internal affairs backs him up. The kid has a couple of priors, too. Problem is there's no weapon at the scene, okay? Kid didn't have a piece. Jimmy starts asking around on his own. Turns out the armed robbery was a shoplifting dispute. The kid stole a U-NO candy bar. You ever seen a U-NO wrapper, Guerrero? Silver foil. Real shiny. Kid got popped for flashing a loaded chocolate bar."

Guerrero waited for Hooks to finish the story.

"What happened?" he said at last.

"You know what happened, Guerrero."

"I don't."

"Jimmy wrote up his interviews. Drove downtown. Maybe it went upstairs. Maybe it didn't. A year later, he was off the force."

"Fired?"

"Quit. Drove down to LA, got into private security. The kid was still dead. The officer who shot him, Bobby Ellis, got kicked up to lieutenant."

"*Chief* Ellis?"

Hooks sighed, his wrinkled throat swelling.

"What did *you* do?"

Hooks opened his eyes and surveyed the office it had taken him three decades to earn. "You're a good cop, Guerrero. The force is better off with you on it."

"You're going to bury this, aren't you?" Guerrero said, almost in wonder. Like all cynics, he was an idealist at heart.

"The defendant confessed," Hooks replied calmly. "Charged and pled. You cuffed him yourself."

"But Marcus Stallworth is alive." He jabbed his finger into the package he'd retrieved from the desert; must swirled between them, like the miasma from which some malignant genie might appear. "There's a good chance, a decent chance, which means—he has a wife, children."

"Man disappears down a trail of his own blood. You want to be around for that family reunion?"

"You're trying to confuse me," Guerrero said.

"No, I'm trying to get you straight."

"This is about evidence, Captain, exculpatory evidence. With all due respect—"

"Under whose jurisdiction are you operating?"

"Jurisdiction?"

"You entered the home of a homicide victim and his survivors. Did you have a warrant to do so, Guerrero? Did you have permission to visit an FBI lab? To secure an affidavit from a senior scientist at that lab? Under whose aegis did you travel to Fresno and Imperial to conduct interviews? Pursuant to what open investigation?"

"You're trying to put me on trial. This is about Saenz. He could be innocent."

"That's not what he says. It's not what a jury would say. He's a felon. Parties with crackheads. Drives stolen cars. Runs guns out of basements. Where you think his life is headed, Guerrero?

You think he's going to straighten himself out, like you did? He's lucky he's not on death row."

"Lucky?"

Hooks looked down at his lap and began emitting raspy little barks of laughter. "Ninety percent of life is luck. Justice is a luxury item."

Hooks was working him. Guerrero knew that. But his chest had been gripped by a flailing sensation, one he associated with childhood, the years when he had come running to his mother, betrayed by some offense, eager to display for her some wound he might trade for love. His mother would usually offer him a hug. But if he went on too long, she would shake him loose and mutter, *Soñar no lo hace así.*

Dreaming doesn't make it so.

"What'd you think was going to happen here?" Hooks asked. "The FBI was going to take one look at all this and send a search party down to Mexico? Does that accord with your understanding of how justice operates?"

"You're making excuses," Guerrero stammered.

"And you're making it personal. Don't. Show some humility. It's bigger than you, son. Before you were a cop, you were just an invisible number. But you made something of yourself. You chose to protect and serve." Hooks had closed his eyes again. He was speaking slowly now, almost tenderly. "I see you, Guerrero. The world's a better place with you doing this work."

Guerrero glanced at the clothes Marcus Stallworth had stripped off his body and, inexplicably, folded. "What are you going to do with this evidence, Captain?"

Hooks smiled, though his sorrow was evident. "You want to believe we're on opposite sides of this thing. But there's only the one side."

GUERRERO STORMED OUT of the office and found his way to a pay phone. Nando's voice was in his ear, murmuring, *"Tranquilo. Respira hondo."*

"I am calm," Guerrero seethed. "I *am* breathing."

"I warned you about Hooks. He's part of the machine. That's how he learned the gears."

"Didn't matter what I showed him, he was going to find a way to ignore it."

"Now you're sounding like our little friend, Lorena."

"Do me a favor," Guerrero barked. "Shut the fuck up for once."

"Okay. Just don't do anything stupid, *primo.*"

"This isn't over."

"El diablo nos tienta a pecar," Nando murmured. The devil tempts us to sin.

"I'm not gonna do anything stupid."

Why was everyone talking to him like he was a child?

HOOKS TOOK NO pleasure in admonishing Guerrero; his police work had been exemplary. But Hooks knew how the department worked, and he knew how far beyond the department this case had gone. He knew the president of the United States would be traveling to Sacramento in twelve days to deliver a speech to law enforcement officials in which he would outline a sweeping anticrime initiative.

This speech would, in turn, help define the Reagan Revolution, an era dedicated to the promotion of private enterprise and the defamation of the needy. Reagan's optimism was genuine—who but an optimist would crack wise with a bullet lodged an inch from his heart? But behind his bright smile lay the conviction that the poor were destined to enact the violence housed within their souls. The state's essential task was to protect the law-abiding, their boulevards and bright mansions. Even if the Stallworths no longer lived there, the eternal dream of America did.

Captain Hooks could not have known about the First Lady's role in conceiving this plan. But he had good reason to believe that the president would cite the Stallworth murder, as an example of the moral chaos unleashed by career criminals and crack cocaine, as well as the outrageous lenience of the criminal justice system. He was basing this hunch on one indisputable fact: the First Lady—who was taking the unusual step of attending this speech—had demanded that she be seated beside the brave officer who had arrested the Death Valley Killer.

THE TEARFUL RELIEF Graciela Saenz had expressed at the return of her daughter was real enough. But her behavior in the presence of Nando Reyes, the ways in which she had made herself small and abject, were part of the larger performance she staged each day, as an undocumented person. She peered through the shades as Nando drove away, then turned and addressed her daughter. "I assume he took the maps under your bed."

Lorena looked up from her plate of eggs.

"Don't treat me like a simpleton, Lorena. Just because I pray doesn't mean I can't think."

Lorena had underestimated her mother's guile. It was what teenagers did, what allowed them to perpetrate betrayals and to react with indignation when they got caught.

"I got on the wrong—"

"*Cállate*," Graciela said. "Don't tell me about some bus you missed. You went down there looking for something to help your brother. You wanted to play the hero. And what's the result? My daughter in police custody. What do you think happens to this family if he files a report? *Think*, Lorena."

Graciela came and stood behind Lorena's chair. It was something she did when she didn't want her daughter to see her face. She took hold of Lorena's shoulders. As she spoke, her grip tightened steadily until Lorena let out a whimper; Graciela paid her no mind. She was a tired woman with powerful hands. Her life was a small box of disappointments lit by the blood of Jesus. When she allowed herself to daydream, it was of her daughter graduating from college and becoming a nurse.

"No more lies. Your father gave me enough for one lifetime. Then came your brother. Enough. If something had happened to you—" Her voice broke off. "I want you to listen now. Tony was weak. He gave in to temptation, to vice. You can't save him. You're fourteen, Lorena. You have a mind for studies. It's a gift God gave you. You're a citizen of the United States. That's the gift we gave you, your father and me. You are not to throw away these gifts. Do you understand? I won't let it happen."

They spent the next few days in an uneasy silence. Graciela had arranged time off from work. Each morning, they took a bus to the federal lockup, where they joined a line of glum relatives that stretched around the building. They wore baseball caps and kept their heads down to avoid being identified as kin of the Death Valley Killer. Inside the dingy, smoke-filled lobby, a guard behind bulletproof glass scanned his clipboard and denied their request. Lorena asked him what this meant. He shrugged. "I'm just a guy with a list, sweetie."

They arrived earlier each day, but the response was the same. Antonio Saenz was not taking visitors. Lorena spoke to a secretary in the public defender's office who said that prisoners often behaved this way during the initial phase of their incarceration. They were ashamed. Visits were one thing they could control. He would soften up as his sentencing hearing drew closer.

"Could I meet with his lawyer?"

"I'll pass along the message," she said.

Lorena was no longer allowed to make calls at home. Graciela took the phone with her into the bathroom and snatched up any incoming calls. Most of the time, it was a friend from church, to whom she whispered for hours, while Lorena sat at the kitchen table, staring at the take-home packets sent by her teachers, affixed with desperately cheerful little notes—*Do your best! I'm here if you have any Qs!*—that somehow made everything worse. There were other calls, too, which her mother took in the halting, petrified English she used with officials. Officer Reyes, perhaps, or even Guerrero.

Lorena was forbidden to leave the house unaccompanied. Graciela took her to Bible Study in the evenings, where Pastor Jorge exhorted the group to direct the power of their prayers to uplift the Saenz family.

Lorena had watched this process play out with Tony before he enlisted: the improvised house arrest, the trips to church; the glowering meant to disguise Graciela's distress. She wanted Tony to understand how fragile his destiny was; the INS didn't care how long he'd lived in the United States, how gringo he believed himself to be. They had a list and he was on it. They both were.

It never ended well. After a few days, Graciela would return to work and her son would slip outside to the cracked avenues, ready to take foolish risks for the older boys he mistook for friends. Lorena would hear them out there, gathered under the addled streetlights, spitting, cracking knuckles, calling Tony *maricón, pendejo*, mockery that filled him with the pride of being seen.

Lorena was thinking about all this on the night her mother crept into her room, dressed in her work uniform. "You don't have to pretend to be asleep," Graciela said. Lorena understood the situation at once: her mother had taken the midnight shift.

She came and sat on the edge of the bed and told Lorena that she would be back in the morning. In the meantime, she had arranged for neighbors to check in, to make sure she didn't run away again.

"I didn't run away," Lorena murmured.

Graciela stared down at the daughter who had somehow, in her absence—while she was at work or worrying about Tony or praying for deliverance—become a young woman. She wanted to touch Lorena's cheek, to anoint her with forgiveness. She thought of what awaited her in the hospital rooms she was paid to clean, the new mothers, rosy with exhaustion, clinging to their precious cargo. "Don't do anything foolish, my daughter. We need to stick together now." She wanted to sound commanding, but she couldn't squeeze the fear out of her voice.

Lorena lay still below her, inhaling the scent she had come to know as her mother's, industrial detergent, cooking oil, hair spray, the sweet loam of her skin. Later, she would think back on this moment: I should have hugged her.

It was still dark when the knock came. Lorena shook herself awake. She sat up in the dark and cursed her mother and whomever she had enlisted for this humiliating bed-check, probably the widow Gomez, who reveled in such tasks. But the figure in the doorway was a man. It took her a second to recognize him. He was dressed in sweatpants and new hiking boots and looked genuinely astonished to see her. Lorena knew at once why he had come. She could feel the sting of her betrayal.

"Where are we going?"

Guerrero dipped his chin. "To find him."

LORENA AND HER mother had been left with the impression that Tony had turned them away. This was not the case. Within hours of their first and only visit—an encounter videotaped and reviewed by federal investigators—the inmate was transferred to a Special Management Unit, which was the formal name for solitary. According to Corrections officials, his gang affiliation, along with his notoriety, placed him at risk in the general prison population. The transfer had in fact come at the request of the FBI, acting on the recommendation of Special Agent Joel Salcido. Solitary softened the mind and weakened the will. Prisoners became more likely to provide additional information about, for instance, the location of a victim's body.

The solitary unit consisted of six cells, each measuring seven by twelve feet. They had been staggered so that it was impossible to see the other inmates. Tony could hear them but had trouble making out their words. The concrete reverberated with muddy shrieks. Once a day, a guard ordered him to slip his hands through the food slot and cuffed him and he was led to an "exercise room" that was the size of three cells set end to end. Inside was an old tennis ball. After an hour, he was cuffed and returned to his cell. Both guards walked behind him. He couldn't see their faces. That's what solitary was: a place without faces.

He was allowed a pencil and a yellow legal pad. His lawyer directed him to write what she called a "biographical sketch" that could be used for the Pre-Sentencing Report. It was essential that the judge come to see him as a person. Tony picked up the pencil and stared at the yellow paper. He saw some old man in a white wig and black gown peering down at his story through bifocals. He was being ordered to perform his misery, to beg for mercy.

At night, he lay on his bunk, stabbed by memory, as if in retaliation for his silence. He remembered the night of the beating, the stony weight of his father's head resting on his lap in a darkened desert. He remembered staggering through a cold dawn toward a mythical place called Needles and then being there, in Needles, and his father cursing him for shitting his pants. He remembered begging his mother for a treat from the vending machines in some industrial basement, and not telling her what he wanted most, which was for her to come home. He remembered the whore who called herself Trina, the scorpion tattoo that rode the loose skin of her belly, the gleeful panic of his blood, which he had confused with love.

He obsessed over all the people who had played him for a fool, the guys who had put him up to shit in Fruitridge. The recruiter who promised him that the navy was his best bet for a green card. ("We might have to finesse a few things on your contract, Antonio, but Uncle Sam always takes care of his own.") He was supposed to learn sea-to-air missile systems. But he'd wound up marooned at China Lake, poking at a computer keyboard in a basement with an A/C unit that coughed cold air on him all day.

He thought about Lorena, with her straight As and her white-girl dreams. He'd tried to protect her but she'd ratted him out. His own blood had done that. He punched the walls until his knuckles swelled. He joined the howling chorus of men trapped in a loop of grievance.

But at night, precisely an hour after lights out, the hollering stopped and mysterious whooshing sounds prevailed. Tony thought he might be imagining it. He peeked under the crack of his door just in time to spot a magazine sliding across the unit. It vanished, miraculously, under the threshold of the cell beside him. The recipient tapped three times on his meal slot and a small rectangle came rifling back across the floor—a pack of playing cards. This was how the unit conducted trade.

The next night, a small white triangle flashed beneath his door, a tightly wrapped sheet of paper with a hole in one corner that had been strung with dental floss. He untied the floss and held it between his thumb and forefinger and his heart fluttered as he felt the tug of the human being at the other end. Then the floss was gone, plucked back by its rightful owner. Tony un-folded the paper, which contained several yards of dental floss, then crouched in the corner where a little pool of light from the common area seeped in. The note was composed in a tight, controlled script, in pencil, with multiple erasures and corrections, as if in accordance with a penmanship workbook.

I hear we got royalty among us. Soak the ground and rejoice, brother. The TRUE REVOLUTION of the LKN is at hand.

This called fishing.

2 knocks = sending. 3 knocks = returning. Practice. DO NOT attempt till you learned for real. CO will confiscate everybody shit if U get caught. Fishing hours: 7:45-8 AM & 10-10:30 (shift switches)

Get a ROUTINE. Don't watch the clock. Your head will play tricks on you. Don't listen to that shit.

Is it true you popped some rich motherfucker?

Darius X., LKN (Stockton, CA)

Darius X included a diagram of the unit, showing the location of his cell, catty-corner from Tony. The diagram included a dotted line showing the path the note had traveled. At the bottom of the note, Darius had drawn an intricate portrait of the Sacred Crown, the Latin Kings' logo. The three tips of the crown were emblazoned with the letters *M*, *Y*, and *D*; a miniature lion curled in the middle. Tony read the note a dozen times.

He spent the following day composing his response, working through a dozen drafts in search of the words and phrases that would make him sound assured. He edited himself down to a paragraph, offering thanks and respect to the Almighty LKN, describing how he'd been framed up, how he wanted to change his plea but couldn't reach his lawyer. He signed the note: Antonio S. (Sac, CA)

He folded the note razor sharp and affixed the dental floss and perfected the flick along its hypotenuse, a technique he recalled from the games of paper football he'd played in detention. That night, at 10:00, he tapped twice on his meal slot. Two sharp raps sounded across the unit, and a magazine came rifling out from somewhere. There was a protocol to this, an order. It made sense. He was new to the unit. It was 10:25 before his turn came. Tony flicked his note out, heard it skitter along the floor, the faint thud as it hit something on the other side. He tugged the note back, tried again. The floss kept tangling. His fingers went slick with sweat. Then time was up and the others started hissing at him. He needed to respond to Darius, but he couldn't figure it out, couldn't manage it, and he was taken with a terrible humiliation. As he lay on the floor of his cell, silently convulsing, something pricked at his cheek—a note, approximately the size of a cockroach.

You'll get it, brother. Try again tmw. D

It took him six tries the next night before he felt a tug from the other side, which connected him to Darius. It was almost like touch, as close as he could get, and so he held on for a few seconds, letting the floss cut into the pad of his thumb, until he heard three knocks and released his grip and by then joy had wet his cheeks.

Thus began a brief and volatile correspondence, one that would eventually be sealed from public view, within an FBI file. The two men exchanged a dozen notes over the next week, 2,813 words in all.

Darius wrote about his life as a banger, dealing weed, flashing his piece, playing the big man on a little corner. He described this period as his "primitive stage." He had been unwittingly enlisted into an army of poor boys who turned their rage on one another. It was all part of the larger scheme: to keep brown people imprisoned in poverty. Joining the Kings had taught him that. He'd absorbed a few beatings, which he now appreciated.

The LKN had rules, consequences. He retired from the streets. Then a friend from those days turned on him and he caught an old charge, aggravated assault on a cop. He wound up in solitary for defending himself from a pair of skinheads who jumped him. He missed his queen and his son. But he knew he was an instrument of the True Revolution; this phase of his life was a necessary step. MYD. *Make Your Destiny.*

His notes were full of such abbreviations, aphorisms, icons, all of which fit into a larger system of thought, a kind of fervent mysticism that Tony associated with the storefront preachers his mother revered. With Darius, though, the gospel wasn't about some skinny blond God bleeding out for your sins. It was about facing the truth of your circumstance, where you came from, what you were up against. Make the mind strong and the body will follow.

Darius understood Tony's life. He, too, had been raised by a single mom, part of the larger system he called the Immigration Slave Trade. It was like on the plantations: tearing families apart was how you turned proud men into angry drunks and queens into servants. It was how white people programmed brown people to pick fruit and dig ditches and clean toilets. The un-documented had no voice. Sometimes, they even got tricked into becoming soldiers, dying on behalf of regimes that treated them as subhuman. *That recruiter chumped you,* Darius wrote. *He was just making his quota. They pulled the same shit on my little bro.*

Tony had never thought about his life in such sweeping terms. He felt honored to be the recipient of such wisdom, and he studied each letter closely. He began to hear the words in his ears, a gruff and knowing whisper, like Peña, but without the bluster. It was Darius he was hearing. His friend Darius.

For the first time since his arrest, Antonio Saenz began to feel that there might be a life on the other side of this ordeal. Be-cause Darius wasn't just offering friendship. He offered a kind of enlightenment, a path from the ruin of his past. To get there, Tony would have to endure the present, to absorb injustice without losing hope. He needed a belief system to do that, and someone to believe in him. He had that now.

It was precisely at this point that the tone of the notes from Darius began to shift, from benevolence to gentle confrontation. *I was just like you when I first got here,* Darius wrote. *Everything was someone else fault. But there's a reason you're here. You got to own what you done.*

Tony acknowledged his sins: the drugs and fights and lies. He knew he needed to atone and he could see now that prison afforded him the chance to do so. He sent this letter off but received no response.

He began to fear that Darius had fallen ill, or been moved off the unit. He lay with his cheek pressed to the floor and stared out at the common area. On his march to the exercise room, he called to Darius. Kissing noises and shouts of *faggot* rang out around him. Tony sent a second note, then a third. *You still there? We cool?* Tony never made the conscious connection, but the terror that coursed through him was the same as in the months before his father left for good, the urge to say just the right thing, to keep an idol from slipping away.

AFTER THREE DAYS, Darius replied:

> *Live by the Manifesto. Come clean or you stay dirty. You got a body on your record now. A man buried somewhere. A True King carries that. A True King takes care of his people on the outside. You know what I'm saying, T. MYD.*

Tony stared at the note for a long time. He knew what it meant, what he was being told to do. For a few hours, he found refuge in the cleansing rage of the boy who'd been played again. Then came the tender ache of bewilderment. He couldn't understand why Darius didn't believe him. He felt he must have done something wrong, something that made him unworthy of faith, and justified his abandonment. Long ago, his father had disappeared and his mother had stopped believing in him. He did not understand these events as losses that might be mourned. They had become a part of who he was, a merciless doubt that attached itself to everything he touched. Tony could not forgive. The want of it took him under.

He sat on the floor of his cell and the silence pummeled him. After a time, he heard a dull bellowing for silence; with a start, he realized that he had been producing a low keening noise.

Corrections officers gathered his untouched meals and led him to the exercise box. In the logbook filled out for the next shift, they described Tony as *withdrawn, sluggish, disoriented.* These words elicited no great sense of alarm. They were common on the solitary unit, where inmates, dulled by sensory deprivation, often retreated into private torment.

It was at this point—a week into his solitary confinement, five weeks from his sentencing hearing, three days from his twentieth birthday—that Antonio Saenz began to experience auditory hallucinations. The voice came at night mostly, when the drone of complaint dimmed and the unit settled into fitful slumber.

What, you thought I was just going to ghost on you? Come on, T. You ain't shaking me that easy. We kings for life. We gotta get each other straight.

Tony knew he was going sort of crazy. He had heard other inmates, in the throes of something like madness, pleading for their meds. It never occurred to him to alert the guards. He worried what Darius would think.

YOU STILL UP, *T?*

No.

We gotta talk through this shit.

What shit?

The feds gonna put something on your mom. They done it a thousand times before.

You don't know that.

She got no papers. Look at it.

You're not real.

I know. I'm just saying shit you already know. Don't hate the prophet for telling the truth. Darius laughed. He sounded a little drunk. *She carried you. Brought you into this world. Down there in some dusty-ass village. Think on that. Your dad never did shit but drink and fuck his whores and beat on her every now and then. You gonna hurt her, too?*

Tony rolled off his bunk and did push-ups till his shoulders burned and lay there panting while a rough hand took hold of his piddling biceps and squeezed until the muscles yelped. He let his head thump on the floor.

Andale, Pollito. This was what his dad called him, Little Chicken. He could smell the yeasty fumes of beer, rising from a tongue browned by cheap Mexican cigarettes. Faros, they were called. Lighthouse. At night, as they sought passage through the desert, Little Chicken staggered after the glowing orange tip.

How do you know about my dad?

I know about everything, T. I know you fucked two girls your whole-ass life. I know you're no King. That raggedy-ass home-made tattoo—that don't make you LK. I know what you did to that fucking chester who messed with your little sister.

You don't know shit.

I know what's gonna happen if you don't tell them where you hid that body. That's the whole problem here.

I don't have a problem.

Darius laughed his tremolo laugh.

There is no body.

But that wasn't true. Tony could feel the cutting wind of the desert, could hear his father's moans, the meaty thud of boots kicking the life out of him. He got them to relent and took his father's head onto his lap and promised to keep him alive. His father grinned and blood dripped down his mustache and chin so that his face looked like a tribal mask. *"Me vas a proteger, pollito?"* You going to protect me, Little Chicken?

Then he went limp and Tony was sure he *had* died. He wanted to go find someone who could help him, an adult, but his father had pinned him to the earth and he could only stare at the stars smeared across the distant night, while scorpions tiptoed around them. He couldn't remember what happened next. It occurred to him, obscurely, that perhaps nothing had happened, that the rest of his life, as he knew it, was simply the long nightmare of a boy trapped beneath his father.

You thinking about him again, huh? That fucking borracho. Remember what he used to say about your mom?

Sangre campesina.

That's it. Fucking peasant blood. Like he was some kind of royalty. With that stupid mustache of his. She made the same journey he did, T, with a baby inside her. You chose the wrong God to worship.

I don't worship him.

You wanna be a True King, save your queen. Show them where the body is.

There is no fucking body. I told you.

Then give them another one.

The night pressed down like a stone.

What are you talking about?

Darius sighed, abruptly bored of the whole topic. *Do the math, Little Chicken.*

TONY BEGAN TO notice the more obscure aspects of his cell. He had conducted a basic inventory when he arrived: the wooden bed frame with its wilted mattress, the conjoined stainless-steel toilet and sink, the concrete slab that was supposed to serve as a desk. Now he looked farther up the walls, his gaze snagging on a fire sprinkler head some ten feet off the ground and bolted into the cinderblock. It was housed in a steel mesh cage.

He began toying with the idea of prying off the mesh cage. He didn't think about why he wanted to do so. It was just a problem to solve, a distraction from the empty hours and the voice. He had no tools, aside from two pencils and a few yards of dental floss. But he could see that it might be possible to weight the floss with the pencil and use it as a kind of lasso. He used a noose knot to attach the pencil and a lariat knot for the floss itself and swung it in wild little circles, aiming for the bent prongs at the top of the mesh cage, as if he were a tiny vaquero in a tiny rodeo. It took a dozen tries, but he finally figured the optimal wrist action and release angle and the lasso sailed up and caught on a prong and Tony let out a yelp of triumph.

So what if the floss snapped at the first sharp tug? The basic method worked. He doubled up the floss, then braided the strands into a slender rope, and this time he tore the mesh cage from one of its hinges before the floss shredded.

An hour later, he sat with the mesh cage in his hands, holding it like the delicate bird nests he had lifted from the crooks of trees as a child. He hated school back then, being small and clumsy and unable to decipher the words flying out of the mouths around him. The classroom was a place of solitude and shame. But there were moments in science lessons when he felt the spark of competence, even a shy sort of wonder.

That was what had led him to the navy, the promise of what the brochures called "applied science," calculating launch thrust and trajectory, the silent music of physics applied to missiles sent hurtling through the atmosphere. That plan had turned to shit, like everything else. But at least he'd learned his knots. For the first time since he'd arrived in solitary, Tony ate every bite of his meal. He sat at his desk, scooping powdered eggs into his mouth, glancing from time to time at the sprinkler protruding from the wall, then at his bedsheet, which measured nine feet, two inches along its hypotenuse, rolled tight and properly knotted.

So long as he set his mind to the task, Darius didn't say shit. But at night, he started up again.

Clever work, Little Chicken. But you still gotta find a way to get yourself off the ground.

I know.

The storage locker, right? You can do a jump kick, ninja style. Time it right or you're fucked as a fish. I know one guy—

Shut up already.

I'm just saying, if the guards catch you, they put you on a special watch. Then we're both fucked.

I don't need a bedtime story.

Calm down. I'm just here to help.

THE NEXT MORNING, Tony slid the "locker" from beneath his bunk. It was a hard plastic bin, actually, the kind his mother had lingered over in Kmart, before deciding they were an indulgence. He took out the socks and underwear and stashed them under the bed, with the prison-issue Bible, and positioned the bin below the sprinkler. It would take some doing, to leap and kick at the same time, to make sure the head came forward just as the body was falling.

Darius was right. A botched job would mean hours of writhing, a trip to the looney bin, doctors watching over him like a specimen. He had one shot to get it right. Back to science: mass, force, trajectory. He practiced all day. Leap. Kick. The syncopated skitter of the little plastic bin.

There were no cameras to capture this macabre ballet. But the staff had been keeping a close eye on Antonio Saenz. In fact, they had taken the remarkable step of enlisting an inmate to send Saenz notes under the alias Darius X—notes that had been composed by Special Agent Joel Salcido. This plan was approved by the Bureau of Prisons, at the direction of the Department of Justice.

The goal of this correspondence was to extract information regarding the location of his victim's body. In Salcido's professional assessment, Saenz had been broken, psychologically, and was prepared to provide the necessary details.

Salcido was unaware that his operation had been commissioned by the attorney general of the United States. Nor that the president himself was scheduled to deliver a major speech just a few miles away, in which he intended to cite the grisly slaughter of Marcus Stallworth as evidence of the need for a crackdown on violent crime. It was the president who needed a body.

Salcido knew only that there was "pressure from above"—his superiors had made that abundantly clear. And so he planned to visit solitary the very next morning, to interview Antonio in person, to see if, together, they could resurrect the dead.

LORENA SAENZ HAD no reason to expect that Officer Guerrero would appear at her door. And yet some part of her had been anticipating his arrival. For years, she had pledged allegiance to the flag and the republic for which it stood, while a portrait of the governor (who had been a movie star and was somehow now the president) watched over her. His smile was a sunny thing, full of eternal promise. There were moments when it reassured Lorena, as she imagined a kind father would.

She had grown up in a one-bedroom apartment with pipes that smelled of sulfur and carpenter ants that no amount of scrubbing could defeat. But like Guerrero—unlike her mother and brother—she had been born into certain innocence. Deep down, she believed that a man proved innocent in America would be a man set free.

THEY STOPPED AT Denny's on the way out of town. Guerrero unfolded a copy of the map Nando had taken from her and laid it across the table. His version had a blizzard of indecipherable notes, recording his contacts with police in the little towns around Yuma. Now he was explaining the plan to Lorena. They would locate the final supply drop—that was where she came in—to gather additional evidence and any clues as to the whereabouts of Mr. Stallworth. Guerrero had traced out a route that would bring them within five miles of the drop, provided the roads were passable.

The waitress came by with their food and Guerrero pulled the map onto his lap, where it sat like a giant, dirty napkin.

"Big plans, huh?" The waitress smiled down at Lorena. "Where are you and your dad headed off to this morning?"

Lorena glanced at Guerrero, then down at her pancakes. "It's just, like, this thing for school. A science fair."

"How exciting! You must be excited, too, Dad!"

"I am," Guerrero replied.

"What's your project about, sweetie?"

"Navigation," Lorena murmured. "Like, using the stars to navigate."

"Cool. The only thing I know about the stars is my horoscope! And half the time, even that turns out to be wrong." The waitress aimed a giggle at Guerrero. "Freshen up your coffee?"

"We're actually running kind of late. Any chance we could get the check?"

"No problema," the waitress chirped. "Good luck today!"

"We'll need it," Guerrero said.

The waitress looked at him curiously, then smiled. "Well, I just think it's real nice to see a dad who's so involved."

The two of them sat in uneasy silence and waited for her to tally the bill. A puffiness showed under Guerrero's eyes. Lorena realized, in some vague manner, that he was no longer acting in an official capacity. "Eat your pancakes already," he snapped. "We're going to need energy. Don't worry about your mom. Nando will keep her calm." This was an absurd thing to say; they both knew it.

Then they were back on the highway, whizzing down the Central Valley with its neat rows of withering crops. The signs read Fresno 27, Barstow 265.

Lorena sat in confusion. She was young and shy, a girl conscripted into action by a cop. It took her some time to pose the question on her mind.

"Why are you doing this?"

The dawn sun sliced through the windshield. "New facts have come to light," Guerrero said stiffly.

"I guess the blood on those clothes wasn't Tony's."

"Good guess."

"But if we're doing this, I mean, isn't that reasonable doubt?"

"That's a standard that applies at trial, Lorena."

"Couldn't his lawyer—have you told her?"

"Tony pled guilty. That's how the system sees him."

"The *system*?" Lorena spoke the word with more force than she intended. It was the word her mother had invoked a thousand times, the reason she couldn't get days off for birthdays, the reason she couldn't complain to the landlord or make parent/ teacher conferences. Her mother spoke of the system as if it were some vast machine, in which the human beings were merely parts, twirling gears, dizzy cranks, soft valves. "Aren't *you* the system?"

"I don't have some magic wand, Lorena. That's not how it works."

"How does it work?"

Guerrero saw Hooks in his office, the benevolent mask he had worn as he took possession of the evidence laid before him. He thought of the corrupt thrill he'd felt wheeling Antonio around and latching cuffs onto his delicate wrists.

Lorena could sense that Guerrero was off-balance, and because she hated him at least as much she trusted him, she pushed harder: "You can lock my brother up but you can't set him free?"

Guerrero had been gunning the Buick, but now he mashed the brake and swerved onto the shoulder so that the seat belt cut into Lorena's belly. "What did you just say?"

Lorena stared out the windshield. They were into orchard country now, the endless rows of trees, frisked of their fruits by seasonal workers who came north each spring and vanished by Thanksgiving.

"You want to make me into the bad guy in all this? Take a look at your brother. You think he's some kind of saint?"

"I didn't say that."

"Where did you think Tony was going to end up, with his stolen cars and his *pistoleros* and his coke parties? Come on now. You're a smart girl, Lorena. Do the math. You think he was going to clean himself up? Become a real success story? Dreaming don't make it so."

Guerrero was staring at Lorena, at the spot on the lower lid of her eye where a tear balanced. Its trembling enraged him. He wanted her to stop sniveling. He wanted to ask her what the hell she had been doing in that house in the first place, flirting with a rich white dad three times her age. He wanted to stop yelling at her. "I'm the one who listened to you! I'm the one running around trying to save his ass! I could have left him to rot in prison! Do you have any idea how much trouble I could get into here? Hell, if it wasn't for me . . ."

Amid this shouting, Lorena had assumed a watchful stillness, which Guerrero recognized from the years he had spent overseeing domestic disputes. It was the posture certain children learned to adopt, to keep themselves safe from the bad weather of a drunken father or boyfriend. He had been one of those children.

Pedro Guerrero was not the sort of person who held on to the past, at least not that he could tell. Police work suited him because it kept him facing forward, toward the next call, the next clue; he had a procedural path to follow. He had needed the uniform at first, and the gun, and the power that came with them. But that power was hollow, or worse, indecent, without the impulse to protect the innocent.

His hand slowly reached out toward Lorena; the girl flinched. He had no right to comfort her. But at least he had stopped yelling. The sun drilled into his eyes, so that he had to wipe at them furiously. "I'm sorry, Lorena. Okay? I don't know your brother. I've got no right to speak about him like that. Okay?"

Lorena knew what she was supposed to say to this cop, the absolution he was demanding. Her father had pulled the same maneuver. She couldn't remember the words he had used. She was too young for that. But she recognized the tone—the menace lurking within its imploration—and her mother's sighs, each one cast into the small, bottomless wishing well of her life.

"You want me to say it's alright?" Lorena said. "It's not alright. None of it is alright."

"I know."

Guerrero dipped his chin, an effort at humility that came off as a sulk.

Lorena closed her eyes and saw Tony, the sullen brother who had held her in photos. He was the one who needed to be held, the little boy who had been dragged away from his life, across deserts and borders, unable to protect himself, and later, his mother, and her. He loved weapons, but he didn't have the guts to kill. He would sooner harm himself.

"If something happens to him, it's on your head," Lorena said.

"I know."

IN FRESNO, THEY ditched Guerrero's Buick for a Jeep, borrowed from a friend of Nando's who worked for the National Park Service, a rather morbid loaner, given the make and model of the vehicle found a month earlier, splashed with blood. But they needed four-wheel drive, and it would help to have an official vehicle, with an insignia and a radio.

They sped south, through Bakersfield and Vasalia and Indio, onto Route 111, then east on 78, which carried them into the blasted wasteland north of Yuma. He had entrusted Lorena with the map, and from time to time she offered directives, but otherwise said nothing, only stared out the window. She had the inscrutable manner of a child accustomed to being alone, at home in the company of her own thoughts. With every mile marker, Guerrero felt his ambivalence giving way to inevitability: he had taken them too far to turn back.

They passed the old Tumco Mine, where men in search of gold had carved the earth into tiers that resembled Mayan temples. Wild burros clustered in the stingy shade of verde trees, nibbling at the brittle blossoms of Mormon tea. Higher up, the slopes turned to cobbles of rusty orange and brown.

Guerrero stopped short at a turnout. A thick chain stretched across the fine yellow dust of the road, affixed with two signs, one in English, the other in Spanish:

DANGER | KEEP OUT | WARNING

U.S.N.R. MILITARY RESERVATION

NO CIVILIAN ACCESS BY ORDER OF THE

INSTALLATION COMMANDER, CHINA LAKE

Beneath were a series of criminal codes.

"What the hell?" Guerrero grabbed a pair of binoculars and examined the road, which looked sturdy and flat as it winded up into the Picacho Wilderness. He called back to Lorena. "How far away are we?"

"Seven miles; seven point four."

"Jesus Christ."

"There's no military reservation here. Not according to the map."

"Of course not. It's bullshit." Some turf battle, bureaucrats squabbling over barren land. Or maybe they'd found treasure beneath the earth—oil or gold or water. Lorena watched him grab a pair of bolt cutters from the trunk. It wasn't a graceful operation, but he got through the chain.

"I'm deputized as Park Police, but you should stay here."

Lorena shook her head. "You said it yourself. It's bullshit."

"Don't curse."

Up and up they went, into the ripping breeze. After a few miles, strange features began to appear in the landscape: cobbles that had been blown apart, churned earth, pale circles blasted onto the slopes and rimmed in ferrous rubble. The farther they went, the worse it got. Trees tossed sideways and charred to ember, the bleached bones of animals like ivory sculptures. A great desert tortoise lay overturned by the side of the road; they got out to inspect this stinking curiosity. It was as if they had entered some province of biblical ruin. Lorena thought of the phrase Pastor Jorge used in church, *el Apocalipsis*, uttered always with relish, as if God's damnation would be his final dividend as well.

Guerrero could see that the area had been used for bombing runs, and recently.

"We're three miles away," Lorena said. "Not even. Two point eight."

"It's too dangerous."

"You're just going to give up?"

"I'm not giving up," Guerrero said. "I'm keeping us from getting blown up. Or maybe you want to end up like our friend here?" He nodded at the tortoise's cracked shell, picked clean by vultures.

Lorena stood clutching her compass and pedometer, studying the road.

"Don't even think about it," he said quietly. "Get in the car. Now."

"Look," he said, a few minutes later, "I'm responsible for you." In fact, he had abducted her, for the second time if one wanted to get technical, which a prosecutor might. "This is how police work goes, Lorena. There are setbacks."

"What do we do now?"

"We drive home and hope your mom isn't too freaked out." He was disappointed but also secretly relieved. He had done what he could to honor his promise. In time, she would see that.

"But he's down here. You saw the map."

"He could be in Mexico City by now, Lorena. He could be in Tahiti."

They drove out of the wilderness, retracing their route in silence, passing through Bard and Ross Corner. It was late afternoon. The folly of what he'd done was dawning. It would take ten hours to get Lorena home, at which point the questions would start. They stopped at a Circle K for food and gas, and while Lorena was in the bathroom, Guerrero tried Nando from the pay phone and got nothing.

He knew his chief duty at this point was to see Lorena safely home—that had been his duty all along, actually—though he took a last idle look through his notes, where he came across the name Ricky Stark, an old friend of Jolley's from their days in the Border Patrol, who handled missing persons down in Yuma.

HE FIGURED STARK would be white, but he was one of those Hispanic dudes who had reinvented himself as a good old boy: aviator shades perched atop a crew cut, Tony Lamas hoisted onto his desk, a lump of Skoal bloating his bottom lip. The photo on his desk showed a couple of little blond princesses holding him hostage with toy rifles. "Doug Jolley. Well shit. That lazy sumbitch called me, what, a month ago. You guys had that bruhaha up there, the Death Valley thing. What brings you to God's little furnace?"

"A missing person," Guerrero said, carefully. "We got a report that he may have been camping up in the Picacho Wilderness."

"Not recently, I hope. They started bombing that place a few weeks back, no warning or nothing; you could hear the jets screaming."

Guerrero grinned stupidly.

"Don't tell me you drove up there." Stark spit into his coffee cup. "Shit."

"Isn't that federal wilderness?"

"Supposed to be."

"Are they done with the bombing?"

"Good luck getting a straight answer. Who's this guy you're looking for?"

"Stallworth. Marcus. But he'd be traveling under an assumed name."

"The good old gringo runaway."

Guerrero handed him a Xeroxed photo and recited the rough particulars: white, early forties, from the Sacramento area.

Stark cocked his head and spit again. For a moment, Guerrero felt sure that Stark had recognized the name, or the face. Instead, he swung his boots off the desk and reached for a notepad behind him. "Doubt this does you any good, but I got a call last night. A woman from a ranch just across the border. Said there's some Americano who wandered down there, after getting robbed in the desert. She put him at forty, thereabouts. But this guy is from Tempe, supposedly."

"What's the name?"

Starks checked his notes. "Tennyson. David Tennyson."

Guerrero felt the skin on the back of his neck prickle. Tennyson. Professor Tennyson.

"And this is on a ranch?"

"Taylor Ranch, they call it. More of a compound, really. They do plural wives down there. Mexican Mormons. What'll they think of next, right?"

"Where is it?"

"South of the Yuma Reservation, mile marker four or thereabouts. But you can't go down there. You know that, right? It's a federal jurisdiction situation."

"Who would I contact? Border Patrol?"

Starks shook his head. "That's sovereign territory, friend. You gotta establish a diplomatic channel. Try the FBI. They've got a relationship with the *federales*. But these Mormons—they don't trust outsiders, especially guys with a badge."

"You ever been there? Doug told me you worked Border Patrol together."

"We stuck to this side of the river."

"Did she say anything else about this guy, Tennyson?"

"Not really."

"Why did she call you?"

"Sounded like she wanted him off the property. Who knows, really. They got their little dramas down there, like the rest of us."

Stark neglected to mention one detail to Guerrero: the caller had sounded scared to death.

HER NAME WAS Sariah Taylor. She was the first wife of Ammon Taylor, the guardian of his legacy. Her own son had gone astray up north. She knew God would call him back to take his place as inheritor of his father's prerogatives and property. But she worried about the girl who had been married into their family to sire a second son.

Alma was a Romney, among the most ambitious of the Mormon clans to settle northern Mexico in the nineteenth century. She had been steadfast, even arduous, in her procreative efforts. Yet eighteen months passed with no result. Then the stranger had appeared in their midst.

They all tended to him. But it was Alma who had volunteered to take extra shifts, who snuck glances at the stranger when he appeared for the Sabbath meal shaved and formally dressed, like a younger, more virile, version of Father Ammon. Sariah began to ponder the unthinkable: Alma hoped to conceive by adulterous means. She concealed these suspicions within a public attitude of sisterly amity. But a few nights after that Sabbath, she paid a visit to the cabin where her sister wife slept and found it empty.

Sariah was hunched in the dark when she heard footsteps. Alma appeared in her traveling cape, hurrying from the main house. Sariah felt her pulse ease: the girl was guilty of nothing more than laying with her husband. Rather than returning to her cabin, though, Alma hurried on toward the stables.

Sariah considered pursuing the girl. But the cold bit at her joints, and she couldn't bear the thought of what she might witness. She knew the proper course would be to alert Father. But this, too, felt untenable—a humiliation too intimate to disclose.

The problem was Tennyson himself. He had come from a kingdom of heathens and brought iniquity with him. In the end, Sariah stole into Father Ammon's office and quietly dialed the
Yuma police.

GUERRERO WAS DESPERATE to reach Nando, but he didn't want
to use a police dispatcher, didn't trust where that might lead,
so he left word with a secretary in the Fresno substation and
skulked around a pay phone. It didn't ring until nearly five.
"Where the fuck you been all day?" He growled these words
while smiling broadly at Lorena, who sat in the Jeep eyeball-
ing him.
    "That's what I was going to ask you, *primo.*"
    "I'm in Yuma, okay?"
    "I'm still in Sacramento, looking for Graciela Saenz."
    "What?"
    "She never came home. Neighbors haven't seen her, either."
    "You check with her church people?"
    "Next on my list."
    "Should I ask Lorena?"
    "Just get her back here."
    "That's the thing."
    "What's the thing?"
    Nando listened to his cousin relate the strange events of
their day. "Tell me you're not considering what I think you're
considering."
    "Okay, I won't tell you."
    "I'm serious, Pedro."
    "It's five miles away."
    "In Mexico! You're talking about entering Mexico. No,"
Nando said. "You're driving back here. With the girl. *Now.* Then
we figure out what to do next."

Guerrero turned away from Lorena and closed his eyes. He hadn't slept properly in a month. He wanted to curse Nando for turning him into a cop, for convincing him that men could be policed when their hearts ran wild with temptation. The voice of his cousin was still in his ear, like a tiny metallic drill.

"Don't go gangster on me, *primo*. You'll wind up in jail. I'm serious. I'll turn you in myself if you fuck around."

"Okay," he said. "Okay. But I can't drive back tonight, Nando. I'm too wiped."

"Find a room, then. Call me from there. I'll give you an hour. And get back here quick as you can. I don't like this situation with Graciela Saenz. I got a bad feeling about it." Nando hung up the phone and looked at Captain Maurice Hooks, who'd been listening in on the extension in his office.

"You did the right thing, Reyes."

"Fuck you, Captain."

HOOKS HAD PUT a tail on Guerrero as soon as he turned up with his evidence. Tapped his calls, too, which is how they got wise to Nando. The moment Guerrero took off with Lorena, he'd committed a felony, and the department had the leverage they needed. Nando didn't argue. He could see it at once.

"Let him have his little goose chase," Nando counseled. "When he gets back, I'll talk him down. Nobody wants this to become a scandal, right?"

Hooks sneered his accord. He'd always liked Reyes, the smart mouth aside, was sorry to see him ship off to Fresno. He liked Guerrero, for that matter. It was disappointing, the way things had turned out. He was trying, in his own way, to help Guerrero. Cops didn't do well in prison, especially skinny little rats.

The situation had gotten beyond him, beyond all of them. It was another Jimmy Grinnell, only this time the FBI was involved, and the media, and the goddamn White House from what he could tell. The Death Valley Killer had arrived in their midst, a kind of modern folklore. The monster had been apprehended, arrested, imprisoned. That was the story. And it needed to stay the story.

LORENA SAENZ KNEW none of this. But she understood that something was afoot. Officer Guerrero had emerged from his meeting with Ricky Stark looking damp and jittery. When she asked what he'd learned, he frowned unconvincingly and made his thumb and pointer finger into a zero. Then he stopped at the first phone booth he found. He knew she was staring at him, so he pretended to be having some kind of breezy chat, leaning against the glass, slipping a hand into his pocket, with an idiot grin pasted on his face like a catalogue model.

She recognized this particular form of deceit from her mother, who had exuded the same fraudulent, slightly frenzied calm every time she lost a job, or they were evicted, or, later, when Tony got busted.

Guerrero hung up and ambled back to the Jeep and announced that they would be driving back to Sacramento the next morning. She merely nodded.

They took a room in an Econo Lodge west of the city, and ate at the McDonald's across the parking lot, receiving their meal from servers in desperately bright pastel uniforms. In a couple of years, Lorena knew, she would be one of them, grateful for the chance to get out of the kitchen at the old age home, to make food rather than scraping it off plastic plates. They prepared for bed awkwardly, each of them taking turns in the bathroom. There were two queens in the room. By nine the lights were out and they lay listening to the dull roar of eighteen-wheelers zooming past on the interstate.

"It was always going to be a long shot," Guerrero said.

"I know," Lorena said quietly.

"I'm not giving up."

"I know." She didn't trust him exactly, but she could see he was trying.

"Did your cousin say anything about my mom?"

"We talked about the case." He sounded tired.

Guerrero was silent for long enough that Lorena thought maybe he'd fallen asleep. Then he asked a question that neither of them quite expected.

"What happened to your dad?"

The truth is, she didn't know her father, not like Tony did. He was just a jumble of sensations, a restless lap she was continually climbing into and being pushed from, the smell of cigarettes and beer, a crooked nose and dark eyes, a mood of violent dispute. As much as she remembered him, she remembered her mother in relation to him, the cursing and crying, the throwing of shoes. Her mother had exhausted her capacity to fight ridding herself of her husband, only to find that Tony had inherited his habits. They weren't criminals so much as delinquents, vandals of calm.

"He took off when I was little," Lorena said.

"How little?"

"Five, I guess. He drank."

"Where's he from?"

"El Salvador. He came to Honduras for work. It was his idea to come to America."

"But you were born here?"

"My mom came over while she was pregnant with me."

Guerrero whistled softly. "Tony was here already?"

"My dad brought him up six months before I was born."

"How old was he?"

"Four."

"Any other family here?"

"Some cousins in San Jose."

This was what cops did. They asked questions. But there was something unsettling in it, as if Guerrero were making a record, taking possession of her history.

"What about you?" she said. "Where's your family from?"

"Morelia. Michoacán state, to the west of Mexico City."

"Are your parents legal?"

"They were. My *abuelo* made sure of that. He came over back in the fifties. Worked in the pecan orchards. Made enough to move the family to Fruitridge."

"Sounds like a good guy."

"Not really. He was an abuser. Where my dad learned it, I guess. Any other questions?"

"Did you always want to be a cop?"

"No. I was headed the other way, if you want to know the truth."

"What happened?"

"Nando saved me. I got lucky."

Lorena wanted to ask if Guerrero was married, or had a girl-friend. She hadn't learned yet about checking for rings. She tried to imagine this rat-faced little man holding hands with a woman, escorting her into a movie theater, presenting her with a bouquet of flowers. She couldn't do it.

"Lucky how?" she said.

A silence ensued. It became clear after a time that Guerrero had fallen asleep.

Lorena waited until his breathing had grown deep and mea-sured. Then she got up and tiptoed to the far side of his bed, where he had set down his holster. It was empty. He had slipped his gun beneath his pillow. Because of how he'd shifted onto his side, she could see the blunt outlines of the weapon. She saw herself taking hold of the butt, the object sliding along the sheets, its weight in her hand. She imagined Officer Guerrero waking to the eye of the barrel staring down at him.

Lucky how, she whispered.

His mouth was slightly open, as if he were on the brink of answering.

She reached out and touched the gun, ever so lightly, with her fingertips. It was cold and dense and her heart pumped wildly.

Lucky how?

AT 4:00 A.M., Guerrero got up and took a shower and dressed quietly. The girl was dead asleep, burrowed beneath the covers. He wrote her a note, just in case—*Getting breakfast. Back soon. Wait here*—then hopped into the Jeep and headed for the Yuma Reservation.

From her spot in the backseat of the vehicle, tucked beneath the camping tarp they hadn't needed this time around, Lorena listened to the door whine open and felt the weight of the driver settling in. He hadn't thought to check for stowaways in the bleary darkness. Why would he? Lorena had carefully arranged her bedding, using extra pillows to create a life-like lump—the way Tony had taught her years ago—then slipped outside while Guerrero was in the shower. She felt the Jeep pitch into motion, the grinding of the clutch, a few choice profanities. Wherever he was sneaking off to, he was in a hurry. And she was coming, too.

Guerrero drove to the border crossing that abutted the Yuma Reservation and went inside to chat up the INS agents. He emerged a few minutes later, blowing on a Styrofoam cup of coffee. The parking lot afforded a view of the Colorado River. It was the commuting hour for the day maids coming over from Morelos. They emerged from buses in gales of drowsy laughter and massed on the river's far edge, where they haggled with the burly men who waited to ferry them across the river on flimsy rafts. The women balanced plastic bags on their heads and scampered up the embankment on the other side and peeled back the chain-link fence and invaded America. They stood in the low desert scrub and stripped down to their underwear and pulled on the carefully folded clothes stashed in those plastic bags, shivering, balancing on one foot, performing this wardrobe change as briskly as possible, to avoid the possibility of being chased down by the green *migra* vans that occasionally roared out of the parking lot where he stood. Guerrero watched all this, with a peculiar sadness, as he waited for dawn.

He knew his grandmother had been one of these young women once. Back in the fifties, you could simply walk across the bridge. She bragged about it: the size of the houses she cleaned, the miracle of electric fans, the appliances she scrubbed in hope and wonder—*el refrigerador! las lavadoras!*—which reminded her how far she had traveled in life already. She had been ambitious, eager to earn money, to learn the language and habits of the great country in which her destiny lay cradled. Guerrero, half raised by this staunch woman, had been subject to the gravity of her aspirations; perhaps that, too, was why he had become a cop. They were believers.

He drove east to mile marker four. Here, beyond the city limits, the demarcations of the border fell away. No one saw him cross into Mexico, except Lorena. She waited a full minute after he'd locked the vehicle, then climbed out of the Jeep and tracked him on foot. Like Guerrero, she was traveling with ghosts. Fifteen years ago, in the half dark of another dawn, her father and brother had made their way north, crossing a mile to the west, sprinting headlong into a promised land that would doom them both. Lorena came later, a kind of secret cargo, floating untroubled inside her terrified mother.

AFTER TEN MINUTES, the beam of Guerrero's flashlight found a barbed-wire fence held up by weathered wooden posts. He got out his binoculars and scanned in each direction, then headed west along the fence, toward the rising sun, Lorena a hundred yards behind him. It made her think of the night, nearly a year ago now, when she had walked out into the desert with Mr. Stallworth and he had revealed to her the hidden world of scorpions.

Perhaps it was the narcotic sway of this memory that led her to step on a twig. Guerrero wheeled around and peered through the mottled dawn. Her first impulse had been to throw herself onto the ground. But there was nowhere to hide, so she just stood regarding him.

"Goddamnit," he murmured. "You want to tell me what you're doing out here?"

"If you tell me first."

"That's not how this works."

Lorena stopped five feet away from him; she wouldn't come any closer.

"I'm pursuing a lead, okay. It's probably nothing. But it could be dangerous, so you're going to need to walk yourself back to the car. *Now.* This isn't some game." Guerrero reached for his handcuffs. "If you won't do it yourself, I'll escort you."

Lorena's eyes drifted to the gun strapped to his hip.

Guerrero stepped forward and reached for her arm and she twisted away from him. "You don't get to order me around anymore. We're not in America."

"Calm down," he said. "I'm trying to protect you."

"I never asked for your protection."

The edge of dawn was burning off, revealing them bit by bit. He didn't want to wrestle her into custody. His job was probably dust. And yet, retracing his steps, Guerrero couldn't see what he might have done differently. He took hold of Lorena's wrist. "Honest to God," he muttered, "you should have just shot me last night, when you had the chance."

Into the stunned silence that greeted this comment—before Lorena could respond, before Guerrero could slip the cuffs onto her—came the strange tinny sound of music emanating from a radio. For a brief moment, Lorena saw an image of herself at age seven or eight, standing silently in the doorway to her room, watching her mother sway to the music of that cheesy norteño band she loved, dancing, quite beautifully, and alone. Then she snapped back to the present.

Both of them turned. On the other side of the fence, perhaps twenty feet away, was a young caballero perched atop a bony mule. He clicked off his transistor radio and looked down at them in sweet befuddlement.

AS THE COWBOY approached, Guerrero stepped away from Lorena and smiled and dipped his chin and called out a greeting in Spanish and scanned the man for weapons. His dress was oddly antiquated, a leather-tooled vest and chaps, a holster beneath the rope coiled around his shoulder and a bowie knife looped through his belt. Guerrero angled his body to hide the weapon on his far hip. "Praise God!" he said. "I was hoping he would send us a sign. And here you are. My name is Pedro Guerrero. This is Lorena, my daughter. What's your name?"

The young man frowned. "Josiah," he said timidly. He glanced at the daughter. She looked Mexican, or maybe something like it, but wore gringa clothing, a cotton sweater and jeans and white sneakers. Guerrero was dressed in a windbreaker with a strange insignia. "What are you doing here?" he said, in rather formal Spanish.

"We're on a mission of mercy, you could say. My brother-in-law got lost around here."

"Your brother-in-law?"

"His name is David Tennyson."

Josiah's eyes, partially obscured by a scruffy Stetson, darted away. "I don't know anything about that. I'm sorry."

"Please. Mr. Tennyson has a family, a wife, two children. This is his niece."

"I'm sorry, sir," Josiah replied, in consternation. "This is private property, you see. If you have questions, you can go to the front gate. It's no problem. Down that way. A quarter mile, more or less." He gestured. "Maybe someone there knows." He began to turn his animal away. Guerrero knew the boy would alert whomever he worked for, and things would turn south from there. Before he could think better of it, he pulled out his service pistol and leveled it at Josiah, who froze. "I don't know anything about that, sir. I swear to God. You have to ask Father Taylor."

Lorena stepped backwards; her face had drained of color.

"It's okay," Guerrero said quietly, to both of them. "Everything is fine. Let's just stay calm. Josiah, I need you to come off your animal. Nice and slow. Right, just like that. Now come over to the fence, to where I am. I'm sorry about this, okay? I'm trying to keep us all safe. Do you understand?"

The boy nodded.

Guerrero patted him down, took the knife and an antique six-shooter with no bullets. He set them on the ground, narrating his actions all the while in the way he had learned to over the years, quick and matter-of-fact, so that suspects would be able to assimilate what was happening to them. "I'm going to put these restraints on you, Josiah. But just for a little while, so I can see what's in the saddle bag on your animal. It won't hurt if you don't struggle, okay? Nod to show me you understand. That's good. Does he have a name, your animal?"

"Midnight," Josiah croaked.

"Midnight? That's a funny name for a gray mule." He emptied the bag of its contents: the portable radio, pliers, a hammer, a cattle prod, a pack of Faros cigarettes, a flint lighter, a leather water bag, a ceramic bowl wrapped in a cotton towel with the kid's breakfast inside: two homemade tortillas filled with beans and onions. He took the cattle prod and left everything else in the bag.

"I'm doing this because I know Mr. Taylor doesn't like strangers on his property. I don't blame him, by the way. I don't like strangers on my property, either. But, you see, I promised I'd find my brother-in-law. Can you understand that, Josiah?"

The kid was struggling not to cry. He was maybe twenty; a wisp of beard clung to his chin like dried moss.

"Try not to be frightened, Josiah. All you have to do is lead us to where he is, to Mr. Tennyson."

"You have to ask Father Taylor, sir. I just mend the fences."

Guerrero didn't want to do what he did next. He worried, curiously, that it would upset Lorena, though he knew also that her distress would be useful, so he raised his gun and aimed it at Josiah and she burst into tears. "Don't shoot him!"

"I'm asking you, Josiah."

"He's in the room by the stables. I think it's him. The American."

"Good," Guerrero said. "You're going to lead us there now, quick as you can. It's still early, you see? So we can get Mr. Tennyson and leave and no one will get hurt."

The kid nodded. He had wet himself.

SARIAH TAYLOR KNEW that calling the police department in Yuma without her husband's knowledge, let alone approval, was a betrayal—both of her marital bond and the laws that bound her community. She spent the night in tribulation. At first light, she slipped into Father Ammon's bed chamber and confessed to him.

In previous years, Taylor might have beaten her with the strap prescribed for that purpose. But she was an old woman now, bent low by their decades together. He could only bring himself to glower at her, which might have been worse. At last, he called Sariah over and took her hand and assured her that Alma was incapable of such a subterfuge, that he had dispatched the girl himself to check on Tennyson. "The man has infected wounds," Taylor explained.

This was technically true. Alma was obedient to her marital vows. But above all she was obedient to her husband.

From the moment Stallworth had appeared, Ammon Taylor had contemplated why God would dispatch this battered soul to his property. He pondered the clues: the heaven-sent injuries; the cash; the tiny, hidden phone number. The stranger, he deduced, was recompense for the injuries the United States had inflicted upon his bloodline. His call to Van Dyke had served as confirmation.

And yet there had to be something more than money at stake. As he pondered the matter, his mind kept returning to the strangest of the items found on Stallworth's person: the photo of the naked girl, just a few years younger than Alma herself. The stranger's lustful intentions must have been integral to God's plan. He explained this to Alma, so that she came to understand: her body was the soil in which the Taylor bloodline would be replenished. She was to lay with Ammon on her fecund nights, then with the fugitive. Let heaven decide the matter.

Now, however, Sariah had alerted the American authorities, and no good could come of that. He needed Tennyson off his property as soon as possible. For a moment, Taylor's fatigue did battle with his vigilance. Then he rose from bed and did his business and shaved his face and dressed. Sariah had set a kettle but he waved her off and slipped a small pistol in the pocket of his trousers and ventured out into the raw light of sunrise.

On his way to the stable, he passed by the cabin where, he assumed, his youngest bride had returned from her final assignation. It did not occur to him that Alma, exhausted from the exertions of her week, might fall asleep in the fugitive's bed.

TO GET TO the stables, where Tennyson had been staying, Guerrero and Lorena would have to enter what Josiah called "Father Taylor's Domain." He struggled to explain what he meant, but Guerrero understood the moment he looked through his binoculars: a patchwork wall of cement and brick that rose twenty feet. It was topped with broken glass. The heart of the Taylor ranch was a fortress.

"It's to keep evildoers out," Josiah mumbled. "There's another way, anyway. A tunnel. Not far from the stables."

"Would anyone see us?" Guerrero said.

"Not if we hurry."

Guerrero couldn't leave Lorena unattended. But he didn't want to bring her along. "We don't want trouble," Guerrero said again. "If there's trouble, I have to use this." He lifted his gun. "I don't want to do that, Josiah."

"It's safe," Josiah said. "Nobody is up yet."

"You sure?"

"It's the Sabbath, sir."

They left the mule tethered to a fence post and moved swiftly across the prairie, toward the northern edge of the wall. "Stay behind me and stay close," Guerrero whispered to Lorena, in English. "You understand?"

"Yes."

"Say it."

"Stay close," she mumbled. "Stay behind you."

The tunnel was more of a trough, but it got them inside. Josiah led them to a small courtyard, ringed by cottonwoods. He pointed to a low-slung building that had been divided into stalls. "He's staying in that one, with the window."

"Lead us there."

Before Josiah could advance another step, they heard the creak of a wheel. A horse and buggy emerged from behind the far side of the building and began to traverse the courtyard. For a few seconds, Ammon Taylor rode into the ruddy dawn without taking notice of them, bouncing along like a liveryman from the last century. He clicked his tongue and the horse came to a halt not twenty yards away. Guerrero pushed Lorena behind him and raised his pistol. "Put your hands up, please," he shouted.

Taylor sat up and turned slowly to face Guerrero.

"Your hands," Guerrero said.

Taylor shook his head, as if he had been awaiting an ambush of this sort. "You may speak English, if you prefer," he said politely.

"Please step down from the carriage, sir. Nice and slow."

"That is an unnecessary directive at my age." The old man clambered down from his seat, moving gingerly. His strange beard and formal dress made Lorena think of the illustrations in her history books. She found the man's genteel manner oddly soothing. For the past half hour she had been on the point of throwing up.

"Are you Father Taylor?" Guerrero said.

"I am. May I ask you to identify yourself?"

"My name is Pedro Guerrero, sir. I'm a police officer."

"That may be so, but you are threatening me with a deadly weapon on my property, which is a religious sanctuary within the sovereign nation of Mexico."

"I'm looking for a man who identifies himself as David Tennyson."

Taylor stared in puzzlement at Josiah, whose hands remained cuffed, then at the girl behind Guerrero, who looked oddly familiar. "Who is the young lady with you? She looks rather alarmed."

"I'm going to ask the questions, Mr. Taylor. Are you armed?"

"It's the Sabbath, sir."

"Your employee tells me Mr. Tennyson has been staying here for some time."

Taylor glanced at Josiah. "He is my tenant, not my employee. Please give him leave. He has no part in this."

"I'd like to see Tennyson. Now."

"Certainly," Taylor said. "As I say, there is no need to threaten me, or my tenant, Mr. Guerrero."

"I am sorry to go about it like this," Guerrero said. "I was told you can be wary of strangers."

Taylor smiled ruefully, as if encountering a familiar bigotry. "On the contrary. Mr. Tennyson showed up here some weeks ago, grievously injured. We offered him care and shelter. This is a place of God. If he is in some sort of trouble in the United States, I am happy to see him gone. Are you from the Yuma police?"

"Please, Mr. Taylor."

"Very well." As he drew closer, Ammon Taylor spotted the insignia on Guerrero's windbreaker. He was from the Sacramento police. For a moment, he wished to dispense with all the subterfuge, to speak honestly about the desperation of men in exile. But he knew this would only complicate matters, so he led the little officer toward the room where the fugitive slept. "We'll need light," he whispered. "There's no electric."

Guerrero nodded and Taylor dipped down and lit the kerosene lantern placed outside the room. It did not escape his notice that the lock on the outside of the door had been released. But he stepped inside anyway. It was too late to do otherwise.

AS AMMON TAYLOR entered the room, his lantern illuminated the scene. Stallworth at the head of the bed, his back against the wall, Alma, curled below him, the sheets wound around her like a sheath. Taylor stood stunned before the scene he had engineered. The rank aroma of what they had done hung in the air.

For a moment, no one moved. Then Stallworth reached for something on the table next to the bed. He rose up and lunged at Ammon Taylor. Taylor saw a flash of silver. He reared back and drew the pistol from his pocket, as if he were shooting a venomous snake in his own barn. Because he was a man of God, and thus averse to murder, Taylor closed his eyes as he fired. The gun jerked in his hand. He did not see the bullet strike the man before him. Nor did he consider the man behind him, the little police officer who had trespassed upon his land. He heard the lamentation of two young women and felt, in the mystifying fraction of a second before he lost consciousness, the bolt of God's fingertip laid upon his ear.

PEDRO GUERRERO PROCESSED the events in question as his training required. His job was to secure a positive ID, then to usher Lorena safely off the Taylor property. For this reason, he had holstered his gun and taken up the cattle prod. If necessary, the authorities could return to the ranch to retrieve Marcus Stallworth. Had he a bit more time to consider his dilemma, he might have recognized the irony: in pursuit of a fugitive, he had become a fugitive.

But he clung to the present, a step behind Ammon Taylor. Through the dim light, he spotted two figures on the bed, a white male and a young Hispanic female, both quite naked. Then a flurry of movement. The man appeared to leap at Taylor.

Guerrero stepped forward to intercede; a shot rang out. The muzzle flash cast the figures into sharp relief: Taylor staggered by the discharge, the girl cowering in a nest of sheets, and, at the center of the tableau, at long last illuminated, Marcus Stallworth, his naked torso mottled with bruises, his jaw fringed in neat whiskers. The force of the bullet knocked him back onto the bed.

Guerrero swung the cattle prod, watched the old man go down, then kicked his tiny gun away. He advanced through the smoke and shrieking to the victim. Stallworth was gurgling, coughing out a bright pink froth; dark liquid surged onto the floor, as if his chest were nothing more than a lake of blood.

For a long minute, Guerrero tried to stanch the bleeding. He reached for a pulse but the wrist kept slipping away. The victim's eyes turned filmy and vacant and the limbs began to stiffen, until it seemed the only machinery still in operation was his ruptured heart. He could feel Stallworth passing to the other side, the rasp of his breath relenting, faint, then gone. Guerrero lifted the bedsheets away, shocked at the delicate dimensions of the entry wound. It looked as if Stallworth had been stung.

Guerrero struggled to assess the situation. The naked girl had crawled off the bed. She lay clinging to Ammon Taylor, cradling his head and imploring him to wake up. *Padre,* she whimpered. *Mi padre.* Josiah was gone. Guerrero located Lorena; she was stooped in the hallway with her hands over her eyes. He kneeled before her and softly raised her chin, so that her eyes would meet his and she would know the truth of what he was telling her, that it was okay, it was all over, that she was safe, but that he needed her to take his hand, *right now*, and not let go. Did she understand?

He led her outside and they sprinted together, back the way they had come. He heard the anguished honking of a mule behind him. There was a distinct possibility they would be pursued, perhaps on horseback. There was nothing he could do about that but run and hope and run.

Guerrero was a police officer, a good one, and because of this training, he felt he had some understanding of what had transpired. It was obvious to him, for instance, that Marcus Stallworth had sexually assaulted the young girl in his bed, who was Ammon Taylor's granddaughter, or perhaps his daughter, and that Taylor, upon encountering this defilement, and despite being under armed guard himself, had flown into a rage and shot the assailant dead. That was what the facts suggested, and the version he carried with him for the rest of his life.

There were aspects of the story he didn't understand—how Stallworth had reached the Taylor ranch, for instance, or how the girl had wound up in his room—but these mysteries did not obscure the basic facts, which allowed him to offer some solace to Lorena Saenz, once they had reached American soil. "Mr. Stallworth was a predator," he said gently. "That's his nature. You were right, Lorena. You saved Tony."

LORENA SAENZ WAS the last person Marcus Stallworth saw before he slipped away. The empirical part of him recognized that she was just a vision, fed to him by his perishing soul. God knew what he was: a scientist desecrated by lust, a father who destroyed his family, a man who preyed upon children. Still, he felt a surge of awe. Lorena had found him. By some miracle of mind and will. He wanted to show her the strange specimen he had discovered, a creature with the courage to kill itself rather than live in captivity. He wondered, in his final moment, what she would make of it.

LORENA HERSELF PERCEIVED almost nothing of the fatal encounter. From the moment Guerrero produced a gun and took Josiah captive, she had been a state of shock, following his directives, but dissociated, as if she were watching herself in a movie. She watched herself watch Guerrero enter the room behind the old man called Taylor. She saw the naked man inside, though it had taken her a moment to recognize Mr. Stallworth beneath his strange new beard. She did not know who fired the gun or why but the shot sent her reeling to the ground. She heard a body drop, smelled gun smoke. Then a girl's voice was crying *father, my father*, and she considered, briefly, whether she herself was the one uttering those words. Then Guerrero was squatting before her. His fingers were sticky and smelled of iron and she didn't want him to touch her face but he was doing it anyway. *Run,* he kept saying. *We need to run.*

HAVING REVEALED MARCUS Stallworth to be alive, only to witness his homicide less than a second after this revelation, Pedro Guerrero was determined to alert the Stallworth family, and his superiors. But he was even more worried about Lorena Saenz, who was clearly disoriented.

He found the Jeep and drove toward the Yuma police station, then pulled into a gas station to get Lorena food and water, and to determine whether she required medical attention. It would not have occurred to him that *he* might need medical attention because, like most police officers, he did not understand the impact of traumatic events on the mind and body. These were to be absorbed in the line of duty, and only later disgorged onto those around them, cloaked in drink and violence.

He knew enough, though, to call the number Nando had left him. The first words out of his mouth were these: "He's alive. Marcus Stallworth. I saw him get shot."

"You saw Stallworth get shot?"

"It just happened. You need to call FBI, the regional guys down here."

"Slow down," Nando said. "Take a deep breath. Where the hell are you?"

"Yuma."

"Jesus. Where's Lorena?"

"Here. With me."

"You got to get her back here," Nando said.

"Did you hear me? Antonio Saenz didn't kill him. Stallworth was down in Mexico. On a ranch. We have to get Antonio out of prison."

For several unnerving seconds, Nando didn't say anything. "Okay, calm down. Just tell me what happened, the whole story."

Guerrero did as he was told, confiding even to Lorena's presence, and glancing every now and then across the parking lot, to where she sat in the front seat of the Jeep, staring blankly at a package of frosted donuts.

When he was done, Nando sighed deeply. "I need you to listen careful, *primo*. You have to drive back here immediately."

"But I'm a witness—"

"You're not listening—"

"I can get transport from the Yuma—"

A third voice suddenly cut in.

"Get the girl back here," Captain Hooks snarled. "Or I'll lock you up myself."

"What the hell?" Guerrero said. "Why is Hooks—"

"We fucked up," Nando said softly. "Big time, *primo*."

FOR THE FIRST few minutes of their drove north, Guerrero tried to comfort Lorena, however awkwardly. She didn't respond. When he looked over, he found (to his considerable relief) that her eyes were closed, her head slumped against the window. But Lorena was not asleep. She had been remitted to the sudden senseless violence of her earliest years and responded in the only way she knew to keep safe: by making herself invisible.

Most of all, Lorena wanted to see her mother. She had a keen sense, no doubt also a vestige of those years, that her mother was in danger. She wanted to see Tony, too. She pictured them waiting for her in the doorway of the apartment where they had lived together for four years, before he shipped off to the navy. Her mother would prepare *baleadas*, the kind with crumbly cheese and scrambled eggs, and Tony would tease her for putting ketchup on her plantains. She knew it wouldn't happen like that, but the scene soothed her.

She wanted to thank Guerrero, for believing her, for keeping her from harm. She also wanted to forget he existed, to travel back in time to the era before he had come into her life, when she had been happy to believe that a new hairstyle, or a pair of designer jeans, or the loss of ten pounds, would grant her access to the careless pleasures she found in the Stallworth home.

Guerrero had reminded her that Marcus was a *predator*, as if to mitigate the horror of what she had witnessed. But every time he spoke she felt dragged into the world of adulthood, with its rigid ideas of power and weakness and right and wrong. She wanted him to understand how it had felt at first, when Mr. Stallworth had reached across the Jeep to unlock her door and the hairs on the back of his forearm brushed the skin of her belly. He hadn't seemed like a predator at all, but a shy man fighting, somewhat blindly, against desires stronger than his resolve.

She had desires, too. She had wanted him, inasmuch as she understood wanting. She wanted the obvious things: his strong arms, his soft lips. And she wanted the less obvious things: the quiet power of his regard, the precision of his mind, his reverence for the natural world. Above all, or beneath it, she wanted what he saw in her, the trust he seemed ready to tender in fleeting moments. She thought of him as a scorpion, not the kind trapped in amber, but the kind that had scampered across her skin, so dangerous and alive that she had wanted to capture it in her fist.

IT WAS DARK when they arrived at the Sacramento police station. Nando escorted them to the conference room on the second floor. Lorena spotted an older cousin of hers from San Jose, sitting at the table with two women she didn't recognize. The cousin's cheeks were streaked in black, where her mascara had run. Nando opened the door and nodded to Lorena and closed the door behind her.

Guerrero stared through the window as the cousin burst into tears. Then Lorena fell to the ground and began retching.

"What the hell?"

"Come on," Nando said. "You're late."

"Late for what? Why is everybody staring?"

"You've got blood on your pants." He hustled his cousin over to Homicide, where Hooks shut the door to his office and lowered the blinds.

Guerrero's windbreaker was filthy and rumpled. He looked like someone who had been buried and dug up again. "Will somebody tell me what the fuck is happening?"

"Antonio Saenz died last night," Nando said.

"What?"

"The feds put him in an iso unit. His body was found this morning."

"His body?" Guerrero closed his eyes and saw Lorena, collapsing. He heard a ringing sound, then absolute silence, like the quiet after a plague. Nando's hands were on his shoulders, sort of holding him up. He feared he might get sick.

"Take a few minutes if you need them, *primo*."

"Cause of death unknown." This was Hooks again. "Coroner just finished the autopsy."

"He was innocent."

"It's a shit show alright—"

"We *told* you," Guerrero shouted. "We brought you the evidence."

"You brought me a pile of bloody clothes," Hooks replied quietly.

Guerrero's body began to rock. He could feel the savagery vibrating outward, ready to strike. For a moment, he saw himself leaping over the desk. Nando's grip tightened on his shoulders. "Don't make your situation worse, *primo*."

"*My* situation? Tony Saenz is *dead*. That's the situation. An innocent kid. Because this motherfucker sat on his hands." Guerrero was trying to twist away from Nando, to get at the Captain. "We told you. We handed you everything on a fucking platter."

"Lower your voice," Hooks said.

"The chief must be mighty proud of you, Hooks. He really owes your ass now, doesn't he? Or maybe you'll go into business with Van Dyke, that scumbag. Earn a fortune making rich people's mistakes go away." Guerrero went on this way for a minute, while Hooks sat, vast and impassive, waiting for his adrenaline to run down. An eerie calm settled over the small office, which was filled with cheap plaques and commendations.

"Even if I believed you—" Hooks said.

"*If* you believed me? Where do you think this blood came from, Captain?" Guerrero thrust his hands out for inspection;

tiny brown crescents rimed the skin under the nails. "This blood came from Marcus Stallworth's body."

"I heard the story," Hooks said.

"I'll bet you did."

Nando and Hooks exchanged a glance and all at once the true dimensions of the situation came clear. Guerrero felt the sting of it. He turned slowly and stared at his cousin. "You let him listen in the whole time. You're on their side now."

"*Tranquilo, primo.*"

"Don't *tranquilo* me, you fucking Judas."

"He was trying to keep you out of jail," Hooks snapped. "Still is. You acted in violation of direct orders, Guerrero, as well as about 150 state and federal statutes. You led a terrified teenage girl into a fortified compound in Mexico. Any idea how much legal exposure we've got here?"

Nando began to speak, but Hooks wagged a finger. "You're a pit bull, Guerrero. And a pit bull can run and jump and bite your nose off. But you know what a pit bull can't do? It can't unlock a fucking gate. And the confession is that gate. Saenz is guilty because he *told* us he was guilty. The Mexican government isn't going to approve a raid on a private ranch. Even if they do, that body is long gone."

Guerrero was pressing his thumbs into his eyes. "I'll go to the *Bee*."

"And tell them what? That the Death Valley Killer was just an innocent victim who accidently confessed? That Marcus Stallworth staged his own death? Whatever happened down there, you can't undo the past, Guerrero. All you're going to do is ruin the future."

"Are you threatening me?"

"You're already fired." Hooks sighed and stared directly into Guerrero's eyes. "You no longer have any formal relationship with the Sacramento Police Department. So you can do what you damn well please. But you better think through the consequences.

You better think about the Stallworth kids having to read the story you're so eager to tell. Dead is dead, son."

Guerrero could feel himself starting to panic. Hooks had this power over him. There was something monstrous and tranquilizing about the way he spoke. The more you struggled, the deeper the venom swirled in.

"And that poor thing downstairs—you want to make a public spectacle of what she just lived through? What *you* put her through? Who does that help, Guerrero?"

He could see her in the darkness of the dingy motel room they'd shared, reaching for the gun under his pillow, taking aim. He had been terrified that she might actually try to shoot him. But he could see now why he had given her the chance.

Hooks was still casting words into the air between them, strangling justice with the serenity of a monk. "Isn't that why you got into this line of work," he was asking now, "to help people?"

Guerrero tried to reignite his rage but it kept slipping away. He looked to Nando, that great pocked face of his, the one he had loved as a young man, and he remembered what it had felt like at first, how badly he had wanted to be like his cousin, a somebody, a cop, the hero of the story. Lorena should have murdered him. She had damned him by her mercy, left him adrift and desolate.

"Lorena needs her mother," Guerrero said. "Someone better find her."

"Easy now," Nando said.

Apparently, he was weeping.

"Get some rest now. You're all fucked-up from the adrenaline."

When he got home, Guerrero drank seven beers, one after another, and wrote down every single detail he could remember in an official incident report, including his conversations with Captain Maurice Hooks. The account filled twenty-three pages. His hands were plagued by the shakes. It was like stabbing the paper.

At some point, he must have fallen asleep, because he woke to find his cousin standing over him. "You're wasted," Nando said softly. "We need to get you cleaned up." He remembered Nando peeling off his clothes, easing him into a scalding bath.

The next day, Guerrero woke to a blaring behind his eyes. He stumbled into the closet he used as a home office and picked up the report he'd written. He couldn't read a single word. With a growing sense of dread, he began to search for the clothes he'd worn on his trip south, the ones covered in the blood of Marcus Stallworth. What he found, instead, was a note from his cousin, taped to his front door.

You'll thank me for this someday, primo.

GRACIELA LEFT HER graveyard shift early for the federal building, to see if the government would allow her to visit her son. Under normal circumstances, she would have returned home and enlisted Lorena to serve as a translator. But this was a special occasion, and she was determined to arrive at 7:00 a.m., an hour before the office for visitors opened. Being first in line, she believed, would compel the guards to look favorably upon her request. Lorena had explained that the system didn't work like that. Tony was in a solitary place; he wasn't allowed visitors. But Graciela had prayed on the matter. In her hands, she held a box of pastries from his favorite bakery.

She was waiting outside the office, on the sidewalk, when a tall white man in a three-piece suit approached her. He was so neatly groomed that she assumed him to be a lawyer. She would remember thinking to herself: this is the sort of gentleman who would convince the guards to let me visit Tony. She remembered thinking: how proud his mother must be! She didn't quite recognize what was happening, even after he smiled pleasantly and asked, in impeccable Spanish, if she was Graciela Saenz.

She had known this moment was coming, had been waiting for it, in one way or another, all along. On the eve of her departure for the United States, her great aunt had read the entrails of a pullet and warned her not to go. The journey, she announced with solemn grandeur, would end in sorrow.

And here she was, fourteen years later, listening to this handsome stranger, as he explained that he was a special envoy from the Office of National Repatriation of the Immigration and Naturalization Service and showed her a small golden badge and a laminated ID and asked if she would please come with him and that it would be a lot nicer if they could do this in a friendly way and trust one another because he certainly didn't want to have to put restraints on such a lovely woman.

He escorted Graciela to an unmarked van parked just around the corner and helped her inside. It was an expensive model, with a crushed velvet interior, and she was the only passenger. She expected to be dropped at a detention facility, but the tall gentleman pulled onto the freeway heading in the opposite direction.

"Where are we going?" Graciela said.

"It's all in your packet," the driver said, matter-of-factly.

She examined the shiny red folder on the seat next to her. It was embossed with raised lettering, which read *Office of National Repatriation* in a dignified font. There was a letter personally addressed to her and written in formal Spanish, which stated that her presence in the United States was a violation of the Immigration and Nationality Act of 1965, specifically the US criminal code, sections 1325 and 1324 ("improper entry by alien" and "harboring an alien" respectively). These federal crimes, compounded by the homicide charge brought against Antonio Saenz, "the harbored alien in question," necessitated "an expedited repatriation process." However, because of her outstanding conduct as an undocumented resident, the recipient qualified for assistance from the Office of National Repatriation

(ONR), including transport and up to $1,000 in resettlement funds, and assistance in applying for legal residency.

"I don't understand," Graciela said. "Am I being deported?"

"Temporarily repatriated," the man said.

"But where are we going *now*?"

"Did you read the letter, ma'am?"

"I have children," Graciela said. "A daughter. She's only four-teen." She began to hyperventilate. "My daughter is waiting for me!"

"I understand," the man said, in his unflappable manner. "But I need you to calm down, Mrs. Saenz. I realize you're frightened. But you are in violation of federal law, as you have been for many years now. I don't view you as a criminal, ma'am. And I don't wish to treat you as one."

Graciela began to weep.

"Your daughter will be looked after. I promise you. The ONR has made those arrangements. You have cousins in San Jose. The office has contacted them. They will stay with her for as long as necessary. The United States government is not going to allow a minor to be without familial support."

The driver glided onto the off-ramp that led to the airport.

"Please," Graciela sobbed. "Let me say goodbye to my daughter."

"Believe me, ma'am, I have children, too. We're on the same side here. You have to look at this as an opportunity. Wouldn't it be better for you, for your children, if you applied for legal entry into the United States? Once you get to Honduras, you can do so. The ONR is prepared to help you with that."

"The ONR," Graciela said faintly.

"Yes, ma'am. The ONR will assist with all of it. But you need to sign the form in your packet, ma'am. If you don't sign, we can't help you."

Graciela thumbed through the forms. She came to one, printed in English, that had been affixed with a transparent sticker in the shape of an arrow that pointed to the line she was required to sign. Although not marked as such, it was a voluntary consent decree, in which the undersigned granted the INS indemnity in the process of her deportation, voluntarily waiving her right to legal representation, a court hearing, and the provisions entailed by a writ of habeas corpus.

The driver glanced at Graciela in the rear-view mirror and smiled. "As recently as fifty years ago," he noted, "the federal government subjected Central American nationals to kerosene baths at the border. To delouse them. Can you imagine? Those days are over, thankfully. We are all human beings. We all deserve dignity. That's why the ONR was established."

Graciela murmured something unintelligible.

"In time," the tall man said, "you may come to see all this as a blessing."

BY FOUR THAT afternoon, as her daughter was approaching the outskirts of Sacramento, in the passenger seat of a vehicle driven by Officer Pedro Guerrero, Graciela Saenz was weaving through the damp customs hall of the Toncontín Airport in Tegucigalpa, Honduras. She had no luggage to declare, not even the packet provided by the ONR, which had been quietly procured from her in the moments before she boarded the plane. The sole item in her possession was a box of pastries, which she had clung to, inexplicably, during the flight. At the urging of an airport official, who took note of her disorientation, she handed the box to the customs agent, a woman roughly her age in a gray uniform that sagged around her.

"This is all you're declaring?" She peeked inside the box. "Oh, *pan de coco! Rosquillas!*"

Graciela replied politely: "They're for my son. From his favorite bakery."

The customs agent nodded hesitantly. Had this little woman brought nothing but pastries from the United States? Was she that wealthy?

The agent handed the box back, but the traveler didn't seem to understand that their interaction was over, that she needed to move on to the next checkpoint.

"It's his birthday," Graciela informed her brightly. "He's turning twenty today."

"Oh, how nice! He must be full of mischief."

Graciela flinched, as if she had just been startled awake. "Why would you say such a thing?"

This question was posed with such a sudden and inexplicable vehemence that the agent took a step backwards. "It's just his zodiac, Señora. He's a Scorpio, after all."

THE OFFICE OF National Repatriation was created by agents of the FBI's Special Operations Unit, with the singular aim of removing Graciela Saenz from America as swiftly as possible. The execution of this plan required the coordinated efforts of agents from the FBI, INS, and Honduran Consulate. They were told that the target was a high-level foreign operative who had been instrumental in funding the efforts of a Honduran leftist group, which had recently hijacked a jet bound for New Orleans. All records of the operation were destroyed upon its completion. Officially, the ONR never existed.

ON NOVEMBER 30, Ronald Reagan traveled to Sacramento to deliver an address to the International Association of Chiefs of Police. He was expected to outline a narrow set of proposals arising from his Task Force on Victims of Crime. But the president, still riding a wave of public adoration that began with his shooting eight months earlier, offered instead a robust and sweeping vision of American law enforcement.

"There are two absolute truths of human nature," he observed. "That men are basically good but prone to evil; and that society has a right to be protected from them." The implication, though subtle, was profound: individuals turn to crime not in response to social conditions but because of personal defects. It was the government's role to punish the wicked, not aid the poor. "There has been a breakdown in our criminal justice system," he noted. "The people are sickened and outraged. They demand we put a stop to it." The police chiefs met these declarations with thunderous applause.

Reagan's broader agenda was to reduce the powers of the state through deregulation. When it came to law enforcement, though, deregulation meant just the opposite: casting aside the bureaucratic rules that shackled police and prosecutors. He wanted the rules of evidence seizure loosened. He wanted felons to compensate their victims. He wanted judges to deny violent offenders bail. Most of all, he wanted prosecutors to seek the death penalty.

It was here that the president (or more precisely, his speech writers) had hoped to invoke the story of Antonio Saenz and Marcus Stallworth. Early drafts of the speech described the assailant as "a savage who stalked his prey, dragged him from his family home, then slaughtered him in a drug-fueled rampage." The passage continued, "Thanks to our so-called *justice system*, the Death Valley Killer was never tried, nor executed. Instead, he was given a plea deal that could usher him back onto our streets within a few short years."

These lines, regarded as the heart of the speech, were struck from the final draft, after tense discussions with officials from the Department of Justice. The president was told the edit was made in deference to the family of the victim.

Faced with this unfortunate rhetorical elision, Reagan did as he was prone; he ad-libbed. He told the police chiefs that his central regret as governor was that he had not invoked the death penalty more often. His cowardice had allowed seven killers to return to the streets; they had killed thirty-four more people. Any reporter who bothered to ask for documentation of these claims would have found none. The president had made them up.

FOREMOST AMONG THOSE gathered for the president's address was its chief instigator. Of course, Nancy Reagan had not ordered her husband to deliver this speech, or any other. That was not how they operated, despite what the vultures in the media were so fond of insinuating. Instead, at the end of each day, Nancy joined him in bed and they talked. She listened to his drowsy complaints, the dull cabinet meetings and feuding staff, and smiled at his corny jokes, occasionally interjecting a sympathetic comment or observation, assembling the elements he would need.

She mentioned the galling details of the Stallworth case only once, after he himself brought up the task force. She reminded him of how he had cracked down on criminals and hippies as governor, had restored order to a lawless state. She told him how much she looking forward to returning to California, and mused aloud as to whether they might prolong their vacation if he traveled there with some official purpose.

In the moments before slumber, Nancy cast these notions into the dark air above him—like stars he might connect into a constellation—and waited, with the loyal patience of a Cancer, as they took root in the world of his dreams. She saw her husband as he needed to be seen: the intrepid navy captain, standing tall in his crisp uniform, barking out commands while others dove for safety.

THE FIRST LADY of the United States entered the auditorium a minute before the address was to begin. She wore a Bill Blass original, in a shade he insisted on calling incarnadine, accented with a white sash and judicious epaulets. Although she was physically dwarfed by her escort, the Sacramento chief of police, she appeared—by some illusion of celebrity—to loom over him as she was led from the wings of the stage to her seat in the front row.

Before sitting down, she turned and offered a sly salute to the assembly of police chiefs. This gesture elicited a standing ovation. The First Lady set a hand upon her heart and smiled, a dab of red in the sea of blue.

Nancy was delighted to be back in California. The sun reminded her of their years in Hollywood. She recalled the buzz of delivering lines into the giant black eye of a movie camera, smoldering on command, coming to know Ronnie, the giddy intertwining of their lives. Their wedding had been glorious, even though it was just a private ceremony, hurriedly arranged, even with the nausea that salted her tongue. They stood in that chintzy little church in the Valley, the five of them, she and Ronnie, William Holden and his wife Brenda, and the secret guest floating inside her.

The move to Sacramento had been a comedown. But she had endured the tawdry holiday pageants and dismal boutiques, as part of the path that had led Ronnie to his fate. Even the shooting had served its purpose. The stars had revealed his mettle.

Beneath the tinseled charm lay a cord of steel that bound him to his role in history.

Nancy had hoped Rosemary Stallworth would attend as her special guest, but this request was quietly vetoed by the US attorney, who wanted no further media attention paid to the case. The First Lady was informed that the widow Stallworth, though grateful, wished to move on with her life. That was fair enough. The speech had been a rousing success, even without any mention of the Stallworth murder. For the first time in months, she felt her husband was perfectly safe in a public space. All it had taken was an auditorium with three thousand law enforcement officials in full dress uniform.

Afterwards, the First Lady received the attentions of the police chief, who eventually introduced her to the burly officer seated on her other side. "This is detective Douglas Jolley, ma'am. He was the lead investigator on a case you might have read about, the so-called Death Valley Killer."

"Oh yes."

"Jolley arrested the suspect."

She turned and looked up at Jolley. "Is that right?"

The officer nodded diffidently. He had a big frame and a wide Irish face she found reassuring. Behind him, Denise was approaching, eager to hustle her off to the next event. But Nancy was seized by a question and, more remotely, by the conviction that only Jolley could answer it definitively. She grasped his arm with unexpected force. "What would make him do such a thing?"

"Ma'am?"

"To torture and kill an innocent man, a husband and father?"

"It's like the president said: sometimes the evil inside us wins out, I guess." He knew it wasn't a very good answer, that the First Lady of the United States deserved better. "The other thing, he was under the influence of crack."

"Crack?"

"It's a solid form of cocaine, ma'am. More potent than the powder. Cheaper, too. So what you've got is someone with a ghetto mentality, and the drugs send them over the edge. They kind of lose the human part of themselves."

"I see," Nancy said quietly.

All around them, thousands of men with guns and badges churned in a kind of rhetorical ecstasy while reporters flung questions at her from the press box. Denise was tugging her sleeve, gesturing at the Secret Service agents who had readied her exit route. But the First Lady lingered a moment. She felt comforted, almost to the point of tears, by the phrase Jolley had used. *The human part of themselves.* It was like a smooth white veil slipped between the mayhem of this world and the one she had dreamed into being.

OWING TO THE ambiguous and upsetting nature of his demise, along with the family's relocation to Philadelphia, no memorial service was ever held for Marcus Stallworth. In keeping with what they understood to be their mother's wishes, her children avoided mentioning his passing, even when they spoke to friends from Sacramento. When the subject came up with new friends, they would say only that he had been a shy man who died suddenly. In this way, he was erased from the record of the living.

His colleague, Joseph Tennyson, edited the paper he was working on at the time of his disappearance—*Toward a Theory of Parasitic Mating in the Order Scorpiones*—and donated the bound manuscript to the Zoological Archive housed in the library at Sacramento State. This tract represented his lone contribution to the field of scorpiology, aside from his anonymous authorship of *Prince of the Desert Night.*

None of his children followed in his footsteps. His son, Glen, went into financial services, taking a job arranged by his grandfather. For a decade, he denied what had been apparent to him from a young age. In his thirties, he moved to New York City and began dating men, though never for more than a few months.

After an uninspired college career at Temple, Jennifer settled down with a wealthy classmate and bought a house in the same neighborhood as her mother, where, with the help of several caretakers, she raised two children. She became involved in Republican politics and worked as a precinct coordinator for Mitt Romney's 2012 presidential campaign.

Neither Stallworth child was ever made aware that they had a half-sister named Sariah Taylor who was, in fact, a distant cousin of Romney's.

ONLY A HANDFUL of people on earth knew that Marcus Stallworth had died by the hand of Ammon Taylor, not Antonio Saenz. Pedro Guerrero often vowed to go public with the story, out of duty to the Saenz family. But he knew that it would be impossible to prove this claim, and he worried that Captain Hooks—who had been promoted to deputy chief, the first African American to reach such a rank—would bring the powers of the department down upon him.

His failure to speak out caused Guerrero to feel like a coward and a fraud. He racked up a series of DUIs, the last of which culminated in an accident that caused minor injuries to a family on their way home from a Sizzler restaurant. Nando picked him up from jail and drove him straight to an alcohol recovery program.

Guerrero didn't like the meetings but accepted them as necessary. He declined to share his own story but sat in back, listening, quietly awed at the variety of ways human beings found to ruin their lives. It was like being a cop in some ways: absorbing the language of shame that led people into bondage.

One Wednesday night, he spotted a woman across the room who looked eerily familiar. Lisa Catalis had grown stout in the intervening decade; her hair was streaked with gray. She had drunk her way into and out of one marriage and a few teaching jobs. She spoke plainly about all of this, and Guerrero recognized the story she was telling, which wasn't about sin or failure so much as the erosion of faith.

Guerrero was under no illusions. He was an ugly man with a friar's fringe of hair, an ex-cop who worked security at a failing mall. It took him a month to screw up the courage to introduce himself, and for a long moment, after she had recognized him, they both stood in silence. "We have some catching up to do," Lisa said, at last. "I guess grabbing a drink isn't really an option."

They took to sipping coffee and eating pie at a diner near their meetings. Guerrero didn't like to talk about his life. It made him ache for beer. But Lisa was good at waiting him out. When she laughed, he felt less alone. A year later, they moved to Oakland together. It was nothing either of them expected, as much a reprieve as a romance. Lisa took a job teaching science at a private school in Alameda. With her encouragement, Guerrero earned a teaching certificate and taught social studies at a middle school in Fruitvale where the students were mostly the children of Central American immigrants.

OVER THE YEARS, Guerrero made efforts to track down Lorena Saenz. She proved more elusive, in the end, than Marcus Stallworth. For one thing, she formally changed her name to Maria Lopez, adopting the surname of the cousins into whose apartment she moved. This was not a decision borne of loyalty but an effort to elude her past.

She remained devoted to her mother, speaking with her twice a week and sending money to help her re-establish a life in Honduras. But the news of Tony's death, which Lorena had had to convey in a chaotic phone call that took place a week after the deportation, transformed Graciela. She moved back to the village outside San Pedro Sula where she had grown up. Her thinking became scattered, irritable, riddled with non sequiturs.

She worried that the US authorities were targeting Lorena for some unnamed persecution and sometimes hung up abruptly, claiming to have heard suspicious clicking noises. Lorena dismissed such talk as delusional. In fact, her phone had been tapped for several months, at the direction of Special Agent Joel Salcido, who hoped the women would eventually reveal the location of Marcus Stallworth's remains.

Although Lorena was an American citizen with a valid passport, it would take more than a year to convince Graciela that it was safe for her to travel to Honduras. She found her mother living amid the sort of filth she had never tolerated in their Sacramento apartment. Her white hair was knotted into a rope that swung wildly as she spoke. Her first words to Lorena were, "Where's Tony?" It became apparent that Graciela was giving much of her money to a local herbalist whose ritual cleansings promised to restore good fortune to her family.

Lorena consulted her aunts, who lived in San Pedro Sula, and summoned a doctor from the city who concluded that Graciela was suffering from a "mental collapse" brought on by the hardships she had suffered. He recommended sedatives. Lorena could not connect the woman who stood haranguing this doctor, vowing to bring a curse upon him, with the quiet, indomitable mother she had known as a child.

She did not give Graciela sedatives. Nor did she scold her for squandering money on an herbalist. She offered patience and companionship: phone calls, letters, a visit each year. Her mother eventually emerged from the fugue of her grief. She found work at a local clinic, performing the basic nursing duties she had witnessed for many years. She began attending a Bible study group. She spoke with great pride about her daughter and showed her off during visits, hosting small fiestas in her honor, walking arm-in-arm through the market, across the plaza, announcing to anyone they might encounter, "This is my daughter, the one who studies in America."

As Lorena's visits drew to an end, however, her lucidity often gave way to troubling episodes. One year, on the eve of her return flight, Lorena was awoken by her mother's voice outside her window. She found Graciela kneeling in the dirt near the wood pile, murmuring an incantation of some sort. The beam of Lorena's flashlight revealed the creature she was addressing: a small rust-colored scorpion.

"These little ones speak to me," her mother explained, in a haughty manner. "They tell me secrets."

For a moment, Lorena could feel the weight of all that she had kept from her mother, like the ghost of a scorpion on her palm. She had been drawn to the Stallworths initially by their wealth and ease. But it was their secrets that ensnared her: secret cigarettes and secret drinks, secret lusts and transgressions, which they pressed upon her, sensing, perhaps, that she had arrived in their midst bearing her own ruinous secret. Perhaps that's what family was, in the end: a unit bound by blood and torn asunder by secrets.

Her mother was now extending a dainty hand toward the creature, as if asking for a dance.

"Come away from there," Lorena whispered.

Graciela stared at her daughter in bewilderment, then smiled knowingly. "They only hurt the ones who don't listen. You know that." She began to nod. "You loved them once, didn't you? But it was your brother who got stung."

Lorena staggered; the stars above her lurched.

"Switch off that light," her mother commanded. "They prefer darkness."

Lorena did as she was told. She fixed her eyes on the scorpion, which sat perfectly still, its pincers glistening in the moonlight.

"You hear that?" Graciela whispered patiently. "You have to listen, *mija*."

ROSEMARY STALLWORTH SPENT the remainder of her life on the Main Line. She married again, moving into the home of a widower considerably older than herself, a gentle and tiresome man who had worked with her father. The days yawned before her and she filled them with remodeling projects, civic work, gossip. Her grandchildren visited, though never quite enough. They regarded her as a cloying presence, the fount of rambling, possibly drunken yarns, which they gradually learned to evade. Her children remained remote, Glen in particular. Although she was often lonesome, Rosemary took pride in having seen them into respectable lives.

As for her first marriage, and the catastrophic events surrounding its demise, she tucked these away, like a soiled linen folded into an attic trunk. Only in sleep did her powers of containment falter. She suffered a recurring dream in which scorpions had been unleashed in her home. Her mother was sometimes present, casting useless blandishments; once or twice Nancy Reagan appeared. She stood on the landing, immaculate and horror-stricken, surveying the bedlam from above.

In time, these night terrors became so disruptive that Rosemary upped her dose of sleeping pills, which left her listless and disoriented during daylight hours.

ANTONIO SAENZ MADE his final preparations in the dank hour that preceded morning bed check, working with an industry that might have struck the casual observer as exuberant. He rolled his bed sheet tight and tied ligatures into it, then tossed one end over the sprinkler mechanism, which was composed of a pipe stub crowned with a deflector plate shaped like a steel daisy. It caught immediately; the ease of it sent a ripple through him. He looped the rope around the pipe twice and yanked, to make sure it wouldn't pry off the deflector plate. He was left with nearly five feet of rope, more than enough to construct a hangman's knot. He knew that a greater number of coils would increase the mass of the knot, and thus the force of the upward snap. But he found that each new coil added friction to the knot, as well, a problem he solved by smearing ChapStick along the contact points.

Because he had lost track of the date, Tony had no idea that it was his twentieth birthday. He knew only that a guard would saunter by at 6:30, which gave him thirty-nine more minutes. He sat at the concrete desk and wrote a short note, in careful Spanish, which he left on his pillow:

> *Dear Ma,*
>
> *It is hard for me to put into words, but it is better if I go. Please trust me. I know I caused you a lot of pain but I always loved you. You were a great mom. Tell Lorena to stay in school. She always had the brains. Please forgive me.*
>
> *Your son,*
> *Antonio*

At the direction of the warden, the letter was passed along to the FBI. It never reached Graciela Saenz.

Tony emptied his bladder and bowels. He stepped up onto the plastic bin and practiced his leap half a dozen times, to make sure his head would come through the noose at the optimum pitch. He didn't know how much force would be required to break his neck, but it struck him as terribly important that his final effort in life be dignified. He wanted to get death right. To that end, he tucked the Bible he'd been issued into the waist-band of his jumpsuit and secured it there by pulling on two pairs of underwear over the jumpsuit. He did this because the Bible was the heaviest object in his cell, but also because he liked to imagine that his mother might eventually learn this de-tail and feel gladdened in her heart. As a final measure, he stuffed each hand into a pair of socks, then doubled up, so that even if he panicked and tried to grab at the rope he would be unable to work his fingers under the noose.

He needn't have worried. When his autopsy was released, the coroner detailed the victim's meticulous preparations in rhapsodic detail. In twenty-seven years of work for the Depart-ment of Corrections, he had never witnessed a self-suspension so ingeniously executed, particularly given the Spartan nature of isolation units. He made note of the complete ligature mark that ran below the thyroid cartilage in the shape of a sickle, and listed the cause of death as cerebral hypoxia.

That Antonio Saenz would leave behind such an impeccable crime scene was especially striking, given the grisly allegations that had led to his incarceration. As a result, the FBI declined to classify his death as a suicide. It was ruled an "unsolved death," possibly an execution carried out by incarcerated members of the Latin Kings.

IT WOULD BE inaccurate to describe the final moments of Tony Saenz's life as peaceful. His body, after all, began to convulse.

But his mind did produce a rush of thoughts that nonetheless culminated in a state of wonder. He could feel the weight of his father's head, cradled to his narrow chest. They were in the desert, traveling north though a wilderness without mercy, toward America. Tony needed to wake his father up. He tried digging his fingers into the soft flesh where whiskers gave way to skin. Then he realized that his father had slipped from his grasp and floated into the dark sky above so that he was choking himself now and had been for a long time and even though he wanted desperately to breathe he could see that he would have to surrender that pleasure if he wanted his father back. It was a kind of trade: in exchange for his mortal breath he would be allowed to ascend, to take his place amid the riot of dead souls and flickering stars that disappeared before dawn lit the world.

IN THE MONTHS following her brother's death, Lorena devoted her energies to re-establishing her life as a high school student. She moved to San Jose, into her cousin's basement, and took a job cleaning an office after school, so she could chip in for rent and groceries and pay for her visits to Honduras. There was no one to help her process what she had endured; even if there had been, she wouldn't have confided in them. She saw it as her duty to transcend these misfortunes, not to wallow in them. So she stored them away inside her, each memory in a secret box, all of them blindly thumping at their lids.

It was mostly at night that the memories would break loose. She would see Tony shackled to a table, or hear his soft growl. *You did something. I can hear it in your voice.* She would recall the lies she had told Jenny Stallworth, or wake up panting, a phantom hand on her cheek, sticky with blood. She would feel the flesh of her hips grasped and the warmth of Mr. Stallworth's breath upon her pubic bone.

The world was littered with invisible triggers, too: the bang of firecrackers, the scent of chlorine or wine coolers, even a casual mention of the zodiac. Any of these might send her body into a panic, which she would have to disguise by finding the nearest bathroom and setting her head against the tile until the ringing stopped.

She began to attend church services, not in deference to her guardian, but because she hoped a relationship with God might help her manage these attacks. She found that the rituals of worship made her feel closer to her mother and more patient in the face of her trials. She could not bring herself to believe that a divine father dwelled in heaven, awaiting her supplication. Nor did she view the stories in scripture as historical events. They read more like grotesque fairy tales crafted to mete out moral instruction.

At times, though, Lorena saw faith in a more expansive manner, as a means of locating forgiveness. Religion helped congregants accept the most vexing aspect of the human arrangement: that most people made terrible decisions, even when they acted with the best of intentions. Her parents had come to America seeking opportunity. Tony had sought to protect her from Marcus Stallworth. The list went on forever.

As a student, Lorena still possessed the inclinations of a scientific mind. She understood that a sustained application of empirical principle marked the surest path to truth. But her own experiences had revealed a world that operated in precisely the opposite manner; those in power bent logic and circumstance to serve their beliefs. She was not skeptical of science, but of the human ability to honor it.

HAD SHE ATTENDED high school in a more prosperous section of San Jose, Lorena might have been urged to apply to college as a senior. Even with the disruption of her freshman year, she ranked among the top one hundred students in a graduating class of seven hundred. She scored well on the standardized tests, though not as well as she might have, because of her work schedule. But her school employed only one college counselor, who catered to those at the very top of the class, students who felt entitled to a college education and knew how to advocate for themselves.

Lorena enjoyed learning, but she did not think of herself primarily as a student. She focused on money, the supervision of her mother, how to keep anxiety at bay. Later in life, she would come to understand that she had held herself back, perhaps as penance for the sins committed against her brother. At the time, it simply felt like survival.

After high school, she took a job as an administrator in an office that distributed medical devices, and was quickly promoted to shipping and receiving. Within a year, she was running the department. The woman officially in charge, her supervisor, Mrs. Stochansky, had been with the company for forty-one years, through three divorces and two cancers. She was battling a third tumor now. She smoked with a ferocious impunity and spent her days dozing in her office.

Late one afternoon, as she prepared to depart, Stochansky turned to Lorena, who was entering data into a computer she had programmed to cross-reference bills of lading with each product's SKU.

"Can I ask you something, Lopez?"

"Of course."

"What the hell are you doing here?"

Lorena had tried to explain the computer program to her supervisor already. "It's just something to simplify the inventory process."

Stochansky fixed Lorena with a look that was both impatient and frankly tender. "Do a dying woman a favor, okay? Quit playing dumb. God didn't give you that brain so you could design inventory sheets." Stochansky unleashed a violent cough and hid the blood in her palm. "The world loves to overlook girls like you. Don't make it any easier."

MRS. STOCHANSKY NEVER returned to the office. Lorena received a promotion and a small pay raise and enrolled in night classes at the local community college. She focused on subjects that would lead to a nursing degree. In her second year, she allowed herself a single elective: a course called Science of the Sky, taught by an eccentric amateur stargazer who enjoyed dressing up in the costumes of Renaissance astronomers. Of the seven students, Lorena was the only female. The professor loaned them his own personal telescopes and set up celestial scavenger hunts. He encouraged them to spend as much time as they could looking into the night sky with no particular agenda. "Let your mind wander around up there. See what shakes loose."

One night, her professor announced that he had astounding news. Vera Rubin, one of the most famous astrophysicists in the world, would be delivering a lecture at Stanford. The name had a familiar ring to it. But Lorena found the prospect of visiting the Stanford campus daunting. She told her professor that the talk was during her work hours, which happened to be true. He doffed the floppy beret by which he transformed himself into Copernicus. "The cosmos has delivered Vera Rubin unto you, Ms. Lopez. Seize the opportunity. I implore you."

Rubin was a petite woman with a crop of short white hair and oversized glasses. She looked like a librarian. Lorena assumed she would use highly technical language. But she spoke rather plainly about her area of study, which concerned the movement of stars on the outskirts of galaxies. "We assumed these bodies would be rotating slowly, like the planets at the edge of our own solar system. But they were spinning very quickly. So quickly that the entire galaxy, by the known laws of gravity, should have flown apart. Astronomers call this the galactic rotation problem.

"Now I happen to think—I am making a little editorial comment here, with your permission—I happen to think this is a terribly unfair name. Human beings tend to classify anything that doesn't fit into our current version of reality as a problem. It would be much more precise, and productive I think, to use the word *riddle*. It was a great *riddle* to all of us. And that is what makes science so pleasurable, isn't it? Solving the riddles!" Rubin smiled with an undisguised delight.

She went on to detail the theories her colleagues put forward in response to her data. Some believed that different physical dynamics obtained in the outer regions of galaxies. Others suggested that irregular patterns of light absorption had distorted her measurements. And still others claimed her data were flawed.

"One night I was out at the observatory and I remembered something that my favorite astronomer, Maria Mitchell, once said: *The universe veils its secrets in darkness.* The reason these galaxies were rotating so fast, I realized, was the presence of nonluminous matter. We now know that more than 80 percent of the matter in the universe is hidden in darkness. It is out there, keeping us from flying apart, though we will never see it. I find this idea quite elegant. It has a theological aspect, I suppose."

Rubin took a sip of water and gazed fondly at the mostly empty seats. "I must pause here to say a few words about Maria Mitchell. Most of you know she was the first female to discover a comet. You will not find her name in many textbooks. But she is the reason I became an astronomer. She made it possible."

Lorena suddenly recalled sitting in her eighth-grade science class as Miss Catalis rhapsodized about Maria Mitchell. She had no doubt mentioned Vera Rubin, too. That's why her name had sounded familiar.

MOST OF THE questions came from male faculty members and grad students, who treated Rubin with a grudging respect. They involved the intricacies of spectrographs and velocity curves. But toward the end of the session, a middle-aged woman seated a few rows in front of Lorena asked Rubin if it was true that her first paper on galactic rotation had been rejected by the American Astronomical Society.

"Oh yes! Rejection is a vital part of the scientific process. We stand atop the summit of our failures, don't we? I happened to be terribly pregnant at the time, too, which probably didn't help my cause. I suspect the women in the audience—there are a few of you, I see—will understand what I am saying here." Rubin winked at the men in the first few rows.

"There is another saying in astronomy that comes to mind. *It's not the size of the telescope that matters, but whether your aim is true.*" This remark drew a few muffled laughs. "It gives me enormous pleasure to see things I've never seen before. But it requires the humility to admit that human attention is imperfect. We still fail to apprehend most of the known world.

"I see some of you are confused. Allow me to elaborate. Earlier, your department put on a little reception for me. It was a lovely party and the food was scrumptious. There were scallops wrapped in bacon. I must have eaten a hundred. And yet, at no time amid this gluttony did I think, even once, about where those scallops came from, the reef from which they were harvested, the fisherman who did so, the worker in the slaughterhouse who butchered the hog, any of the hundreds of people who helped deliver these little morsels to my tongue. I gave no thought to the catering staff either, beyond wishing they would bring out more scallops. Nor the janitor who would dispose of all the greasy napkins I produced. I didn't think about whomever set up this lovely microphone for me, or the people who will clean this auditorium when we leave in a few minutes. I know that they exist, theoretically. But my inattention rendered them invisible." Rubin paused and squinted into the crowd. For a moment, her eyes settled on the young woman seated in the last row of the auditorium.

Then a young man in the front row, unable to contain himself, asked if harnessing the energy of dark matter might ever play a role in the weapon systems that President Reagan had proposed building in space.

Rubin smiled at her inquisitor, somewhat somberly. "I appreciate your question, but I am ill-equipped to discuss technologies of aggression. As I have sought to convey, science is about the great pleasure of seeing new things. It is a torch. As such, it can illuminate our world or it can burn us down."

She glanced at her watch and smiled again, this time warmly. "It has been an honor to spend time with you this evening. If you will allow me one final thought. I am not a medical doctor, or even a biologist. But it is my belief that the central challenge we face as a species arises from dark matter within us, the regions of ourselves that we cannot see or confront. I recommend that you look into the sky as much as you can. Perhaps the answers lie there."

LORENA SAT IN her chair for a long time. She felt a damp buzzing beneath her ribs. Everything she looked at—the students clustered around Rubin at the front of the room, the green velvet curtains behind them, the swooping vault of the ceiling with its spiraling filigree—shimmered with an aura, like a photographic afterimage. She could smell the solvent of her pen, and the cherry Life Saver someone nearby was sucking. The clasp of her bra was digging into her back; she could feel the crimped welt it would leave. This was not the inward plunge of anxiety. It was more like the vivid sensations she had experienced with Mr. Stallworth.

At a certain point, she realized that someone was standing in front of her.

"Are you okay, my dear?" Her professor wore a robe of royal blue, meant to evoke the Greek astronomer Ptolemy, against which a prick of red stood out just below his earlobe, where he had nicked himself shaving.

Lorena nodded. Blood spun outward from her heart, into the galaxy beyond.

"Are you sure?"

"It was beautiful."

"Oh, I see. Good. Let's go say hello before Ms. Rubin gets swallowed up by these Stanford brats."

"That's alright," Lorena said. "I should get back to work."

The professor shook his head, as if she had missed the point. He touched her hand, very gently. "Don't you understand, my dear? You must meet her. You're my star student."

IT TOOK LORENA five years to receive enough credits to earn her bachelor of science. She applied, and was accepted, to a graduate program in astronomy at New Mexico State University, in Las Cruces. A week before she was to depart, she found herself standing on the grand concourse of Great America, a garish amusement park off the 101, watching children from her church group hurtle through the air in brightly colored rocket ships and shriek with delight. Across the sea of asphalt and sun-burned necks, she spotted a woman she knew holding hands with a little Hispanic guy in a baseball cap. For a moment, she felt again the elation of hearing her named called out, followed by that of the most popular girl in her entire eighth grade class, and grinned without realizing it. She wanted to tell her old teacher about her graduate work, perhaps even thank her. But before she could cross the concourse, Miss Catalis was gone, along with the man on her arm, Pedro Guerrero.

LORENA SPENT THE balance of her years in Las Cruces, devoting herself to the study of dark matter and gravitational fields, at the university's observatory. The Blue Mesa Observatory sat atop Magdalena Peak in the Sierra de las Uvas, thirty miles northwest of town and a mile above it. The observatory's dome housed a telescope lens two feet across, along with a spectro-graph, spectrophotometer, and photoelectric photometer.

As much as she enjoyed capturing data, Lorena felt most alive outside. At around midnight, the generators shuddered to a halt and a profound silence descended. She would wrap a sleeping bag around her shoulders and hike through this silence to a nearby promontory, with a thermos of hot tea and a notebook.

For some, the night sky was a canvas on which to paint their national glory with fireworks, or the boundary of a fortress that could be made impregnable with magical missile systems. But Lorena saw a different sky. By training and inclination, she understood that the brightest bodies of the Milky Way—Sirius, Rigel, the sparkling Pleiades—were nothing more than specks of dust bound together by a pall of dark matter. Science could not proceed without faith in the unseen. And the unseen revealed itself only with patient observation.

It took a number of years, but she came to an understanding with the dark matter inside herself. She gazed upon the girl she had once been—the one who starved herself into designer jeans and basked in the radiance of the Stallworth family—and saw a child whose yearning to be seen left her vulnerable to exploitation. She saw in Mr. Stallworth a man desperate to conceal, and helpless to contain, his foulest urges. At the same time, he had been the first person to recognize her for who she really was, to set a scorpion upon her skin and aim her gaze at the heavens.

There were others to whom she owed a debt of gratitude: her mother, Miss Catalis, even, in his own irascible way, Officer Guerrero.

In moments of tranquility, she was able to discern that her brother had been dragged under, not by her misdeeds but by those of the police, and even before that, by humiliations heavier than his hopes. She would never be free of his death, or her mother's anguish. These losses had become a part of her. They bound her together.

If the wind wasn't too harsh, she would bundle up and sleep under the stars and wake to find dawn flaring off the geometry of the cliffsides, a hundred shades of red and brown, and later, the grays and greens of the desert floor stretching to a sharp blue horizon. Her life was not without these joys.

AS PART OF her duties as a research fellow, Lorena was required to teach Intro Astronomy once a year. She wasn't much good in the classroom. It was hard for her to accept that she had the right to lecture anyone. She struggled to convey her passion for astronomy to a room full of yawning freshmen, most of whom had no sense of what might excite them.

But the class did include an overnight to Blue Mesa. And occasionally, on such trips, Lorena would discreetly invite a favorite student to stargaze with her. If she was feeling mischievous, she might even share her secret hobby with them, drawing out a purple light and revealing how scorpions fluoresced. Most students responded with polite disgust. But once in a great while, she would encounter the other sort, a young woman struck by enchantment.

The last time this had happened was shortly before the college tore down the Blue Mesa Observatory, to make room for a radar installation. The student in question, Gloria Calero, had a habit of slipping into class and taking a corner seat in back. No speaking, no eye contact. Lorena knew that she had grown up in a home where her guardians, or guardian, was undocumented. Only in her written work did Gloria's formidable intelligence emerge.

Lorena hadn't expected Gloria to come on the Blue Mesa overnight at all, and she was even more surprised to find the girl milling around after dinner, pretending to fiddle with the hot cocoa machine. Gloria had a question about astronomical scintillation—the atmospheric interference that makes stars appear to twinkle—and why it didn't apply to planets. In fact, she had a whole slew of questions, which she had apparently been accumulating all term, about galactic curvature, gamma ray bursts, the Big Bang.

Lorena eventually set her mug down. "Did you bring any other clothes with you, Gloria? A warm coat, maybe?"

She led the girl to a rocky hillside where she knew stripe-tailed scorpions liked to hunt and clicked on her UV light. The girl let out a soft gasp. "They're like little stars, aren't they?"

"Actually, they don't twinkle. So they must be planets."

Gloria kneeled to get a closer look. "My *abuela* says they're kind of like tricksters, that they carry secrets from one house to another in their tails. She lives down in Oaxaca, so she's into superstitious stuff."

"My grandma said the same thing. Scorpions have all the secrets. That's why they only come out at night." Lorena kneeled next to Gloria and together they watched the creature scurry under a rock.

"There he goes," the girl said.

"Actually, that was a she."

"Why do they glow like that, anyway?"

"Nobody knows for sure. My guess is that their exoskeletons are super sensitive to shifts in ambient light, which helps them find shelter from predators."

"Like an alarm system."

"Right. Scorpions know that it's a dangerous thing to be seen."

For a few seconds, neither of them said anything. Then Gloria turned away. Her shoulders began to shake, very gently. It dawned on Lorena that whatever burden the girl was carrying had been jarred loose. Maybe her father was in custody, or she had no father, or someone she loved had fallen ill, or she herself was ill with love.

"Can I tell you something, Gloria?"

The girl wouldn't look directly at Lorena, but she gave a slight nod.

"You've got an incredible mind. Don't be afraid to share it with the world."

Gloria Calero smiled without meaning to. Down below, at the observatory, the generators chuffed and fell still and suddenly they could hear their own breathing.

Lorena clicked off her flashlight. "Let's leave these little guys alone. They're never going to spill the beans anyway." Above them, a billion stars lay scattered across the cosmic mantle, each held in place by forces beyond their seeing. "How about this," Lorena whispered. "Why don't we go see what the stars will tell us tonight?"

ACKNOWLEDGMENTS

I t took three decades, and many failed lightbulbs, but here we are. Special commendation to the brilliant and unlucky recipients of early drafts (Victor Cruz, Jenn DeLeon, Karen Lynch, Paul Salopek, Matthew Zapruder, Billy Giraldi, Sorche Fairbanks). Also: the everyday saints at Grub Street, Hugo House, Lighthouse Writers Workshop, the Nieman Fellowship, and Wesleyan University, who have allowed me to teach remarkable writers and steal from the buffet. Thanks to my long-time lifelines: Tom Finkel, Camille Dungy, Clay Martin, Karl Iagnemma, Keith Morris, Laurie Pomeranz, Cheryl Strayed, Tom DeMarchi, and Pat Flood. A big hug to Jenni Ferrari-Adler for believing, to Emily Bell for editing the hell out of *Secrets*, and Molly Stern and the Zando gang for putting it in the world. Eternal gratitude to my wife, Erin Almond, who recognized what the book was striving to be and found the language to explain it to me. Over and over. Patiently. And to my children—Josephine, Judah, and Rosalie—who are all amazing readers and even better people.

ABOUT THE AUTHOR

S teve Almond is the author of eleven books of fiction and nonfiction, including the *New York Times* bestsellers *Candyfreak* and *Against Football*. His essays and reviews have been published in venues ranging from the *New York Times Magazine* to *Ploughshares* to *Poets & Writers*, and his short fiction has appeared in *Best American Short Stories*, *The Pushcart Prize*, *Best American Mysteries*, and *Best American Erotica*. Almond is the recipient of grants from the Massachusetts Cultural Council and the National Endowment for the Arts. He cohosted the *Dear Sugars* podcast with his pal Cheryl Strayed for four years and teaches creative writing at the Neiman Fellowship at Harvard and Wesleyan. He lives in Arlington, Massachusetts, with his family and his anxiety.